Christmas Eve in a Gum Tree
and Other Lost Australian Christmas Stories

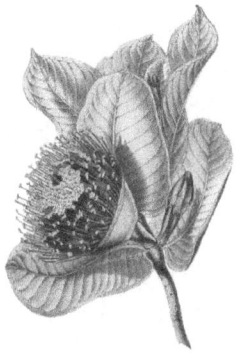

Edited and introduced by Imelda Whelehan

Obiter Publishing

Published by Obiter Publishing
PO Box 5133
Braddon ACT 2612
info@obiterpublishing.com.au
www.obiterpublishing.com.au

NATIONAL
LIBRARY
OF AUSTRALIA

A catalogue record for this book is available from the National Library of Australia

ISBN: 978-0-6481742-5-7

Cover design by Giraffe
Design by Karen Downing
Printed by Ingram Spark

'To Be Continued ...'

Series editor Katherine Bode

The 'To Be Continued ...' series publishes fiction discovered by literary scholar Katherine Bode and bibliographer Carol Hetherington. They used new digital methods to search the National Library of Australia's *Trove* database to uncover over 21,000 stories published in Australian newspapers between 1828 and 1914. Although fiction is a rarity in newspapers today, prior to World War One Australian newspapers routinely published fictional works, and in the nineteenth century, were the main source of fiction for colonial readers. Some of the stories discovered in this project are short, amounting to only one or two columns on a newspaper page; some are lengthy novels, published over multiple newspaper editions.

Fiction in Australian newspapers came from around the world: from Australia, Britain and America as well as France, Germany, New Zealand, Russia, and beyond. All of the titles discovered – with an interface for readers to interact with *Trove* to discover new stories and correct the newspaper text – are available at http://cdhrdatasys.anu.edu.au/tobecontinued.

The 'To Be Continued ...' series focuses on Australian fiction not previously published beyond the original newspaper pages. It thus uncovers lost pieces of the nation's literary heritage enabling new understandings of the way Australian literature developed and how early Australians understood themselves and their world.

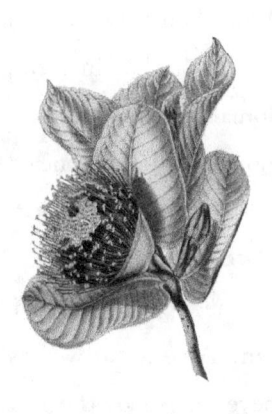

Contents

Publisher's note

'Christmas Eve in a Gum Tree' appeared in the *Illustrated Sydney News* in 1877; 'Linlarra Station and the Christmas Day I Spent There' appeared in the *Queenslander* in 1879; 'A Christmas Message' appeared in *Australasian Sketcher with Pen and Pencil* in 1879; 'Clare's Christmas Eve' appeared in Adelaides' *Evening Journal* in 1880; 'The Bushman's Revenge' appeared in the *Liverpool Herald* in 1902; 'Uncle Tatbury's Ghost!' appeared in Sydney's *Empire* in 1864; and 'The Rightful Heir' appeared in the *Bowral Free Press* in 1884. No changes have been made to the original formatting apart from obvious typographical errors.

Ghosts of Australian Christmases Past

Imelda Whelehan

Thinking about Christmas stories perhaps inevitably brings to mind the most famous of such tales, Charles Dickens' *A Christmas Carol*, first published in London in 1843. Dickens wrote *A Christmas Carol* at a time when Victorian Britain was re-evaluating past Christmas traditions and introducing new ones, such as the Christmas Tree. Christmas, as captured by the fiction of Dickens, is a time of charity and remembrance – dressed in the melancholy colours of a dank, grey English winter. British and European migrants to Australia during the nineteenth century inevitably took their traditions with them, anachronistic as some were, and impossibly ill-suited to an Australian summer, its flora and fauna. Marcus Clarke found it absurd to try to keep the English version of Christmas celebration in the colonies and saw Dickens' stories of Christmas conversions, such as that of Scrooge, as unseasonal because 'cold weather is the proper time for sentiment; charity is proverbially cold – but in a hot-wind-ravaged-dust-hole like this city, it is preposterous.'[1]

For all Clarke's protestations the influence of Dickens, who was widely circulated, serialised, and read in the Australian colonies, and the themes of the English Christmas, are present in Australian fiction and journalism of the period. Whether or not 'Christmas was an umbilical cord with the mother country',[2] the experience of Christmas in the southern hemisphere was informed by the iconography of the northern winter solstice, even if those traditional images of reindeer, snow and holly were humorously subverted. For instance, an image in the *Illustrated Sydney News* of 1869,

---

[1] Kylie Mirmohamadi and Susan K. Martin, *Colonial Dickens: What Australians Made of the World's Favourite Writer* (Melbourne: Australian Scholarly Publishing, 2012), 47.
[2] Maisy Stapleton and Patricia McDonald, *Christmas in the Colonies* (Sydney: David Ell Press, 1981), 7.

'The Bushman's Dream', depicts a slumbering selector, dog at his feet, boomerang and gun mounted on the wall, dreaming of an English Christmas, with an image of a wintry scene of a family emerging from a carriage and being greeted and welcomed in to a cosy looking house suspended above his head. A paper dropped to the floor may suggest a letter from home has prompted this particular dream.[3]

---

[3] *The bushman's dream* from an original drawing by T.S. Cousins; engraved by S. Calvert, *Illustrated Sydney News*, December 1869. The image can be viewed in colour at: https://nla.gov.au/nla.obj-135891983/view

Having travelled so far, one imagines that Christmas was a time of nostalgia for new migrants, no doubt exacerbated by the wait for parcels and mail from overseas, particularly when Christmas cards came into vogue in the 1840s. In 1879 the *Sydney Mail* lamented, 'what is Christmas without the grey or steely sky, the grim twilight, and long black night? How can the roaring Yule-log, the mighty baron of beef, the tremendous pudding in its fiery shroud of flaming spirits, the reeking wassail bowl, be suggestive of comfort in a country were the thermometer oft-times marks ninety degrees in the shade at Christmas Tide, and where, instead of trusting Robin-redbreasts and blackbirds, tamed by hunger, flocking before the window for eleemosynary crumbs, a host of blood thirsty mosquitoes settle upon perspiring guests.'[4] The virtues of a northern versus southern hemisphere Christmas were also a topic in *The Queenslander* Christmas Supplement of 1883, which notes that Christmas will come to 'scorch our Queensland and freeze old England', but reaffirms Dickens as a defining force in its celebration, wherever one is: 'who can speak of Christmas and not straightway think of Charles Dickens, its modern exponent in story and carol?'[5]

As towns and communities grew, so Christmas holiday celebrations diversified and adapted themselves to the climate and culture. Maisie Stapleton and Patricia McDonald assert that 'Australians have learnt to live with the strangeness of it all. Christmas cards with their scenes of snow, the department stores decorated with reindeer, Santa Claus sweating on street corners; it is a fantasy of Europe in exile. Every traveller, every migrant who has come here since the early 1800s has noticed the incongruity'. Although they claim that 'little has changed, and no one seems to want it to change,'[6] their study of Christmas in the colonies

---

[4] Cited in Stapleton and McDonald, *Christmas in the Colonies*, 23.
[5] Anon, 'Some Christmas Fantasies', *The Queenslander,* Saturday 22 December 1883, 16: https://trove.nla.gov.au/newspaper/article/19795367 (accessed 28/10/18).
[6] Stapleton and McDonald, *Christmas in the Colonies*, 7.

notes multiple accommodations: seasonal picnics, sporting Boxing Days, carols by candlelight and bush dinners improvised at remote stations are all examples of Christmas events that have taken on a distinctly antipodean slant.

During a period of intense migration and increasing national prosperity, Australian Christmases, like those in Britain and Europe, became increasingly commercialised with the growth of urban markets and Department Stores, and the expanding practice of giving and receiving presents. Christmas supplements, pull-outs and other special features became common in December editions of Australian newspapers and periodicals in the 1880s and 1890s. There is evidence of early Christmas anthologies, such as J.F. Hogan's *An Australian Christmas Collection* (1886). This collection of stories, book reviews and profiles is introduced by its author as a 'selection from my contributions to Australian periodical and newspaper literature during the past few years', and he thanks 'several hundred subscribers throughout the colonies, who have done me the honour of ordering copies of the book in advance of its publication.'[7]

Dickens' *A Christmas Carol* has been 'credited with transferring the Christmas of the literary imagination from the English countryside to the modern urban world.'[8] Just as Dickens adapted representations of country traditions of feasting, charity and family togetherness and transplanted them into the urban home, the writers in this collection appropriate the Christmas story for a multitude of Australian locations – the bush, the sheep station, the suburbs and the cities. The stories collected in this volume are from both well-known and lesser-known writers. First serialised between the 1860s and early 1900s, they are not all literary masterpieces, by any means. But these stories offer fascinating insights

---

[7] J.F. Hogan, *An Australian Christmas Collection* (Melbourne: Alex McKinley & Co, 1886), preface (n.p.).
[8] Neil Armstrong, *Christmas in Nineteenth-Century England* (Manchester: Manchester University Press, 2010), 10.

into the themes and preoccupations of nineteenth-century Australians, and show the many ways Christmas as a significant festival was perceived, and its traditions and themes repurposed for the city, the country town and the bush. As we read them – all available in print for the first time since their original publication – it is pleasant to imagine how they were first received, nestled in the newspapers and periodicals of the time, with avid readers waiting for the next chapter in the next issue. We have access to them once more thanks to the work of literary scholar and specialist in digital collections, Katherine Bode, who mined the National Library's Trove database to uncover a new history of Australian literature and literature in Australia among the pages of Australia's metropolitan and provincial newspapers.

In these stories we find themes that echo those of Dickens' stories: there are travellers, family reunions, feasting, romantic encounters, kindness and reconciliation, the uncanny and stories of hardship endured and sometimes overcome. They vary in length and our title story, 'Christmas Eve in a Gum Tree' (1877), is hardly more than a 'yarn', in which two novice stockmen retreat up a gum tree, survive a devastating Queensland flood and live to make their fortunes on the land. One of the brothers concludes, having enjoyed the 'queerest sort of Christmas fare', that 'I am not sure that lizard stew, sour Johnny cake, and washed tea are not to be preferred to turkey, plum-pudding and champagne' (page 7). The author, A.J. Boyd, was born William Alexander Jenyns Boyd (1842–1928) in Paris and educated in England, Germany and Switzerland, eventually migrating to Queensland in 1860. He is primarily known as an agricultural journalist, schoolmaster and solider.[9]

Ada Cambridge and Catherine Martin were both acclaimed authors of their time and continue to be celebrated for their commitment to broader social issues. Audrey Tate writes that Cambridge is frequently

---

[9] See *Australian Dictionary of Biography*: http://adb.anu.edu.au/biography/boyd-william-alexander-5325 (accessed 19/10/18).

described as the foremost novelist of her sex in this country, and various aspects of her work were likened to names such as Thackeray, George Eliot and Charlotte Brontë,'[10] though notes that her reputation was later tarnished by negative associations of her work with romance fiction. Like Catherine Martin, Cambridge critically explored women's social and domestic roles in her fiction and for years juggled her own twin identities as author and clergyman's wife. She was born in England and travelled to Australia shortly after her marriage – the complete works of Dickens being one wedding gift she brought with her (Dickens actually died while Cambridge was en route to Australia).[11] She had written hymns by her late teens, which were published and circulated to a degree of recognition. In common with other women writers of the period, the income from her work provided an important supplement to her husband's meagre clerical salary. After the publication of her serialised *Up the Murray* (1875) her reputation soared; while 'A Christmas Message' (1879) collected here is noted in her bibliography, it has not been published since its original serialisation in *The Australasian Sketcher*.

'A Christmas Message', set in the Western District of Victoria, introduces two visitors to a country home where the daughter of the house has recently returned from a long stay in England. Nelly Charteris is well-known to the older man, but Frank Townshend, having heard about her charms, ventures to wager £100 that he will never propose to her, because 'I flatter myself I am proof against the machinations of a flirt. I know one as soon as I set my eyes on her, and I've never been taken in by one yet' (page 41). This hasty bet threatens to compromise the growing affection between the two, despite a seemingly mystical link between them, presaged by the reason for her premature return from England – 'A Cooee that I fancied I heard. And the smell of a bit of wattle; but for that

---

[10] Audrey Tate, *Ada Cambridge: Her Life and Work 1844-1926* (Melbourne: Melbourne University Press, 1991), 1.
[11] Ibid, 45.

I should have been in Rome at this moment, probably, instead of sitting here' (page 49).

Townshend's own memory of cooeeing in Paris and Tasmania – the latter a call to his future, as yet unknown, love – adds an uncanny air to their first meeting, reinforced by an eclipse of the moon. These portents lead the reader to hope that, despite the obstacles between them, they will reach an understanding, just as Jane Eyre, hearing Rochester's eerie cry from afar, returns to Thornfield to search for him.[12] The bleakness of the weather the following Christmas – 'it was felt by everybody that those time-honoured institutions so religiously clung to by the British householder, irrespective of the state of the thermometer, would be more entirely in harmony with the occasion than usual' (page 62) – echoes the miserable rift between the two, which perhaps one more 'cooee' might heal.

Unlike in Jane Austen novels, the best suitors are not always in possession of a fortune: such is the case with Harleigh Roxburghe, a clergyman Clare Rutherford meets and falls in love with on board ship from Europe in Catherine Martin's 'Clare's Christmas Eve' (1880). Just as Cambridge's Frank has to learn from his quick judgement of Nelly, so Martin's Clare is circumspect in love. Clare has the self-determination to defy a controlling older sister but harbours a secret that she is reluctant to reveal to Harleigh and which may threaten their future happiness if revealed by another. Beyond the plot of love and perseverance, Scottish-born Martin demonstrates a 'sharp eye for social pretension and injustice' in her writing.[13] This is aptly demonstrated by a terse exchange in the drawing-room where one self-important guest pontificates on the state of the modern novel only to be publicly humiliated by her interlocutor when it is re-

---

12 Charlotte Brontë, *Jane Eyre* (1847), Chapter XXXV.
13 Katherine Bode, 'From Adelaide to Genoa: Locating Catherine Martin's Lost Fiction', *How I Pawned My Opals and Other Lost Stories* (Braddon, ACT: Obiter Publishing, 2017), vi.

vealed she is simply parroting a published article.

Martin's story also offers strong social commentary. During a lengthy exchange Harleigh is at pains to illustrate to Clare the plight of the poor in his former London parish and disabuse her of any idea that poverty is correlative to criminality: 'I knew men and women who lived in foul rookeries – I cannot call them houses – in crowded courts and alleys, constantly surrounded by the depressing grim monotony of the streets, who lived honest, true, and brave lives; who were cheerful and kind and capable of real heroism in the way of unselfish helpfulness to others' (page 123). We understand that Harleigh has chosen to forego his own fortune to support such people, but his new clerical position in a working-class district presents a less than attractive future home for Clare. To be happy the couple need to agree to find common ground, which involves Clare spending her Christmas Eve in an unexpected place.

Salian Muir's 'The Bushman's Revenge' establishes the weather before it introduces its main protagonists, and the weather and its destructive potential is a powerful theme in a number of these stories. A lengthy period of drought and heatwave is 'compared to the terrors and inconveniences of the historic plagues of Egypt' (page 167) where 'the once bright flowers and verdant herbage bowed their blighted heads in sheer enervation; the gasping birds were voiceless and inert, and the countless carcasses of the larger animals which strewed the plains, told only too eloquently their own tragic story' (page 168). John Maclean, originally from Scotland and owner of the sheep station, is not well-liked, being bad tempered and tight-fisted. The heatwave has made him more irascible than usual and the arrival of 'Sundown Bill', a well-known swagman and popular raconteur, less a jobbing labourer and more a beggar, further irritates him. Maclean won't even let him fill his waterbag before the 20 mile journey to the next property, so Bill vows revenge – an opportunity for which presents itself very soon. Maclean, like Scrooge, has to learn to value his neighbours, but at a tragic cost.

In 'Linlarra Station and the Christmas Day I Spent There' (1879) bush meets 'civilisation' in the beautifully tended gardens that surround the house and provide shade to the Christmas party gathered there. Yattie Ingledon, like Clare Rutherford and Nelly Charteris, has been broadening her horizons in Europe. Stiff English courtesies are perhaps implicitly contrasted to the open hospitality of the bush station as the narrator remarks, 'Oh how pleasant is the hearty hospitality of the Australian bush! ... Send in your name, and it is taken for granted that you are a gentleman; no matter what creed or nationality, you are made welcome' (page 20). The fragility of the colonists' control over their environment is emphasised as a cyclone – 'nature's avenging Nemesis for man's invasion of her domain' (page 33) – tracks the path of Yattie Ingledon and her beau George Moreton. The author, Manchester-born Price Fletcher (1836–1906) published this story under the pseudonym 'Bush Naturalist' and was a regular nature columnist and fiction writer whose focus was Queensland.

Little is known about E. Charles (aka Mrs. W. Morrice), author of 'The Rightful Heir: An Australian Christmas Story.' But an E. Charles (aka E.C. Morrice) is listed in the Austlit database with twenty other works of poetry and fiction to their name.[14] The story begins in a pleasant establishment in the Sydney suburb of Woolloomooloo Bay, with Marion Halstead in conversation with new arrival Frank Northbrook, on his way to a sheep station in Queensland. Marion is travelling to her Uncle Clovelly's place which neighbours Northbrook's property, and conversations reveal Frank's mother's dread of the journey as well as of preparing a full Christmas dinner on arrival, not to mention her fears about the local Aboriginal community. Clovelly's 'super', also called

---

[14] See AustLit database: https://www.austlit.edu.au/austlit/page/A8629?mainTabTemplate=agentWorksBy&restrictToAgent=A8629 (accessed 21/10/18)

Northbrook, cuts an enigmatic figure with descriptions focusing on his physiognomy: 'the keen, dark face, with eyes whose deep lustrous darkness reminds us of the natives of Spain and Italy; so does also the clear, olive skin and crisp-raven hair; and so do also the clearly-chiselled features, regular as those of a statue. But when we look closer at that striking face we see that the jaw is too massive, and the lips, shaded by a dark, drooping moustache, are too full and defiant for classic beauty' (page 235). These descriptions hint at the mystery of Norman Northbrook's parentage, with the dreadful secret it represents linked to broader themes of injustice and dispossession: 'The white man has come and taken what was the rightful possession of his weaker fellow-creatures, and now expects him to look on quietly while he enjoys the ill-gotten wealth' (page 245). In its portrayal of an Indigenous hero and a love story that traverses racial boundaries, this story also exposes some dominant attitudes to Indigenous Australians during the period, portraying them as at once childlike and yet potentially doomed: 'tomorrow perhaps lying at rest for ever, shot down by the gun of the revengeful white man' (page 270).

In keeping with the spectres and hauntings of many a Christmas tale, Frederick Sydney Wilson, a prolific writer of poetry, songs and prose, narrates a ghost story with an urban setting in the Sydney suburb of Paddington. The evocative description of the bustling food markets trading on Christmas Eve recalls those revealed to Scrooge by the ghost of Christmas Present:[15] 'Business went on brisker than ever – butchers

---

[15] Though Dickens' prose is hard to beat: 'The poulterers' shops were still half open, and the fruiterers' were radiant in their glory. There were great, round, pot-bellied baskets of chestnuts, shaped like the waistcoats of jolly old gentlemen, lolling at the doors, and tumbling out into the street in their apoplectic opulence. There were ruddy, brown-faced, broad-girthed Spanish Onions, shining in the fatness of their growth like Spanish Friars, and winking from their shelves in wanton slyness at the girls as they went by, and glanced demurely at the hung-up mistletoe. There were pears and apples, clustered high in blooming pyramids; there were bunches of grapes, made, in the shopkeepers' benevolence to dangle from conspicuous hooks, that people's mouths might water

chopped and sawed, and cut off giant joints. Joints that would persist in looking out of their owners' baskets, in spite of all endeavours to keep them confined; grocers made up dainty little parcels, giving the change, and the compliments of the season, to pretty girls, in a manner pleasant to behold, while the poulterer's shops exhibited lines of long-necked fowls, like rows of notes of admiration at the plentiful cheer provided for all—who had money enough to pay for it.' (page 211). Tatbury, like Scrooge, needs to review his own past and the loyalties he has betrayed in his treatment of his niece's beau, if he is to rid himself of the spectre haunting his home. Christmas Day for Tatbury brings a transformation and the promise of many happy Christmases to come, celebrated in the Australian way: 'the Australian bush is bright with a thousand hues, and merry with the whistle and clatter of birds with restless wings. The creek which in its windings nearly surrounds the station, is lined with the 'mimosa' or wattle-tree covered with the gorgeous garments of scented golden flowers' (page 227).

These collected stories reclaim Christmas as a precious time for reunions, charity, revealing truths and falling in love. With many featuring characters newly arrived to Australia, and still at odds with their surroundings, they encourage readers to imagine their own confusion at spending the festive season in settings where adaptation to the conditions is required, and not always predictable.

I grew up in England where Christmas was shaped by Dickensian images of Victorian English celebrations, recycled on chocolate boxes and

---

gratis as they passed; there were piles of filberts, mossy and brown, recalling, in their fragrance, ancient walks among the woods, and pleasant shufflings ankle deep through withered leaves; there were Norfolk Biffins, squat and swarthy, setting off the yellow of the oranges and lemons, and, in the great compactness of their juicy persons, urgently entreating and beseeching to be carried home in paper bags and eaten after dinner. The very gold and silver fish, set forth among these choice fruits in a bowl, though members of a dull and stagnant-blooded race, appeared to know that there was something going on; and, to a fish, went gasping round and round their little world in slow and passionless excitement.' *A Christmas Carol* (1843).

biscuit tins, accompanied by adaptations of *A Christmas Carol* on film and television, and even in festive comedy sketches. It is easy to imagine how Scrooge thinks he sees the face of Marley in a door knocker when darkness falls by 4pm during the height of the British winter solstice and anyone might see a shadow and think it is a ghost. Christmas lights, however, brighten up the end of a working day and add lustre to the damp twilight streets. There is nothing like curling up with *A Christmas Carol* or some other uncanny seasonal tale during the holiday period. In my family the giving of Christmas stories, to be opened and started on Christmas Eve, is something of a tradition. As they multiply annually we box them up with the Christmas decorations, the better to savour them afresh the following year.

Eight years ago we moved to Australia and those Christmas boxes travelled with us. We muddled through our first Australian Christmas and, as usual, spent part of the time curled up on sofas reading our Christmas books. But we were soon distracted by the sun on our backs, the absurdity of being indoors when long walks and beachside reads beckoned, and of course, there is always a much longer wait for darkness before the Christmas tree lights can work their magic. Like all migrants we gradually acclimatized and adjusted our family traditions to make the most of a beautiful Australian summer, where the Christmas holiday blurs into summer holidays – which I associate with quite different reading habits.

This collection is for everyone who wants their Christmas stories to mirror their Christmas location – with the heat on their backs, perhaps wondering if lowering clouds presage a storm or more extreme weather event. They will be best savoured as the barbecue sizzles or while dipping a toe in the water, enjoying fresh raspberries, cherries or apricots, or during lunch at the cricket. It might be a tonic, too, for those travellers who find themselves in the northern hemisphere longing for the characteristic smells and sounds of an Australian summer holiday. By 6 January (Twelfth Night) one thing is certain: this book will be tucked away in my Christmas box with the likes of Charles Dickens, Anthony Trollope, J.R.R. Tolkien, Jeanette Winterson and other tellers of Christmas tales. Every year it will re-emerge, along with the Christmas decorations, once more to be enjoyed and shared and to become an essential part of our changing family Christmas traditions.

Christmas Eve in a Gum Tree

A. J. Boyd

Rain, rain, a pitiless downpour from the leaden skies, drenching the lonely traveller; swelling the creeks and rivers till their swollen torrents came roaring down, bearing on the yellow turbid flood hurrying masses of timber – giant trees, uprooted by the rush of the passing waters to the far off blue ocean, whose tides were discoloured for miles by the volumes of flood water poured into them from countless streams.

Such a rainy season had not been experienced in Queensland for many years. It seemed as if the waters above the firmament and the waters under it had combined for the purpose of sweeping mankind from the face of the earth.

Travelling inland by any mode of conveyance became a sheer impossibility. The roads were no longer roads, but fathomless bogs. Where the rude bridges constructed by the settlers were not carried away bodily, they were reduced to such a ruinous condition that crossing them was fraught with greater danger even than an attempt to stem the boiling current by swimming.

This was not the sort of weather which any one would choose to start on a journey northward of a thousand miles. Nevertheless, numbers of travellers who had commenced their journey under favourable auspices were overtaken by the rainy season when too far advanced to make it a matter of choice whether to return or push on.

It was during this terrible season that the 14th of December found three travellers camped on the Dawson River, west of Rockhampton. They were driving a large mob of cattle to a station in the far North, when, overtaken by the rains which had set in earlier than usual, they decided to camp for a day or two, hoping that the weather would clear up.

The spot chosen for the camp was selected more on account of the good feed and natural features of the country than from any idea of its safety in case of flood.

The Dawson River on one side formed a barrier impassable for the cattle; a dense scrub fenced them in in front, whilst the only side which required watching was bounded by a creek with rather steep banks, which appeared to take its rise near one portion of the river, and run in a semicircular form to empty itself into the same stream below the camp.

If George Miles and his brother Harry had been older hands, and a little less thoughtless, they would at once have listened to the counsel of their stockman, Jim Everest, and camped anywhere but where they were. Just before deciding to stop at this point, Jim had said: "Mr. George, I think we'd best not camp here. I don't like the place."

"Why, what's wrong with it, Jim? There's plenty of grass, and the place is a good twenty feet above the river. Besides, there is plenty of water in the creek, where the cattle can get it easily, without scrambling down to it."

"That's just it, sir; there's too much water, and I'm mistaken if we don't find it out when it's too late."

"Oh, rubbish, George," said Harry. "Let's camp here, and get under cover from this confounded rain. I'm drenched to the skin, and as cold as charity. The sight of a steaming pot of tea would just now be more to my mind than the Christmas dinner at Rockhampton I'm looking forward to."

George was half inclined to agree with the more experienced stockman, especially when the latter pointed out the nature of the ground.

"Don't you see, sir," he said, "we shall just be jammed in on an island if this weather holds; and to my mind it means to keep on for a month. Do you notice the ant-hills? The ants know when a flood is coming, and they build up good high walls round the entrances to keep off the water. Look at that nest at your feet. It's just as I said; they have built round the holes, and that's a sure sign—not that the flood we're going to get will stop there, but it's a sign we ought to take warning by. What do you say, sir! Will I round up the cattle, and find a safer camp?"

George sat on his horse, musingly. He was in considerable doubt as to what sort of country was ahead. It might be all scrub, where some of the cattle would be sure to be lost. Perhaps they might fall in with a wild mob, and lose a good many head in that way.

But this indecision soon changed to prompt action. A blacker cloud than usual rushed across the dull, murky heavens, and a perfect deluge descended. The horses turned their tails to the merciless blast, the cattle crowded together for shelter, whilst the darkness was so great that even the anxious stockman thought it would be as well to camp, at least until the rising of the water in the creek gave notice of impending danger. This point decided, and the cattle settled down comfortably, Harry busied himself with making a fire, whilst the others unpacked and unsaddled the horses, and after hobbling them turned them out to make themselves as happy as the miserable weather would allow them to be. The fire was soon burning brightly, thanks to an abundance of stringy-bark growing on a ridge not far away. The quart pots were set before it, a small tent erected, and all gave themselves up to the enjoyment of the grateful warmth and of dry clothes. As soon as the tea was made, and the beef and damper were produced, the discomforts of the situation were almost forgotten. After the meal pipes were lighted, and lots having been drawn to decide who should take the first turn at watching, two of the tired drovers lay down in their blankets on the saturated ground, and were soon in a deep sleep.

Harry, who had drawn the first watch, sheltered himself as well as he could under the lee of a large tree, and gave himself over to his pipe and a soliloquy.

"Well, this is a rum go," he said to himself. "Here am I, who could have stayed comfortably at home, drawing a good screw, and waiting patiently till Maud Summer said "Yes" to a certain cabalistic question (which I mean to put when I get back to Brisbane); here am I, I say, like a great laughing jackass, wandering over the country at the tails of a lot of stupid bullocks, when I could be kicking my heels and waxing fat at home with the governor. It's all very well for George; he's not the fellow to live in a town. Now, I bet he prefers knocking about with cattle in the bush, in all sorts of weather, to lying comfortably back in a cane chair, with a good cigar, and just enough work to keep one out of mischief; but I always did think he was mad, although he is such a rattling good fellow. Now, this cursed weather is just about the thing to make a fellow commit suicide. I wonder, by the way, how we should all look if the flood rose so high as to compel us to squat up in one of these trees. Rather cold quarters, with a log for a bed, and a bunch of wet gum leaves for a pillow, not to mention the probability of its being a harbour for tens of millions of snakes, centipedes, scorpions, soldiers, jumpers – – – Jumping Jehosaphat! What's that?"

Harry's soliloquy was brought to a sudden termination by a roar, which awoke the two sleepers in the tent. This noise can be compared to nothing less than the bursting of an enormous dam, and the rush of its lately-imprisoned waters down a narrow gorge.

This was very much what had happened. A glance in the direction of the creek showed the catastrophe which had taken place, and then only did a knowledge of their fearful danger dawn upon the two men.

Jim Everest was perfectly cool and collected. He merely said: "There's just what I felt sure would happen if the flood came down heavier during the night. The river has risen above the level of the creek, and has raised it eight or ten feet. In half an hour the island we are on will be under water."

"Well, all I can see for it," said George, "is to make a dash for it, and swim the creek before it is too late."

Both brothers were splendid swimmers, and might possibly have succeeded in getting across, although the chances were nine to one against their crossing that boiling torrent, encumbered as it was with floating timber rushing past at the rate of ten miles an hour. But what was to become of Jim? He could not swim a stroke, and must inevitably perish unless he succeeded in reaching the upper branches of the trees. There was no possibility of getting him across with them, so they nobly resolved to remain, and trust to Providence to get out of the perilous dilemma. There was no time to save anything but a little flour, beef, and tea, and their blankets. These things were hastily got together, and then the stockman, assisted by the others, climbed into the lowest fork of a flooded gum, and lowering a line made of three surcingles, hoisted them into a place of safety and made them fast. The two brothers then climbed up—an operation which was greatly aided by the surcingles. Seated firmly on the limbs of the tree, they looked at each other, and then burst into a hearty fit of laughter. When this had subsided, George said: "It's all very well to be jolly, but I'm afraid we shall soon laugh on the other side of our mouths. Look at the horses."

The other two peered through the misty atmosphere, through which the struggling moonbeams threw a dim light on the scene. The horses, abandoned by their owners, had left off feeding, and were wandering restlessly up and down the bank of the creek, as if looking for a ford. At last one of them plunged in, and was quickly followed by all the rest. The water was tolerably still at the point where they entered it, and the stockman determined to try and bring them back.

"I am bound to get them horses again, sir. If we lose them, we shall have a job to reach Overinga, let alone Rockhampton." And in spite of the remonstrances of his companions, he slid down the tree and made towards the animals, who were now battling with a swift current and were almost out of sight. Scarcely had Jim disappeared when a stampede amongst the cattle announced another catastrophe. The solitary watchers in the tree soon became aware that the river had risen above its banks, and was rapidly covering the island. They cooeyed loudly to warn Everest;

but, had the latter possessed wings, he could not have reached the tree before the whole island was two feet under water.

"Poor Jim!" said Harry, sorrowfully; "I'm afraid he is drowned. He could not swim, and I don't recollect a tree down the creek where he could find shelter."

"No; the trees there are all a hundred feet high. God help him! Both he and the horses are long past help."

"And there go the cattle, George! We shall not save a hoof. All our savings gone like this! What will mother say? And we were going to make things so comfortable on the station for her. It's misery to think of it."

"Never mind, old fellow. It can't be helped. We might have been lost, like poor Jim; and at worst we shall have our arms to work with when we get out of this trap. I wish we had some covering overhead. It's deuced uncomfortable to have the rain coming down on a fellow like this."

"By the by, George, we don't know how long we shall be stuck here. What is there in the dilly-bag?"

"About enough beef and flour for a day's feed, and a pound of tea; but the tea won't be much use. One can't get up a fire in a green gum tree."

"Well, look there: there's one of the calves drowned in the branches of that wattle. Let's get it. The water is still enough hereabouts to swim."

So the calf was safely brought to the tree and made fast, and it was well they had secured it. The water gradually rose—ten, fifteen, twenty, thirty feet—till they expected to have to change their haven of rest for one more secure. Day after day the flood crept up the straight butt of the tree. On the seventh day the carcase of the calf, which had sustained them, became so offensive, that they cut it adrift, and were now without any means of supporting life beyond a small modicum of flour, which, with a strange pertinacity, they had determined to keep until Christmas Day, if they could possibly do without touching it. It was only a few spoonfuls, and the wet had soured it, but still it would serve to make a Christmas dinner. When the calf was gone, they looked about for something to appease the pangs of hunger. The logs, as they floated by, were alive with snakes and lizards. Occasionally they caught some of these latter, and ate them raw, but they had no fancy for raw snake. At last the flood began to abate, and in three days more they were able to descend from their perch, and once more tread terra firma. Their first business was to find something which they could cook. A fire was soon got with some dry matches they had guarded with the most anxious care. Then commenced an extraordinary hunt. Lizards were running about in all directions. They caught a pint pot full of these little saurians, and boiled them down into soup. The flour was kneaded up; the tea, out of which the long spell of rain had washed all flavour, was made; and the two famished men sat down at the fire to enjoy the first warm meal they had had for eleven days.

"Well, this is the queerest sort of Christmas fare I have ever partaken of," said George. "I am not sure that lizard stew, sour Johnny cake, and washed tea are not to be preferred to turkey, plum-pudding, and champagne."

"Yes," rejoined his brother; "when you are starved, and not within cooey of a meat-safe or a bread-bin. For my part, I prefer the ordinary style of doing things, and don't want any repetition of Christmas Eve in a gum tree."

Next day they started for the nearest station. They had lost all they possessed – cattle, horses, saddles, everything was gone. They could scarcely crawl, so weak had they become by their long sojourn in the tree, but in two days they managed to make a station, living meanwhile on grubs, lizards, and bandicoots. They were received with great hospitality, and, remaining long enough to recruit their strength, were provided with horses, and at last reached Rockhampton. Since then both have thriven, and are well-to-do men; and, above all, Maud Summer did say "Yes:" but they have never forgotten the Christmas Eve they spent in a gum tree.

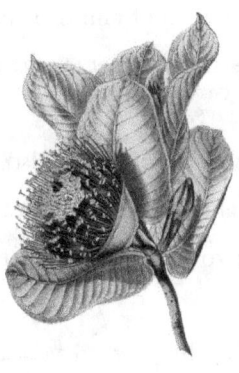

Linlarra Station and the Christmas Day I Spent There

"A Bush Naturalist"

Chapter I

Linlarra, and Introductory

"The old place looks as pretty as ever." So thought George Moreton as, on emerging from the box forest on to the "big" plain, Linlarra homestead could be seen in the distance. Certainly the young man was right, for Linlarra was one of those old-established country residences only to be found on the western slope of the New South Wales mountainous country. To Moreton it looked particularly cheery, for he had come a long distance over brown plains and still browner forest land, and, as the fresh green color of the many fruit trees that surrounded the house came in sight, even a person less interested than was the rider would have thought as he did. How pleasant indeed is the sight of any homestead to the Australian traveller after a weary day's ride of forty or fifty miles, especially at Christmas time, with its accompaniment of a hot sun!

George Moreton was the owner of a run some 160 miles lower down the Murrumbidgee river than Linlarra was situated. Let me describe him a little, for he is my hero. Like so many of the "Sydney natives," he was tall, being quite 6ft., and well and strongly built; his age was about seven-and-twenty; his hair a light brown, with whiskers of a lighter color and of which he wore sufficient to give a manly look; and they were carefully trained too, for he did not believe in burying his handsome face in a bramble of beard. His smile was particularly pleasing; there was an openness about it which, when coupled with the honest look of his fine brown eyes, made many a young damsel think how pleasant a fate it would be to be the sharer of those smiles and of "Wollondoo" station as well. However, he was as yet quite heart whole, so he said, though deep down in his inner self there remained the recollections of his former little playmate, his "bush queen" of long ago, which we, who know him better than he does himself, fancy are something warmer than mere recollections; for, now that he anticipated meeting her again, unconsciously strange feelings of pleasure quickened his pulse. No wonder the "old place" looked pretty, for the fire of love was slumbering, only waiting for one little spark to start it into such life as it had never had before. At Linlarra he had lived many happy years; it had been his adopted home, and there it was that he had been such friends with little Yattie Ingledon, the elder of the two daughters of the owner of Linlarra.

William Ingledon was one of the early settlers in this district of New South Wales. He was an educated English gentleman; but being only a "younger son" he had left the old manor-house in Buckinghamshire, come out to Sydney, and invested his capital in a sheep station. He had prospered even beyond his utmost expectations, and now was owner of a larger and fairer domain, and in receipt of a far larger income, than was his elder brother at home. However, he had no intention of quitting the land that had favored him so; but, on the contrary, was one of those few squatters who had remained faithful to their first choice, and had not been tempted to sell and buy and sell again, as is so generally the case. The consequence was that Linlarra was a model of comfort, a "snuggery" indeed, for its owner was a man of taste and refinement, and aimed at making his home as comfortable as had been the old manor-house of his boyish days.

Ingledon and Moreton, senior, had been early friends and near neighbours for years, and on the latter's death, some ten years before the date of my tale, Mr. Ingledon had taken, at the request of the dying father, young

George, who was also motherless, into his household, and accepted the executorship of his money matters. A kinder, wiser guardian the young man could not have had. After five years spent at Linlarra, by the advice of his guardian, who well knew that the lad would be the better for it, young George had gone travelling and roughing it in the other colonies, and, although travelling with stock or exploring, all the time keeping his eyes open for any good station he would like to buy; but he was in no hurry, as by his father's will he was not to have his money until his twenty-fifth birthday. In no other way can a knowledge of the capabilities of country be so satisfactorily attained as by the practical experience of droving, and George had profited much by his three years' journeyings. He had seen and been delighted with the grassy downs of Queensland, her extensive prairies and magnificent cattle runs; the close short-grassed swards of Victoria, and the clover estates of New Zealand charmed him by their greenness, but somehow—being a "sheep man," he said, was the reason—he had returned to his native colony, New South Wales, and some two years before had purchased Wollondoo; "for," as he remarked to his guardian, "what better sheep country could a man possibly want than the borders of the saltbush country of the Murrumbidgee." We, who know his inner self, may perhaps detect yet another reason—the desire to be in the neighborhood of Linlarra and its fair inmate. But how was it that George had not seen Yattie for so long, although he had been a near neighbor (160 miles counts for nothing in the Australian bush) for two years? This is easily explained; she also had been sent travelling. Her wise father— her mother was dead long years before—thinking that it would do his girls no harm to have the rusticity of bush life a little knocked off, and to enjoy for a time the benefit of female society, had taken advantage of a friend's voyaging to England to send them to his brother, their aunt having written that she "would be glad to take the little savages and ci-vilise them a bit." But the bright Australian flower, Yattie, somehow did not thrive in the cold climate of England, and so, after an absence of two years, she gladly returned to Linlarra, and took upon her the charge of her father's house. Her younger sister, Linda, quite shocked her aunt by saying "She detested England; it was a fusty old place; all small paddocks and townships; no bush; could not go for a gallop except along a road." She called her aunt the "old dowager," and was always getting into scrapes.

Yattie, on the contrary, had fallen easily into "home" ways. Although always bright and cheerful, she was less impulsive than her younger sister; she inherited far more of her father's refinement and of his gentleness of manner. Her extreme beauty had caused many to wish to win the hand of this Australian heiress; but she had refused all offers, at which her aunt was very much disappointed, and expressed her opinion, in a letter to her brother, that Yattie was by nature cold. She had done her best, but the girl would always haughtily check any approaches, even from the most eligible of suitors. The old man's heart was glad when he read this, and somehow he thought of his "boy" George.

As George drew near the homestead he could not help wondering if Yattie was looking out for him. Silly fellow, she did not even know for certain that he was coming. Then he speculated as to what she was like, and whether she had grown; and the pleasant picture of the bright young girl, just budding into womanhood, cantering by his side on her cream colored pony as she used to do in former days, arose in his mind. Yattie was just sixteen when he saw her last; she would now be twenty-one; and he wondered if she would be changed, and whether he ought to call her "Yattie" or "Miss Ingledon." Why was he thinking so of her? She was nothing to him. Most likely some English swell, knowing she had plenty of money, had persuaded her that he loved her and had won her affection by his fine talk and grand English ways. Well, well, it did not matter. He had come determined to spend a jolly Christmas, and not to moon and spoon with girls.

The governor, as he called his guardian, had written to him, telling him to come without fail, as he intended keeping Christmas right royally, this year, in honor of his daughters' return; that the Laylands from the Murray, and the Gardiners from St. Kilda, were visitors for a month; and that for Boxing Day all the neighborhood were invited, and races, including a steeplechase for a ladies' purse, and athletic sports, were to be the order of the day. But the great novelty for the bushmen was a bicycle race, two of which iron steeds the young Gardiners—being townsfolk, and wanting to astonish the dwellers in the bush—had brought up with them. It was now the day before Christmas Day; he ought to have arrived a week ago, but had been busy starting a mob of fat sheep for Melbourne.

Moreton was mounted on a fine dark bay mare, his special favourite, and with which he intended to win the Ladies' Purse, for she could and would go, and jump too, when her master wished her. Lurline he had named her, and the quickening of her walk and pricking up of her ears now reminded him that he was close to the paddock fence.

The gate into the home paddock was some half-mile from the house, which faced the river, so that anyone arriving and going straight to the stables, as George now did, could not be seen from the verandah except just at the time of opening the gate. So, his arrival being unnoticed, he dismounted, put the mare in the stall, removed the saddle, and himself carefully washed her heated back with cool water from a tank by the stable; then, giving his favourite a pat on the neck, he took off the halter, and away she trotted to the good feed in the bend of the river, never even thinking of such a thing as corn or hay, and none the worse for the 150 miles she had journeyed during the last three days.

Our hero, taking his valise in his hand, walked towards the house, and opened the little gate in the creeper-covered fence which surrounded the exquisitely-kept garden; for gardening and horticulture was Mr. Ingledon's favourite recreation and delight. From this little gate, and extending to within a few feet of the verandah, was a long, broad, arched trellis of vines, now in the full luxuriance of their summer's growth, and many in fruit. The coolness of this glorious shade was particularly pleasant to our hero after his long hot ride, and the sight of the luscious bunches of fruit hanging around and above him was refreshing indeed. Only a "saltbush country" resident can appreciate to its utmost such a temple of verdure.

Just at this moment there appeared at the opposite end of this covered walk a fair girl, evidently engaged in cutting flowers for the house, for she did not notice the visitor. One glance told George that it was Yattie; but, Heavens! how beautiful she had grown! Could it be possible that that lovely creature was his old playmate? Had indeed the bud bloomed into such a flower—his little bush queen into such an exquisite woman? The rays of the setting sun of that Christmas Eve fell full upon her, lighting up the bright hues of her golden hair; the "mountain purple"—that glorious blush of nature which, at sunset, in the pure air of our Australian alpine and semi-alpine country, envelops the hill-tops and fills the dales with its liquid ether of rosy purple—cast its full flush upon her. It was as a halo of glory, rendering even more beautiful that most lovely of pictures—a young and fair maiden. To George, who saw her thus, and through the telescopic vista of the green vines, she looked fairy-like—ay, even, he thought, divine.

Just at this moment a young man joined the fair florist. It was evident that he had been her attendant squire, for he had a large bunch of cut flowers in his hand, and George saw her give him those which she had just cut; and also he noticed that she selected a particular one and gave it to this companion, who gallantly acknowledged the present, and carefully placed it in the button-hole of his coat. Poor George! At sight of this not very extraordinary act he felt a pang shoot through him. He knew not what it was, nor had he time to think, as he was now close upon the pair. Young Fred Gardiner, for it was he, had never seen George Moreton, so it was with a somewhat supercilious annoyed look that he greeted the stranger who appeared so inopportunely upon the scene.

George broke the ice with, "Beg pardon; had no intention of intruding, I assure you."

Miss Ingledon, turning and seeing who the intruder was, cried out impulsively, "Why, it's George!" Then, feeling conscious that she had been surprised in a little mild flirtation, and noticing Moreton's cross reserved look, and remembering the sneer that was in the words he had just spoken, said stiffly, "How do you do, Mr. Moreton? We are all glad to see you. You will find papa on the verandah." And George, not making allowance for the girl's natural confusion, raised his hat and walked towards the house. Poor little Yattie, she could have bitten off her tongue for saying those cruel words.

Hearty was the welcome Moreton received on the verandah; cordial the grasp of his late guardian's hand; friendly the introductions to the strangers present. "Why, George lad, we thought you had forgotten us. Have you seen the girls? Here, Yattie! Yattie! Linda! where are you? Yattie! What on earth's become of the girl? Oh! here's Linda." And with a bound into his arms and a host of kisses did the merry girl welcome her old playmate, her "handsome brother" as she liked to call him.

But then she was not in love with George.

Chapter II

Christmas Eve in the Bush

A merry sociable party was the one gathered at Linlarra on that Christmas Eve. Times had been "good" of late years for the squatter; wool high, ready sale for all fat stock; and this year there had been abundant winter rains, and, consequently, plenty of feed. But the summer had set in hot, very hot; the grass, as is always the case at Christmas—except in tropical or semi-tropical parts—was brown and dry as tinder. This day had been intensely sultry, and the smoke of distant bush fires was to be seen in all quarters of the compass. George thought he had never had so hot a ride, even during his Queensland tour, and congratulated himself on the prospect of rest for the morrow.

The usual luxuriant dinner-tea of the well-to-do squatter's household was over. George and Yattie were more friendly, for the young lady had come up and shaken hands with him, saying she was sorry she had been so cross, but that he had surprised her so. And George thought that without doubt he had; at the same time he felt that he would like to get "that swell Gardiner" out after cattle; he would put him on a bucking horse—that he would—and then he could show off his town riding and town airs before Yattie.

However, of course, he said nothing of this, but apologised for his stiffness, and they were friends again. Presently his quick eye noticed a ring on the engaged finger of her band, and his heart sank once more. All hope fled; the cup of happiness, just found, had been knocked from his hand and broken. Nevertheless, he bravely determined not to spoil fun, but to enjoy himself as best he might, and so proposed a dance. A dance! Always welcome to all Australian girls—how heartily they do enjoy it! Hot night or cold, it is all the same—dance, dance—keep it up till daylight. Then the morning drive home in the easy light buggy, drawn by good horses; or the ride home in the cool dawn with "somebody else's brother" for an escort. Oh! there are pleasures in the bush, whatever townsfolk may think to the contrary; but a dance at such a house as Linlarra was perfection. The main home—the "old" house as it was called, to distinguish it from the many additions that had from time to time been made, till at last they formed a quadrangle at the rear—contained only four rooms, a dining room, drawing or sitting room, as it was called, the girls' bedroom, and Mr. Ingledon's library. This building was a square; the roof was of thatch, and sloped on all sides towards the edge of the verandah. This verandah was a glorious feature of the old house, for it was 12ft. wide and extended all round the four sides, and it also being roofed with thatch kept the house cool. The floor being of good sawn boards was, as the girls said, "splendid for dancing," and, as all the rooms opened by French windows on to it, the dancers could glide in or out, and so had abundant room. The dining and sitting rooms were both of them large, and were well and comfortably furnished. Choice engravings, a few good water colors, and one or two rare old paintings, the especial pride of Mr. Ingledon, for they were left to him by his father, adorned the walls; elegant little statuettes and scroll brackets were to be noticed in odd corners. The latest books too were always to be got at Linlarra, and the hospitable and refined owner studied in every way to make his home comfortable and his guests at ease. His daughters inherited their father's taste and love for the place, and supplemented his efforts by those indescribable but effective touches which betoken a lady in the house. That the love for flowers, music, drawing, and beauty pervaded the establishment was apparent at a glance. The exterior of the house showed as much tasteful thought as the interior. Let me describe it, for I was one of those guests who saw its prettiness on this the last day of its glory.

The house faced the east, and the view on this side was a fine reach of the river, which, fringed as it was with our noble Australian red-gum trees, made a magnificent natural avenue, surpassing in beauty even that of which Mr. Ingledon's elder brother was so proud at the manor-house in England. That afternoon while I sat in one of those sloth-begetting, too comfortable, Indian basket chairs, which in all parts of this cool verandah were always tempting one to indulge in their ease, I had passed the time noting the beauty of my surroundings. Clinging up and around the posts of this front verandah were a variety of those climbing plants which thrive so well in our sunny clime; these were carefully trained, and instead of the too luxuriant mass which is what one usually sees on "bush" houses, harboring vermin and shutting out pure air, there was no overcrowding, and dead shoots or brown leaves one might have sought for in vain. Each pillar had its particular kind; on this the gorgeous scarlet jacsonia showed its brilliant flowers, which contrast so beautifully with its own light green foliage; on that the homely dolichos, which is always pretty when kept neat and within bounds. Then there was a fine pillar of old English honeysuckle. This was honored with a corner post, and allowed somewhat more the privilege of spreading. Up the opposite corner, the cool corner of all, was English ivy, a rootlet from the old home, which even in this hot climate, by the aid of abundant irrigation, revelled in existence, and seemed to like things better than in cold England. Elegant hanging baskets of wire and wickerwork filled with delicate creeping ferns, others from which in rich festoons depended the white clematis, intertwined with the beautiful scarlet kennedia of our own woodlands, vied with the pillars in adding elegance to this pretty retreat. Between the front verandah and the river was the lawn—the novelty of the district, the talk of the neighborhood, and the astonishment of all bushmen when they first saw it; for it was green, really green, even on this hot day. It takes an Australian traveller to appreciate the greenness of a grass-plot. After the glare of saltbush plains—the mirage of the interior dry downs—how refreshing to the eye is the cool green of a sward of buffalo grass! At Linlarra the garden was only kept up by abundant irrigation. Situated on a sandy cliff above and close to the river, water could not be given in excess and a windmill was constantly going, night and day, supplying tanks placed above the level of the house, from which a stream always trickled through the garden. The beauty of the lawn was caused by the constant operation of the Californian sprinkler—a little machine of four arms which, revolving on the top of a standard of light iron pipe, by the pressure of the exuding water sent a spray of rain over the whole of the plot. On this hot afternoon, as I gazed, through this artificial shower, at the river beyond, and noticed the sunlight play a perpetual but ever-shifting rainbow on this misty mimic rain, I could not help thinking with what a little trouble can man, if he only likes, make this world pleasant.

The north verandah was differently treated; on this came the fall blast of the hot winds and of the noonday sun. Some few feet from the veran-dah posts was a trellis of vines, which were thence trained up to the edge of the verandah roof, and, being luxuriant and healthy in their growth, they formed a dome wall and an extended roof to the verandah which kept this part of the home cool; from these vines now hung bunches of ripe grapes, tempting, indeed, as was the apple in Paradise.

No wonder that dancing was a pleasure in such a ballroom, or that Linlarra had a good name.

Mr. Ingledon divided his time between the library and the garden; riding he did not now care about, and the practical management of the station was entirely left to his overseer. He was also somewhat more than a mere dabbler in scientific pursuits. Thermometers—maximum and minimum—dry bulb and wet bulb; barometers, rain gauge and wind gauge, were dispersed about the place; and he had contributed some exact and valuable meteorological details of that part of the colony to the Sydney Philosophical Society.

There were other visitors there that evening than those already men-tioned; but as they do not come into my story I need not particularise them more than by saying that there were young girls from the neigh-boring stations, a governess just up from Melbourne, and a stray "super." who had popped in uninvited, but nevertheless heartily welcomed. Came looking for lost horses, "one of which was a brown mare with a snip down the nose." And mischievous Linda put the poor fellow to terrible confu-sion by asking him aloud if he expected to find the brown mare with a snip down her nose in their drawing room. Of course the girls were the attraction, the strayed horses being a mere excuse; and well they knew it, so he must stay and enjoy the fun.

"Plenty of room," old Ingledon said. "If the beds are all full there are the hammocks in the verandah, and the girls will find you blankets."

Oh, how pleasant is the hearty hospitality of the Australian bush! How often have I experienced it! You arrive a stranger and unknown, glad of a night's rest, and you are not allowed to go away under several days, or a week perhaps. Send in your name, and it is taken for granted that you are a gentleman; no matter what creed or nationality, you are made welcome.

George Moreton had not yet danced with Yattie; he had made several attempts to secure her for a partner, but somehow he was always check-mated; she was engaged to someone else, or she was wanted in the house, or some such excuse. He thought she was avoiding him, and so she was; for, poor girl, her heart was as sore as his. If it had not been for that unlucky bit of flirtation with Fred Gardiner how different things would have been! She had been looking forward to this meeting with intense joy, for she had long and secretly loved her old playmate—that was the reason the English swells seemed insipid to her; that was why she fretted when at her aunt's, and was called cold; that was why the Australian flower did not thrive in cloudy England.

Poor love-sick little Yattie, she only wanted to get back so as to be near George; she often wondered if he cared for her; somehow his letters were addressed to Linda and not to her; he had never sent a fresh photo., although he had promised one; and it was five years since she had seen him. Linda had more than guessed the state of affairs, for Yattie had had a miniature taken from an old photograph of George, and had placed it in a closed locket which she always wore, and which for a long time she would not let her sister see; but it all came out one day, much to the satisfaction of Linda, who said "George was a good fellow; she would like him much for a real brother, but for her part she would not marry a big man for fear he would be master. She intended to get a little whipper-snapper that she could trot out as she liked." The evening was slipping away most pleasantly to all but the two love-sick ones. It was after 11 o'clock. Mrs. Gardiner had just sat down to the piano for the fourth time, and was rattling off a lively galop. George snatched up Linda, and away they went; Linda gloried in a galop—"left square dances for the sober folk," she said—so round and round the house they went. "Oh! George," she said, "this is delightful; so much better than the tiresome balls we had at auntie's—had to wear horrid long trains; stiff quadrilles, and we were crowded and 'scrunched'."

Linda had noticed something was wrong between George and Yattie, and she could not understand it. "What a pair of silly things they are!" she thought, for, by George's letters to her, she felt sure her pretty sister was as much in his thoughts as he was in hers. "It's all that Fred Gardiner's doing, I believe;" for although she knew nothing of the flirtation scene, yet she had noticed his very marked attentions to Yattie that night. As they for the third time whirled round the house, Yattie and Fred stepped on to the verandah from the vine-walk. She felt George start at the sight, and her quick wit saw a chance of putting things right. Disengaging herself when just by her sister, she said, "Oh, Yattie dear, George has so improved in his dancing since we put him through his first quadrille, just try;" and before the astonished couple could recover from their surprise she had seized hold of Fred Gardiner and was galoping round with him. George put his arm round Yattie, and away they went too. Round and round that long verandah they galoped, now by the ivy corner, now under the fern fronds, now flitting in the moonlight, now in the shade. Only these two couples remained. If Mrs. Gardiner imagined either of these would tire before she would she was much mistaken, for Linda, from pure enjoyment of the exercise, and "to give," as she said afterwards, "George a chance," would not give in; besides she liked Fred Gardiner, and did not quite approve of his attentions to Yattie. George and Yattie were in such a daze of happiness that they felt they could never tire. At last the piano stopped. Mrs. Gardiner thought "those girls had had quite enough," she said, and the cheery voice of Mr. Ingledon was heard saying, "Now, girls, it's quite bedtime. Save some of your dancing for Boxing night and the woolshed ball. We men are just going to have a smoke in the verandah and then retire."

As Yattie went up and kissed her dear old father she looked flushed and happy and very pretty. "You look well, little one," he said.

"Oh! Papa, dear, we have had such a pleasant evening!"

"That's right, Pussy. Who have you been dancing with?"

"With George, and"—

"Never mind the others, dear; good-night;" and the old man's heart was glad, for he dearly loved his "boy" George, as he called him.

Somehow Yattie felt that she had her father's confidence, and she was happy, although she and George had hardly spoken a word during the dance.

"Was not that a nice galop?" said sly Linda from under the coverlet.

"Dear Linda, you are such a kind good sister;" and Linda knew that her move had been successful.

"The barometer is still falling, we shall have a hot north wind to-morrow," said our host as he rose from his smoking chair, tapped at the weather-glass, and wished us all good-night.

I, the favored guest, the family friend, slept in a hammock slung from the house corner to the verandah pillar; and, as I lay and looked through the leafy screen of the climbing passiflora, and saw the light of the rising moon reflected in the rippling of the running water of the river as if it had been a floor of liquid silver and glittering gems, I could not help envying the lot of our genial host, with his fair daughters and his fair home.

Alas! it was the calm. On the morrow came the storm.

Chapter III

Clouds

Christmas morning broke close and suffocating. The sun, red with the smoke of the late bush fires which hung close to earth, seemed to struggle to rise. A gentle north wind arose with the sun, and by the time breakfast was announced it had increased into a strong hot wind. We all met at the table with that feeling of lassitude upon us which is an invariable accompaniment of Australian north winds.

"Good morning, everyone," said the cheery voice of our host as he entered the room and took the head of the table. "All well, I hope? Going to have a roasting hot wind today. Never saw the barometer so low before. The thermometer is even now 90 degrees, and that when under the ivy corner. God help those whose grass gets on fire to-day!"

"I hope you are secure," said George.

"Pretty well, boy. You know I always burn strips as soon as the grass will take fire, and there is a good broad patch burnt on our north boundary; from the east the river protects us but we are open to the south. I hope travellers will be careful of their camp fires to-day."

"What are your plans for the day?" continued Mr. Ingledon, who was one of those truly hospitable hosts who let their guests do just as they like, yet at the same time study to make occupation for them.

"I think it too hot to do anything," said Fred Gardiner, "and so intend to sit and smoke and lounge in the verandah." The truth was that he had been so enraptured by that last galop with Linda that he began to think her ten times as jolly as Yattie, and by staying at home he thought he might get a chance of a little flirtation with her.

"Well, you are a lazy thing!" said Linda; "I thought you men were going to practise bicycling for tomorrow's race, and I anticipated fine fun seeing how awkward our crack buckjumping riders would be on this town horse that cannot buck but only run away or tumble down."

Fred Gardiner, who was a good bicyclist, would not have minded this opportunity of showing off before the lively girl; but the other "males" who did not care to make exhibitions of themselves, voted it too hot, and backed up the first proposition of the verandah and laziness.

"Yattie," said our host, "be sensible, and do not give us a hot heavy dinner in the midday, although it is Christmas Day. Let us have one of your nice fruit luncheons."

"Very well, papa. I will tell cook not to serve dinner till sunset; by that time perhaps the wind will be from the south."

"I think you are wrong there, little one; except there come a cyclone this wind will keep on till tomorrow night."

George Moreton had managed to get a place near Yattie. They had shaken hands that morning and were good friends. He had picked a pretty little bunch of two or three flowers and a spray of leaf, and as he sat down had slipped it by her plate. She took it up, pinned it with her brooch, and—their eyes met. Oh the language of the eye! how much, yet how quietly, it talks! It was their first love look—their first drink at that intoxicating fountain—the insertion of one link of a chain which they little thought would that very day be rivetted fast by a scene of mutual peril and trouble.

Breakfast over, Mr. Ingledon went down to his overseer's hut to tell him to keep horses ready harnessed and saddled all day in the stable, in case of a fire breaking out; also, to have the water-keg in the light waggon, and the beaters—old bags fastened on to sticks, with which the burning grass is beat out—all ready. But the trusty McAndrew had already seen to these things, and had started an hour previously to see where that fire was the smoke of which was now plainly visible to the south-west.

About 11 o'clock Mr. Ingledon entered the verandah where we were all sitting, the young men lounging in net hammocks and Indian chairs, doing nothing, and saying "silly nothings" to the ladies, who were trying to make us believe that they were doing "fancy work" of some sort.

"A frightful day this," he said; "the thermometer is already up to 110 degrees. There is a terrible fire to the south-west. It is to our leeward certainly, but if the wind should change it might turn back again if no rain falls, and it is our weak quarter."

"A good thing for me," said George, "that so many travelling sheep have this year passed over Wallondoo; it relieves me of much anxiety, for they have left it quite bare."

"I am afraid, papa," said Yattie, who had gone on to the lawn and seen the direction of the smoke, "that the fire is on Thompson's selection. Dear me, I do hope not, for his wife is sick and they have a large family of little ones."

"I fear you are right, Yattie, and the long grass of the river bend where he has just built his new house extends close up to his door. I told him ten days ago he ought to burn it at night-time; if he has neglected to do so he is done for. But," he resumed, "I see McAndrew at the paddock gate. By his hurry I should say something was amiss."

In a minute or so the overseer walked up to the verandah. He was almost unrecognisable from smoke, dust, and perspiration. It was evident he had been through hard times already that morning, for his fine whiskers and beard were singed to the cheek.

"Fire got away," he began, without noticing anyone but the master, "from a traveller's camp in our bottom paddock, crossed over Sandy creek, then the strong north wind turned it south, and it has cleared Thompson out—fences and house all gone. He made for the river, carrying his sick wife, and telling his little children to follow. I rode up just as the fire caught the house; noticed little Willie crying inside, so I rushed in and got him out; then followed the fire to the river, where I found Thompson coming out of the shallow lagoon where they had taken refuge. The poor wife was in a great way when she found little Willie had stopped behind. Was she not glad to see him again all right!" And the hardy fellow's begrimed face actually looked cleaner as the pleasure of the good deed he had done recurred to his mind.

"Well done, McAndrew, well done indeed!" and as our host said this he took a bottle of beer from the water-bag cooler in the corner, knocked off the top, and handed it to the thirsty overseer. "Here, man, drink this; we will talk afterwards."

Bass' ale never, no not even in our Queensland Gulf country, was so appreciated as by that man, who, without waiting for tumbler or seeming to be aware of the presence of ladies, hastily put the big bottle to his lips and there kept it until it was entirely empty.

"That was good, sir, and no mistake. I only wish my throat was as long as a native companion's," he said, laughing.

"Start Dick off with the waggon, put in one of our spare tents, and take out a bag of flour, some tea and sugar, and meat," said the warm-hearted Ingledon. "Send him round here first, and Miss Ingledon will put up some little things as well."

"And, Mr. McAndrew, will you please get up my mare Whitefoot?" added Yattie. "I will go and see poor Mrs. Thompson and what I can do for her," she said to her father.

"I am afraid it is too hot for you, little one; still I should like you to go."

"Mac, get Lurline up as well; she is down in the bend. If Miss

Ingledon will accept me as an escort I shall be happy to go too," said George, as he turned enquiringly to Yattie.

"I shall be very glad," said Yattie in return; and indeed she spoke the truth.

Chapter IV

The Ride for Life

Yattie looked simply perfect in George's eyes as some two hours after she stepped off the verandah and walked under the vine trellis towards the back gate leading to the stables. When she placed her tiny foot into his hand, and lightly sprang into the saddle, George thought himself in Paradise; and as he turned and caught sight of her pretty figure, shown off so nicely by a well-fitting blue riding-habit, down which her golden hair hung in long wary curls, his conquest was complete.

"Here, George, give this to Thompson," and Mr. Ingledon placed a cheque for £20 in his hand; "and, Yattie, if that poor woman can be shifted, arrange for the trap to bring her in; she can stop here until her husband has a new house up."

And they started, little thinking that, but for their being mounted on two trusty horses, they would never again have seen the dear old place.

"It is frightfully hot for their ride, a regular furnace blast, not fit for a man to be out in, let alone little Yattie. I hope she will take no harm." All this Mr. Ingledon muttered as he turned towards the house, after gazing for a long time at the retreating couple. A strange foreboding of coming evil passed through his mind, but he dismissed it as foolish.

It was indeed a furnace blast; actually in the cool shade of the ivy corner the glass told 115 degrees of heat; such a thing had never before occurred at Linlarra. Reader, if you are a bushman, and have ever travelled in the saltbush country on such a day, you will know that it was not a pleasant ride this young pair had undertaken; it wanted all their fresh young love to compensate for the discomforts of that hot sun and that scorching wind. Conversation was not brisk between them; both felt rather awkward, and did not know what to say. It was only seven miles to Thompson's, but that would take them an hour and a-half, for it was too hot to canter; walking was quite enough exertion for either the horses or their riders.

"Look at those poor dear birds," exclaimed Yattie, as from a box-tree in full bloom she saw some paraquets fall to the ground, struggle for breath, and die. "The heat has actually killed them."

"Yes," replied George, "I have seen that sort of thing before, but only once, and then I was in the dry Darling river district. Even water does not always seem to save them; they are actually suffocated by the dry hot blast. Look at those honeyeaters under those shady leaves and that big laughing-jackass up yonder tree, how they all pant with open beak and evident exhaustion, and yet the river is only three miles off. I have known on days like this crows, magpies, hawks, and even some of the smaller birds boldly seek the shelter of the men's huts, and perch on the rafters, even when the men were at dinner."

"Poor things! I hope the men did not hurt them."

"No likelihood of that," replied George. "I have met with very few cruel men in Australia—except to horses," he mentally added.

"Do you believe in presentiments, Mr. Moreton?" She did not like to call him George, as of old. "I somehow have a strange feeling of coming evil."

"No, I do not. This hot day is enough to make anyone feel presentiments."

"Well, I hope it is that;" but to herself she was not satisfied.

On arriving at Mrs. Thompson's they found the dray already there, the tent up, and the sick woman snugly housed and as comfortable as circumstances would admit, so Yattie thought it better she should not be moved to the station—a most lucky decision as things turned out. The cheque was given to Thompson, who was as astonished as he was thankful for this help, just when it was so greatly needed.

As they started for home, George looked at his watch and saw that it was just 3 o'clock—about the hottest time of the day. After they had gone a mile or so on their return Yattie complained of faintness, and said she would so like a drink. As there was no water on the road till they got home, George suggested a detour by the Billabong swamp which was about half a mile distant; so they turned off on that track, thus making their journey a mile or two longer—nothing of any moment ordinarily, but on this day nearly a fatal mistake. After having obtained a drink, which George managed to get tolerably cool by putting the little pannikin (that used always to hang at his saddle) as far below the surface of the water as he could reach, and having watered their thirsty horses as well, they started up the track that led to the main one they had left.

"I cannot make the weather out at all," said George; "the hot north wind has dropped entirely and suddenly, and yet no southerly 'burster' has come up, and it is hotter than ever. If we were in Queensland I could understand this calm close heat, but down here it is most unusual, particularly on a hot-wind day."

"One could almost fancy an earthquake coming," said Yattie.

"Just so," replied her companion; "there is a feeling as if everything wanted to burst—an oppressiveness unaccountable. Clouds we cannot see for the smoky haze over everything."

"What is that noise, George?"—the old name slipped out then, and quite naturally too, for gradually a fellow-feeling, a sympathy of interests, was springing up between them—"is it the south wind coming?"

"It sounds like it; but, by Jove! it is from the west!"

Just then they reached an elbow in the road and were on a slight eminence; it could hardly be called a hill, but from it, on a clear day, was a very extended view over the heavily-timbered country surrounding them. Moreton turned and looked towards the west, and in the far distance, in spite of the smoky atmosphere, was to be seen a dense black cloud. But it was not like the blackness of rain clouds, as in a southerly "burster," or as in a thunderstorm. No; it looked like dust and smoke; in fact, for a moment our hero was puzzled.

"What a strange phenomenon!" said his fair companion, "and how it roars even at this distance!"

Another look at it and Moreton knew what it was, and shuddered as he thought of the terrible danger they were in.

"Yattie," he said gravely, "it is no common southerly burster, no ordinary gale; it is a cyclone, a whirlwind! It will clear everything before it, and apparently we are exactly in the centre of its track."

The girl's cheek turned pale; well she knew their danger. She had seen the strange tracks cut by such cyclones in years gone by; tracks of from half to three-quarters of a mile in width, in which every tree and shrub had succumbed to the terrific force.

Moreton had actually witnessed one, had almost been in it; had seen even the supple mallee scrub twisted up and wrenched from the ground; had known a woolshed to be coiled up in a minute's time, and scattered far over the plain; even men actually lifted up and carried some distance. Nothing can stand against them if in the vortex of the whirl. Thank God they are not common. I, the writer of this little history, have seen one, and the tracks of several, in the course of my travels, so cannot but think that as the country gets settled—more particularly Queensland—their frightfully destructive effects will be oftener heard of.

"George, we must be off home at once: we are both well mounted and may outrace it."

"Yattie, dear," replied he, "that will never do. It is yet five miles to home-station plain; all the rest of the way is forest land. These cyclones travel at the rate of from thirty to a hundred miles an hour; it would overtake us before we were half the distance. There is only one way of escape, and it is to go back to the Billabong swamp; there is a little plain there."

"But it is coming that way; we should be going to meet it."

"Yes, dear, we should; but it is our only chance. We are three-quarters of a mile from the swamp; at any rate, I think if we gallop hard we can get there in three minutes. Once there we are safe. We cannot run away from this danger; then let us face. Will you try?"

"Yes, George, I am ready." But the plucky girl's face turned pale as she thought of the peril and of home.

All this talk had not taken half as long to say as it has to read, for there was no time for indecision.

"One minute, dear. Let us be sure we are on its track. The bend in the river near Thompson's may perhaps change its course. It will cross that directly. Let us see; if it does not it will then have two miles to go, and we a short mile. We can do it unless it quickens its pace."

"George, dear, you take the lead. Whitefoot heartily enjoys a race; she will try and head Lurline. Don't be frightened for me, you know how I can ride. See, it is across the river!"

"God help us!" exclaimed Moreton; and with a cheery word and a touch of his spur away bounded Lurline on this terrible ride; and Whitefoot was not behind in the start. The earnestness of the riders was apparent to the horses, who put it down as a race, and each did its utmost to get or keep ahead of the other. The roar of the whirlwind came louder and louder. George ventured a look back at Yattie, and by a pleasant smile quite reassured the trembling girl.

"We shall do it," he shouted; "only another minute." The pace they went was alarming, but it was for life. Although it was through heavy timber they were galloping, yet the track they were on was made by the bullock drays, which usually turned off the main road in order to camp at this water, and both horses and riders knew the road well, so there was no danger except from the hurricane; the horses were not likely to bolt from the track, and, as long as the riders kept tolerably near the middle of the road, the slight turns caused by trees could be easily avoided. Yattie and George had had many a youthful race, but never such a ride as this.

The long grass of the billabong they could now see; another quarter of a mile and they would be safe—would they, could they, do it? The whirling leaves and twigs, the forerunners of the vortex, they could see had already crossed the swamp; they felt the first rush of the exterior whirl. "Steady, Lurline, steady!" exclaimed George, as he took a slight pull on the reins, "we must clear it," and he again looked at the brave girl beside him. She caught the glance and nodded assent; then with an "Up! lass, up!" a gigantic gum-tree that had already succumbed to the first blast, and whose huge trunk lay fairly across the path, was cleared simultaneously by the two horses; another fifty paces and they were in the hollow of the billabong, and free from timber.

"Off, Yattie, off, and lie down!" shouted George—and they were safe! The frightened girl lay down and hid her face in the grass. George sat by her. They were not a minute, scarcely a second, too soon; the roar of the cyclone was upon them, the air was dark with dust, leaves, twigs, and branches, which even the journey of half-a-mile over the swampy plain had not ceased to drop. The horses now seemed to know by instinct what was coming, and stayed down in the hollow of the billabong, crouching themselves up into the smallest possible space and turning their backs on the storm.

With Yattie's little hand held tightly in his did Moreton sit out that frightful, that terrible, gale. Once he felt himself almost lifted off the ground by the whirling force of that mighty wind. The main centre, the vortex, passed some two hundred yards to the south; when it reached the timber again the tree-tops were twisted off the stoutest gums, whirled round in the air, and dashed to the ground. The strangest part of this phenomenon to our hero was that it was done apparently quite noiselessly; the general roar was so great that the uprooting of a forest giant and the twisting off of his head made no individual noise. And the black mass whirled on, carrying death and destruction to everything it touched—Nature's avenging Nemesis for man's invasion of her domain. At length it was past, leaving a cool gentle breeze in its wake.

"Yattie, darling, it is gone; look up;" and the poor bewildered girl raised herself, gave one loving look at her companion, and fell fainting into his arms. Even her good nerves and strong common sense had been overtaxed, and no wonder. This was a climax little expected by George, and he was now fairly puzzled; but gently laying her down he ran to the water, filled his hat, and, returning, bathed her face. It soon had effect, and as the gentle breeze played with the golden ringlets of her long hair, and he gazed on the pale face, George thought he had never seen such beauty.

As she opened her fine blue eyes and encountered George's anxious look, the crimson blood returned to her cheeks, quickened into circulation by the sight of her lover, and she soon was herself again.

"Thank you, George," she said, "you have saved my life by your courage and decision. How can I ever repay you?"

"By trusting yourself to me always, darling," he replied, encircling her with his arm.

No need for words; all was understood. Still George said, "Yattie dear, I have always loved you." For answer she showed him the locket with his own boyish portrait in it that was suspended from her neck.

"But that engaged ring, Yattie?" said he, pointing to the one on her hand.

"Oh, I only wore that because I did not want you to think that I—that—"

A kiss from George finished the sentence.

This pretty scene was put an end to by Yattie, who said, "Let us hasten home, George. I do so hope they are all well at home. Do you think the storm has missed them?" And George said "Yes," although he saw that it had gone straight in the direction of the Linlarra homestead.

Chapter V

Linlarra Again

That afternoon we at Linlarra sat and lounged out in the verandah. The fruit luncheon had been a great success, and the tables in the parlor were still covered with peaches, grapes, sugary watermelons, and luscious rockmelons, all grown to that perfection which only a horticulturist like our host can attain to. Numbers of empty bottles that had contained Kaludah and Irrawang, those delicious light wines of New South Wales, testified to the heat of the day and the thirst of the guests; these when full had been exhumed as wanted from the depths of the water-cooler. The little lawn-sprinkler had been busily revolving all day, sending its refreshing spray over the sward in front. Never had the snugness of the homestead been more apparent, never had Linlarra looked pleasanter.

About 3 o'clock our host anxiously walked on to the verandah; he had had an hour's "coil" on the sofa in his study.

"I cannot make today out at all," he said; "I have never seen the thermometer so high before; it has actually been up to 115 degrees, and is now 110 degrees, and the wind has dropped to a dead calm. I never knew such a thing happen on a strong hot wind day. The barometer it rising too rapidly. I don't like it; I am uneasy."

"Why," I exclaimed, "does it not always rise before a south wind?"

"Yes. But in this district generally not till it comes, or there are plain indications of it in the clouds; and I can detect no sign of a change in that quarter. I expect a hurricane or a cyclone," he resumed, "and probably from the west. I do so wish Yattie was here."

"Why from the west?" I asked.

"Well, I have no good reasons; but this north wind has evidently met with a strong south one, and the meeting of the two causes this calm; and, like two waters meeting, although they stop the current, there is always a whirl somewhere. As our south winds here generally have a westerly inclination, I expect this whirlwind will be on that side of the compass." And the old gentleman paced up and down, and anxiously glanced at the gate, as if by that he could bring his pet daughter to him.

Excavated out of the sandy cliff on which the house was built was a spacious cellar, or rather underground room. Before the adoption of the extensive garden irrigation, when the verandah was bare of creepers, and no lawn was to be seen, this room used to be the favourite sitting place of the family on hot days, for the door into it was from the river side, and it was pleasant to sit there and see the water glide by. They called it "the Cave," for the entrance was reached by a slanting path cut in the face of the cliff. Latterly this retreat had been abandoned and converted into a wine cellar.

The timepiece in the hall had just chimed half-past 3 when Mr. Ingledon again appeared. "It is coming!" he said hurriedly. "God grant it may miss the house and poor Yattie!"

"What is coming?" we all anxiously asked, for by the manner of our kind host we saw that it was no trifling matter.

"The hurricane! the cyclone!" he replied and taking us all on to the lawn he pointed to the dark moving column of cloud, whose spiral movement could be traced high up into the sky by the accumulated gathering of dust and leaves. It was the same which had overtaken our two lovers.

None present but the owner of Linlarra and myself knew the terrific force of that pillar of cloud, so the others were rather astonished at the anxious and somewhat peremptory tone with which Mr. Ingledon continued: "It is coming direct to the house. Linda, take all the ladies into the cave, and stay there. Quick, girl, there is no time to lose!"

"McAndrew," he said to his trusty overseer, who seemed always to be where difficulties were, "do you know what is coming? Never mind, you will soon see. Off to your own house and the men's quarters. Turn everyone out; the stockyard will be the safest place. Let the women folk lie down and hold on to the rails, or the wind will blow them away. Run, man, run!" Then turning to us, he said calmly, "Gentlemen, we will retire below the level of the bank a little and watch this grand demonstration of the wind's power;" and the brave old man led the way to the sloping walk in the cliffs.

Alas! fair Linlarra, with your cool verandahs and hospitable recollections, your lovely flowers and elegant surroundings—without even a minute for a farewell glance—we had left you for ever! On came the whirling roaring mass of cloud straight for the house. One moment and we thought it would miss it—no, it was not to be. The black pillar enveloped the building, smothered us with dust, blinded our eyes as we, new in fear, crouched down below the level of the bank. There was a frightful crash, and then a continuous rushing roar, and over our heads, as we lay close to the ground, we felt this fearful wind—dense with earthy materials—whirling, flying round and round, in that terrible vortex; it was a maelstrom in the air, a whirlpool of the skies!

Five minutes afterwards, on what had been the lawn, but was now a rubbish heap, stood a frightened group of persons, aghast at the destruction around them.

The whole place was destroyed; house, quadrangle, stables, vines, and trees gone! The plain as far as could be seen, and the surface of the river, were strewn with pieces of furniture, thatch, wearing apparel, and papers, sheets of iron, and rubbish. The heavier beams and the brick walls of the nearer buildings were moved and felled into an extraordinary mass— destruction was utterly complete. The very centre of the whirl, the vortex of that maelstrom, had passed over the house; but the men's huts, the woolshed, and the overseer's house, being a full quarter of a mile to one side, had escaped with the loss only of their iron roofs and windows.

One sentence only did our dear old host say; it was: "Yattie; may God help her!" We could give him no comfort, so remained silent.

***

It was an hour or so afterwards, as the old man again stood, with folded arms and sorrowful anxious face, gazing at the ruins of his own fair homestead, a young girl came quietly up to him, kissed his tear-bedewed cheeks, and said, "Dear father, never mind, for we are all safe and well."

"Pussy, dear, is that you? Oh, how glad I am to see you!" and he hugged her to his heart. "How did you escape? McAndrew has gone looking for you. Are you hurt?"

"No, papa; George was with me."

"George with you!" and the old man laughed. "Why I knew that, but how does that help the matter?"

Things were soon explained, for George came up and helped Yattie out of her difficulty.

"Ah! I see how it is," he said gaily; "I have lost a house but found a son. I am so pleased, lad. I always wanted this to be," and he again kissed Yattie warmly, and shook George by the hand.

"Linda, lassie," he continued; "come here, girl, I have news to tell you."

"I know what it is, papa dear. I went with Fred and McAndrew to find Yattie, and it all came out."

"Fred, Fred—who is Fred?"

But the awkwardness of answering this question was avoided, for just then a four-in-hand drag entered the paddock and dashed up to the ruins.

"Ingledon, old fellow," said the handsome driver, as he jumped off his seat directly his man had the horses by the head, "my boundary-rider was met by your overseer, who started him off at a gallop to tell me, so I harnessed up at once. You must all come to Dunrobin. I'll drive the girls—I beg pardon, the ladies I mean; the gentlemen can ride." The speaker was the jolly owner of the next station.

"Ugh! what a smash-up!" he exclaimed, as his eye fell upon the heap of ruins. And so it turned out that Dunrobin was full to overflowing that Christmas night.

Chapter VI

Conclusion

The Boxing Day fête at Linlarra was necessarily postponed, but only till the next year. By that time a new home was erected, and it was then held. As many of the guests who were at the "smash-up" as possible could come were there, including the stray "super." and the young governess, for on this Christmas Day a double wedding had taken place, and it was the event of the district. The reader can guess as to the respective brides and bridegrooms when I say that Linda had gone on a visit to St. Kilda with Mrs. Gardiner and Fred, and had a gay season in Melbourne; and that our dear old host, anxious, as he said, to see what the saltbush country was like, went back with George Moreton and stayed at Wollondoo till the trusty McAndrew wrote to him that "the place was somewhat itself again." Need I say that Yattie went with her father—and George?

A Christmas Message

Ada Cambridge

Chapter I

It was in the middle of February last year, late on a Saturday afternoon, that two young men tramped home to dinner, with their guns over their shoulders, after stalking wild duck since daybreak. They carried one small bird between them, which was an object of deep interest to the retriever at their heels, and they did not seem by any means dejected at having achieved so little success at so great an expense of time and toil. The drought had broken up, but the fertile undulating downs of the Western District were still parched and brown, and the hot air had a pungent smell of smoke in it, quite as strong as the smell of the wild peppermint blossom which they crushed under their tired feet. The hum of a threshing-machine stole through the evening stillness from a distant farm-yard; like the hum of a bumble-bee. The sun was beginning to paint some far-away hilltops with lilac, and the dusty bush track with faintest flakes of shade. A rosy flush of oleander flowers broke the dark monotony of garden foliage, which, half a mile off, indicated that haven of rest, and iced brandy and soda, towards which the faces of the pedestrians were set. A fair haven it was—a charming country-house, of that order of bush architecture which one grieves to think must pass away, while perhaps we are ourselves alive to see it go—like nothing so much as a dozen or two of rustic cottages growing together, embellished, with as much care as if it had been a queen's palace. All higgedly-piggedly as to roofs and gables, and windows and doors, built here of weatherboard, and there of brick, with ivy on one wall and Swiss woodwork on another, French casements in one room and diamond panes in the next, the beauty and harmony and picturesqueness of the whole would have driven an artist wild; and those who were not artists, but practical people; fond of ease and comfort, of cool rooms luxuriously appointed, of leafy verandahs to smoke and flirt in, of pleasant society and good dinners, thought there was no such "nice place" anywhere about. It stood in the midst of smooth lawns and speckless gravel paths, with wide belts of shrubs and trees about it, as sweet an oasis in that desert of sun-parched paddock as weary eyes could wish for.

Our two young sportsmen entered the garden by a side-gate, and went straight to the smoking-room, the French windows of which stood wide to the shadow of a great dark pine-tree at a far corner of the house. They were late additions to a large party of guests, which, according to annual custom, had assembled under that hospitable roof as soon as shearing was over. The elder, Mr. Robert Yorke, was, or had been, a police magistrate, whom Black Wednesday had thrown upon the world a month ago—fortunately, with a little money of his own, and no wife and children; the younger, Mr. Frank Townshend, was a neighbouring landowner, lately settled on the paternal station after a few years' travel —a handsome young fellow, with a large estate and plenty of brains and breeding, whose society was considered an acquisition in all well-regulated households. They disposed of their guns and game, flung themselves into long-armed wicker chairs, with great puffs and sighs of satisfaction, and watched the butler, who had followed at their heels with his tray of tumblers and bottles, drawing corks and ladling out lumps of ice, with an ardent wistfulness that was very touching. There was no word spoken for several minutes, while they drained their glasses, and smacked their lips and wiped their moustaches, and leaned back to enjoy the delicious sensation of assuaged thirst and rested legs. Then the butler, pausing at the door, broke the silence with these words—"Mr. Yorke— sir, she's come."

Evidently the announcement was unexpected and startling. "You don't say so, Wills!" Mr. Yorke exclaimed, suddenly springing up from his lounging attitude, with an air of pleased excitement.

"Yes, sir. Mr. Charteris wanted her to rest in town a little while, but she insisted on coming straight home to her ma tonight. The telegram to order the buggy came just after breakfast. She's gone to her room till dinner-time, sir. All the other young ladies are out riding."

When the man had left them Mr. Yorke began to fill his meerschaum, talking volubly the while. "Pretty little Nelly!" he exclaimed. "How glad I am she's back. If she's anything like what she was when she went home with her aunt to England two years ago—and she can't have begun to go off yet—there will be the devil to pay with some of you."

"Not with me," said Mr. Townshend calmly, hunting for a cigarette.

"Don't you boast too soon," retorted his friend. "You have never seen her. You'll be as bad as anybody in a week's time. You've no idea what a way she has of getting round a fellow—I don't care who he is."

"So I have heard," said the young squatter, composedly puffing and stroking his beard. "But I flatter myself I am proof against the machinations of a flirt. I know one as soon as I set my eyes on her, and I've never been taken in by one yet. There's nothing in this world I detest so much."

"Did I say she was a flirt? I don't believe she has an ounce of coquetry in her."

"How can that be, by your own showing? No, I have heard men in Melbourne going on about her, as if there was never another woman in Australia. I know what she is by the way they talk. And I know I am not destined to swell the number of her slaves."

Mr. Townshend was a fine young man and a born gentleman, who would as soon have cheated at cards as cast a slight or a slur upon a lady, if he knew it; but his own excessive popularity had made him a little autocratic in more ways than one. He had had a large experience of women, and they had as a rule been kinder than was good for him. Moreover, the Divine passion had not awakened in him yet, to humble the pride of that well-balanced judgment which he brought to bear on all their little foibles. Mr. Yorke, too, had had a large experience of women, comprehending that special knowledge which he lacked, and now he laughed derisively. "My dear young friend," said he, taking his pipe from his mouth, and waving his hand with an air of fatherly superiority that was certainly rather irritating, "I don't mind telling you something considerable—that you'll either marry her before the year is out, or be fit to cut your throat because you can't."

And then Mr. Townshend did a very foolish thing. He was a proud young fellow, and it ruffled him to be treated like a boy. "I'll bet you £100," he answered hotly, springing up from his chair and striking a table near him with his clenched hand, "that I'll never ask Miss Charteris to marry me." As soon as the words were out of his mouth he was ashamed of having uttered them. And the next moment he would cheerfully have given £100, and a great deal more, to have them unsaid. For his eye fell upon a face in the doorway, the expression of which told him that they had been heard by other ears than those of his companion, in whose honour and friendship he had safely trusted for many a long year. It was one of those dreadful children who have a knack of presenting themselves at the most untoward times; the youngest son of the house, who had just escaped from his tutor, and was casting about to see what mischief he could find for his idle hands to do. Mr. Townshend certainly did not go the right way to work to remedy his. "What do you stand grinning there for, you young idiot!" he burst out savagely, with a white and angry face.

"I'm not doing anything," whined the boy, shrinking a little from this unexpected onslaught; and then he added maliciously, "But I know Nelly wouldn't marry you if you did ask her. Mother says there was a lord wanted her when she was in England, and she wouldn't even have him."

Mr. Townshend strode across the room, and dragged in that boy by the collar of his jacket. "Look here," he said, with sharp distress in his rough words, "if ever I catch you telling your sister that I said that—and I was only joking, I did not mean it seriously—that is to say, I only meant I shouldn't presume to ask her; hang it, it's no business of yours what I meant? You want a good hiding for coming prying about when you're not wanted, and listening to what you've no right to hear. If you ever tell her, mind, I'll—I'll make it a caution to you, and so I tell you."

"Well," said Mr. Yorke, when the two men were alone again, "I gave you credit for more sense, Frank. You might as well have told that boy to go and report your little speech to his sister straight off. He'd have been much more likely not to have done it."

Frank Townshend said nothing. He stood by the table mechanically uncurling his cigarette. It had come home to him as suddenly as his freak of insolence and temper had arisen, that he had been speaking and acting like a snobbish schoolboy—he who had been considered almost infallible in all matters of taste and breeding—and he was ashamed and mortified to the last degree. "It is time to go and dress," he said, after a gloomy pause, as the brazen boom of a great gong began to swell through the house. And he walked off to his room with a more stately step than usual.

Half an hour afterwards he came slowly into the drawing-room, with the quiet self-possession of a man who knows he is welcome wherever he may go, and a rather more haughty air about him than he had worn last night when he crushed that young travelling Englishman—the son of a baronet—who appeared amongst the ladies in coloured clothes and a striped collar (under the delusion that he was conforming to the customs of the country), by politely reminding him that the dressing-bell had rung.

Two or three gentlemen were in the room and six or eight ladies, all gathered round the hearthrug, where stood the newly arrived daughter of the house. "Here is our dear child, of whom you have heard so much," said the delighted mother, leading her forward. "This is Mr. Townshend, Nelly, our nearest neighbour, you know, love."

Mr. Townshend bowed calmly, and as he raised his head he looked at her with cold and critical eyes. Was that the notorious Nelly Charteris, with that grave and noble face—that gracious and gentle dignity of manner, which, to the experienced man of the world, indicated instantly the pure and proud and high-bred woman, whom no one would dare to flirt with? Mr. Yorke was watching the introduction from a distance, and he knew what was happening to his self-confident young friend, who was only himself vaguely conscious of a great shock of surprise and pain. He had fallen a victim already.

Chapter II

To fall in love at first sight—to do so, moreover, against one's determined wish and will—is not a very common occurrence, perhaps, but it does happen now and then. It is not beauty that does it—the striking beauty that is patent to the world. Who can tell what it is? Something, not in one face, but in both; something not seen, but ever so dimly felt; an instinctive recognition of natural fellowship between his spirit and hers, as they look at one another out of strange and purblind eyes. So slight a thrill of sympathy that probably neither of them are aware of having felt it if, afterwards, they see each other's faces no more; but, if otherwise, distinct enough to indicate the true birth-moment of the passion that grows up to be one flower and fruitage of their joint lives.

Frank Townshend and Nelly Charteris fell in love with one another that night in this latent and unconscious way. Neither was in the least responsible or prepared for such a contingency. He was thirty-three, and she was ten years younger; both had read and travelled much, and were experienced in the ways of the world; had enjoyed popularity and admiration, had had love affairs in plenty, had been engaged to be married, and, as the result of it all, were now disposed to regard both past and prospective sweethearts with a little weariness and suspicion. He was an utter stranger to her, she was worse than a stranger to him, for he had made up his mind to dislike and disapprove of her. It was Fate. Or, rather, it was Nature.

They were mutually attracted to begin with, no doubt, by reason of a certain beauty and distinction which in different ways they both possessed. They had opposite seats at dinner, and each stole a gravely intent look at the other when he or she was not aware of it. He had a remarkable "presence," both as to stature and bearing—that lordly air of the man born to rule and dominate, which has a more potent fascination, even with the women who feel that they have themselves a vocation in that direction, than perhaps any manly virtue. She was no longer a child—she was not even girlish; but a nobly developed woman, tall and straight, with the free step and graceful carriage of a wild creature, and the serene and stately manners of a queen. She had a sunny and vivacious nature, a sensitive face that changed its expression continually, yet she never lost that air of repose and strong self-possession which was so essentially regal and so peculiarly her charm. They were a surprise and a study to one another.

The children came in for an hour after dinner, two little girls and a boy—the boy; and Mr. Townshend set himself to propitiate the latter. He challenged him to a game of draughts, and allowed him to win, and he promised to get a holiday for him and take him out shooting on Monday. The boy was immensely delighted, and the young man flattered himself that all fear of his indiscretion rising up in judgment against him was over. When the children were dismissed, the little girls unlocking their arms reluctantly from their sister's waist, after listening in a far corner to one of the most lovely stories they had ever heard, Mr. Townshend did the very last thing he had intended to do. He sidled round to that far corner, before the vacant places were taken, and began to talk of the weather with much earnestness. From this topic, as everyone knows, it is very easy to get on to others, especially with some people. The general company entertained themselves with much animated discussion of the alarming Eastern crisis far away, and the more alarming eccentricities of the Berry Government at home. He and she discoursed of books and pictures, of foreign places and people, of things that some he's and she's never talk of together, though they may live under the same roof for years—questions of abstract morality, enigmas of fate, mysteries of human life and destiny, near and dear thoughts that lay close hid from the light of common day—with a growing sense of companionship and a confidence of fellow-feeling that was none of their seeking, and that they were not consciously aware of. They did not know how the time went; they looked out from their quiet corner upon the moving life and colour that filled the room, and listened to music and laughter, and consumed bread and butter and tea, without knowing what they did. The interest of their talk absorbed them. Though they were scrupulously courteous and respectful in speech and manner—though they only lifted the outer veils from the sanctuary of emotion and thought—they were at heart old friends before the time came for bowing a formal good-night to each other. Father and mother watched the beginning of the acquaintance with furtive satisfaction. They did not want to lose their child as soon as they had recovered her; but when the time did come, in the course of nature, it would be pleasant to have her living near them, the wife of a handsome, well-connected man, whom everyone looked up to, and who owned one of the finest properties in the district. Mr. Yorke, too, watched the tête-à-tête in the corner, and did what in him lay to prevent anyone from disturbing it; but he was discreet and held his tongue. Even when he found himself alone with Mr. Townshend in the smoking-room, on the verge of Sunday morning, he refrained not only from gibes but from comment, which the reader will allow was very noble of him.

It did not take a week. In twenty-four hours Mr. Frank Townshend had fulfilled the predictions of his friend, and was perfectly aware of it. It was after the family high tea of Sunday, and the whole company had come out of doors to seek for a whiff of cool air in the twilight. Some roamed about the garden paths, some lay outstretched on the lawns, some sat in low chairs under the creeper-covered verandahs, and congregated in congenial groups upon thresholds and doorsteps. Amongst them Miss Charteris shone conspicuous in a soft white gown, resting herself easily in a bamboo chair under a great oleander-tree, which spread out over her head like a pink umbrella inside out, and Mr. Townshend squatted Turk-wise on the grass at her feet. Her mother had been sitting with them, but the discreet matron had retired after a decent interval. And the two talked together in musing undertones, she looking at the sky, and he at her lovely face. She was telling him how she came to return home suddenly, against the wishes of her aunt, who had brought her out in London, and had hoped to keep her always as her own adopted child. There was no girlish naïveté, either real or affected, in the style of the narrative, still less any trace of the careless cynicism of the hardened woman of the world.

"We were driving home from church on Christmas morning. Aunt and I were going to a little party at night, and we called at a friend's house to get some flowers that had been promised us. Aunt went in, and I sat in the carriage and waited. While I was sitting, quite still and thinking, all at once I heard someone cooee from a long way off. Aunt said it was a preposterous fancy; we were in London streets—Queen Anne's Gate—and no one about but people going home from church. But I heard it quite distinctly. I daresay it was some Australian in the park. One long musical cooee, not repeated nor yet answered—indeed, I felt the strongest impulse to answer it myself. I can't tell you what a shock it gave me. All the rest of the day I was thinking of Australia, and I could not get rid of a fancy that somebody there wanted me. In fact, I determined to start off there and then, and, as you know, I did. It was very silly, but really I couldn't help it. I am not in the least superstitious."

Mr. Townshend was not superstitious either; but it flashed across him that on that very day, at 10 o'clock in the evening, he had been telling his friend Yorke how he had cooeed once from the window of an hotel in Paris to a friend who had an apartment on the other side of the street, and how no less than seven Australian strangers had called on him in consequence; and Mr. Yorke had been telling him how he once cooeed into the night, from the top of the old Buffalo, to a woman whom he loved in England, and had heard long afterwards that at that hour she had been married to another man; and then he remembered that they had both cooeed over the sea (they were spending Christmas in Tasmania), each to the unknown mate whom destiny had selected for him, whoever and wherever she might be. They were smoking and drinking coffee after a convivial Christmas dinner, and were in the mood for nonsense. Still it was a strange coincidence, and some day he would tell her of it. She went on with her story.

"While I was in the carriage, looking out of the windows all round to see where that cooee could have come from, Aunt returned, and a servant with her carrying a little box of flowers. As soon as we drove off, and before I could tell her what I had heard, she put a bouquet into my hand, which some one—the husband of our friend—had specially prepared for me. It was a lovely bouquet, and it had a scent about it that was like the scent of that violet of William Story's—

"Yes," said Mr. Townshend softly, "I know"—

"'Oh faint, delicious, spring-time violet,

Thine odour, like a key,

Turns noiselessly in memory's wards—to let

A thought of sorrow free.'"

"It was not a thought of sorrow, though something like it, for it made me cry; but thoughts of my home and people, and my dear country that I had deserted—a whole rush of memories that, coming just at that moment, quite overpowered me. What do you think it was?" she asked, looking down into his face with almost tragic earnestness.

"I don't know. What?"

"A little sprig of silver wattle. It was set just in the middle, with lovely ferns and hothouse flowers round it—indeed, it was a hothouse flower itself for once in its life. Mr. Kingscote had begged it out of a ducal conservatory, I believe, on purpose for me. I had never seen it since I left here."

"And that was like another 'cooee' to you, I suppose?"

"Yes. It seemed a message to me to come home, I wore it that night, and have kept it ever since. I feel that it represents my fate somehow, and that it would be unlucky to destroy it. From the moment that I got it I began my preparations for a start, and I was able to sail directly, as it happened. How queer it all is!" she said, breaking off with a laugh. "A cooee that I fancied I heard, and the smell of a bit of wattle; but for that I should have been in Rome at this moment, probably, instead of sitting here."

Mr. Townshend was looking at her strangely, and thinking the wildest thoughts. "I believe," he said at last, "that someone in Australia did cooee for you that Christmas day."

"The person who did so had to cooee in the middle of the night, then," she replied lightly.

"No, not in the middle of the night—it was about 10 o'clock."

In the deepening dusk—beginning now to be faintly illuminated with summer moonshine—he saw that her attention was arrested by that latent significance in his tone and manner which he had tried to keep back, and that she was a little disturbed and startled.

"What nonsense," she said, with a laugh, and yet in a gentle tone. "You are as bad as the spiritists. By the way, I wonder where those children are gone off to. I promised to tell them a story before they went to bed." And she rose from her chair and glided away in her white gown, leaving him fully awakened to the tremendous consciousness that he had met his Fate at last.

But this idyllic evening had a most disastrous end. At 9 o'clock the moon was eclipsed, to help the sense of abnormal gloom that at that hour seemed, to the prosperous young squatter, to have suddenly overtaken him and all the world. It hung low over the dim shrubberies, like a dark fat face with a little white skull-cup on, and all the tender radiance had burned down, like a dying lamp, into a strange darkness that was not at all like the ordinary darkness of a crescent moon. In this weird twilight shone a few pale, lost-looking stars. Plovers were crying in the distant paddocks, the birds in the garden were awake and restless. There was an uncanny feeling—a sense of misfortune—in the very air. Yesterday had come the tidings that the Russians had gone to Constantinople, and that the English fleet had entered the Dardanelles; the men were all talking of the wholesale catastrophe that the morrow's telegrams might have to tell in hushed tones of despondency. All but Frank Townshend, who had withdrawn himself from the rest, and he leaned on a gate with folded arms, thinking bitterly of his new-found love already lost—how she had swept by him just now with a rigid, beautiful, scornful face, in which he had clearly read her knowledge of the fact that he had betted another man £100 that he would never ask her to be his wife.

Chapter III

The next morning Miss Charteris came to breakfast rather late, looking very stately as she moved through the room to her seat. She exchanged friendly greetings with the guests as she passed them, but took such infinitesimal notice of Mr. Townshend that he would rather she had taken none at all, though it was he who rose to place her chair for her. After breakfast she retired somewhere with her mother; she had to unpack, she said. Mr. Townshend loafed about restlessly, breathing savage anathemas to himself upon that wretched boy who had betrayed him, until the long forenoon was over and the gong sounded for lunch. At lunch he met her again, and, urging himself upon her notice indiscreetly, she snubbed him in such a pointed manner that Mr. Yorke noticed it, and became aware of what had happened. In the afternoon there was a tennis match, and instead of playing in it or looking on, she went to her room to write her English letters. At 5 o'clock the whole party went out riding and driving, and Miss Charteris joined three other ladies in the pony carriage, and there was no getting near her. After dinner she sat in the same corner where Mr. Townshend had had his tête-à-tête with her on Saturday night, and discoursed pleasantly with the young bar-onet's son (who had hurriedly supplied himself with the white tie and swallow-tails of civilisation, a sadder and a wiser man)—so pleasantly, indeed, that her deposed cavalier felt himself justified in reverting to his original opinion of her, and declaring to himself that, after all, she was a flirt, and not worth bothering after. With but slight variation, this was the daily programme for a week. In a house full of guests it was easy to avoid the society of any particular person, and Miss Charteris ignored Mr. Townshend completely, without transgressing any conventional pro-prieties in so doing. But the same conditions enabled him to see much of her, to hear her and watch her constantly, to study the beauty of her face and the noble womanliness of her ways, to gather up her thoughts from scattered talk, to learn her nature, which was of a special quality that he was specially fitted to understand; and at the week's end he had come to the conclusion that to think of her in connexion with flirting was an impossible profanation, and that she was the fairest and sweetest woman in the wide world.

On the following Monday Mr. Townshend went home to look after his own affairs for a day or two. On his return the weather was excessively hot, and Mrs. Charteris and her guests were all physically demoralised, so to speak, in consequence—lying about in cool corners, gasping on sofas in the thinnest and loosest raiment, sustaining life on salads and iced claret and water, and feeling themselves incapable of anything beyond the passive occupation of killing time. In this state of things Miss Charteris, being human, was obliged to melt a little; and when her admirer showed his anxiety to combat the general prostration, so far, at least, as the ladies were concerned, she delighted him by suggesting that he might read aloud. It happened that this was one of his accomplishments, and that he not only knew how, but exactly what, to read; so for several afternoons he sat in the darkened drawing-room, with large fans swinging to and fro around him, and held forth in sonorous, rich tones, pleasantly modulated, for hours at a stretch. Some of the ladies he invariably read to sleep, but Miss Charteris never. He felt, rather than saw, that of all his auditors she was the most attentive, losing herself often in her own reveries, in dreamy abandonment to the spirit of the poem, or essay, or romance that she was listening to, but never detaching her interest from it. Sometimes she was so absorbed that he would look up and catch her softened eyes fixed, full of thought, on his face, with an expression of enjoyment and appreciation in her listening air and attitude that refreshed his soul—beginning to hunger for her favour—as rain would have refreshed the parched earth outside. At such moments she would recover herself with a sudden flush of colour, and a sudden stiffening of relaxed limbs and features; but she could not undo their effect on them both, which was to deepen the sense of natural sympathy between them, whether she liked it or not.

So the second week went by, and the hot season culminated on the 4th of March in a terrible sultriness that was a sort of "dispensation of Providence" to the little company in the way it drove them to sink all personal matters in the common cause of suffering. "It is too cruel to ask you to read to-day," Miss Charteris said, with unwonted gentleness, when Mr. Townshend and his book appeared in the drawing-room at the usual hour.

"I shall not want asking, if it gives you any pleasure," he replied, smiling, and feeling absurdly happy. And he read away until all but she had gone to sleep, and, when tea came in and woke them up, he read on till dinner-time; and he felt himself amply repaid when she said, "Thank you—I have enjoyed that," as she sailed out of the room before him while he held the door open for her.

However, next day the weather changed. At 5 o'clock in the morning the thermometer stood at 86 in the coolest room in the house, but a lovely rain began to fall while they sat at breakfast, and before night it was almost cold. Then came pleasant cool days for a while, when all the out-door pursuits—walks, rides, tennis matches, &c.—were resumed; and Miss Charteris froze up again, and became more unapproachable than ever. Three things, just at this time, combined to harden her heart against her unfortunate lover. In the first place, Mr. Yorke, on the eve of his departure from the house to enter on a new appointment in a distant col-ony, undertook to explain matters on behalf of the delinquent, privately, as an old and privileged family friend. Of course, he met with the usual success of a go-between when he ventures to meddle with such very del-icate affairs. The mere speaking of the bet that had been made about her, irrespective of the way it was spoken of, was a fresh outrage and insult to so proud a woman—which he did not understand until it was too late; and then he was so confounded at the enormity of the mistake he had made that he did not dare to tell his friend about it. In the second place, Mr. and Mrs. Charteris began to see in their young neighbour a suitor for their daughter's hand, and to show by slight signs, unmistakable to the interested parties, though perhaps not to the general public, that they were well-disposed to favour his pretensions, and thereby they poured oil upon the flame of her resentment in no small measure; and, lastly, Mr. Townshend himself was too much in love to hide it—too anxious for her favour to let her alone. While he was able to efface himself discreetly she did not mind showing herself complaisant, to a certain extent, for she could not help knowing that he had that in him which made life more interesting to her than it would otherwise have been; but as soon as he began definitely to assert his claim upon her notice—to obtrude the love which she never meant to recognise—then the indignity he had put upon her began to rankle afresh, all the more bitterly as she grew more clearly conscious of what it was likely to cost her.

And so a new phase of intercourse set in. First, a restless pursuit of her on his side, and an obtrusive avoidance of him on hers; then daily contact, forced on her, sometimes by accident, more often by strata-gem, which was something like the contact of flint and steel, resulting in mutual aggravation of all sore feelings, and at the same time in the kin-dling of passion on both sides. The guests began to drop off one by one, opportunities multiplied, the situation became more and more keenly tantalising to him, and painful to her, and intolerable to them both; and then the crisis came. It was on the last day of that month of March, exactly six weeks from the Sunday on which he had first discovered that he loved her, and she had first known of the bet he had made that he would never ask her to be his wife. It was pouring with rain, so that nobody could go to church. The household assembled for a short service in the schoolroom at 12 o'clock, and then there was an interval of half an hour before the early dinner. Mr. Townshend took a stroll round the verandahs, remembered he had left a favourite Prayer-book lying about, returned to the schoolroom to look for it, and there found his lady-love all alone, toasting her feet on the fender, and reading her English letters, which had arrived from the township only the night before. He paused irresolutely at the door, half afraid to come in; then advanced boldly, and began to hunt for his lost property with much ostentation. She, on her part, made a movement as if to rise and leave the room, but, recovering her self-possession instantly, continued to read her letters more assiduously than before, rustling the sheets as she turned them over in an apparently absorbed study of their contents.

"I hope you have had good news. Miss Charteris?" the young man presently remarked. He had found his Prayer-book, and was lingering over the operation of fitting it into his pocket, and taking wistful looks at the back of her head the while.

"O, yes, thank you," she replied coldly.

"And was your aunt still going to Rome?"

"I believe so. She had made all her arrangements."

"You would have been there now, I suppose, if you had stayed with her? Holy Week is not far off."

"Most likely. I was exceedingly foolish not to stay, for I shall probably never see Rome at all now.'"

"You would have found it rather dull this season, the Pope being just dead." As she vouchsafed no comment upon this suggestion, he added persistently, "Wouldn't you?"

"I really don't see how the Pope's death would have affected me," she replied, gathering up her letters and pulling out her watch. "At any rate, it would have been pleasanter than being at home—for some things."

"I know what you mean by that," he said, fencing no longer, but coming to close quarters with a rush. "Why are you so hard and cruel? No, don't go," putting his back to the door and stretching his hands towards her as she rose to leave the room. "You always want to go away as soon as I begin to speak; but I can't bear it any longer. You must listen to me for once—I must say it?"

"Say what?" she asked, coldly, but with a flaming face, as she drew herself up before him like an outraged queen.

"You know what, as well as I do—that I love you—that I want you—that I can't bear my life in this suspense—that it isn't worth having unless I can have you too."

As he broke down here with a sort of deep sob, still holding out his arms as if to take her in, she turned quite white, and her mouth twitched, and her indignant eyes quailed; but the insulted woman in her was obdurate.

"Oh no," she said, with a tremulous smile, that was half a feeble sneer, "you are mistaking your feelings, Mr. Townshend, I am sure. You quite forget the good resolution that you made before you saw me. If you are so weak as to sacrifice your principles, not to speak of your money, in a moment of temptation, I am certainly not so weak as to take advantage of it."

"Oh, curse that unlucky day!" he broke out, despairingly. "Am I to be ruined for ever because of that? I know that is what you have been thinking of all along. And doesn't it ever occur to you that people make fools of themselves sometimes without knowing what they are doing? Oh, my love, forgive me—I had never seen you—I will atone for it fully if you will only give me the chance! Will you?"

If they had had five minutes more it might have been all right; but at this fatal juncture the gong began to hum and vibrate through the house, and a child's voice to call, "Nelly, where are you?" along the passage that led to the schoolroom. In the emergency he seized her hands, and demanded eagerly, "Say yes—be quick, darling—say yes!" And she, not having time to collect herself, resenting the too familiar action and too obvious readiness to take her "Yes" for granted, snatched away her hands, and said, passionately—"No, I will not. I made a bet, too—a bet with myself—that I would never marry you, after what you said about me. And I never will."

"Is that your final answer?" he inquired, with a sudden stiffening in face and voice.

"It is my final answer," she replied recklessly.

So that afternoon, all in the chilly autumnal rain, the unhappy young man, pleading pressing business, rode away to his own lonely house. And Miss Charteris, pleading a bad headache, shut herself up in her room and lay on her bed and cried. And each felt that the flavour of life had gone out of it.

Chapter IV

We are all familiar with the old proverb about misfortunes—how they seldom come singly. Experience teaches us from year to year that, even in such small matters as broken crockery and torn flounces, it rarely rains ill-luck but it pours. This was the case with Frank Townshend. Hitherto he had been a prosperous man, never knowing what it was to be sick in mind or body, or to want for any pleasant thing that he was not abundantly supplied with. But being, as we are after all, pretty fairly handicapped in the great race of life, his turn to suffer came, and the tide of his fortunes began to ebb on the 31st of March, 1878, the Sunday on which Nelly Charteris refused him. He found, when he reached home, that a valuable shorthorn which he had lately imported had been taken ill, and was not likely to live. Next day the bull died, and he was £2,000 out of pocket in consequence. The day after, his favourite thoroughbred, which he had some thought of putting into training, sprained a back sinew; and some greyhound puppies broke into the enclosure containing his fancy poultry, and amused themselves for two hours tearing all his prize birds to pieces. He bore these reverses with calmness, as he did the loss of his diamond breast-pin, and the destruction of a whole cask of rare Amontillado by the man who was entrusted with the bottling of it going to sleep over his work and leaving the tap turned on. But when, in the course of a few weeks, his brothers-in-law began to press for the payment of certain legacies which his late father had left as charges upon an estate already much encumbered, and his banker simultaneously reminded him that an old-standing mortgage would shortly have to be attended to, and day by day the bad times which, under the 'Berry Blight,' were bad for everybody, grew worse and worse for the landed proprietors, then his ill-luck took a darker aspect. There is no need to go into details, and describe the several downward steps in his fall from prosperity to adversity; more than one well-to-do country gentleman shared his fate at that time, and the process is being repeated still. It was only a little more rapid than usual, owing to those legacies, the amount of which had been fixed by his father in prosperous times, when no one could have foreseen what the colony was coming to. His sisters' husbands wanted their money, which drained him of all his capital; the firm that held the mortgage was itself "hard up," and, with all the will in the world to be accommodating, was driven by its own necessities to foreclose; the banks were suffering with the rest from the prevailing depression and insecurity, and were more cautious than enterprising. And so on all round. It began to be whispered about that even the envied owner of that fine place, which old Mr. Townshend had spent 30 years in making—years of hard work, and privation, and danger, of which the whole country reaped the benefit that he and his only were begrudged—was finding it all he could do to carry on. And by and by it was openly talked of that young Townshend's property, which in happier times he might easily have preserved to be an inheritance for his children's children, was less his own than the bank's. It looked very bad for him indeed when, just before the shearing, a part of it was advertised to be sold; and when, at the auction, it fetched, as everyone knew it would, about half the price that his father had refused for it 18 months before, nobody was surprised to hear that he was "done for." This final blow fell in the latter end of October, and the Kelly murders happening just then, his ruin was not so much talked of as it might have been. Nelly Charteris did not know of it till sometime after, though her father and mother did. There had been a dropping of intercourse between them and him, partly because the pride of the young lady would not permit her to acknowledge how thoroughly—to use a vulgar phrase—she had cut off her nose to spite her face, partly because the troubles of the young man pre-occupied him and kept him away from balls and races and places where he might have met her, and partly because Mrs. Charteris had found a more eligible suitor for her daughter in the person of that baronet's son whose two elder brothers had lately died, leaving him heir to a title and estates, and who lingered on in the colony because he was so desperately in love with our heroine that he could not bring himself to put the seas between them. Mrs. Charteris might have known better. She had had her own romance in her youth; she had made her own woman's sacrifice, and had learned the cost of defying nature. When she was herself a girl she had given up her true love for the sake of a favourite sister who wanted him, and during long years four people had had to suffer for that act of immorality, which she had fondly imagined was virtuous and Christian heroism of the highest order. And yet—so little wisdom do we learn from experience—she was now scheming to do away with that young fellow whom her child, as she knew, still loved, and to encourage her to mate herself with a good-natured, brainless noodle, because he was going to be a baronet and rich. She was thinking over her plans one afternoon, lying on a sofa in her drawing-room, and fanning herself (for it was the 13th of December and one of the hottest days of the season), when the butler opened the door and announced Mr. Townshend.

"I have come to say good-bye, Mrs. Charteris," said that young man quietly, sending a quick glance round the room as he strode up to her couch. "I daresay you have heard that I have been unfortunate, and have had to part with my property. I made over everything this morning to the new man, and now I am going away to Queensland, where I have a share in some back country, to begin the world afresh."

Mrs. Charteris was a kind woman, and she loaded her visitor with genuine expressions of sympathy and motherly good wishes and encouragements, which he found very comforting, but at the same time she was thinking how dangerous it would be for Nelly to have any share in these parting interviews, and wondering what she could do to prevent it. He was looking much altered, thin and sunburnt, and graver and older; and there was a quiet dignity in the way he bore himself under his misfortunes which seemed to show that they had developed and ennobled him—as, indeed, they had. "I am so sorry Nelly is out," she said; "she will be distressed to hear you have gone without her seeing you again. But I hope you will soon be back, with a good report of yourself. Queensland is the land of promise now-a-days, everyone says."

"I thought I should be sure to find Miss Charteris at home on such a hot day," he said, with a pretence at carelessness which did not deceive the mother's ear.

"She ought not to have been out, of course. But Mr. Wrayburn asked her to ride with him, and she did not like to refuse. I must make him promise to take better care of her before I consent to give her into his hands altogether."

"Are you thinking of doing that, Mrs. Charteris?"

"Well, it depends, of course. There is nothing settled yet." (To do her justice, she blushed as she thus deliberately deceived him, and did not like doing it.)

He rose to go. What was there to wait for? It was better for him not to try to see his beautiful sweetheart any more. "Tell her," he said with solemn earnestness, as he shook hands, "tell her from me that I came to know if she had forgiven me for something—she will know what—before I went away."

"Shall I tell her?" Mrs. Charteris asked herself when her visitor was gone, wiping a little moisture from her eyes, and feeling angry with her young fledgeling baronet that he was not more like this man whom she had discarded. "No, I think I had better not. It might unsettle her." And she didn't.

But Nelly was duly acquainted with the fact that Mr. Townshend had been to say good-bye, and that he was going away to the wilds of Queensland, and never coming back any more. Her informant was the same dreadful boy who had done them that ill turn nearly a year ago.

"And such a lark, Nelly—he hasn't two sixpences left to rub together, father says, though he used to be such a swell that nobody was good enough for him. Such a jolly come-down for him after all his cheek!"

Nelly turned round sharply and boxed that boy's ears—to his intense astonishment; then she begged his pardon, and kissed him; then pushed him out of her room and locked the door; and then she flung herself on her knees by her bedside, and sobbed and cried like a weak-minded schoolgirl for that lover whom she would not take when she might have had him, and whom she could not have now that she was ready to give up the whole world for his sake.

Chapter V

S o Christmas Day came round again. As everybody knows it was a
Christmas Day that was equally unworthy of comparison with the
average British and the average colonial article, as far as weather was concerned—at any rate in that part of Victoria where the Charteris family
lived. It was neither a festival of snow and holly berries, nor of sunshine
and summer flowers. It rained in torrents all the previous night, spoiling
the roses and the strawberries that were to have adorned the breakfast-
table; and in the morning the sky was so grey and the wind was so chill
and fresh that Miss Charteris was fain to go to church in the same seal-
skin jacket that she had worn in London the Christmas Day before. At
luncheon they sat down to eat their lamb and green peas, and their cool
fruits and salads, before a fire of blazing sheoak logs that would have put
an English grate—even a Christmas grate—to shame; and towards the
evening, when the fumes of roasting turkeys and brandied puddings and
mince pies began to steal about the house, and preparations were set on
foot for the brewing of punch and the firing of snapdragons, it was felt by
everybody that those time-honoured institutions, so religiously clung to
by the British householder, irrespective of the state of the thermometer,
would be more entirely in harmony with the occasion than usual. The
little girls of the house, in white frocks and blue sashes, went to their
sister's room at 6 o'clock to see if she was ready for dinner. The honour
of dining by lamplight with her and a dozen more grown-up people (the
near friends and relations who habitually swelled the family circle at this
season) was a special indulgence granted to them for the first time, which
they greatly appreciated. They rushed in suddenly, full of life and mirth,
and surprised her in a motionless attitude of dejection, leaning out of her
open window, with her head resting on her hand. She was looking far
away over the misty hills to a distant dark patch on the horizon, which

she could hardly see for tears (it was the plantation of English trees which had grown up round the house which had been Frank Townshend's a year ago); and altogether she presented a listless and spiritless appearance that the children felt to be an outrage upon Christmas Day.

"O Nelly, you have got your dressing-gown on yet!" exclaimed little May, the eldest, in a tone of indignant remonstrance.

"And she's crying!" whispered Gerty, in dismay and alarm. "O Nelly, how can you—and after all the nice presents you have had! Why, everybody is happy on Christmas Day, always"

"Not always," replied Nelly, shutting the window, and beginning to make her toilet hurriedly. "I was just thinking of some one—some people—who are all alone, with no one belonging to them; no Christmas Day, you know, like ours—only sad things to think of—" And she broke off with a little angry sob, as she pictured her lover in his comfortless Queensland hut, all the bitterness of his changed lot made doubly bitter by the memories that this anniversary would bring him. Then, seeing the wonder and alarm in the children's faces, she shook herself together with an effort, and began to talk to them as she dressed herself with a sort of hysterical animation which passed very well for the seasonable hilarity that they desired.

"And how does the schoolroom look, Gerty? Did Mr. Wrayburn get the Union Jack to hang straight after all?'"

"Yes, Nelly, it's lovely; and they have been putting more flowers into the evergreens, and mother has lent them the silver candlesticks, and Wills has waxed the floor. It will be the grandest servants' party we have ever had."

"Mr. Wrayburn says we must go and dance with them, because it will be such fun," put in May. "There is a man with a violin coming from the township to play."

"Because they have covered the schoolroom piano with coffee cups," said Gerty.

While they chattered, Nelly, putting in a question now and then, dressed herself rapidly, thinking her own thoughts the while. A white dress, like the children's, only of creamy Indian silk—the same she had worn 12 months ago with the sprig of silver wattle—and a quantity of soft old lace about her white neck and her dimpled elbows. This was her costume to-night—too good, she said to herself, with a sigh, as she saw in the glass how lovely she looked in it, considering there would be nobody to see her.

"Now, put on Mr. Wrayburn's flowers," said May, taking up some scarlet rosebuds from the dressing-table. "You want them to brighten you up. You look quite pale to-night—like mutton fat, you know."

"Thank you, May; I don't think so. And you may take the roses, with my kind regards, to cook, and tell her I sent them for her to wear at her party tonight. They will suit that brilliant blue silk of hers beautifully."

"What, Mr. Wrayburn's roses, Nelly?"

"My dear girl, Mr. Wrayburn never made them. Do as I tell you, and fetch me a bit of deutzia and a few fronds of maidenhair."

She came to dinner presently, like a tall lily, all in white, smelling sweet wherever she went. She had flowers in her hair and in her bosom, and a chain of pearls round her throat. Mr. Townshend had once told her mother—at a time when Mrs. Charteris did not fear to "unsettle" her—that she was the only woman he had ever seen whom a white costume perfectly suited, and who could wear pearls next the skin with impunity. Since then she had had a fancy for white dresses and for pearls, especially as her necklace happened to be an heirloom and valuable. Her general whiteness—and she was paler than she knew— was set off rather strongly by the richness of colour about her in the costumes of the other ladies and the decorations of the table.

"Nelly reminds me of those girls who were confirmed the other day," said her precocious brother, in a pause between turkey and pudding, when he had nothing better to do than to look at her.

"She reminds me," said little May, "of a bride, only without a veil on. O what a pretty bride you would be, Nelly! Wouldn't she, Mr. Wrayburn?'"

The young man said, "Yes, indeed," and sighed and gazed at her tenderly, whereat she metamorphosed herself into an iceberg, and her father called out sharply, "Pass the burgundy, Wrayburn."

The long dinner came to an end, and the usual toasts were drunk— "The Queen" first, and "Absent Friends" last; and then there was an interval of rest and waiting while the servants finished their work and set their own entertainment going. The gentlemen, though it was Christmas Day, saw an opportunity for cigarettes as well as coffee; the ladies (all of them, save Nelly, being married and intimately connected with each other) for one of those confidential gossips which matrons love; and the children for fresh enterprise in the servants' hall and schoolroom, where country maids and men were beginning to assemble from the township and stations round. Nelly, who was hot and restless, stole away to refresh herself with a little quiet ramble in the garden, and knew that for half an hour she would not be missed. The rain was over, though the night was damp and dark, and the air was still and soft, if not very warm, and sweet with the smell of new-washed earth and flowers. The wet laurels brushed her bare arms as she paced the gravel with her skirts tucked under them; a tangle of rose boughs caught her hair, and dropped diamonds amongst her pearls, as she paused at a little gate, and leaned over it to listen to the stillness of the night. It was the same gate on which Mr. Townshend had leaned, what seemed now so long ago, when she had begun to revenge herself, and to make him unhappy. She did not remember that; her thoughts were busy with the talk they had had together under the oleanders, when she had told him of the cooee that had startled her in London, and had been the mysterious message that fetched her home.

"I believe someone in Australia did call you," he had said; and how grave he had been! as if he believed it. "I wonder who it was," she said aloud, with a little smile at the absurdity of the idea. "It could not have been himself, since he was probably not aware of my existence." And then she begun to muse sorrowfully on the hopeless distance that now separated them from one another. If only a cooee could reach him—if he could hear it, and know it was she who called—would he come back to her? Without thinking of what might be the consequences, with so many people about—obeying one of those unaccountable impulses which now and then take possession of the most reasonable beings, she lifted her face in the cool darkness, and uttered a long, clear, musical cooee that must have travelled at least a mile on such a night. To her intense surprise and fright she was answered immediately by someone not more than two or three hundred yards away—so immediately, indeed, that the one note took up the other without a break. It was as if her own cooee had been prolonged by an echo stronger than itself. She stood rooted to the spot, with distended nostrils, like a hind that has got scent of the hunter, and listened, wondering if her ears could have deceived her. It was none of the men, she knew; even a cooee has its individuality, and this was not one that belonged to the place. And yet she was sure she had heard it before. As she stood, like a spectre, amongst the laurels, grasping the rail of the gate, with trembling knees and a singing in her ears, she heard quick footsteps brushing over the grass, the long stride of a tall man, and presently saw his shape looming dimly in the darkness before her.

"Is that you, Miss Charteris?" came a voice, low and eager, across the paddock.

She did not answer. She waited for him to come up to her, thrilling with expectation from head to foot. She knew who it was now—unless it was his ghost. As he approached the gate she held out her hands impulsively, and it was not so dark that he did not see the gesture. He reached her with a bound and seized them both, and they stood together, so closely that they could hear each other's hearts beating, with the gate between them.

"Were you calling anyone?" he asked, between deep pants of breath. "Were you calling for me?"

"How did you come here? I thought you were in Queensland," she answered, in a sort of sighing whisper, feeling as if her strength was gone.

"But you called, dear; I am sure it was you. Tell me who it was you wanted? Were you calling for me to come back?"

Her lips said "Yes," but she had no sound in her voice. However, speech was superfluous. In another moment her lover was over the gate beside her.

***

Dancing had begun in the schoolroom. The squeal of the fiddle floated out upon the night, with the sound of the revellers' shuffling feet; and Mr. Wrayburn and the children were hunting high and low for Nelly. She could see their shadows on the window-blinds going from room to room; now and then she could hear a faint "Nelly, where are you?" echoing up and down passages and verandahs; but she made no sign. She sat on a garden bench all amongst the wet laurels, curled up warm in her lover's arms, perfectly indifferent to everybody but herself and him.

"And you were not gone away after all?" was her whispered reply to Gerty's loudest shout.

"No; I was looking for some lost cattle. I had found where they were, and was riding home, when I saw the lights of your house, and I dismounted to have a look at them—like Mr. Guppy, you know. I was thinking how I should like to cooee for you to come out to speak to me; and wondering, if I did, whether it would have any effect."

"Oh, how strange! So was I."

"I was just going to cooee, really, when I happened to remember two or three things—that I was so poor, that Wrayburn was in possession—"

"He has never been in possession for an instant."

"And at that very moment I heard you. I knew your voice, Nelly, though I never heard you cooee before. And, somehow, it was 'borne in on me,' as they say, that you were calling me."

"I wonder if you would have heard me—heard me in spirit, I mean—if you had really been in Queensland."

"I am sure I should," he answered confidently. "You heard me further off than that. Didn't I call you home from England just a year ago? I shall always believe that it was my cooee that you heard in London, now."

"Well, I shall like to think of that when you are really gone—if you must go. When must you go, Frank?"

"Never, dear, unless you should happen to have a fancy to go yourself. It is arranged now that I stay on, the other man having left, and manage my old place for the bank until I have time to turn myself round. Three hundred a year and rations—that's what I've got to offer you, Nelly."

"I don't care if it's only three hundred pence. We will go and be free selectors, if you like, and I'll bake the bread and milk the cows for you."

"I should like to see you at it. No, no; it will go hard if I can't do something better for you than that. I've got a thousand or two left, and the Queensland place is doing well. And, thank heaven, I've no debts."

"Yes, you have. You owe Mr. Yorke a hundred pounds."

"Don't, Nelly."

"Well, he's welcome to it. Only, as we are going to be so poor, you might have been content with a smaller stake. But you men have no idea of economy."

Clare's Christmas Eve

Catherine Martin

Chapter I

"Home, Sweet Home."

"I stretch my spirit forth to the fair hours,
the purplest of the prime."

The view from Calthorpe Park was beautiful at all times, but more especially so in the lengthening days of spring, when the breath of the approaching summer was warm and fragrant in the air; when the rosebuds were opening out their pink, creamy white and crimson petals, when the fruit-trees were in flower, showering down floods of snowy and delicately tinted blossoms, and the whole country round was as fresh and green as an English meadow. Then, indeed, it was a joy and a delight that lingered long in the memory to sit in the balcony, to stand on the terrace or wander across the lawn in front of the large, handsome, well-appointed house that stood in the midst of the grounds. Looking eastward, one saw the hills crowned with trees, the radiant sunshine sleeping on their green slopes and quiet sweet curves, the mysterious valleys between them filled with deep shadows, and here and there in the vales and on the hillsides, surrounded by vineyards and well-tilled gardens, stood comfortable-looking homesteads, that had an unmistakeable air of cheerful prosperity. At these hills, rising range beyond range, standing as it were on tiptoe to look over each other's shoulders, further than the eye could reach, one might look for hours without satiety or weariness. The still blue heaven arching over them, with now a wandering cloudlet pallid and distant as the remembrance of a regretted past, and anon swept by great masses of clouds, full of life and colour and motion, that marched swiftly onward like victorious armies, casting fitful shadows full of subtle pathos and tenderness across the silent hills. Looking northward, beyond the rapidly-extending suburbs of the city, one saw the level stretch of plains which would soon be yellow with broad acres of ripening wheat. But the fairest sight of all was when the golden light of sunset streamed over valley and hill and wood, over plain and city, and lit up the distant troops of shining waves that encircled the land to the west and to the south like a great belt of liquid silver, and where the white-sailed ships coming into havens of rest or sailing away to distant lands, stood out with startling distinctness between the great calm sea and the glowing sky.

It was not, however, in a white-sailed vessel that Clare Rutherford returned to her home from her two years' visit to the old country. It was in the great black-funnelled swift Lahore, which steamed into port three whole days before any one looked for her coming.

"Fancy papa and mama's delight to find you safe and snug at Calthrope when they come home tomorrow," said Dolly the stay-at-home to Clare the wanderer, as they sat enjoying the luxury of a long uninterrupted tête-à-tête a few hours after the arrival of the latter.

"Matthew will be quite disappointed that he, too, was from home when you came. He always said the fatted calf must be killed when we got you safe back again."

"As if I had been wasting my substance in riotous living," laughed Clare, lying back luxuriantly in the recesses of a great patriarchal looking armchair, which was her special property and delight.

"No, we didn't think you did that exactly," returned matter-of-fact Dolly; "but I'll tell you what we did think," she said confidentially. "We really thought—Matthew and I—that you would never leave that old Dresden again. As long as you raved only about the music and the scenery we were not alarmed, but when you said you could tolerate sauerkraut and enjoy worst Mat declared papa ought to look into the matter, as the next thing you would like might be a Count with a rent-roll of an English shilling a week, who kept up conversation by ejaculating 'Mein Gott' twice a day."

"Matthew no doubt has deteriorated through not being properly snubbed during my absence," said Clara, with a somewhat unsuccessful attempt at a frown.

"What sort of passengers came out, Clare? Were there any on board you knew besides the Chardingles and the Listons?" asked Dolly presently.

"None that I knew till I met them on the Lahore," returned Clare with a faint colour rising in her face. "The passengers, with one or two exceptions, were the average set one meets travelling. There was the large overdressed, bejewelled woman, who slights the aspirate, and holds you like the 'Ancient Mariner' till she has told the tale of her first and second husband; there was the lively widow, who dresses with exquisite taste, gets up tender confidences with half a dozen men, and is mistrusted by her own sex. There was a Melbourne family, who indulged in loud recollections of sweet intercourse with the British aristocracy, and would have been regarded by unsuspecting souls as people of distinction had not another passenger, alas, deposed that the wealth of the family was chiefly due to pawnbroking—but there, enough of such gossip. It is awfully nice to be at home once more," broke off Clare, looking round her room with affectionate recognition at the pictures—radiant summer landscapes, for the most part, with white and gold frames—at the pale blue hangings with cunning touches of dead gold in them; the low easy chairs, the thick carpet with its deep harmonious shades, and the fleecy-white long-haired mats lying before couch and easy chairs, inviting you sociably to bury your feet in them, and forget all weary pilgrimages.

Dolly looked at her sister as she leant back in the deep easy chair, in her creamy French cashmere, with soft lace falling about her white throat and delicate hands; her dark brown hair coiled in thick satiny plaits, and fastened up, with one or two scarlet rosebuds and dark leaves.

"What a nice picture you make, Clare," she said admiringly. "There is more rose colour in your face than you used to have, and that soft dress and the dark blue velvet of the chair make just the right framing for you. Do you know you are really much prettier than when you went away."

"If that were possible say, my dear, and then your compliment will leave nothing to be desired," said Clare with a mock bow and the slow glad laughter which came to her so readily.

"Tell, me, Dolly," she said, suddenly becoming grave; "is there really anything seriously wrong with mother's health?"

"Oh, no," answered Dolly brightly; then, as if recollecting herself— "At least nothing that we need be alarmed about. But Helena seemed very anxious when she had palpitation of the heart so much, and so thought it was better you should be at home."

"Now, I said that over and over to myself," said Clare, sitting upright with a glow in her cheeks. The younger sister looked a trifle uneasy. Poor Dolly in the old days used to have rather a hard time of it, what between her loyalty to Clare and her forced subjection to Helena, the eldest daughter. Helena, the imperious and commanding spirit of the family, who was always hatching little plots and nursing petty intrigues to mould Clare into a more submissive and irreproachable young lady. Dolly had always been more in sympathy with Clare, both by nature and affection; but Helena was so determined—so desperately bent on mastery—that she had an irresistible knack of coaxing, cajoling, and frightening Dolly into a kind of vagabond allegiance against her inclination and dawning judgment. When this masterful eldest sister married three years previously an elderly and rather vulgar man, who was supposed to possess vast hoards of wealth. Dolly was in a measure emancipated. But her enjoyment of the sweets of liberty was short lived. In less than a year after

Helena's marriage Clare had gone to visit some relatives in England, and subsequently an aunt in Germany. This was Mrs. Rutherford's only sister and the wife of a German Professor in Dresden, where Clare stayed and studied music, which she excelled in and loved passionately. And thus it came to pass that Dolly had fallen once more under the sway of Mrs. Joseph Hartingdale, nèe Helena Rutherford.

"What did you say over and over to yourself?" she enquired, trying hard to look as if she could have no possible conception of Clare's meaning.

"Why, that it might be a little melodramatic plot of Helena's to make me break off my musical studies and return so abruptly."

"Is it such a hardship for you to return to your own home and all of us?" said Dolly plaintively.

"Good Heavens! you are going to be another Mrs. Joseph. I could have vowed that was Helena's tone and look when mounted on her great moral elephant," cried Clare in a voice of comic despair.

Dolly pouted and picked up her crewel work which as usual was lying in placid folds at her feet. She generally had a piece of needlework on hand that had an invariable habit of sliding gracefully to the carpet, only to be resumed when she was vexed or felt conscious that a lecture from Mrs. Joseph was imminent. "These birds and flowers are scapegoats that wander into the drawing-room laden with Dolly's remorse," Clare used to say in the old days.

"Never mind, Carassima," she said, stroking Dolly's fuzzy fair hair. "I'm very glad I have come home, but I think it was too bad of Helena to alarm me by throwing out vague hints about darling Mutter's health, writing mysteriously of the Doctor's "not speaking openly," and the symptoms which seemed to threaten heart-disease. Dearly as I loved Aunt Juliet and Dresden, I cannot now wish that I had stayed away longer, but I do wonder why Helena has wasted all this diplomacy to secure my return just now."

"Oh, perhaps she was afraid that you would be too much like a professional musician, and fall in love with some musical genius," said Dolly, with one of those sudden bursts of confidence by which she usually threw off allegiance to Mrs. Joseph.

"Oh, is that the last enormity I am supposed to meditate said Clare with a merry laugh. "'Concerts for the people. Million prices,' &c., &c."

"Clare, how is it that you liked Aunt Vahlberg so much more than Aunt Marshland?" asked Dolly, by way of leaving a dangerous subject.

"You might as well ask me why I like an Australian spring better than an English autumn, why I like hills and the freedom of the winds and clouds better than monotonous flat and low-clinging fogs!" answered Clare warmly.

"Well, Aunt Marshland and the girls always seem very nice, to judge by their letters. I am sure aunt is a very good woman," said Dolly, stoutly.

"Yes, of course—good to excess, with the kind of virtue that gives coals, and recipes for eternal salvation, with an ungrudging hand, but narrow and conventional to an extent that makes all the little demons one has cast out return with endless processions of big demons. 'Oh! my soul, praise Thou the Lord!' she says so solemnly in her pew on Sunday. You would never imagine she was thanking God so devoutly for six hundred a year, a bad collection of foreign pictures, and two daughters even more prosaic than herself."

"Clare, you are too exacting," said the younger sister, laughing. "I really don't think a very prosaic person would write such letters as Aunt Marshland sends papa—about politics and charity and the High Church and things."

"But then, you see, you never lived with her for five months," returned Clare, with the calm assurance of superior knowledge. "I have seen the very rosebuds that were near her grow stout and commonplace in half an hour. You may laugh, but it's true nevertheless. They puff out, and get a look of dull content, as if they thought, 'How much better it is to be in here, where there is a plump sham Madonna on the wall, sage green chairs about, and a warm atmosphere redolent of Ess bouquet, than to be out in the fresh cold air, with big stupid clouds floating about in the sky, and little birds singing to the east and to the west, without a mission or useful purpose in life!'"

"Oh, Clare, I do believe you're worse than ever," said Dolly, with a look of amusing reproof on her pretty rosy face. "At any rate, I'll be able to see for myself when I go to England. I told you in my last letter, didn't I, that George and I are going for a trip as soon we are married. We are going by Francisco; won't it be delightful. We are both going to keep journals and illustrate them. But if there is anything extraordinary, I must get George to draw it for me. You know I draw faces, and birds, and flowers, and insects better than anything else."

"Well, perhaps Providence will be kind and send shoals of butterflies round you on your travels, and then George will have to come to you for help," said Clare gravely.

"Clare, I hope you will like George better than you used to," said Dolly, a little severely.

"Why, child, I always liked George very well. What put it into your head that I didn't?"

"Oh, I remember you used to laugh at his verses, and say they were like primeval reptiles with an uncertain number of feet."

"Did I really say that?" said Clare remorsefully. "But then you know, dear, one may laugh at a man's verses and even opinions without any feeling of dislike."

"I wonder what your lover will be like when you condescend to have one," said Dolly, looking at her sister critically. In Clare's face these simple words wrought a curious change. Over brow and cheek an impetuous overwhelming colour mounted and deepened; the mobile lips quivered, and the long thick lashes drooped persistently. The whole face glowed with colour and feeling. Now the most remarkable characteristic of Clare Rutherford's face was that though capable of swiftly varying expression, it would often remain for hours almost impassive. Unless stirred by some emotion, the fair clear cut face, the large dark steady eyes, and the sweet somewhat pensive mouth would remain quietly unchanged. The merest stranger, therefore, would have been struck with the sudden deepening of expression, the vivid flush of colour, and the obstinately lowered eyes. As for Dolly, these signals of confusion were simply "confirmation strong as Holy Writ."

"Clare, you mean Sphinx!" she cried, and then paused, feeling that the English language was hopelessly barren of words that could fitly describe the sisterly defection of a girl who would for four hours conceal such a secret. "Clare, you are engaged, and you have been speaking to me all this time without telling me!"

"No, I am not engaged," answered Clare slowly.

"Oh, you are married, I suppose, and never even sent us a morsel of wedding cake, nor wrote for your mother's and father's consent, let alone Helena's. Did you find him frightfully commonplace, and leave him after a few weeks?" asked Dolly, calmly. "Or perhaps you have him wrapped up in wadding along with the blue china bowls, so that he might not bore you."

"Dolly, if you are such a plague I'll tell you nothing at all," said Clare; and if the truth must be told, this is what she would like to have done. She would like to have folded the sweet secret in her innermost heart a little longer, as a dove protects her young with sheltering wings from each cold breath and careless passer-by.

"But who is he? What is his name? When shall we see him?"

"Oh, Dolly, you are worse than a Professorial Board. Even they would not expect one to answer three questions at once. Well, he is a clergyman; his name is Harleigh Roxburghe, and I suppose you'll see him tomorrow."

"A clergyman—Oh," said Dolly, in an indescribable sort of a tone. "Is he High Church with a lot of money?" she continued, charitably seeking for some extenuating circumstances.

"I don't know," answered Clare, with the sound of suppressed laughter in her voice.

"But, Clare, are you joking? You know you used to dislike clergymen more, oh far more, than people who wrote weak poetry; and as for sermons, when you're married you'll never be able to go to church twice a Sunday. Is he very handsome, Clare?"

"Oh, you must not ask me, I'm not an impartial judge you know," said Clare softly, with a blush and a sweet conscious look, which became her wonderfully.

"Well, never mind, tell me all about it. I suppose you did not flirt with him at first just for fun, and then find he was awfully jolly, did you?" said Dolly eagerly.

Instead of answering this mild suggestion with a saucy retort or a quick rebuke, as Dolly expected, Clare looked desperately grave, if not pained, and remained silent.

"But go on, tell me from the very beginning," cried the impatient Dolly, sitting on an ottoman at Clare's feet. "When did you first speak? How long were you on board before you became friends?"

"About two weeks. Harleigh had a cousin with him who came out for his health. Two or three days after we sailed this young man—Patrick Dunstan is his name—had an attack of haemorrhage of the lungs. Harleigh was with him constantly till he was better. A short time after Mr. Dunstan was able to come on deck he was lying one day on a stretcher, and Harleigh read to him. After a while Mr. Dunstan fell asleep, and then Harleigh left him and went below. While he was away Mr. Dunstan awoke. He half sat up, and looked around as if in want of something. I was sitting, near, and I went and asked him if I could do anything for him. He complained of thirst, so I got a glass of water for him, and then sat down beside him. I had a volume of Heine's works which I had been reading. He said he had only Heine's poems, and knew nothing of his prose works. So I read a few extracts, which amused him very much, especially that malevolent little passage in which Heine asserts that he is a man of pure and simple tastes, and goes on to say that he would like to live in a humble cottage in the quiet country, where he could have fresh butter and sweet milk, where the birds would sing their songs, and the flowers would peep in at the windows, 'and, if the dear Lord would make me quite happy, where there would be a large tree growing before the door with four or five of my enemies hanging on it'."

"What a delightful idea," said Dolly, laughing merrily.

"So Mr. Dunstan thought, and he was laughing as you are now when Harleigh returned. He thanked me for looking after 'his boy,' as he called Mr. Dunstan, who said, 'I'm not quite sure that I am your boy now, Harleigh. Miss Rutherford, will you kindly adopt me henceforth, and come and read Heine to me when you want to do a particularly charitable action?' We all laughed at this proposal, and I then gravely consented to 'adopt' Pat till further orders. Then he said, 'I was very grateful to you when I was so wretchedly ill.' 'Why?' I asked in surprise. 'Oh, because when I could not even bear to be read to you used to play such heavenly music. There was one piece in particular that was grand. I'm an awful duffer about music in general, you know, but this piece seemed always full of a story.' 'Tell me what story, and then perhaps I'll know what piece you mean,' I said. 'Well, it seemed to me the tale of a beautiful little angel who got tired of Paradise, and slipped out when St. Peter had opened the doors very wide to let in some swell saint. This little angel was ambitious to feel her feet on earth instead of the wings she left in heaven, but no sooner had she got down among the children of men than she found what a tremendous swindle this world is. She used to be out in the drifting snow and in storms, by the sea when the waves were roaring, and in the street full of discordant cries; and in the midst of all she used to have glimpses of the green pastures and still waters, with the great white throne of God in the midst. Then the conclusion comes quite suddenly, and I can't make up my mind whether it means rapture, or rebellion, or resignation.' 'I wonder if you mean Schubert's unfinished Symphony,' I said. 'Suppose you play that for us now, and then Patrick can decide,' suggested Harleigh.

"So from that our acquaintance grew, and we became fast friends. I used to play a great deal for them, and then Harleigh and I used to talk about Germany. He was at Bonn and other places in his student days. I was surprised to find how in a short time I could talk to him frankly about myself, the people I like best, and my favourite books and music."

"Oh, that's because you were falling in love with each other," said Dolly, nodding her little head sagely.

"No, it is not that," returned Clare; "it is an influence he has with him. You feel that he is really interested in your affairs and thoughts, and that if there is anything he can do for you it will give him real pleasure to do it. Even Mrs. Provost—you remember the old woman who had a large fancy shop in Kleinstreet?—"

"Oh, I remember; when we went for anything she always used to pull out huge pieces of Berlin woolwork with Patriarchs and camels and angels in vivid greens and blues."

"Yes, the same. Well, I have seen Harleigh sit and talk to her by the hour. The old lady knew hardly any one, and she just used to beam with delight when he used to speak to her, and pour a perpetual stream of talk on him. Of course I spoke to her sometimes, but I never knew what to say after we had spoken of the weather and the passage. One day after we had become good friends, I said to Harleigh—'When I see you talking and listening to Mrs. Provost do you know I cannot help wondering whether you do so just because you are a clergyman, or because you are really interested in her.'

"'Why do you think I should speak to any one just because I am a clergyman?' he asked, with a smile. 'Oh, for the same reason that you preach sermons and go to see people who may be your parishioners, whether you think them interesting or not.' 'Well, I do not do any of these things because I am a clergyman,' he said, 'but I became one because these and such offices seemed to me the best worth doing of any work I was fitted for. But do you think Mrs. Provost very uninteresting?' he asked. I admitted that I did. Then he said 'I suppose you will think me very humdrum; but I hardly meet any one in whom I do not find something to interest me, to speculate about, or to wonder at. There is always something so wonderful about a human being when one thinks of it, even those pitiful souls of whom no lifting up is conceivable—to whom no heaven is rightly credible.' Some flippant remark rose to my lips, but there was such a sad earnest expression on his face as he looked across the waves, that I felt constrained to keep silent. The more I saw and knew of him the more I felt that he was different from any man I had ever met before. When we talked together he was constantly saying something that made me think about things in quite a different light."

"Isn't that rather uncomfortable," said Dolly suspiciously. "Now George always sees things just in the same light that I see them. Only the other day we were talking about the alterations that are to be made at Pintoul Cottage—"

"Oh, yes, Dolly; but I don't mean wall paper and bead trimmings, and things of that kind," said Clare impatiently. Then seeing her sister's somewhat disconcerted look, she went on—"You know, Dolly, how selfish and impatient I have always been of a great many people."

"Aunt Marshland, for instance," said Dolly brightly.

"Yes," said Clare, somewhat ruefully, reflecting that, after all, her old besetting sin was strong with her still.

"Then do you think that by-and-by you will see everybody in a new light, and consider every one interesting and charming? Oh, don't, Clare it won't be half such fun; and of course there really are a great many foolish and stupid people about. I daresay Aunt Marshland even is very tiresome," said Dolly, struck with dismay at the thought of hearing no more of the heavy pompous men, and the inane, hopelessly common-place women whom her sister was wont to burlesque so happily.

Clare looked at the eager upturned face, her brows knitted in comic despair. Then she burst into a hearty ringing laugh.

"Look here, Dolly, I'm quite hoarse with chattering; order some tea, and don't be in the least alarmed that I am going to be a reformed character all in a moment."

"Yes, I'll give you some delicious tea—my own particular brew—and then you'll finish. For not a word have you yet told me of the love making."

"There was not much of what you call lovemaking," said Clare reflectively. "I felt that it was becoming more delightful day by day to be near Harleigh," she said, speaking in a low tone; "I used to wake up in the morning with a strange feeling of utter gladness, because as soon as I went on deck he would be the first to meet me, to bring my camp-stool into a cosy corner, to point a distant sail on the horizon, some wandering birds that had alighted on the masts in their long journey across the sea. I used to note with a feeling of pride how unselfishly considerate, how exquisitely courteous and kind he was to all, and more especially to those who needed any help, who were less attractive and less sought out by others. But I did not imagine that he could think of me in any way but as a passing acquaintance; or at most, a friend. I sometimes used to picture the sort of a woman who would be worthy to be his wife, especially after Patrick told me of Harleigh's early life."

"Is he elderly?" asked Dolly, her face falling.

"No. That is, unless you consider a man middle-aged at thirty-two."

"And he has a history? Tell me what it is Clare."

"He is the youngest son of a Colonel Roxburghe, and when quite a young man Harleigh also went into the army. At twenty-five he got engaged to Patrick's half-sister—a very lovely girl. Patrick showed me her miniature one day. A few months after this engagement Harleigh's mother and fiancée went on a visit to some relatives in Ireland. When they were returning to England the vessel was lost in a frightful storm, and not one was saved, except two or three of the sailors."

"How terrible!" murmured Dolly, in an awestruck tone.

"Yes; you may imagine what a dreadful shock it was to poor Harleigh," said Clare in a low wistful tone. "He left the army, and devoted his life and means to works of charity. Then he studied for the Church and took orders. For the last five years he worked incessantly in one of these dreadfully poor parishes in the east of London. He has a sister, a very rich widow—Lady Lisdale—who helped him and worked almost as hard as himself. Patrick, when he was telling me of this, said, 'There is a strain of insanity in the family about money. Sooner or later they squander all they have on people who steal spoons or live in garrets'."

"Which may be at once saintly and aristocratic, but I wonder how it will suit you, Clare? You have always had heaps of money for yourself. Perhaps, though, if you steal things from Harleigh he'll keep his money for you as if you were an institution; and then, I suppose, papa will endow you too."

"I hope papa will be nice," said Clare anxiously.

"I wonder what Victor Maylands will think of it," said Dolly, as if struck by a sudden recollection. Clare crimsoned painfully. "Oh! Dolly, that's the thing which troubles me most. How am I to tell Harleigh of that episode?"

"Don't begin by confessing every little peccadillo, Clare. Life is too short for such trifles."

"But accepting a man's offer of marriage and then breaking off the engagement in two days is hardly a trifle," said Clare ruefully.

"The worst of it," began Dolly, and then she suddenly subsided. "What is the use of annoying Clare," she thought. "But I do wonder what she would say if I were to tell her that no one except her own family knows she broke off the engagement with Victor, and that Helena always speaks as if their marriage were a dead certainty."

"What were you going to say about the worst of it," asked Clare, finding that Dolly stopped short so abruptly.

"O, that you cannot go to hospitals or very miserable people—it would make you so wretched," answered Dolly, seizing on the first decent substitute that came into her head.

"Ah! but now it will be different, Dolly. I am sure I could do anything to please Harleigh. That is not the highest motive; but perhaps by-and-bye I may improve."

"Clare, you are very hard hit. I never thought you could be so humble. Before this you thought men were either idiots or prigs, and now—Well, I must put you to bed. I suppose Harleigh—I can't think of him by another name—you linger on it so lovingly—will come at an unearthly hour in the morning."

Chapter II

The Old Story

"With angels planted in hawthorn bowers,
And God himself in the passing hours."

There are few lives in which there do not come one or two rare days marked off from all the rest by the wonderful emotion we call happiness. It may be the exultation of self-surrender to some great purpose; or the dawning of a new mental life, lighting the way out of the house of bondage to some far-off and supremely beautiful Land of Promise; or it may be the actual, realization of some dimly looked for joy, which has come to us at last large and, unmaimed, a perfect gift from God. And for some hours—nay, for some days, perhaps—we thought that this large and serene horizon, this "light that never was beheld on sea or land," were to be our daily portion, our everlasting heritage. Fate was to be henceforth like one of the angels of Signorelli, who, with radiant faces, scatter roses for elect souls. The monotony which had so oppressed us, the perpetual chafing of trivial cares, the wearing sense of loneliness, these had passed away, and in their place there were these rosy hours fresh as the very breath of Paradise, golden with the light of coming achievement or happy love. It is impossible to imagine that in the drear evenings of a future autumn-tide the love and the hopes which are now so vivid and victorious will then be lean and lifeless as the leaves that the wailing wind blows whither it listeth.

It was with some such feeling that Clare Rutherford stood enjoying the fresh brightness of the spring morning the day after her arrival. The keen, almost intoxicating, "perfume of the things of God," the breath of thousands of open roses, of unclosing buds and of fruit-trees in full blossom, seemed to welcome her back to each well-remembered nook; to the pleasant seats under spreading trees where she had passed so many hours in company with her best beloved authors; to the little creek at the bottom of the large velvety lawn, that ran so blithely on its way till the fierce suns of summer had drunk up its waters and stilled its infantine prattle. And a few miles away, beyond the intervening slopes and valleys, which were dotted with houses rapidly spreading between the hills and the eastern suburbs, lay the town clearly outlined in the light of the morning sun. Clare remembered with something akin to wonder how often she had looked on that rapidly enlarging colonial city, almost with repugnance, and thought it a mushroom growth of ugly buildings without historic associations, devoid of any instinct of harmony and beauty. Now she saw in it countless habitations, with an infinite wealth of life and human interest; she saw in it churches for worship, halls for national and civic government, and theatres where the spectators were moved to tragic pity or light laughter; and away still some miles beyond the town, the sea, mystical and restless, mailed in sunshine and stirred by the air, lay clinging to the borders of the land. That sight at least had never been trivial or wearisome or wanting in beauty. But how much more tolerant and tender were the feelings which henceforth it would awaken in the heart of the girl who looked at it with a smile of supreme gladness parting her red lips, with the light of love shining in her beautiful dark eyes. Clare wandered away across the lawn down to the creek, humming snatches of the Volkslieder she had learned from the peasant girls of the Harz mountains.

No vexing thoughts of the past, no anxiety for the present, or mistrust of the future dimmed the deep joy, the blissful content, of these bright morning hours. The laburnum bushes, with their summery trailing blossoms rising in the soft air, seemed as if they were crying "Hosanna;" the swallows with shining pointed wings, buoyant, eager and swift, darted about and made sudden dives into the fountains, then suddenly assumed quite a solemn air, and lifted up a tiny scrap of material as if the care of a coming family lay heavily on their minds.

Here was a rustic bench beside the talkative little stream, beneath the shadow of a patriarchal gumtree—a tree that looked with lordly benignity on the surrounding country; and though far from being by nature haughty or overbearing, it could not choose but see that there was no other tree near or far which could claim equality of stature with it. This was a spot which had grown to be looked on as Clare's special domain. Seated on the bench one heard the soft dash and fall of the water from a cascade on a miniature scale, which had been formed with considerable skill by Matthew, the sole son of the house; as also the humming of bees, hovering above and amidst the bushes of sweetbriar, banks of periwinkle, the Fior da morte, with pale-blue flowers, the clumps of native lilac, lavender, and other fragrant and flowering shrubs which grew luxuriantly along the banks of the little creek.

With hands folded idly on her lap, Clare sat in a waking reverie, vivid recollections of her eventful voyage back to her Australian home succeeded by swift memories of her late life in Germany. "Can it really be only three days ago since Harleigh and I stood talking on the deck of the Lahore?" The talk had been first of the merest trifles—the change of atmosphere as they neared land, of the birds and seaweed that went floating by. Then there had been a pause. Some dim instinct had brought the colour throbbing into her cheeks. She could hear the words again as they were spoken in a low tone—"I suppose you can hardly realize that I look forward to the end of our voyage with dread." "It has been a very pleasant trip," she had answered, trying to speak lightly, unconcernedly, but feeling that she failed horribly, knowing that there was a tremor in her lips, a false note in her voice; wishing yet dreading that Mrs. Chardingle, who had been an ideal chaperone—confined to her cabin most of the time—would pace up slowly to the vacant seat near her, and say languidly "Thank Heaven! we shall be home tomorrow." But neither Mrs. Chardingle nor anyone else had approached that vacant seat. There seemed to be no one within miles and miles but the man who stood beside her, looking into her face with beseeching earnest eyes—her telltale face that always played the traitor when it should remain calmly impassive. "A pleasant trip," he had repeated with a sudden change of voice. "Yes, I suppose so, only—" he broke short and laughed a little, and she laughed also, hardly knowing why. "What I want to say is that there are some things which are either too dear or too bitter to be called 'pleasant'." What a vindictive hatred this grave, calm man had taken to that unoffending adjective. In the midst of her agitation this thought had flitted through her brain. Then, looking up, she saw with a sudden pang that his face was very pale, and as if possessed by another will, stronger and more instant in sincerity than her own, she had said in a low, distinct voice, "I think I know what you mean." "Are you sure that you know?" he had said in a rapid, shaken voice. "What I mean is that you are so dear, so precious to me that if we are to part merely as strangers ... and if—if you say that we are not ... Was that what you understood?" Trembling, happy, ashamed, thrilled through all her being with a rush of bewildering emotions, she had looked up and answered "Yes." "My darling!" To the last day of her life she would remember those low, passionate words. They could not even clasp each other's hands, but they drew a little nearer and stood in blissful silence looking over the restless, limitless sea, across which the sun's lady rays were gleaming red and warm.

Though Clare could not speak of this unreservedly even to her own sister, yet it was delightful to recall it when alone in her old familiar haunt with the lisp of falling water so near. What did the sound remind her of? Ah, that day in the Bavarian Alps when she heard the ringing of distant bells and the running of swift mountain streams blending in an exquisite melody.

There was a sudden sound of swift movement, and a lithe little figure in pale blue, with coquettish golden tassels all down the front came rapidly across the lawn.

"Clare, Clare, I've been looking for you everywhere," cried Dolly, breathlessly. "He has come; and oh, isn't it fun, with only me to look after you. I was crossing the hall, when I heard a gentlemen ask if Mr. Rutherford was in. I guessed who it was even before I saw his card. I went and shook hands with him, and said, I am Clare's sister: and oh, what a smile I got."

Poor Clare, confused and happy and silent, listened with a loud-beating heart as she went back to the house with Dolly, who was brimming over with excitement and delight.

"And, Clare, do you know he decidedly looks more like a soldier than a parson. He is not handsome, exactly, but he is distingué. I think I should be a little afraid of him. Oh, not a bit like George. Well, I won't play the duenna so far as to go in with you. I suppose we will have luncheon at the usual time, so you have only an hour for spooning."

"Oh, Dolly, you horrid little thing," cried the elder sister, in a tone of dismay and disapproval.

"Well, of course it's rather irregular, without father or mother, or even Helena, to sanction the proceeding. That soft Carmelite grey, with touches of cardinal, is really a sweet dress—did you wear it on purpose? Oh, you'll be like anybody else now, mailing o'er life's solemn main with a young man, like every other common-place girl. But, Clare, what makes you so pale and your eyes are quite big and dark—just as they look when you're going to cry, which I must say is very seldom."

How much Clare heard of this incessant chatter it would be hard to say. She was, in truth, very pale and nervous when she paused at the drawing-room door to regain some measure of composure before passing into the presence of the man to whom she had given her whole heart, but with whom she had never before stood face to face alone.

Harleigh Roxburghe, on his part, stood with his eyes fixed on the door with a look of strained and eager expectation. Dolly was right in saying that he was not exactly handsome, but distinguished, in his whole bearing he certainly retained traces of his military training and service. His face was one which always struck the observer with a sense of unusual power—one in which largeness of soul as well as of intellect was very legibly written. The eyes were dark and clear, with a keen far-sighted look; the brow was broad, with dark and rather heavy eyebrows; the mouth, which was clean shaven, was firm and noble, but somewhat stern. It was a face that struck one at first sight, and grew on the observer as the face of a man keen in spirit and unselfish of heart—of a man not faultless in temper, not particularly patient and longsuffering, but never wanting in fearless, instant sense of the right. There were lines about the mouth and eyes which seemed to have been graven there more by some heavy sorrow than by time—and, indeed, the whole face was in repose rather grave and set for a man of thirty-two; but this fault, if such it could be called, was not now apparent as he waited with fast-beating pulses for the woman who in so short a time had taken tyrannous possession of his heart.

He sat down by a little square medieval-looking table, on which stood a tall vase of antique form, containing a bunch of white moss rosebuds and a few sprigs of heliotrope. The sweet subtle perfume of the latter touched some dormant spring of memory, and in a moment a troop of recollections of other days and far distant scenes filled his mind. He thought of that hour which seemed at once so curiously near and far away, when he was struck to the very soul with a sorrow that seemed impossible to be borne. Then the sudden awakening to a new ideal, the elation of heart and soul in realizing that faith was not a mere dogma, but had suddenly become to him an immense governing power—a lever which raised him above his own immediate despair, and taught him to live, not for himself, but for others. He remembered how for a time his faith had been hard and absolute, without speculation, almost without enquiry. And then the time had come when with a desolate heart and a spirit darkened with questioning uncertainty, it seemed to him as if religion everywhere were strangled by theological systems, and crystallized into dead formulas—a time when the messages of life and healing which he had so often spoken to others with fervent and undoubting joy were becoming party catch words, repeated with parrotlike indifference, or forged by ecclesiastical pride into heavy chains to bind the human intellect. After well nigh five years of unremitting work—work of mind and body—this strange torpor fastened on him, till at last the travailing brain and intense nerve called for relief. It was then that Harleigh Roxburghe left the scene of his labours—his daily services, his nightly meetings, his incessant ministrations among the poor hopelessly chained down with poverty, the weak and vicious still more hopelessly kept down by their ungoverned passions, their undisciplined instincts. He found a fellow-labourer to take his place, a man who had the dauntless courage, the strength and the unshrinking energy which fitted him well for to carry on the work of a poor London parish.

At first to his overwrought mind and irritated nerves the sight and the sound of the sea with its haunting memories had in them something of torture. But by degrees the complete rest, the change from the clanging haste, from the monotonous streets crowded with mean abodes and squalid lives, to the free impassioned splendour of the sea stretching to vast limits that seemed to find no shore on any side, wrought a steady cure. The days that dawned serene and unclouded as the eternity from which they came, the pungent salt air, the swift coarse of the gallant ship over the great deep with its mysterious sounds and colours, its passing shadows and swift changes, filled his nerves and brain with the old delight of living, and braced mind and body alike. And in the midst of it all this beautiful girl, with her frank smile and untroubled brow, became his friend, his intimate companion, his love. Yes, without a moment's warning, without a sign of conquest, she had taken possession of his heart. After the overwhelming sorrow of his early life he had been so sure that the passion of love would henceforth play no part in his existence. In the heart of London he had lived the life of an anchorite, neither desiring nor dreaming of a woman's love. But now! At last the door opened and Clare, very pale and grave, feeling as if there was a heavy mist before her eyes, slowly entered the room. She had vaguely wondered what she would say, how she would hide the shrinking shamefacedness which was so new a sensation to her. Harleigh met her with outstretched hands, his face radiant with happiness, and when she felt his strong firm fingers close over hers, the recreant blood rushed red and hot into her face.

"Clare, it is no dream, then; you do really love me a little."

She looked up, her lips quivering, the tears gathering in her great dark eyes.

"Tell me, darling," he repeated in a low entreating tone, drawing her nearer to him.

"No, not a little, a great deal," she said, with the most charming distinctness, the old habit of quick retort coming back to her as the glad sense of unalloyed happiness vanquished her timidity. Their lips met in a long lingering kiss, and the great measure of that day's strange happiness for both was reached.

"Clare, I feel almost dazed at my new-found joy, it seems so sudden and bright, like a dream that one fears to drive away by moving or speaking too loud," said Harleigh after a long pause, which to both seemed more eloquent than any speech.

"And we are such strangers to each other," said Clare with mock gravity, as if suddenly recollecting that till they met on board the Lahore a few weeks ago they had been oblivious of each other's existence. Yet the observation, though quite true, seemed so absurd that they both laughed—the glad laugh of happy lovers which comes so lightly, and is so unexacting as to its cause.

"Mr. and Mrs. Rutherford, I find, are from home. I suppose no one expected the steamer so soon."

"No, they are to be back tomorrow, and they thought that I would be home the day after. Mother has not been very well for some time back, so papa took her for a week or two to Nillanilla, one of our sheep stations—such a nice old place in the heart of the bush. It is nearly 200 miles from town."

"I am afraid you are very rich people," said Harleigh, with a half comic smile.

"Is that because of the camel?" asked Clare seriously.

"The camel?" repeated Harleigh, in amazement.

"Yes, the camel who can go through the eye of a needle—you know the comparison."

"Oh! I am not thinking of the future world, but of the present. I am not at all a rich man, Clare. I am not absolutely dependent on my calling for a living. I might have a great deal more money, but I had no use for it; and I have not been looking forward to marrying. I can never give you a home like this."

"Nor two magpies that bite the legs of unwary strangers, and swear now and then for recreation?"

"Are these included in your present possessions?" asked Harleigh, smiling broadly.

"Yes, and likewise a pony getting well on in years. I have other horses to ride of course, but I never feel any of them belong to me but Tony— the first one papa gave me when I was ten—that's thirteen years ago. Two magpies, a pony, and my dresses. Do you think I am too rich?" said Clare, with her bright catching smile. "Because, if so, I might send the magpies into a convent; they have long stood in need of better morals and more confinement; and the pony, do you think you could make use of him, Harleigh, going about to see your parishioners? He would do anything—I believe he would even preach a sermon for a few lumps of sugar."

"Well, when the parishioners are forthcoming we may give Tony a fair trial," said Harleigh. "I suppose you would like better to remain in Australia, for some time at least, than to go back to England, as I intended doing, in about a year?"

"Yes, I think I would," returned Clare, a little wistfully as the memory of lowering skies and divers people of the type represented by her aunt Marshland rose to her recollection.

"I have always worked in London—mostly among the very poor," continued Harleigh. "By-and-bye I shall want to return there, but in the meantime I suppose I can get an incumbency in the colony. Of course, before we can speak of any definite arrangements, I must see your father. I suppose you know, Clare, that most rich men are, as a rule, not violently prepossessed in favour of sons-in-law who are not capitalists, nor even ambitious to become such."

Clare knew this, and was also perfectly well aware that her father was no exception to the rule. And with this thought came that other unwelcome one of her father's deep displeasure when she had so abruptly broken off her engagement to Victor Maylands. "Of course it was shameful of me, but I know my father would not have been so incensed if Victor had been poor instead of being so absurdly rich." At that moment a strong impulse rose in Clare's mind to tell her lover all. But it was so hard to spoil the first few hours they had together by such a confession of folly, and weakness, and vanity. She herself could never quite realize how it had all come about—how much less would he whose life was full of noble purpose and unselfish work. "By-and-by, when we have known each other longer," thought Clare, "I can more readily speak of it. I am quite sure if I began now the words would stick in my throat. When Harleigh knows me better he can more easily understand how I could do such a thing." Ignoring her disquieting thoughts, Clare said lightly:

"My eldest sister married a millionaire, so my father will have to keep his mind's eyes fixed on her, if he is displeased at your dislike of money."

"What makes you think that I dislike money?"

"Oh, Patrick told me heaps of things about you—among other tales how you had a legacy of ten thousand pounds left to you, and spent it all in buying up some of those awful London rookeries, to have them pulled down, and have decent dwellings for the poor built instead."

"So Pat used to gossip in that way when you sat by him under the awning. How lovely you used to look, Clare, in that low chair, in the blue dress you used to wear, with a soft cloud of lace on your shoulders."

"And you paced up and down, looking so solemn and preoccupied. I am sure I used to think you would not know whether I was arrayed in sackcloth and ashes or decked out in satin."

"You did think about me sometimes even then?"

"I thought about you a good deal, even before we spoke to each other. Harleigh, when did you first begin to—to—love me?"

"The first time your eyes were lifted to mine with a smile. Look at me now, Clare. It is really quite necessary that I should make up my mind as to their colour."

Clare looked into her lover's face, and as she met his long fond gaze, a happy smile parted her lips.

"It is so wonderful," she said in a low voice.

"What is so wonderful, my darling?"

"Why, that all our lives—every hour and day—has quietly gone on bringing us to each other, and we neither of us knew."

"No; two short months ago we were unconscious of each other's existence, and yet today, Clare, you are going to promise—"

"Oh no, Harleigh, don't speak of promises," entreated Clare, a sudden trouble in her face. It was very hard that in the midst of her newfound happiness a stray thought or a chance word should so vividly recall to her that humiliating episode she most wished forget. "To promise a man to marry him, and then in two days to jilt him so shamefully." How Helena, in her bitter wrath had repeated this over and over again, till the word "promise" had grown hateful and sinister to Clare—a word of evil omen which she could not bear to hear Harleigh utter. "Don't think me very unreasonable and whimsical, dear?" she said coaxingly. "Well, take all the vows and protestations for granted, you can even begin to coach me up in my future responsibilities; how I am to behave on divers solemn occasions, &c. I'll never be able to put on a look of wisdom, and talk to people about the commandments and things. Tell me, Harleigh, what you say when you go to see your people. Suppose I were a poor—oh, dreadfully poor—washerwoman without even a potato in the house, and with my two arms broken, what would you say to me?"

Harleigh laughed and drew the girl close to him, saying softly, "You mocking little puss."

"That's what I call shameful conduct, to kiss a poor helpless woman, and call her names likewise," said Clare gravely.

"By-and-by, when you go to see people, my pet, you need not trouble about what to say. Just let them talk to you, and you will soon acquire a vast store of miscellaneous knowledge. For instance, if a child is badly scalded, what is the best thing to be done?"

"Keep out of its way," responded Clare promptly.

In the midst of their laughter Dolly came in looking very demure and responsible.

"It seems a little profane to tell you, young people, that luncheon is ready," she said very gravely.

Chapter III

Mrs. Joseph

There is not the least doubt that Dolly literally observed the golden rule of doing to others as she would be done by in undertaking the responsible duty of chaperoning her elder sister. Even after luncheon she declined to accompany the lovers in a short stroll round the grounds prior to Harleigh's return to town. "I have so many things to do," she said, with superb gravity. And indeed there was more truth in the assertion than resides in most excuses, for Dolly was deep in the delightful mysteries of unpacking Clare's goods and chattels. That is, she sat in an easy-chair, and watched Clare's deft-handed maid as she unlocked trunks, unfolded parcels, shook out dresses, and tenderly opened bonnet boxes. From depths of the unfathomable the girl now and then brought up packages addressed to Dolly herself—wedding presents from friends and relatives in England. As these variously-shaped, well-muffled gifts appeared there would be a subdued "Oh!" of delight from Dolly, then the sharp sound of keen-edged scissors cutting strings, the harsh sound of brown, and the soft rustle of tissue paper, lo! the hidden treasure lay full to view.

Dolly was just in the act of unpacking two little vases of Meissen porcelain, with flower wreaths so wonderfully soft, glowing, and pure, that she was lost in rapturous admiration, when she heard the sound of approaching footsteps and the frou-frou of rustling silk, followed by a low tap at the half-open door, and a well-known voice said. "Are you here, Dolly?"

"Oh, Helena!" said Dolly, with an awful sinking at the heart, though outwardly she was composed enough as she went forward to kiss her sister—a handsome, elegantly dressed woman, who looked round enquiringly.

"Where is Clare? Is she well?"

"Oh, yes, she has just gone out for a little stroll," answered Dolly, motioning the girl to leave the room. "And just fancy, Helena, she is engaged—at least not engaged, you know; but Mr. Roxburghe came to speak to papa, and of course he wasn't in; he won't be back till to-morrow evening."

Dolly was prepared to see her sister pleased, to hear her utter sharp words of disapproval; but she was not prepared to see her stand speechless, the colour retreating from her cheeks, and an expression of positive alarm in her face. "Perhaps she thinks he is a banjo-man, who blackens his face and sings 'On de ole Kentucky shore,'" thought Dolly, and charitably hastened to explain. "Of course he is quite a gentleman, although I suppose not very rich, being a clergyman."

"A clergyman," repeated Mrs. Hartingdale, mechanically. She sat on a chair that stood near, and looked straight before her for some minutes without further speech. Dolly was mystified. She knew that it was wholly due to Helena that Clare had returned so soon; that she had with feverish eagerness seized on their mother's illness, which had in reality been neither serious nor protracted, and cunningly used it to secure her object with half-expressed fears and insinuations. She also knew dimly, in the way that we divine so many things which are neither written nor spoken, that Helena was extremely anxious to bring about a marriage between Clare and Victor Maylands—to knit up the ravelled threads which Clare had so rudely and suddenly snapped. But, after all, why make it a matter of such intense importance; whoever married or was not given in marriage could make but little difference to Helena. She at least had married a man who could clothe her in purple velvet and costly lace, and give solemn dinner parties, to which neither a Shakspeare nor an archangel would be bidden if he had not a large balance at some well-established Bank. Clare could not mar or increase that splendid fortune, and as long as Mrs. Joseph was secure in its possession nothing surely could work her fatal woe. Yet, why did she sit there pale and silent, so utterly unlike her usual imperious, successful, and indomitable self?

"Where is Clare now?" she said, suddenly breaking the curious silence that had fallen on her.

"She went out for a little walk with Mr. Roxburghe. I think wanted to show him the shortest cut to the Vermont Station." This last was a brilliant suggestion that flashed into Dolly's mind as she was talking.

"How long was he here?"

"Oh, a couple of hours. He stayed to luncheon with us."

"But what right had he to come in at all till he had seen papa?" said Mrs. Hartingdale, with a sharp inflection of rage in her voice.

"What! Just ask for papa and then walk away without seeing Clare?" said Dolly, with wide opened eyes.

"Certainly, that's what he ought to have done. But these penniless adventurers are all alike—once let them come across some foolish girl who has the prospect of a fortune."

"Foolish! Do you call Clare foolish?" said Dolly solemnly.

"Well, if she isn't, you'll certainly make up for both," said the incensed woman, suddenly turning on the victim nearest at hand. "You know very well how impossible it is that Clare should be allowed to carry on in this disreputable manner—getting engaged on board a mail steamer to a man she knew only for a few weeks."

Numerous retorts rose to Dolly's lip, but the traditional habit of submission got the better of her as she marked the usual tokens of excitement displayed by Mrs. Joseph, who very seldom showed so much temper. She could be unjust, and essentially unveracious when it suited her; she would say mercilessly unkind things, but in a dispassionate, calmly judicial kind of way, which was far more unanswerable and exasperating than the hot unreasonable words to which she had just given utterance.

"Adam and Eve were more disreputable still—they only knew each other for a few hours in a lonely garden when they got engaged; but there's no use in making Helena unbearably cross by speaking of Genesis—she's bad enough as it is," thought Dolly, as she looked out at the window and kept silence like a diplomat. "Clare is coming back," she said presently, turning as if to leave the room.

Mrs. Hartingdale gave a swift glance, and saw that some moments would yet elapse before Clare could reach the house with the slow medi-

tative steps which bore her through the glinting shadows of the tall gum-
trees, the branching elms, and the dusky cedars that grew in friendly
neighbourhood in the grounds of Calthorpe Park. A very little reflection
had served to show the eldest sister that her outspoken rage at the sudden
frustration of her carefully laid plans was a crude mistake. Whatever was
to be gained by crafty and patience, and careful dissimulation, nothing
could be achieved by candid and barbarous passion.

"Stop, Dolly, I have something to say to you. Of course you can easily
understand that I am very much annoyed at Clare's treatment of poor
Victor. But, on the whole, I suppose it is better not to say much to her
about the matter just now. Indeed, I shall say nothing at all; and you—
you need say nothing either."

"I am not in the habit of carrying tales," returned Dolly, with a good
deal of dignity.

During the meeting and conversation with Clare which followed,
Mrs. Hartingdale showed no traces of the deep displeasure and disgust
that filled her mind.

"I suppose Dolly has told you," said Clare softly, a swift deep flush
rising on her face, after the first greetings were over.

"Yes; it appears that you have become very friendly with one of your
fellow-passengers."

("It must be very hard to smile and speak gently when you want to
swear out loud," thought Dolly, as she watched her eldest sister.)

"I am sorry Harleigh went away before you came, but I suppose you
will see him soon."

"Harleigh!" repeated Mrs. Hartingdale to herself with a gasp. Aloud,
however, she said with serene composure:

"Of course I may speak of the grand secret to the father and mother.
We are going to drive as far as Wandoo this afternoon, and as they expect
to stay tonight we'll meet them."

"Wandoo. Where is that?" asked Clare.

"Oh, I forgot that it was bought since you went away. It is a beautiful little property Hartingdale purchased a year ago. It is twenty miles out of town, between this and Mount Regard. Hartingdale is going there on business, and I am going with him for a few days. I have not been very well of late, so perhaps a little change will do me good."

("How gracefully Helena can fib even when she is as cross as a hungry cuttlefish," thought Dolly. "She never thought of going to Wandoo till she knew about Clare's disreputable conduct on board a mail steamer. I wonder why she is going.").

"I suppose baby is running about by this time," remarked Clare, recollecting that she was an aunt for the second time.

"He would be, if I allowed nurse to set him on the ground," returned Mrs. Joseph. "Marguerite is growing very rapidly. I must send her and baby to see you tomorrow—at least. I'll leave directions with Clayton to bring them."

Clare expressed due gratitude at the prospect of seeing the sacred scions of the house of Hartingdale, and mentally wondered if their Uncle Matthew still dared to call Marguerite Peggy, as he was wont to do, notwithstanding her mother's haughty indignation.

After a long desultory chat, during which Mrs. Joseph still kept up the "taffeta phrases, silken terms, precise," to which she has schooled herself, Clare said, "I must not forget to give you the blue China bowls Aunt Marshland sent to you, Helena. They are of the rarest kind. I believe aunt used to burn a little incense to them daily, so you may imagine how they weighted on my mind, lest anything should happen to them. I'll go and get them now."

When Clara left the room there was that awkward pause which will sometimes occur between two people who are both conscious that one of them has been acting a part. Then Helena said, "I suppose Mr.—what did you say his name is?—Oh, Roxburghe, I suppose he will come here tomorrow again?"

"Yes; he will be here about 4," returned Dolly cheerfully. "We sent a telegram to papa yesterday evening, after Clare came, and we had a reply this morning to say that they would be home tomorrow at 12. I suppose your meeting them at Wandoo will not delay them?"

"No; not that I am aware of."

Dolly wondered whether Mrs. Joseph was not getting more reconciled to the obnoxious stranger, and said by way of a feeler, "It would not do to keep them longer in suspense. I am sure they are both desperately in love."

"In love" repeated Mrs. Joseph with a scornful emphasis, and a sudden darkening of countenance that convinced Dolly no change would lightly take place in Helena's opinion of the utter folly—to call it by no worse name—of which Clare was guilty in finally rejecting Victor Maylands for the sake of a landless stranger. And in truth, under circumstances far less personal than these, few things could rouse Mrs. Hartingdale's ire more completely that the doctrine that it was noble and worthy for women to renounce position, privileges, or possessions for love. The affection of husband and wife, children and parents, relatives to the twenty-fourth degree of cousin-ship—even that was a different matter. That was secured by bonds, made fast by custom, consecrated by law. Such love was regular, decorous, undisturbed by fever heats and passion and dangerous impulses. But the great primeval love of man for woman, of maid for her chosen lover —the love for which so many have sacrificed the best years of their lives, the very blood of their hearts, for which land and wealth and luxurious ease have so often been cast aside like a child's toy, or the cap and bells of a fool—this she held to be a dangerous, almost unholy thing, too fierce and unruly for respectable domestic life. Such a passion was effective for the stage, for ballads, and romances; but to be, as far as possible, quelled and repressed in every well-regulated household—to be, if need were, stamped out by inexorable quarantine measures, like smallpox, and avoided like cholera.

There had been a passage in her life a few years ago when she herself had been well-nigh a victim to the dread malady. She was then a girl of nineteen, bright and accomplished, with some faculty for disinterested admiration and fitful stirrings of enthusiasm, which a rigorous course Mammon worship had since wholly excised. There had been possibilities latent in her character which might have matured into a nature the very reverse of that which now characterized her. In the eyes of John Hamilton she was five years ago the incarnation of all womanly grace, beauty, and tenderness. He was a distant connection on the father's side—a young subaltern, on leave from his regiment in India. In his sight no wandering isles of night dashed the light of her pure womanhood; he was blinded to the calculating worldly side of her nature; he saw not that she was prone to weigh conflicting interests, and decide for the greater advantages with judicial impartiality, to fight shy of self-abnegation in any form, and to appraise at a very high value the luxury, the ease and opulence, which were her birthright. But when the crucial test came, these won the day. True, no other man had ever held so strong a hold on her heart and imagination. They had walked and rode, laughed and read and sung together. He had been in her dreams by night; and when the sun was high in the heavens, and the roses of summer were flaming out in multitudes that no man could number, she had fallen into long happy reveries of him. His kindly handsome face, his frank laugh, the pressure of his hand at parting, his radiant glance when they met—all these things she knew by heart, and read their meaning aright. But though they were pleasant to her, she never in her heart of hearts deceived herself into the belief that for her plans of life, love and a limited income would suffice. These might be good in their own way, but they were not enough.

When the young officer had gone back to India with this as his final answer, a dull chill apathy, almost amounting to despair, had for a season taken possession of Helena Rutherford. It seemed to her during that period as though by her own deed she had turned the goodly and desirable things of life into cruel shards that strewed the road she must follow, maiming her feet horribly; that she had turned the past into a ruthless hunter following hard on her trail to still her very heart-throbs. But she outlived this in a comparatively short time. She did not voluntarily dwell on the episode at any time, nor harbour any sentimental regrets. She was, if the truth is told, rather ashamed that she had been betrayed into such a weakness—in love with a man who had but three hundred a year. The bare mention of these figures was enough to frighten away the lurking remnants of the first and only dream of love in which she had indulged. Two years afterwards Miss Rutherford married Mr. Joseph Hartingdale. He was red in the face, very stout, very middle-aged, and vulgar. But he was considered one of the wealthiest men in the colony. He had recently come to South Australia to take possession of the hoards of wealth which had been bequeathed to him by an older brother—an unmarried man, who had denied all the luxuries and some of the necessaries of life while he added flock to flock, and bought up a fabulous number of shares in copper mines which at that time were regarded as a little less safe than the three per cents. Even Mr. Rutherford, who probably understood the bent of his daughter's mind better than anyone else, and largely sympathized with her, was slightly startled when after a three months' slight acquaintance she accepted her unromantic suitor. Mrs. Rutherford, who was more or less blinded by that maternal love which is apt to turn a common grey goose into a swan of dazzling whiteness, was utterly dismayed to find that her elegant, accomplished, and very handsome daughter was in her twenty-first year prepared to marry a man who, to use Clare's expression, would keep her "picking up his h's all her life," and who had scarcely an idea in his head beyond the value of money, the best way of increasing it, and of his own importance in possessing so much wealth.

"But, Helena, my dear, are you sure you love him well enough?" Mrs. Rutherford had said, looking with tender anxiety into her daughter's face.

"Certainly, Mamma," Helena had answered without hesitation. Privately she thought her mother was very unpractical to ask a question which might have been both disturbing and awkward. But in this matter she was neither half-hearted nor vacillating. When she said that she loved her future husband well-enough she meant that, in consideration of being a leader of fashion, of having a splendid house, rare wines, a retinue of servants, an unexceptionable equipage; and unlimited dresses from Worth, she was resolved to tolerate his society and make the best of his offences against grammar and good breeding. And she did this, but in the process her whole spiritual nature was deadened, her mind was vulgarized, and all her aim in life was to keep an unfaltering, increasing hold of the possessions and privileges to which she had given herself for better or for worse.

And for a time she enjoyed without a fear or a care the state and ostentatious magnificence with which her husband surrounded her. But suddenly, in the midst of her triumphant splendour, when her feast of life was most unstinted and gorgeous, she saw as it were a finger on the wall writing words which blanched her face and smote terror to her heart. It came upon her with such overwhelming suddenness—this discovery that not only a large portion of her husband's money, but nearly all Victor Mayland's fortune, was invested in a copper mine that had suddenly stopped payment. And two days after Mrs. Huntingdale made this bewildering discovery Victor Maylands announced his intention of joining a cousin of his own in New Zealand. "He has two immense sheep stations, and he is just now very short of capital; so he offers to take me as partner on most liberal terms. You know I fancy that, after all is said and done, it's better to have one's money invested in that way. I always thought it was a curious fad of my father's to realize on his property as he did, and entrust it to you on my behalf in hard cash till I attained my twenty-fourth year. Not but what you have always managed it to very good effect—much better, I'm sure than most trustees do." Mr. Hartingdale murmured something about "friendship," and then with a face haggard with misery he told his wife of this new misfortune. Far into the night Helena sat with her husband as he balanced accounts, valued property, and calculated what their position would be if the money held in trust for Victor Maylands must now be replaced. It was incredible, it was appalling. This was the approximate state of affairs. Of the £400,000 invested in the mine, £180,000 belonged to Victor Maylands. In the then state of the market not only were shares far below par, but there was no possibility of realizing them, even at a ruinous loss. If the mine steadily decreased in value—but this contingency Mr. Hartingdale declined to face.

"But you know such a thing is possible," urged the unhappy wife; her heart beating slowly and painfully.

"Copper *must* rise again," answered Hartingdale, pushing the hair from his forehead with a gesture that had in it something of despair. In that moment Helena realised with a feeling of speechless terror that the splendid price for which she had sold herself might yet pass irrevocably away from her. She looked as her husband, her eyes gleaming, words of passionate anger rising to her lips. But seeing him look so grey and bent, his dull eyes heavy with misery, some stirring of womaly feeling in her heart restrained all expression of reproach.

"If Maylands did not require his money for a year or so, all might yet be well. There is the shipping interest, which promises to show a handsome profit this season. I can sell Wandoo to good advantage, if it is not forced into the market; and I can get large advances on the other properties. But to shell out £180,000 on so short a notice—Of course you will always have your own settlements; nothing can interfere with that," added Hartingdale, seeing his wife look as utterly despairing as if starvation stared her in the face. Helena shivered, and said nothing. A vision more terrible than the day of doom rose up before her—a long, nay, an everlasting farewell to all her greatness; an obscure, dull life, without love or power, or the pomp and display and cherished luxury of great wealth. What could be done to avert so cruel and disastrous a fate?

It was then a sudden resolve took form and substance in Mrs. Hartingdale's mind. Next day she saw Victor Maylands and spoke of his new plans.

"I cannot realize your going away," she said, with a pensive air; "and besides"—she hesitated and looked down, and then, as if with a sudden burst of confidence, she said, "I suppose I ought not to tell you, but"—Another pause, longer than the first, and then the young man, with a flush rising on his face, said quickly, "Is it anything about Clare?"

"Yes, it is about Clare," returned Mrs. Hartingdale softly. "It is as I thought it would be. I can read between the lines. I believe Clare never ceased to love you. Now she seems to long to be home again. But if you are gone when she returns—well, it cannot be helped, I suppose."

"Oh, as for that, I am not bound to go to New Zealand, or anywhere else, unless I like. But you know Clare behaved very badly to me, Mrs. Hartingdale."

"I never defended Clare, as you know, Victor; but there is this much to be said, and I have said it before—I believe it was not through indifference she broke off the engagement so hurriedly."

This assertion was at once soothing and easy of belief to Mr. Maylands. Clare had behaved shamefully, but after all, if she came back humble, penitent, and secretly pining for forgiveness—not that he would be in any hurry to offer her anew the affections and the fortune she had so sacrilegiously cast away; no, he would meet her with a firm front—with the easy unembarrassed gaiety of one who utterly forgives because he lightly forgets; and then to watch the proud, firm mouth relax into tremulous smiles at his approach; to see day by day those wonderful deep soft eyes look more tender at his coming, more wistful when he went—there were vivid dramatic possibilities in all this that made the elderly cousin in New Zealand, with his plans for rapid money-making, become a very pallid vision.

"When do you think your sister intends to return," he asked, with a comical assumption of indifference. Even already he began to assume something of the easy disinterestedness with which he would meet the erring and repentant girl.

"O, I daresay she will be here within the next five months," answered Mrs. Hartingdale. She spoke in a calm even voice, but her heart was beating wildly with excitement and a delightful sense of victory.

Victor Maylands said no more of the New Zealand scheme, and within five months of the time the conversation recorded took place Clare returned from Germany.

"And this is the result," murmured Mrs. Hartingdale, as she drove home, leaning well back in her luxurious carriage. But the stake for which she played was too heavy to be easily abandoned. "I can and must at the very least prevent this wretched insane engagement till after next March," she said, low under her breath, her face pale and set with mingled fury and determination.

Chapter IV

The Feelings of a Father

"Do we move ourselves or are moved by an unseen hand at a game
That pushes us off from the board and others ever succeed?—"

The library at Calthrope Park was a lofty spacious room lined from floor to ceiling with shelves of books in choice bindings. The furniture was of a grave and massive character, as befitted an apartment ostensibly dedicated to converse with the mighty dead. In niches round the room there were busts of the great seers of the ages—Shakspeare, Milton, the world-worn Dante, Wordsworth with his calm grand face, and others whose fame is more distinctly British. In the centre of the room there was a large mahogany table on which were piled reviews, monthly magazines, bluebooks, newspapers, and pamphlets in methodical order. Mr. Rutherford sat at this table on the afternoon of the day he returned home, hastily scanning a heap of letters that had been awaiting him. Some after a cursory glance he consigned to the waste-paper basket that stood at his right hand, some he carefully read and put on one side for further consideration, and on others he wrote a hasty minute, and handed them to a well-dressed gentlemanly looking young man who sat near him writing rapidly at a desk.

In the midst of his work the door was opened unceremoniously, and, looking up, Mr. Rutherford saw a fair-haired fuzzy head with a bewitching fringe of close clinging little curls low down on the white brow.

"Papa, Mr. Roxburghe is here, and wants to see you," Dolly spoke in a semi-mysterious and wholly important voice, and when the well-dressed young gentleman at the desk looked up she gave him a significant look, which implied that Mr. Roxburghe had come on very special business. The truth is that Mr. Temple was in full possession of all that Dolly knew about her proposed brother-in-law. It was a way she had of being very friendly and communicative to the people she liked, and as her father's confidential clerk, or secretary as he was sometimes called, was a good deal in the house, Dolly constantly took him into council on all sorts of subjects—from the scoldings administered by Mrs. Joseph down to the colour of a new ball dress. When her father was absent, and Mr. Temple was supposed to be turning his brown curls grey with care, hunting up armies of figures and battalions of depressing statistics for a Parliamentary debate, Dolly would put her head in at the door as she did on the present occasion, and say, "Mr. Temple, mamma will be glad if you can come and drink a cup of tea with us." Dolly always said this in rather a low voice, as if half afraid that one of those grim bluebooks would rise up in judgment against herself and the young man who left them with such cheerful alacrity. It was on such occasions that George Kendall sometimes thought Dolly was a little too friendly with "that fellow." But if ever he said anything about the matter Dolly opened her saucy brown eyes to their widest extent and said, "George, how silly you are getting! I suppose that's what makes it so peculiarly dull when people are married." (An ironical "Oh!" from George.) "They are eternally talking to each other, and their minds get into one groove, so that at last they either say 'Yes my dear,' till one of them dies a lunatic, or else they quarrel and put an advertisement in the paper about not being responsible. Now, I don't mean to do either. I'll always talk to other nice people as well as you." "So perhaps you'll put Temple in one of your bonnet-boxes, and take him with us when we are married," George would remark sardonically. "There will be no need for that," Dolly would calmly rejoin. "There are always entertaining young men to whom one can talk." "The deuce there are!" George was but human, and the prospect of unending relays of young men making themselves attractive to Dolly in her journey through life was not particularly fascinating to him, so that he sometimes went home rather depressed and wrote fluent verses in which dark allusions to the inconstancy of woman were not infrequent.

Mr. Rutherford looked at his letters with a pre-occupied air, and did not at once respond to Dolly's message.

"Will you come to speak to him in the drawing-room, papa?" asked Dolly, drawing nearer.

"No; ask him to come in here, Dolly," returned her father, pushing his unread letters to one side.

Mr. Temple, knowing that this interview was one which did not touch on immigration or the price of wool, prepared to leave the room. But Mr. Rutherford handed him a letter saying—"Did we not write to Cropper and West about this matter before I left home?". Temple referred to a memorandum-book, and before he found the entry he looked for there was a tap at the half-open door. "Come in," said Mr. Rutherford, in his distinct, decided tones. Then Harleigh Roxburghe stood in the presence of the rich man whose daughter he had come to ask in marriage, and his trained, accurate eye took in the picture at a glance. The large, silent, soft-carpeted room, with its tiers of shelves filled with the treasures of ancient and modern literature, the unmoved "faces of the great and wise" gleaming out from shadowy recesses, and in the centre of the room look-ing steadily at the advancing stranger stood a tall, muscular-looking man well past the meridian of life, his dark hair and whiskers plentifully sprin-kled with grey, but his dark eyes as bright and keen, his faculties as vigilant as in the days when he was the sole architect of his large possessions.

"Mr. Roxburghe, I believe," he said with a somewhat formal bow. Harleigh returned the salutation and held out his hand. Mr. Rutherford, in the careful programme he had laid down of this meeting, after a pro-longed talk with his eldest daughter on the preceding evening, had not included so cordial a greeting. He recollected this vividly as he clasped Harleigh's hand. But then he pictured his daughter's suitor as a very different man from the one who stood before him. "A thin enthusiastic looking fellow with a nervous smile and a cough probably." This, if put into words, was the picture Mr. Rutherford had conjured up. And, instead, there was this athletic-looking man with an unmistakable air of high breeding, of command even, with a frank and dignified bearing, perfectly free at once from embarrassment or self-assertion.

"That will do just now, Temple," said Mr. Rutherford, after he had asked his guest to be seated. Mr. Temple left the library with a good sized bluebook under his arm. This had an impressive air of industry and research, but whether statistics or Miss Dolly shared most of the young man's thoughts the following hour we need not stay to ask.

"No doubt you know the errand on which I have come, Mr. Rutherford," Harleigh said, as soon as they were alone.

"Yes, I believe I do." There was a slight pause. Then Mr. Rutherford, who felt that there was a danger of departing very widely from the programme which had been mapped out for this interview, hastened to say with a well-chosen smile—a smile that expressed at once comprehension and toleration—"I believe, as is not infrequent with young people on board ship, where the days are long and there is little to be done, that you and my daughter drifted into—not an engagement—but the stage preliminary to it."

A quick flush rose on Harleigh's face. "I do not know that I would choose the word 'drifted' to describe the state of affairs," he said, speaking rather rapidly. Still that tolerant smile on Mr. Rutherford's face. "However, I suppose it matters little what led to it," continued the lover. "I love your daughter very dearly, Mr. Rutherford. I have reason to believe that she returns my love. I hope I am not altogether unworthy of such a great gift, although the happiness is far above what I have looked for."

"Is it the present or the future that gives you so much joy, Mr. Roxburghe?" asked the father, still keeping up that air of good humoured patience which seemed to say that however absurd this matter might be he was not going to lose his temper about it. From the first moment he had entered the library Harleigh felt that Mr. Rutherford was not over-joyed at his daughter's choice. But the ungraceful irony of this speech fairly startled him. He looked at Mr. Rutherford a moment in silence, and then said with somewhat abrupt directness:

"I have come to ask for your daughter in marriage, Sir. May I ask for your reply?"

"Seriously, Mr. Roxburghe, what reply did you expect?"

Up to this time Mr. Rutherford had been playing with an ivory paper-knife. He now laid it down, thrust his hands into his pockets, and looked full into Harleigh's face.

"I expected that you would sanction our engagement," returned Harleigh very gravely.

"Upon what grounds?"

"I only know two grounds on which any father should give his con-sent to a request such as I have made."

"And they are?"

"That the girl should love the man who makes it as truly as he loves her, and that he should not be undeserving of her confidence."

"Well, that is very good so far as it goes, but don't you think it rather one-sided?"

"Possibly it may be, sir, but I am not aware in what respect it is so."

"Ah, just so. Excuse me for saying it, but that is one of the disadvan-tages of your profession. You are accustomed to lay such stress on the emotional faculties that the more practical considerations of a question are apt to be overlooked. Now, I imagine you will hardly deny that these two essentials you have named may be completely complied with in cases where a father's approval would be ill-advised—nay, absolutely cruel. Let us suppose the case of a man poorer than myself, one who could give his daughter nothing beyond a few dresses and his blessing; and suppose that another man whom this daughter loved, and who loved her, but was quite penniless, proposed to marry her, what then?"

"Pardon me, Mr. Rutherford, but you are misstating my case. I do not consider that a man who calmly proposed to starve a woman was worthy of her confidence, however blindly she might trust him."

"Well, put so strongly as that, perhaps not. But then men who rush into matrimony on nothing a year rarely propose anything calmly. There is what the poets term the 'glamour of love,' and a sublime faith in Providence as some unseen power who will in a mysterious way satisfy the claims of the butcher and baker, and keep things smooth generally. In your work as a clergyman you must have seen a great deal of the wretchedness of this kind of thing, Mr. Roxburghe."

This was thrown in to give an impersonal tone to remarks which might otherwise seem to be made, not altogether for the purpose of elucidating an abstract principle.

"My work as a clergyman has brought me chiefly in contact with people who if they are to marry at all must do so on what you would term nothing, Mr. Rutherford. Do not imagine, however, that I have been infected by such an example," said Harleigh with a smile. "I have no expectation of ever being a wealthy man; but I am not dependent on my calling for a living; I have four hundred a year independently of it. Hitherto I have spent more than the income I received as a clergyman among my people. Now, I suppose, it will be necessary to adopt a somewhat different plan."

It did not escape Mr. Rutherford's keen observation that there was a shade of doubt, of hesitancy, nay, a something of regret about this admission, and his mental reflection was "This scores one in our favour." Aloud he said, "Of course in taking a charge in the colonies you will nowhere find the dreadful overpowering poverty that is so common in large cities in the old country. But to return to the question from which we started, Mr. Roxburghe, I dare say you think it is the money consideration alone which makes me consider your engagement to my daughter would be unwise. That I do think so I candidly admit."

"I am very sorry to hear it, Sir. In that case Clare must decide what our future relations are to be."

"I suppose," said Mr. Rutherford, "you have not much doubt as to what her decision will be?"

Harleigh's head was very erect, and there was a glad light in his dark eyes as he replied:

"I have no doubt what her decision will be."

A thousand set phrases could not have expressed so much unquestioning confidence as was conveyed in his look and tone. This assurance that whether he were ill or well pleased his daughter would be steadfast to the love she had pledged would doubtless have been keenly resented had Mr. Rutherford been a vindictive or essentially unjust man. But he was neither. He was partly actuated by resentment of Clare's past error, partly imposed upon by his astute daughter, and also, it must be confessed, rather prone to be misled by an over-weening opinion of the importance of money. But he perfectly understood the lover's look of tender loyal devotion, and the thought it evoked in his heart was, "Maylands with his blonde moustache and everlasting small-talk has not the ghost of a chance beside this calm military-looking parson."

Aloud, however, he said:

"Well, well, I suppose it is in the order of things that lovers should think they understand each other completely after a few weeks' acquaintance. Still you will allow that I have a right to exercise at least a little authority in this matter?"

"Certainly."

"Then I must tell you that I withhold my sanction of your engagement to my daughter for six months from this time. During that period I wish no one outside my own family to know that there is an attachment between you. You may perhaps think me somewhat unreasonable in this, but I assure you that I act from no arbitrary domineering spirit."

"Do I understand that you forbid all intercourse between your daughter and myself during the time you have named, Mr. Rutherford?"

"My dear Mr. Roxburghe, I forbid nothing. You understand that my daughter is of age, and has for some time made free use of her own judgment irrespective of mine. I do not flatter myself that she will make obedience to my wishes a point of conscience in this matter. In fact I depend almost entirely on your accepting my conditions in a fair and reasonable spirit. Make allowances for the feelings of a father—if I may use the term without trespassing on the domain of melodrama."

There was a pause, and then Harleigh said very gravely, "I will not deny that I am disappointed to find you think it necessary to impose these condition. But I am too grateful for the love I have won to think a six months' probation intolerable; I will even try to think that it may be wise," said Harleigh with a slight smile. Then taking out his card-case, he handed Mr. Rutherford two cards saying, "These are the names and addresses of two gentlemen, who are old friends of my father, and will be ready to answer any enquiry you may deem it necessary to make about myself and my connections."

Mr. Rutherford glanced at the cards; one bore the name of Dr. Westland, Bishop of Exeter, the other was that of a well-known statesman. He put them on the table, saying, "I am satisfied that your position and calling constitute a sufficient guarantee as to your personal character."

Harleigh bowed, and feeling that the interview was at an end he rose. Mr. Rutherford led the way to the drawing-room, but before they entered it he said:

"You will of course be very welcome to our house as a visitor at any time you may feel disposed to give us the pleasure of your company. I presume you intend to remain in the colony for some time?"

"Thank you. Yes, I shall probably be here for some months to come," returned Harleigh as they stood at the drawing-room door.

Chapter V
As a Visitor

In the drawing-room they found several visitors, mostly ladies who were drinking afternoon tea and generally entertained by Mrs. Rutherford, while Dolly divided her attention between the teatray and a fair young man with sandy hair and moustache, and a look of determined earnestness. This was George Kendall, Dolly's fiancé. His mother and one of his sisters were also making a call. They were both very expensively dressed, talked volubly, and had reddish hair, which was, indeed, a peculiarity of the whole family. Perhaps it was this monotonous trick of Nature that Dolly found so tiresome when she on one occasion before her engagement said to Clare, "One Kendall is very well, two are not amiss, three may be tolerated, but as for the whole family, nothing but the grace of God can enable one to endure them."

Mrs. Rutherford had a refined and somewhat fragile appearance. She was close upon sixty, but her complexion was still softly fair, and in her silky brown hair not a trace of grey was yet to be seen; this, with the large quiet eyes, and delicate serious mouth, gave an expression of singular sweetness to her face.

Clare, looking happy and animated, sat somewhat apart from the rest, talking to a young man whose eyes were very like her own, but with a very bronzed face and a heavy dark moustache and beard. Clare cast a searching look at her father and lover as they entered, then motioned the latter to her side of the room.

"Mat, this is Mr. Roxburghe; my brother Matthew."

The two men shook hands.

"Matthew has just arrived," said Clare. "He is a wild man of the woods, who despises the trammels of civilization, and rarely condescends to leave his beloved bush."

"Yes; just now and again when I want a pannikin, or a possum-rug made in the latest fashion, I am obliged to come to town," said Matthew.

"Then do you live far away from your home?" enquired Harleigh.

"It's just the other way," returned Matthew. "My people have deserted the old nest—a beautiful place in the heart of the woods, with breathing space for thousands on it, with growing trees and sweet water, and peaceful flocks of sheep; and here they stay near town—a place hideous with noise, with ugly houses, with want of room and cleanliness."

"And hideous most of all with the concourse of human beings that envy and cheat and jostle each other in it from morning till night, eh, Matthew," said the sister.

"Quite true,'" answered Matthew emphatically. There was no make-believe or exaggeration about Matthew's love of the great unpeopled woods. He was one of those to whom Nature in her large grand leisure, in her deep solitude, broken only by the sound of winds that rise and fall, the music of running waters, the fluttering of branches, and the singing of birds, was almost as necessary as the bread he ate and the water he drank. He did not theorize about the matter, nor tabulate his impressions. But when he came into town periodically and stayed a few weeks the noise, the bustle, the hurrying to and fro, the appointments to be kept, the dances to be danced, and the polite unmeaning speeches which must be made, seemed to him a burden not to be borne. When sick of these things, the memory of the vague mournful cry of waterfowl flying over a waste of sand, gleaming white and still in the deep solitude of a starry moonlight night, of the perpetual hush and shadow of deep gullies in the heart of closely-wooded ranges, would suddenly sweep across his mind, and he would feel that he must return to his flock and herds, to his free simple life in the Australian bush.

But on the present occasion, Clare's return, after an absence of two years, had induced him to come into town the second time within a few months, though it was now shearing time—that Hegira of station life.

"I hope my cousin will find life in the woods as fascinating as you do," said Harleigh, feeling not a little amused at the look of critical enquiry which the young man bent on him.

"My sister has just been telling me that Mr. Dunstan intends to go into the country. If he does not form any more pressing engagement, I hope he will come back with me to Nillanillu and stay a while, to see how he likes bush life in the north."

Harleigh expressed his thanks for this hospitable offer, and Matthew, who knew what the purport of Harleigh's present visit was, found his way to Dolly's side, and tried to convince her that the tea she gave him in an exquisite cup of Meissen china, with frothy cream, sweetened with loaf sugar, was not to be compared to the same beverage made in a quartpot, under the shadow of a gumtree at sunset, after a long day's march. And then he listened with a comic half-wondering look to the talk of two ladies who sat near him. The younger one—Mrs. Vere Brown—was a self-important, rasping-voiced little woman, who "went in" for being literary, and was given to repeating extracts from reviews and art criticisms with an exasperating air of proprietorship, as if the fact of filching them made those oppressively smart, semi-false, and superficial judgments the original product of her own small brains. It was currently reported that one sensitive young artist, who had come for "studies" to Australia, fled the colony one night after she had persisted in talking to him for a whole evening about "harmonies of tone" and the "supreme melody of nocturnes by So-and-so." When not bent on airing her superior talents and penetrating critical insight, Mrs. Vere Brown was prone to dwell on all the ill-natured versions of her neighbours' affairs which she could collect. She did this, however, with an affectation of false sympathy and regret that many people found more intolerable than downright scandal, "Have you seen any of the Lackgelds lately?" she would say; "I am so sorry for those poor girls. What with the father's intemperance, and the mother's extravagance, I really don't know what is to become of them. It is such a pity three nice, nice girls like them should have no prospect of settling. Why, the youngest must be close upon thirty. Oh! I am sure she is. They begin to look very passé. Dear girls, they are very nice. I am so fond of them, &c., &c."

On the present occasion she was in her literary vein.

"The modern novel, like the modern drama," she was saying in her high-pitched unmodulated voice, "is too essentially the reflex of transitory phases or external life. Neither can keep a permanent place in literature. Nor can we wonder"—

"What a good memory you have, Mrs. Brown," interrupted Mrs. Clanaghan, the lady to whom she spoke. "The Major was reading that article in one of the quarterlies the other day; but he thought it was such nonsense he would not finish it."

"What article, dear Mrs. Clanaghan?" asked Mrs. Vere Brown shrilly.

"Oh, just that style of thing about the great creative geniuses of the past, and the dull level of mediocrity in the present—the sad certainty of the writer that nothing which is the product of the nineteenth century can endure—not even its steam-engines, the workmanship being so bad. The Major got out of all patience with the thing. He said the worst of everyone learning to read was that people of shallow understanding, eager to be considered smart and in the van of so-called modern thought, formed a sort of foolish chorus for such ill-digested stuff." Mrs. Clanaghan was a tall spare woman with a commanding Roman nose, a sallow complexion, dark restless eyes, and thin resolute lips, who had a special faculty for bitter speeches, when she wished to wipe out some real or imagined social grievance. She had once or twice heard how Mrs. Vere Brown made remarks of this kind—"The Major and Mrs. Clanaghan are very good sort of people in their way, but what an infliction it is that they can never talk of anything but India. Someone said the other day the Major left his liver there and Mrs. Clanaghan her manners. Isn't it a shame to say such things?" &c. Hence the savage reception accorded by the Major's wife to Mrs. Vere Brown's attempt at profound conversation. Matthew sipped his tea and listened to these amenities of high-bred friendship with half-cynical amusement, musing on the little lives of men, and how they mar that little with their strife. Then he glanced towards Clare, and wondered why there was such a troubled look on her face while talking to her lover.

"You have spoken to papa?" Clare had said, with a certain feeling of uneasiness, as soon as they were alone. With the quick intuition of a keenly sensitive temperament she felt sure that the interview in the library had not been what she wished. Had not Harleigh's face lost something of the expression of glad content which it wore when she had spoken to him a short time ago?

"Yes, and he has spoken to me," answered Harleigh, smiling. "He has not absolutely refused his consent to our engagement, Clare; but he withholds it for six months—if we are constant till then. Do you think we shall be?"

Clare flashed up violently, and then the blood receded, leaving her paler than before.

"Did my father give any reason for not consenting to our engagement?" she said, in a low tone.

"I cannot say that he gave any precise reason. Perhaps he saw some strong signs of fickleness in my face; or is it you, Clare, who is not to be lightly trusted? Are you like the wicked princess in the fairy tale, who sat in a castle with the bones of her rejected lovers bleaching around?"

Instead of responding to this raillery with her usual gaiety, Clare, looked pale and agitated.

"Tell me, Harleigh, did my father speak harshly to you?" she said, with a quiver in her proud mobile lips.

"No, my darling; unless you call the condition I have named harsh. I do not pretend to like it myself; but, after all, I think such a dear little wife as I am going to have is well worth waiting for much longer than that, if need be."

Clare looked across the room where her father sat talking to Mrs. Kendall, and the thought that he had cordially approved of George as a son-in-law, while Harleigh's suit was for the time being rejected, made her heart swell with anger and a keen sense of injustice.

"My father is always unjust to me," she said bitterly; "before I left home—" She paused abruptly. "Harleigh, there is something I want to tell you—something that caused a coolness between myself and my father before I went away. I suppose I was to blame, but"—

"Never mind it just now, darling. But don't think too hardly of your father. He is quite right, to be cautious before he entrusts you to any-one—even to me." Clare looked singularly troubled and annoyed, but Harleigh was bent on making the best of it.

"See here, Clare," he said, taking up a book that lay on a little table near them—a book of modern poetry, bound in pale blue, with slender gold lilies growing on the cover, and turning the leaves as he spoke— "that is one, two, three, four, five, six months from now—that will take us to March. Well, on the 22nd of March your father, seeing our undying constancy, will give us his blessing; on the 23rd, that is the day after, I shall come riding up to Calthorpe Park, I'll borrow Tony for the occa-sion, and here I'll find you waiting to go to church, in a lovely white tulle moire antique."

Despite her annoyance, Clare burst into a laugh at this.

"It is not that we have so long to wait, Harleigh, but that my father should hesitate and place such restrictions; but of course you will come here."

"Oh, yes; you father kindly made me welcome as a visitor. Clare, I wish you would write me a little manual of etiquette as to what one may or may not do in that capacity. A terrible suspicion creeps into my mind that at some unguarded moment I may remember only that I am your lover."

"As 'a visitor.' So that is my father's decree. I dare say he was thinking of Mr. Drumbleton, who pays us a visit every Thursday afternoon with the even regularity of a planet. He always stays fifteen minutes, always says the same thing, and smiles in the same dreadful way, just like a continuation of his last smile, as if he had put it in his pocket when he had done with it, and then taken it out when he wanted it again."

"I have a presentiment that I shall bear a fatal resemblance to this unfortunate man, Clare. I am sure I shall say the same thing each time I see you."

"What is that?"

"Can you not guess?"

Clare reflected a moment, and then said gravely, "I suppose you will say, 'This is not a very good season for nectarines'."

"No; I shall say, 'Clare, I do believe you are the dearest little girl that ever lived'."

"Ah! you think that now," said Clare wistfully, without a trace of coquetry, thinking ruefully of a certain confession that must be made—some time. Harleigh laughed, and just then it struck him that a visitor should not devote himself exclusively to one member of the household.

The Kendalls left, and Mr. Rutherford went out with them.

"Now, Clare, I must not stay much longer just now, and I have a very important piece of news yet to tell you. Last night Patrick and I were at the house of an old London friend, Dr. Sheeness. Among other people there was Mr. Laker, the incumbent of St. Christopher's. Perhaps you know him?"

"Slightly. I have heard him preach once or twice. He always begins. 'It is eventide. Across a plain some sojourners on camels are hastening towards a group of palm-trees, which mark an oasis—a welcome place of rest for man and beast. My dearly beloved brethren, this was in the Holy Land.' And then he pauses, as if to give his hearers a chance of recovering from their surprise at this vividly graphic description. Now, Harleigh, you need not shake your head at me. You know he has a most elaborate way of saying nothing."

"I can see that a certain young lady has a wicked way of saying something. But what I want to tell you is that Mr. Laker is going away for his health for six months, and proposed that I should take his charge during that time. I have not yet decided, but I think I shall most likely do so."

"Oh! then would you live in Barbaja? Or is it at Millhaven St. Christopher's is?"

"The parish—do you speak of parishes here?—comprises both suburbs. I understand they are three miles west of the town. Mr. Laker spoke in rather a desponding way of his parishioners."

"Oh, there is hardly anyone in the place but brickmakers and labourers and people who do something to skins far gone in mortality. I believe the chief amusement of the place is wife-beating. Really, Harleigh, nearly all the dreadful things happen in that neighbourhood. But you needn't live there, need you?" said Clare, in a deprecating tone.

"Yes, of course I shall live there, Clare. I do not suppose it is anything like my London district. You see, dear, I have very low tastes in that way," said Harleigh, smiling.

"Tell me, please, what you did in your London parish—district was it? That sounds more doleful; long stretches of crowded back streets and lanes, with villainous-looking roughs in tattered clothes waiting round the corners to heave bricks at one! Did any of your people become better, Harleigh."

"My dear child, some of the people I knew among the very poor of London were the greatest example and encouragement I found in my work. But you must disabuse yourself of the idea that the majority of even those who are wretchedly poor and disgracefully housed are either paupers or criminals. I knew men and women who lived in foul rookeries—I cannot call them houses—in crowded courts and alleys, constantly surrounded by the depressing grimy monotony of the streets, who lived honest, true, and brave lives; who were cheerful and kind and capable of real heroism in the way of unselfish helpfulness to others. Of course these were the exception; they are the exception in every rank of life. But the knowledge that it was possible for such lives to grow and develop in the face of so much terrible discouragement kept the Devil at bay when he would have one believe that seed sown among masses of partially pauperized and indifferent human beings could bear no fruit. Then in the pastoral work, in the house-to-house -visitation, sick visiting, provident clubs, penny banks, reading-rooms, day, night, and Sunday schools, meetings, lectures, and social gatherings, I had a splendid band of earnest workers as my coadjutors, with my sister Laura—you will love her so fondly, Clare—always to the fore. A great feature in our district was the establishment of numerous mission houses for amusements, social reunions, and quiet evenings. It was a kind of opposition we started to the public-houses, beer-shops, and gin palaces. These are always open, always handy, and we did not expect people tired with their day's hard toil to trudge to us past these ever-open tempting resorts. So as thickly as possible we hired or built rooms (as cheaply as possible) that were well lit each evening, where good periodicals, works of fiction, &c., were to be had, also tea and coffee were supplied at almost nominal prices. In many cases these rooms became self-supporting. We made no distinction of Church or creed: anyone who chose to drop in, and who behaved decently, was welcome. Otherwise these rooms would have been on a very unequal footing with the public-houses. A good deal of my work was decidedly secular. From the first—acting on the advice of experienced fellow-workers—I set my face against alms-giving. There are always numbers of hopeless hereditary paupers in London districts and parishes, who regard the Church as a beneficent institution for giving charity tickets. But these are not the people one hopes to do much with. If I did not believe that life is in itself a moral end, the only remedy I would advocate for such people would be wholesale euthanasia. The larger number of my parishioners were hard-working, but with such a close battle for a livelihood that any misfortune or drawback may suddenly precipitate them into pauperism. A little judicious help in such cases is of incalculable value. You would be surprised to know, Clare, how large my dealings as a money-lender have been."

"And do you charge a very high rate of interest?"

"Oh, I am not going to reveal business secrets. If you want to raise a loan of course, it's a different matter. But haven't you had enough of this just now?"

"No, indeed," answered Clare, who was absorbed not merely in listening but in drawing mental pictures of the life and scenes Harleigh's simple facts suggested. This was Clare's invariable habit when listening to what deeply touched or interested her. It was not an unusually powerful imagination that led to this, but a vivid dramatic faculty, that turned, scraps of conversation, the meagrest description, or even a chance allusion, into scenes that came and went as swiftly as slides in a magic lantern.

"You used to write sometimes, didn't you, Harleigh? You see, Pat gave me bushels of statistics about you."

"Oh, my writing, dear, was chiefly of a very prosaic character. It generally took the form of protracted onslaughts on vested interests that stood in the way of some material or social betterment in our district. I suppose most people get what Herbert Spencer calls a professional bias sooner or later. When I was a soldier my ideal achievement was to lead a charge of cavalry to a brilliant victory against fearful odds. But at St. David's in the East, to level to the ground some of the stifling courts where people are packed from attic to basement in degrading wretchedness, was one of my dearest dreams. And some of them were realized; but, oh! the endless interviews, the official letters, the meetings, the appointments, the statistics, which had to be encountered. And then the abuse that was sometimes heaped upon us. We made more beautiful the Temple of our God, and had daily services; we were Papists in disguise. We lent a helping hand to all whom we could aid, irrespective of creed or sect; our only aim was to proselytize; we struggled to compass the social improvement of the district by having better dwelling houses and mission-rooms for innocent amusements; we were Socialists and Materialists. I remember a writer once in a local evening paper referred to sundry of our methods as being "very carnal." I have never yet, however, had the opportunity of being as carnal as I would like. One of my day-dreams is to see large theatres thoroughly well conducted within the reach of the very poorest."

"Theatres! Oh, Harleigh, how delightfully unorthodox," said Clare, with a beaming face. "Would you have French plays translated with an uneasy air of British propriety performed in them?"

"Now, Clare, that is cruel. More than three hundred years ago God gave us a man whose genius is so rare and splendid that even a partial appreciation of his works is a kind of education in itself. Yet to the people of England they are to this day a sealed book. They always will be till they are properly rendered. So when my ideal theatres, free from the associations that have brought disrepute on the stage, have emerged from the shadowy land of dreams, they need not depend for their attractions on the pert, modern French play, with its sécheresse of soul, its restless attitudinising, and feverish anxiety to make one laugh at everything. Now, don't tempt me into any more disquisitions on this subject. Oh, yes, I can see I am undone. After this, when I want to remonstrate with you—that's a good connubial word, Clare—instead of listening with a contrite heart you will smile, as you do now, and say, 'Tell me a fairy tale; about an ideal theatre, for example'."

"O, yes; one clearly foresees that you will be the most ill-used of men," said Clare, laughing; and then, Harleigh, feeling that no right-minded visitor would linger so inexcusably, made his adieus and went away.

Chapter VI

Barbaja

Barbaja was a low-lying, thickly populated place; which straggled round corners, shot out in irregular lanes, peeped out at unexpected angles, and had a general air of taking up more ground than it could rightly claim. This appearance was chiefly owing to the large number of disused and active brickfields which were to be found in its outskirts. These brickfields were surrounded by small mean habitations, crowded into the least possible space—some of them on the very verge of the worked out pits, which gave them a pathetic air of peering over with their grimy, often broken windows, to see how far they would have to fall when their present precarious foundations would finally give way. A stranger walking through Barbaja would sometimes come on a desolate-looking exhausted clayfield, and fancy that he was at the extremity of the place; but, lo! a little beyond he would find that a fresh architectural start in discoloured bricks and dust-coloured shingles had been made. He would find more two and three roomed little tenements perched up and down on minute plateaus, and overlooking yawning chasms; more low, narrow, endless-looking rows of small houses with dirty windows, with paint blistered and falling off, with tiny yards behind them, and still tinier scraps of land in front, where now and then a few flowers drew a languid existence, till a strong sense of discouragement overtook them, and they faded off in an apologetic kind of way. They seemed to say, "We have done our best to be as white as the moon and the stars, to be as pink as the clouds of sunrise, to be as blue as the far away sky. But hot dish-water thrown suddenly over us is injurious to our constitution. So are goats. So are the little chubby hands that tear us up to see what we are made of. So are the strong-nailed boots of heavy men that stagger and trample on us." Alas! the pale little blossoms were not the only creatures of God mortally hurt by the men who staggered.

The principal industries of Barbaja besides brickmaking were tanneries, fellmongering and boiling-down establishments, gasworks, and aerated-water manufactories—industries which for the most part were either very noisy or very unsavoury. Indeed, the Barbaja, the little river from which the place took its name, and which flowed through the suburb, dividing it into Barbaja East and Barbaja West, was as foul and discoloured as the most civilized stream to be found in the "Black Country." When the establishments named were in full work, when the hides were tanned, the wool scoured, and rancid fat boiled down—besides many a small business which had a fierce perseverance of their own in smelling— the atmosphere was impregnated with odours that more than rivalled the forty smells of Cologne. Perhaps under these circumstances it is not surprising that a strong belief was cherished by the labouring men who comprised the bulk of the inhabitants—in number between two and three thousand—that strong doses of beer and spirits were indispensable to keep the human system in fair working order. Doubtless this was one reason why public-houses were so numerous in Barbaja. They were in the main streets, in the back streets, in the lanes, and by the roadsides. From the tall three-storied, important-looking building with stuccoed front, shining plate glass, and newly hung signboard in the principal streets, down to the old squalid wooden shanty with its ill-omened narrow front, its dreary look of combined dirt and vice, in the midst of a cluster of miserable dwellings—all these public-houses had their customers and made their gains. At the bars, in the taprooms, in the grimy parlours redolent of vile tobacco and viler spirits, there were always to be found after work hours groups of men in their labour-soiled clothes—some in eager talk, others quarrelling noisily, a few in moody silence, but all having something to drink.

On Saturday nights these groups swelled into crowds, the quarrelling ended in fighting, and "something to drink" went on to hard-and-fast potations till a number of the men were riotously or helplessly drunk. No public-house in Barbaja was more noted for these Saturday night orgies than the "Black Panther." It was a low one-storied building facing Chapel-road—one of the main thoroughfares of Barbaja. Exactly opposite to it on the other side of the road stood the "Golden Lion," newly built on the site of the first inn which had flourished in the place, The two houses were not by exact measurement more than 100 yards apart. Five houses beyond the "Black Panther," on the western side going down Chapel-road towards Millhaven, you came to yet another inn—small, grimy, and black-looking, with "The Brickmakers' Rest," gleaming in bold gilt letters above the door. But neither the "Golden Lion," with its glistening bar, its large tap-room, with a green and scarlet wall paper adorned with flaming pictures of Heenan and Sayers engaged in brutal fighting, and similar works of art; nor the "Brickmakers' Rest," with its seductive title, and underneath a legend in small letters of "Good meals for 9d," drew so many customers and drove so large a trade as the "Black Panther." It was reckoned among local statistic mongers that more heads were broken, more constitutions ruined, and consequently more money made in the latter than in any other two inns in Barbaja put together. As a matter of fact, no other inn was haunted to the same extent after nightfall by anxious and miserable looking women and children in their arms and at their sides. They would stand, these wives and mothers, at a little distance and gaze timidly in at the flaring bar, listening with a loud beating heart as voices rose within in boisterous mirth or angry altercation. But as a rule they did not go very near, and few, indeed, were bold enough to go to the bar-door or in at the side entrance to ask for any reveller who might be within. For Host Bampton, with his rubicund nose, his heavy cheeks, his shock of red hair, and his thick gruff voice, knew well how to keep those women with their careworn haggard faces at a safe distance. "A passel o' wimen pokin' round with red eyeses is enough to give any one the mollygrums," he used to say with a fine touch of indignation. From this it might be inferred that "mollygrums," was not the highest form of jollity known to the landlord of the Black Panther.

One Monday evening in the early part of December, just one month after the Rev. Harleigh Roxburghe had taken charge of St. Christopher's, the bar of this inn was half-filled by labourers, mechanics, and others, who in passing from their work had called in to have a glass of beer.

Like all hostelries that make a large trade, the Black Panther had many frequenters who were not always undeviating in their attendance. Among these it may suffice now to note Larry O'Donnell, who was viciously teetotal till he fell into temptation, and after spending his money loudly sorrowed over his fall, vowing amendment with many tears, "It's thim public-houses, me jewel," he would say to his wife Bridget, with solemn certainty. "They blazes into a man's eyes as it were whin he's comin' home from his work, an' wan afther another goes in, an' he calls on the saints to help him; but bedad they're too cosy or too far away to moind. And thin he feels that he's just a poor mane-spirited blackguard if he doesn't take a dhrop o' the crather loike Pat and Mike and the rist o' the bhoyfs."

There was James Glenrice, the broken-down gentleman, who in his sober moments wrote those diffuse, eloquent begging-letters which brought the tears into the eyes of pitiful charitable ladies—letters in which he imprecated wrath of Heaven on himself if he ever again gave way to his "besetting sin," as he glibly termed his drunkenness. But once fairly started again with a pound or two in his pockets, and a tumbler of spirits before him, none so vituperative as he about meddling legislation, and interference with the poor man's liberty. "Let us beware of those who would try to rob us of the 'good gift of God,'" he would say pathetically as he drank Bampton's adulterated brandy. And then when his hand shook with incipient delirium tremens he would give a forcible oration on the text that people are not to be made sober by Act of Parliament. There was, further Dick Brown, a clever house-painter, who in his time figured at many temperance meetings as a man who had seen the evil of his ways, and held all intoxicating liquor as accursed. Dick kept sober sometimes for six and nine months at a time, and then the Black Panther saw nothing of him. But Bampton did not despair. "Dick is making money fast; I'll have a good haul soon," he would say with a chuckle to his more intimate cronies. And poor Dick generally fulfilled this expectation. Yet he was never one of the Black Panther's most desirable customers. There was a moodiness about him, a feeling of sullen discontent which was apt to find expression in savage speeches and in scornful tirades upon his own weakness and that of others. "Dick is one o' them as allays spiles a spree by counting up the cost when he ought to be injying his licker," an associate of his said once; and there was truth in the saying.

On this evening the talk in the bar turned on the innovations the new incumbent of St. Christopher was introducing.

"He's got some chaps round Mason's corner to sign a partition agin another public-'ouse bein' built there," said one.

"Yes," chimed in Dick Brown, "he has the people to meet in the Sunday-school most every evenin'—not Bible classes or Catechism affairs, you know, but just to sit round quite homely like, with views and picters to look at, and coffee to drink, and then he leads 'em on to talk of Parlyment, and the sort of men that ought to be there, and how working men should save money—"

"As if a passon had anything to do with the likes o' that," broke in the landlord, with a voice full of lofty scorn.

"Why, didn't you hear what he said in the pulpit two Sundays ago?" said Glenrice.

"Let's hear it, Glenie," said one or two.

"Well, you see, I was at low ebb—no money, no tobacco, no credit, no shoes to speak of, and no work. So there was nothing left for me but to go in for repentance and the respectabilities—"

"Doesn't agree with your constitootion, that, does it?" said the landlord, winking.

"Not very much," answered Glenrice reflectively. "But you see, though you are a good fellow in your own way, Bampton, you don't overflow with the milk of human kindness when a poor devil is so completely out at elbows. That was my plight. So I just wrote a letter. I was on the brink of starvation; I was surrounded by temptations (that's you, my friends); I was sick of wallowing in the mire (that's scripture); I was sick of myself and tired of life; I wanted one more chance to retrieve myself; and so on. So the old lady I wrote to gave me a nice light job, picking up faded rose-leaves and looking after a couple of ducks. Of course she expected me to read tracts at night and go to church on Sunday. Behold me, then, clothed in a second-hand coat and seated in St. Christopher's, and I'm blessed if that 'passon' as Bampton calls him, didn't pitch with tooth and claw into the national vice of drunkenness. He stood up straight, with his eyes and his voice going through a fellow; and didn't he describe the scenes, that might be witnessed any evening at the Black Panther."

"What?" roared Bampton, his face purpling.

"Well, I'm not sure that he named the place, but one who knows it as well as I do couldn't mistake it. And then he said—'Perhaps some of my hearers may think that on this holy day of rest—this beautiful calm Sabbath—it might be more fitting to speak of the joys of heaven and the blessedness of immortality than of the vice and misery that stare us in the face. Oh! my friends, if the life that is given us here is misused and debased by low indulgence—if God's beautiful earth here is stained with our crimes and our uncleanness—to what purpose should we speak of the eternal city paved with gold, and the white-robed saints who bear palms of victory in their hands? Is not this world as grand and wonderful as any that can await us beyond the clouds? Is not this life as precious as any hereafter?'"

"There, that's what I calls the words of a hinfidel!" cried the landlord in a tone of triumph.

"It's curus prachin', that, to say this woorld, where so many av us has to work at six bob a day and no beer, is as good as the blissed abode av the Almighty and all the Saints," said Larry reflectively.

"And then the cheek of a man like him, as don't know what a 'ard day's work is, to go cryin' out agen us poor chaps injyin' our beer," said a bent elderly man with brick-soiled clothes and red blinking eyes.

"Well, Jim, you've had as much beer in your day as any man going, and I'd like to know what good it's done you in the long run," said Brown gruffly.

"I've been a misfortunate chap, Dick, what with my poor missus in the Destitute and my youngsters scattered about here and there," said the bricklayer, with a quaver in his weak voice.

Bampton did not relish such excursions into the histories of his staunch supporters, and tried to divert attention by saying, "I s'pose if this 'ere new passon gets his way much we poor publicans ull hev to shut up shop."

"True for you, Mr. Bampton," said a newcomer, a short thickset man in the prime of life, whose lime-stained hands and clothes proclaimed his calling to be that of a mason. "True for ye, my boy. If you want to earn an honest penny you must buy some Testaments and tracts and write 'Milk and coffee sold here' over your door. If you do I'll warrant you old Nick will be one of your first customers. He's not so easily taken in as Harry Barnwell."

The men who had paid their score on Saturday night laughed at this, but those who were in the landlord's debt were not prepared to find any fun in the joke till they saw how Bampton took it.

"I takes any man in, Ben Davis, what pays his way and keeps a civil tongue," growled the landlord with a scowl.

"And has a soft head and a full pocket, eh?" retorted the carpenter.

"Well, your head maybe soft, but I'm blowed if your pockets are very full," said Barnwell, in a blustering tone.

"You're right thereabout, Barnwell," returned Davis quietly. "They're never so full that they'll need emptying here, while the man who has filled them is lying helpless with a broken leg, unable to look after his own."

"What do you mean by that?" said the landlord, in a semi-threatening tone.

All eyes were now fixed on Davis, who had finished his pot of beer and was filling his pipe, outwardly calm, but with certain look of indignation about the eyes and a little tremor in his hands, which, to a close observer, would indicate that he was labouring under some repressed excitement.

"You want to know what I mean, do you?" he said, speaking in rather a lower tone than was usual with him. "Well, I'll tell you. Last Thursday Harry Barnwell and his stepson, John Patterson, finished the contract that had from Jenkinson. They were paid the balance due to them, about a hundred and fifty pounds, by cheque. John went to town to have this cashed; when he was on his way to the Bank he saw a runaway horse and trap dashing down the street, and a child of five or six standing directly in the way. He rushed to save the child, but in doing that he got knocked down himself, a wheel of the trap went over his leg, and smashed it just above the ankle. You've all heard that, haven't you?" said Davis looking round.

"Yes," said several voices.

"Perhaps you don't know what took place afterward, though," said Davis. "John taken home; Barnwell, in the confusion, got hold of the cheque, and what do you think he did with it?"

There was no answer to this, but one or two looked at the landlord in an enquiring way, and he, purple with rage, said, with some expletives, which we need not record here—

"I don't want to hear any more of your yarns, Ben Davis, and the sooner you clear of out of here the better."

"Well, my yarn is nearly told. Harry Barnwell, who would be a penniless loafer if it weren't for his stepson, took the money, and after paying something like eighty pounds of it away, he made straight for the Black Panther, and he has not gone home since—not once; and for my part I wouldn't be surprised if he stayed here till his money is done."

"Come, come, Ben, a feller couldn't swaller all that money in a few days," said the man who had been addressed as Jim.

"I've known a man swallow a row of four neat cottages and flower gardens in five days, Jim, when he was under the care of a landlord," answered Davis, solemnly, as he shouldered his bag of tools.

"Now, Ben Davis, you just remember that your room is a deal more valuable not your company here, for the futoor," said Barnwell, as the carpenter went out.

"Well, I don't suppose the loss of my threepence now and again will break you; but maybe if I get a pocketful of someone else's and make up my mind to let the old women and my young uns take care of themselves, you'll give me a sweeter welcome," answered Davis, marching out.

"It's just as I thought," he muttered to himself. "That flathead Barnwell got the money and made up his mind to go on the burst; he trumped up a story about having to go on some business, and now that old villain has him in there. Lord love us, what with the fools and rogues in this world, there's not so very much to be cocky about."

An hour after Davis had left the Black Panther, Harleigh Roxburghe came up Chapel road, on his way to the house in which he lodged, halfway between Barbaja and Millhaven, and as he passed the inn he saw a middle-aged woman, decently clad, coming out of it, her face very white, and the tears falling down her cheeks. There was an air of such hopeless misery in the poor woman's whole appearance—she looked so desolate and helpless that Harleigh's whole heart was moved by pity for her. There was no room for speculations as to the cause of her wan face and fast-flowing tears, as she slowly walked away from the inn, with its group of noisy revellers in and around the bar-door. When she had walked a few paces she stopped and looked at the Black Panther, as if undecided whether to go or turn back. It was then that Harleigh overtook her, and, taking off his hat as he stood beside her, said,

"I am afraid you are in trouble. Is there anything I can do for you?"

"Oh, Sir; I don't know whativver I'm to do," answered the woman, who had a soft, plaintive voice, and spoke with a broad Lancashire accent. "My mon went away o' Thursday neet wi' seventy pounds on him. He said he mun go out to Warrarra, a place fifty or sixty moile out o' town, and that he would be back on Saturday neet or Sunday morn. But he hasn't coom, and we're afraid, my son John and me, that he's in the Black Panther."

"Does he—is your husband apt to be unsteady, then?" asked Harleigh.

"Happen now and again, Sir; but he wor main careful and peaceable for more'n five months back. My eldest son is so hard-workin', and most niver tastes a drop o' drink; he helps to keep his stepfather reet. You see, Sir, Harry Barnwell is my second husband. Oh, if he has broke out wi' the drink now when my poor boy is down wi' a broken leg, and more'n half the money is due to people who worked for them!"

"Have you asked the landlord if your husband has been at the inn since Thursday."

"Yes, Sir; but he just flared up and said he'd have no wimin folks come botherin' about, and he'd no contract to look after my husband. Then I asked him direct, had he or had he not seen Barnwell. But he wunnot answer; he made believe someone was callin' him in, and he went out of the bar. What can I do, Sir, if he spends that money, and my poor boy not able to look after things?"

"Just wait here a little, Mrs. Barnwell. I'll go and ask the landlord whether your husband is on the premises. If not, you must see the police."

"Oh, Sir, I daren't. My husband would be wild wi' me, an' he's so violent when the drink is on him. Perhaps if you're so good as to speak to Bampton, he'll be frighted to turn you away as he did me, Sir."

Harleigh, without further delay, strode back to the Black Panther, and went in at a side door which stood open. He found himself in a long narrow passage, dimly lit by a kerosene lamp that was burning above the door. A red-faced woman in a dirty flounced silk and a huge mass of false hair tied up with a flaming ribbon stood at the door of a room opening on the passage to the left hand.

"I want to see the landlord for a few moments," said Harleigh, addressing this woman.

"Will you step in here, and I'll send him to you," she answered, eyeing the visitor with a half-suspicious glance.

Harleigh stepped into the room as desired. It was a small parlour, with a square table in the middle, on which there were one or two empty decanters, a greasy pack of cards, some soiled glasses, and clay pipes; there were a few cane-bottomed chairs round the table, frayed Indian matting on the floor; on the mantelpiece a tallow candle in a dirty tin candlestick was burning in a low-spirited sort of way. The atmosphere of the place reeked with the heavy fumes of tobacco and spirits. Through the half-open door came the sound of muttered curses and drunken laughter. Presently the landlord came in. He recognised Harleigh at once, and an evil light came into his eyes. Before he had time to say anything Harleigh spoke.

"Excuse me for trespassing on your time; I want to know whether Mr. Barnwell has been here since Thursday last, or if he is now on your premises?" The clergyman's stately bearing, calm manner, and business-like speech rather staggered the publican, so that he did not burst out with the hasty expletives which first rose to his lips. But there was an accent of unmistakable fury in his coarse voice as he answered in a loud blustering tone, "I'd just like to know what right you have to come pryin' into my place arter my customers. If you wants a glass of beer or rum or colonial wine, or any other licker, I'm ready to obey your orders."

As the landlord spoke there was a heavy shuffling step in the passage; it paused at the door, and then, in a state of partial undress, a power-ful-looking man, tall, and stoutly built, with bloodshot eyes, dishevelled hair, and unsteady gait, came in.

"Bampton, Bampton; I say, Bampton, where's that money?" he said in a rapid thick voice, looking round him with a half-frightened stare. One quick glance at the landlord's face, with its look of mingled rage and consternation, told Harleigh all.

"Harry Barnwell, come away home with me," he said in a firm gentle voice, laying his hand on the man's shoulder, and looking him full in the face.

"Home to the old woman, d' you mean?" said Barnwell, with a dark frown, thrusting his hands with a dazed look into his trousers pockets.

"Yes, home to your wife and children; you have been away since Thursday; they are frightened about you; they want you to take care of them, to work for them—to love them." Harleigh spoke these words with slow deliberation, his hand still resting on the man's shoulder.

"If you're soft-sawdered over in that manner you're a bigger fool than I took you for," sneered the landlord, drawing nearer to Barnwell.

An angry flush rose on Harleigh's face. It was at such moments that the old military habit of commanding implicit obedience, of instantly quelling the impertinence of an inferior, was apt to reassert itself. "I don't think you quite understand your position in this matter," he said to Bampton, with sharp incisiveness. "What motive have you for keeping Mr. Barnwell away from his family? He came here with a considerable sum of money in his possession. If it is lost, who is accountable for it?"

"Lost—my money lost!" repeated Barnwell moodily. "But don't you see, it's not my money," fumbling in his pockets with trembling hands. "Gone!" he said with a low cry, as all at once his confused besotted mind grasped the terrible thought. He sank down on a chair trembling in every limb, looking round the room, peering with a terrified air into the corners which the insufficient light of the solitary candle threw into Rembrandtesque shade.

"If you mean's that five pun' note I changed for you yesterday"—. The landlord had time to say no more, when Barnwell sprang on him with the fury of a hungry lion. "You have my money; you have it, give it to me!" he cried, his whole frame convulsed with passion, the strength of a giant in his rigid arms. Bampton had not kept a public-house for twelve years without knowing what the set look on Barnwell's face meant.

"Come, come mate, if you're really sober, and able to take care of yourself and your money, why you can have it," he said in a wheedling tone. Barnwell relaxed his hold while the landlord drew a soiled Russian leather pocket-book from a breast-pocket.

"In coursen now you're sober," he said coolly, handing a roll of notes to Barnwell, "you'd better keep it yourself, and if you take my advice you'll not fool it away on passonses nor churches." Harleigh could not forbear a smile at this thrust, and seeing that Barnwell looked quite sober, as he slowly counted his money over, he left the Black Panther, followed by a look of vindictive hatred from the landlord.

At a little distance from the inn Barnwell's wife still stood, anxiously waiting the result of the clergyman's visit to the house. Her heart sank when she saw him come out alone. But he had scarcely told her that he had seen her husband when the latter came out of the inn.

"Oh, Sir, how can I thank you," she began, the tears starting in her eyes.

But Harleigh took her hand in his, and raising his hat said, "I want to know your son. I shall come and see you tomorrow afternoon, if you will let me."

"I shall be only too glad, Sir, and so will my boy," answered Mrs. Barnwell warmly.

Harleigh gave a glance at the haggard unkempt-looking man, who with a downcast face and lagging steps approached them and with a parting salute to the unhappy wife he went on towards his lodging with a saddened look on his face. "Always the same old story," he thought; sin and misery abound on every side, and when we try to make one little corner less sinful, less miserable, we are for ever confronted with our overwhelming national vice, with places like the Black Panther— licensed centres of pauperism, crime, and lunacy—sown [sic] broadcast over the community, with their desolating trade in human lives and human souls."

Chapter VII

An Unexpected Visitor

Oh, lonely night, art thou not known to me,
A thicket hung with masks of mockery,
And watered with the wasteful warmth of tears?

It was within a week of Christmas, just ten days after the events record-ed in the last chapter, when Harleigh Roxburghe sat one afternoon writing at the open window of his sitting-room. His pen travelled rapidly over the paper, and now and then he paused with a half-smile on his lips. There are some people to whom it is impossible to write without imagin-ing the replies they would make to what we say. Patrick Dunstan was one of these, and it was to him this epistle was written.

"My dear Boy—Your tales about kangaroos and wallabies and natives, about splendid fleeces, cattle-hunting, and buckjumpers, about camping out, damper-eating, and emu-chasing inspire me with due awe and amazement. I have quite a vivid picture in my mind's eye of the old man kangaroo you described as being 'quite like a Christian—he was so spiteful and cunning.' My adventures are in comparison so trite and common-place that I hesitate to dwell on them. If I enlarged on my daily duties you would probably feel more strongly than you did even at St. David's that the most exciting event of a parson's life is when an intemperate washerwoman turns over a new leaf, or a favourite little arab gets ran over. But, stay, there is an element of dire menace in my parochial atmosphere at present which would no doubt atone a little in your estimation for the placid monotony of sermons and pastoral visit-ing. You must know, then, that there is a man here—the landlord of an inn called the Black Panther—who vows that if I go on interfering with his customers he will 'do' for me! He originally honoured me with his enmity because I was in some measure the means of preventing a man from squandering a large sum of money in the Black Panther. This man's stepson, John Patterson, has become an especial friend of mine. He is one of nature's true aristocrats. He is by trade a builder and carpenter, but will one day be a skilful architect. He has a great deal of talent in that direction, and uses most of his leisure in qualifying himself for the profession. Some of the plans he has by him are marvellously well conceived and equally well drawn. He has gradually collected a large number of books—which he has thoroughly read—and digested. Yet he began to work hard when he was a lad of fourteen. A man like this, who has been from his youth surrounded by temptations to coarse excess, who yet has learned to love beauty in nature and art and to hate vileness, and whose passions are curbed with a strong will and a tender conscience, is indeed one worth knowing. He has been laid up with a broken leg for some weeks, and I spend many hours with him. His mother is a gentle amiable woman, whose choice of a second husband has been very disastrous. Well, I suppose I must not inflict more biography on you."

At this point there was a knock at the sitting-room door.

"A lady to see you, Sir," said the clergyman's landlady in a subdued tone. The visitor had driven up in a carriage and pair, with servants in livery, and this unusual display of grandeur, not to speak of the lady's sweeping black velvet and Parisian bonnet—in itself a marvel of costly elegance—had somewhat taken Mrs. Dimble's breath away.

It was with a feeling of surprise that Harleigh recognised Mrs. Hartingdale. She lost no time in disclosing the object of her visit. "Mr. Roxburghe, I must ask you to excuse this intrusion on your time. Yes, I knew you would; I have a special favour to ask of you."

"Pray name it," answered Harleigh as he sat opposite his visitor.

"I have to ask that you will look upon what I am about to say as a profound secret. It concerns Clare, and I can hardly decide whether it is wise or foolish of me to be so candid. But I am sure you will consider my anxiety on my sister's account a sufficient excuse."

A chill fear struck through Harleigh's heart, and for a moment this sharp sudden pang kept him dumb.

"I shall of course respect any confidence you may repose in me," he said at last, speaking quickly; "but if it concerns Clare"—

He stopped because he could not find words to express his meaning without seeming discourteous. What he would have said was that no one—not even a sister—could have a right to say anything to him respecting Clare which must be kept secret from her. No doubt Mrs. Hartingdale divined the gist of the unfinished sentence. Obtuseness of perception was not one of her failings. But it did not suit her just then to be fastidiously sensitive.

"Thank you. I felt instinctively that I could trust you not to misapprehend me," she said with a gracious smile. Then, lowering her voice in a semi-confidential manner, she said, "Of course you know that before Clare went to England she got engaged to Mr. Victor Maylands, my husband's ward."

Harleigh flushed hotly. "I have not heard anything about that," he replied. Mrs. Hartingdale looked surprised, and this at once vexed and irritated Harleigh.

"You are of course aware," he said, in answer to this expression, "that at present our intercourse is very limited, so that many things of which, under other circumstances, we might speak, are overlooked."

"True; and now I have to explain why I speak of the matter. Clare broke off her engagement a day or two before she left for England. I cannot now go into details as to her reasons. Suffice it to say that I believe it was under a cruel misapprehension. I know that she loved Victor Maylands. Since her return their friendship has been renewed. And now you will see why I speak of the matter to you under the seal of secrecy. I have nothing but my impressions to go on, and nothing except the conviction that her happiness may be at stake has led me to speak to you."

"Then, may I ask what you propose that I should do?" asked Harleigh, fiercely sceptical as to the truth of Mrs. Hartingdale's conjectures, yet cruelly tortured by the thought that they might not be foundationless.

"I hardly know what to propose," answered Mrs. Hartingdale, with an accent of distress. "The only thing that occurs to me to suggest is that you should in some way make Clare realize that she is perfectly free at the end of the six months to act as her inclinations lead her."

"But that is so completely understood by the relations in which we stand," answered Harleigh. "I do not say that it is impossible Miss Rutherford may have acted too hastily in breaking off her engagement before going to England. If she has found that she did this under a false impression, she is too true and just not to be penitent for the pain she inflicted. But if, further, she finds, as you seem to imply, that the old love has reasserted itself, and that her engagement to me would be a mistake, I have every confidence that she will be true to me and true to herself."

"Still, you know how from conflicting motives people may sometimes be misled into committing irretrievable mistakes," urged Mrs. Hartingdale. "However, I feel now that as you know the true state of affairs—no, I will not put it in these words—I mean that as you know what my fears are you will be more guarded; and I know you will respect the confidence I have placed in you."

"Certainly, and in return I can only assure you that Clare's feelings in the matter will be my sole consideration."

As Mrs. Hartingdale drove home she reflected sorrowfully that her visit might bring forth but little fruit. A restless and feverish anxiety had driven her to take the step. There was not an hour of the day in which she did not rack her brain with schemes and intrigues to bring Clare and Maylands together. At her own house, at the houses of friends these two met perpetually. At first Clare's manner had been reserved and guarded, but she had speedily taken her cue from the really lofty way in which Mr. Maylands ignored the past. He was evidently far removed from the weakness of harbouring vague regrets or lingering memories of by-gone times. So gradually the old intimacy had in some measure revived between these two. This was excellent, so far as it went. Indeed, Mr. Victor's placid self-complacency, his serene enjoyment of the situation, left nothing to be desired. Only a few days ago he had stroked his ago-nizingly cared-for moustache, and asked Mrs. Hartingdale in confidence whether she thought Clare would expect him to speak soon. "Oh, no; not for some months yet," Mrs. Hartingdale had answered, a cold perspi-ration breaking out on her brow. And then the terrible thought that in some unexpected way the young man might find out how she was duping him led her to devise some means of making a breach, sowing the seeds of a distrust that would at least render Mr. Roxburghe's visits still rarer for the few weeks that would intervene till the family left town. But now that she had acted on the impulse she did not feel as if the stratagem were likely to be attended with any very brilliant success.

Harleigh sat for a long time after Mrs. Hartingdale left, rehearsing and pondering all she had said. He had a wide experience of life, and a keen instinct in estimating the characters of men and women. But after all the keenest of us are apt to be strangely deluded where our affections are concerned. If Mrs. Hartingdale had been an indifferent stranger to Harleigh Roxburghe instead of being the sister of the girl he loved so tenderly he would have been far more likely to gauge her motives at their real worth; and then, again, the feeling that from the first his new-found happiness was something almost too good to continue tempted him to doubt its stability more readily. When the blast of fate has shattered the bark in which our first dreams of happiness were stored, we are ever af-terwards more timorous, more ready to doubt that it is possible we can know the ineffable joy which God grants to his children in a happy love. Far into the night Harleigh Roxburghe sat in his solitary room, the lamp lowered, his pen and books untouched. And then the thoughts that had floated through his mind, the doubts and fears that had assailed him, found expression in the following letter:—

"My dear Clare—You will not, I trust, misunderstand what I am about to write. Half the time of our probation is now over. At first it seemed very hard for both of us that your father should insist on our engagement being postponed so long. But, after all, I suppose he was right, for how little you really knew of me when I had the boldness to confess my love. And even now, Clare, I ask myself as I sit here to-night alone how much have you realized the difference between your easy luxurious life as the daughter of a rich man and the wife of one who never looks forward to anything but a spare competence and hard work, hedged in by surroundings that may not unnaturally be very uncongenial to you?"

Here Harleigh laid down his pen and leant his head on his hand for some moments. Then he wrote very rapidly, "My darling, if on seeing how deeply I love you, you were moved to meet my love as much through tender sympathy as affection; if you have the slightest fear or doubt within your heart that as my wife your lot may be less happy or complete than some other form of life within your reach would be, do not hesitate, I beseech you, to draw back. Do not be swayed by any false feeling of self-sacrifice or pity. I cannot deny that it would be a hard and bitter blow to me." Here the writer paused. "I must guard against this sort of thing," he said to himself severely, "this is nothing but an appeal, flimsily disguised as a renunciation." So he tore up the half-written sheet, and wrote instead—"Nominally, of course, we are both free till we are formally engaged. If, in the meantime, any circumstance or feeling leads you to think that our engagement would be a mistake, do not, I beseech you, hesitate to tell me. Nothing, dear Clare, should weigh with you in finally deciding this question but one conviction—namely, that it is the best and happiest step for each of us equally."

Harleigh read this letter over very slowly, and was far from being pleased with its wording. It seemed stiff and almost harsh. But he reasoned that it was better so, since Clare might thus find it easier to answer if she really were placed in the position that Mrs. Hartingdale had insinuated. But in his inmost heart he could not realize that this was possible. He had such a vivid picture of the girl's deep, passionate eyes as she looked into his face on that glad spring day, and said with an enchanting honesty that she loved him a "great deal." And yet—Well, her answer to this would be decisive. He received it in two days. "Dear Harleigh— Thank you for reminding me that we are yet both free to ratify or annul our engagement. I suppose we ought to be very grateful that we are still in the position of a child who in a certain game stands in the centre of a ring of playfellows and is requested by them to 'choose to the east and choose to the west, choose the very one you love best.' I daresay nearly everyone who marries thinks it at first the best and happiest course. Can you imagine a more cynical commentary on human wisdom? I must confess that I enjoy my present surroundings so well that the prospect of living near a place, say like Barbaja, does not appear to me at all ravishing. No doubt this is the sentiment of a worldly self-regarding nature. Well, it is better that we should know each other's weak points before it is too late. Jack Sprat and his wife, if I remember rightly, got on well in culinary matters, because what one did not like the other relished. A difference of taste in morals is, I am afraid, a more dangerous bar to harmony."

Harleigh read this with a curious feeling of incredulity. The flippancy, the studied coldness, and careful avoidance of any approach to the frank precious avowal of trust and love which he expected so confidently, smote him with a deep, dull pain. For a little he felt inert and stupefied, and yet it seemed as if the most trivial details around him were being slowly branded into his memory; as if for all his life to come he would remember the sturdy roses on a drab ground that formed the pattern of the cretonne which covered the couch and the chairs that Mrs. Dimble was so careful to arrange in a rigid row against the wall, as if under the inspection of a phantom drillmaster. "Did the man who formed that design ever see roses growing?" he said to himself, as if that were just then the most momentous question of his life. And then he again read over that pitiless—one might almost say unwomanly—letter, with a terrible feeling of loneliness creeping over him. "It is true, then," he thought; "Clare has found probably that she wronged her former lover; the old love has revived, and the new, short-lived love is dead. Women sometimes perform these acrobatic feats with their hearts."

He rose, paced up and down, sat again by the table, leaning his head on his hand. Then thoughts of his early love, of his mother, whose memory he worshipped, came crowding in on his mind. When God had taken away the idols of his life before, when in the midst of his careless buoyant life he suddenly found himself bereaved beyond what he seemed able to bear, the first escape from despair, the gradual dawn of consolation came to him with the resolve to dedicate his life to the service of his fellow-creatures. And now again he hungered and thirsted for the love, the constant companionship of the woman who had so suddenly restored to him the passions and the hopes of his youth. Was he not in this like the man who, having put his hand to the plough, looks back—like one who has wearied of the Master's Cross and grasps greedily at the phantom of happiness? It was thus that the strain of asceticism in the man's strong self-contained nature reasserted itself. But, oh! how he had learned to love her; how her face would always haunt him; how the low glad laughter, the warm blush that came so readily to her cheeks, the changing light of her luminous dark eyes—nay, the very colour of the dresses she wore, the faint penetrating perfume that clung to her hands, would come back to him with vivid distinctness. When the moon rose above still woods, when the evening wind wandered upon the wave, when the flowers opened their hearts to the midday sun—everywhere and always would not these disquieting recollections follow him? Could the time ever come when these memories would pass into the quietude of a tranquil remembrance, when she would stand crowned the queen of a quiet land into which his imagination strayed only now and again as if by accident?

The peace of evening fell on the house—the hilltops in the distance were touched with the rose tints of the setting sun; a flock of white-breasted pigeons flew by to their dovecot near a neighbouring house. Kindly bustling voluble Mrs. Dimble came in with a snowy cloth on her arm, and seeing the clergyman grave and silent, with neither book nor writing before him, she at once began a mental review of the most salient features of local history, trying to decide which should be put forward to bring back the animated look which she had been accustomed to see his face wear. At all times when there was an opportunity of using one's tongue Mrs. Dimble regarded silence as a gratuitous addition to the burdens of life, "Some men folk are that backward and helpless," she would sometimes explain, "less you help 'em with a little talk, they'll just sit and stare a hole through your carpet. Sometimes Mr. Roxbery he's one o' them. But I often makes him laugh when I tells him a little about this one and the other, and the early days of the gold diggin's, an' how them butchers is alays trying to put down jints to me I've never had. It don't do to keep on for ever thinkin' about people's souls. Give the flesh its due, says I. The Lord gave us beer as well as hymnses, and a body can have too much of one as well as the 'tother. It's wearin' on the constitootion to be too much in earnest."

"I dessay you know, Sir, as that pore critter Barnwell has broke out again," she said, by way of averting that catastrophe to her carpet which she seemed to think would be the result of a long silence.

Surely not," said Harleigh with a startled look.

"Oh yes, Sir, it's no hearsay. This aternoon I had to go all the way to Briney's gineral store. That limb Scorpion, or Sorophiaa, or whatever her name is—such rubbish, Sir, ain't it, for navvies and bricklayers to give names to their daters you can't rightly name them 'less you've been to a high school or a college? Well, Sir, as I was tellin' you, that girl, though her weekly wage is seven shillings a week and many a dress o' mine, besides as good as new, which I have to give away through gettin' on in life—she never will remember two things at a time. So I just had to go to the store myself, and I took a short cut coming home by Bell's-lane and up by the Black Panther, and there was my gentleman that far gone he could hardly make one foot follow the other. A fine time that pore lad and his mother will have of it. You see, it's the holidays a comin' on, Sir. It gave me a sort of a turn to see so many here and there standing round them publics, till I counted up and found we're within three days o' Christmas. Why, Sir, you're surely not going away before you 'ave some dinner?" said Mrs. Dimble, in an aggrieved tone, as Harleigh rose to leave the room.

"I cannot dine just now, thank you, Mrs. Dimble; but I daresay I shall be hungry when I return. I have a meeting tonight, and I want to call at Mrs. Barnwell's on my way."

"Well, Sir, you knows best; but I can't think it's good for you to go so long without victuals. And there's just one thing I'd like to tell you, Sir, before you go to Barnwell's. Of all the cantankerest men as ever lived he's the wust when he's in licker; and it's my belief Bampton edges him on to worrit that pore woman into givin' him money. I dessay you know, Sir, as she and her son John has about forty shillings a week from a row of cottages—five, I think—left 'em by Patterson, as it's a pity he ever died—not that he could 'elp it, pore man. But still there was no call for 'er to marry again. Men, as a rule, is not such treats that a woman need hanker arter 'em to the toon o' marryin' more'n once."

This latter reflection was made by Mrs. Dimble in solitude as she resentfully folded up the tablecloth which she had spread to no purpose.

When Harleigh reached Barnwell's house he found that Mrs. Dimble's report had not been foundationless. Mrs. Barnwell met him at the garden-gate going out with her youngest boy—a child of six years of age.

"I have had sichan fright. Sir," she said in her low tremulous voice. "I was i' the parlour wi' a bit o' sewin', and John was asleep o' the sofa. He had a bad time last neet, what wi' a headache an' workin late at a plan. I heerd steps, heavy steps; an' when I went to th' door theer was my mon quite, quite drunk. Eh, Sir, but it's hard. He left home quite pleasant an' good-tempered, an' theer he stood, scowlin' at me an' sayin', 'Gie me some o' the money thou hast. Bampton has a score agin me, an' I mun pay it.' Yo mowt ha' knocked me down wi' a feather. I ne'er said nowt, I was so feared he would get mad-like and wake John. I just gied him some mooney I had wi' me, an' he said that would do to morn, an' he would then come for more. Then he went, an' I was just goin roun' to see yo, Sir, for I'm hard put to."

"I am on my way to a meeting at our schoolroom, Mrs. Barnwell. As soon as it is over I shall come here and talk this matter over with your son John. If you are in danger of violence at Barnwell's hands you must have protection."

Chapter VIII

Scheiden, Ach Scheiden

On the same day that Harleigh received the letter which seemed to him like the knell of his dearest hopes, Mr. Hartingdale left for Melbourne. "He has been called away on urgent business, and cannot return for at least a week," Helena explained that afternoon to her mother and sisters.

"I suppose, Clare, you can come and stay with me for a few days? We can of course spend Christmas here as usual."

Clare sat by one of the windows, listlessly turning over the leaves of a new novel. It did not escape Mrs. Hartingdale's quick observation that the girl was pale and weary-looking, with dark rings under her eyes, and that there was a curiously strained inflection in her voice when she spoke.

"Oh, yes, I suppose I can," she said, looking towards her mother.

"There is nothing that I know of to prevent you, my dear. Would you like me to ask Mr. Roxburghe to spend Christmas Day with us—at least as much of it as he can spare?"

Clare coloured painfully. "Thank you, mother dear; I hardly think he could come—he is so much engrossed with his work, and then you see papa has made it so awkward for both of us," she said, suddenly seizing on the old grievance in her anxiety to conceal the true state of affairs. "Mr. Roxburghe feels constrained to make only a few formal calls, while I have no right to encroach on his time."

"What an elaborate conscience you are evolving, Clare," said Dolly, suddenly looking up from a piece of crewel work with a long-legged penitential-looking stork in the centre, which, judging from the scenery round it, seemed to have, like Columbus, discovered an entirely new world.

"No, I assure you it is in a very ragged condition," answered Clare, with a forced smile. Then tossing down her novel, she said, with a yawn, "I wonder people can go on writing such trash. It's eternally the same ingredients, with a few modifications, like the recipes for making plum-pudding—a young woman and a young man, sentiment and scenery, another young man, a little mild villainy, misunderstanding, reconciliation, orange blossom, finis. I suppose I am getting a little beyond the age for genuine enjoyment of novel-reading," said Clare sombrely.

"Oh, my dear, when you have lived half a century you will begin to know what a boon a readable novel is," said Mrs. Rutherford, laughing softly.

Then to-morrow I shall expect you, Clare," said Mrs. Joseph, as she went away. "Bring one of your pretty French dresses to wear tomorrow night. I'll look for you and Matthew between 7 and 8, Dolly."

"Is your Christmas Eve party to be very large, Helena?" asked Dolly, trying to decide on the relative merits of a pale ecru silk with scarlet rose-buds and a peacock blue trimmed with ravishing lace.

"Oh, I suppose between fifty and sixty young people," returned Mrs. Hartingdale, as if she attached no particular importance to the event. But Dolly was suspicious, and a little restless in her mind as to whether she should not tell Clare once for all that Helena's present mood of unvarying amiability was more to be mistrusted than her old habit of assertive authority and constant interference. That, in fact, Mrs. Joseph represented the ingredient of "mild villainy," which, if opportunity offered, might be worked up to fairly dramatic heights. "Clare is as gloomy and *triste* as Eve must have been when she was driven out from the roses of Eden, not but what I think she had her compensation in getting away from the Archangel's theology," mused Dolly as she watched Clare's weariful face. "She is just the sort of girl to keep any trouble all to herself, like that Spartan boy whose vitals were devoured while he kept his cloak in graceful folds. I'll just speak to her about him, and see if I can get any clue."

"Don't you think Harleigh must sometimes find it rather tiresome to be so much among people like the Barbajers, Clare?" asked the younger sister demurely, taking up her long-legged sad stork.

"Not more tiresome than other people," answered Clare, a little vaguely.

"I suppose I have a very small little sneak of a soul, but if I were a parson I am sure I would prefer parishioners who had aesthetic carpets and good cooks—a congregation like that of our own at Thorleaden, for instance."

"What would he do among such a set of wealthy self-complacent people—people who want a clergyman to preach them neat little homilies on the holiness of self-denial, and then help them to consume their over-rich viands at heavy dinner parties? He would be no more than a comfortable fact in their lives, like the policeman who may be called for on an emergency. A parson in such congregations is little better than a well-dressed gamin—a man who earns his bread by posturing, instead of doing real work," said Clare, with a return of her old animation.

"Ah," thought Dolly, "Clare is remorseful about some supposed iniquity."

Aloud she said, "Well, Clarchen, I suppose we are going to have a different standard of morals as well as of literature. I like to peep into your favourite authors now and then, if only for the sake of a new sensation—to be told by Ruskin that England is on the way of being the offscourer of the earth—taking the hyena instead of the lion on her shield, and becoming a field for every kind of sordid, foul, or venomous work which in other countries men dread and disdain. I don't object to be informed by Carlyle that the world is inhabited by so many millions, mostly fools; or to learn from Arnold that the majority of the British race are hopeless Philistines, and after being sat upon by Helena no one can be more delightful than Mill 'On Liberty.' Even when your Comte tells me that Humanity is the only true Divinity I am not greatly shocked. But there is a point at which I always turn sceptical. And just in the same way I decline to believe that a parson's work among the lower orders is superior to his vocation in a church like our own."

"It all depends on the man who has the work to do," returned Clare. "I cannot imagine anything more paralysing to a true man with a purpose in life than to have the spiritual charge of people like myself and Helena for instance. Who could make us practically realize that our own petty rules of self-interested conduct are not the eternal laws of God?"

"Oh, do you think you are prudent like Helena?" said Dolly, with uplifted eyebrows.

"Well, not in the same way," returned Clare, who could not but be dimly conscious that she and her elder sister were parted, not merely by differences of temperament and disposition, but also by totally antagonistic ideals in life—a deep and irresistible current in human nature which has a force of separation more potent than time or distance. "What I mean is that each of us in our plans of life has seen the highest good in what is pleasantest to ourselves. To have unfading heaps of money, Parisian dresses, and be a leader of colonial society is Helena's scheme of the universe. To be a great musical genius; to know great poets, and painters, and celebrated actors; to be bored by no one; to have not even an acquaintance who is not either charming to look at or entertaining to talk to, and to be always surrounded by beautiful things, is mine. Helena has attained her ends. I never shall, and even if I had, I suppose after knowing Harleigh, I should be constrained to take up a new scheme of existence. But just at present I feel like poor Faust, when he cried that two souls dwelt in his bosom. I—" Clare paused abruptly, and Dolly having vainly waited for the confidence she expected, rejoined with a toss of her saucy little chin—"I am thankful I am not such a complex organism; I am sure I have only one soul. I am glad George is not a clergyman," she added, as if struck with the thought that if he were she might be called upon to develop any number of souls.

"Scheiden, scheiden, ach scheiden thut weh!" Clare sat at the piano, and her full, pure soprano voice, with its deep undercurrent of penetrating pathos, rang out as she sang the sweet and tender German song. She sang for an hour, one song after another—her face pale and rapt, her voice rising at times like that of a "winged thing that cries above some city flaming fast to death." She ended with the fiery, passionate little song, "Neue Liebe, neues Leben," and then hastily left the room.

"I am afraid Clare is not very happy of late," said Mrs. Rutherford anxiously.

"Oh, there is hardly any one very happy when one comes to think of it, mother," answered Dolly reflectively, upon which an amused look stole into Mrs. Rutherford's face. If theories stood in the place of experience, many mothers would be forced to conclude that they must really be very impulsive merry young creatures, who should learn deep lessons as to the misery of life and the folly and wickedness of mankind from those sage, deeply tried, world-weary women, their daughters.

Chapter IX

In the Gloaming

Ah, keep near and close,
Thou dove-like help! and when my fears would rise,
With thy broad heart serenely interpose.

As soon as Clare had consented to stay a few days with Helena she was assailed with the fear that Harleigh would call instead of writing an answer to this letter, which she now so bitterly repented writing. She expressed something of this fear to Dolly, and that astute young woman, who, as we have seen, had her own thoughts of the angelic amiability which Mrs. Joseph of late displayed towards Clare, said, "If Mr. Roxburghe calls tomorrow I'll get him to drive with me over to Fingal House to see you—see if I don't!" Dolly gave an emphatic nod of her little head, with a malicious joy in the picture she drew to herself of Helena's dismay at having her little plans so rudely dislocated.

Christmas Eve that year was an oppressively sultry day. The sky was obscured by masses of dull-coloured clouds, yet the atmosphere was hotter than it would have been if the sun had shone with all the brilliancy of a midsummer day. There was hardly a breath of air, but when the foliage of the trees was faintly moved it was by a wind that seemed to come from pitiless wastes of sand lying white and shadowless beneath a fierce sun.

"It is a really horrible day," said Mrs. Hartingdale, resenting the unseasonable heat that threatened to mar the success of her party. But she looked at her great lofty rooms, at the broad verandahs closed in with venetian blinds, at the wealth of shrubs and flowering plants with which the hall and wide, shallow staircase, with its deep piled carpet, were decorated, and she took heart of grace. "After all, it is sure to get cooler towards evening." Then she noticed with some anxiety how white Clare looked, how impassive she was, how monosyllabic were her replies. "It is the weather; she is always sensitive to that," she thought, and when in the afternoon Clare fell asleep in a low easy-chair in the silent darkened drawing-room Mrs. Hartingdale stole softly out, hoping the girl would sleep for some hours to come and then waken up refreshed. At the door a servant met her with a telegram that had just then arrived. She tore open the envelope with an unusual tremor in her hand, and her face flashed as she read. "Accomplished. See G. as arranged. J. Hartingdale." Her heart throbbed with gratitude, for this message conveyed a hope that the disaster which her soul dreaded might be yet averted. She ordered the carriage to be in readiness to take her to town in half an hour. When she went away Clare still slept. It was close on four o'clock when she woke up in a strange fright. She had been dreaming. In her dream she saw Harleigh standing on the edge of a precipice, his hands bound, his face deadly white. She strove to call out to him, but she could not utter a sound. Then she crept slowly and painfully up the steep slippery crags that rose between them; at last she drew near him; she would untie his hands and lead him away from that terrible height. But in the moment that she stood near enough to touch him the beloved face, with its look of pain and sorrow, vanished in the yawning precipice below. It was then that she started up with a cry of horror on her lips. Clare had slept very badly the past two nights, and that day she had been unable to eat anything. Probably this in part was the reason why she now, though wide awake, burst into a violent fit of weeping. The tears fell down her face like rain, while her whole frame was shaken by convulsive sobs. "Oh, my poor old darling," she murmured, brokenly. Then her tears ceased, and she fell into a profound reverie, which put into words ran thus—"I am awfully miserable; but I deserve it all; ever since I wrote that abominable letter I have felt that sackcloth and ashes are heavenly luxuries compared to what I deserve. Harleigh's letter vexed me, but if I had given myself time to think over it I would have seen that it was his unselfish love which urged him to write it. But no—I must always have my own way, always act on impulse, and then repent and suffer. That is what has led to all my trouble. If I had not behaved badly to Victor Maylands my father would not have made himself a nuisance about Harleigh. Well, what do you mean to do now?" said Clare to herself abruptly. In answer to this stern enquiry she rose up with a resolute air, and went to the library to write one of the tenderest, meekest, and most contrite letters which ever rejoiced the heart of man. In passing through the hall she saw the evening papers, which had just been delivered, lying on one of the tables. She took one up and glanced idly over its columns. Presently her eyes fell on a paragraph headed:—"TERRIBLE OUTRAGE AT BARBAJA.—Yesterday evening, about eight o'clock, a rumour spread through Barbaja that a builder named William Barnwell had in a fit of drunken fury shot his stepson dead, and dangerously wounded the Rev. Harleigh Roxburghe." Details followed, which showed that these first rumours were in some particulars untrue—that Barnwell's step-son, John Patterson, was not dead; and that it was hoped Mr. Roxburghe's wound was not of a fatal nature. This much Clare knew, and then what followed always remained in her memory like fragments of a feverish dream—a dream in which faces come and go, in which there are gleams of unrealized scenery, sounds that are vaguely heard as if at a great distance, while an unspeakable dread lives in the heart and overmasters every other emotion. She had a remembrance that one of the servants told her Mrs. Hartingdale had gone to town and expected to be back between 5 and 6; that she had then looked at her watch and found it was a quarter to 5. Then in her misery and perplexity one coherent purpose was formed—to go to Harleigh at once; to leave the house without delay; so that she might avoid the remonstrances and all the infallible reasons which Helena would certainly urge against the plan. Cold, faint, and bewildered as she felt, Clare in an incredibly short time left the house, walked the half-mile across the grounds to the highway where the suburban omnibuses passed on their way to and from town every quarter of an hour. The omnibus passed within five minutes' walk of the railway station from which trains started every half-hour. Barbaja was one of the intermediate stations at which the train stopped. The 6 o'clock train left the city just as Clare reached the station. There was nothing for it but to wait half an hour for the next train. Half an hour! Rather an endless procession of miserable days in which there was neither rest nor peace, and in which despair seemed kept at bay only by a faint gleam of possible hope; in which rattling vehicles drove up and left crowds of people who stamped about with hideous laughter and constantly asked each other if they had heard of "that affair at Barbaja;" in which above all there were shoals of newsboys who followed the poor girl into every nook of refuge, offering her countless evening papers, and tempting her to buy them by shrieking out "Houtrage at Barbaja—two men shot!" So often was this horrible piece of news shouted out to her that Clare at last felt it was the one thing which had been dinned into her ears since the first conscious dawn of intelligence. At last she was safely in the train and away from these hideous cries. But she had not been two minutes in the carriage when an elderly man with a stout red face asked another elderly man who was pale and cadaverous-looking if he had heard anything fresh of the "Barbaja affair." "I believe both are dying, if they are not already dead," replied the cadaverous-looking man promptly, as if he found a grim joy in a catastrophe of such vivid horror. Clare felt for an instant as if she were on the point of shrieking aloud. Her overstrained nerves and sickening fears made her over-credulous. She could not pause to reflect that a hundred wild and sensational rumours are constantly afloat when a tragedy or deed of violence first becomes public property. "Both are dying, if not dead!" The words seemed to fill all space; to rise in surges of sound around her; to stand out in lurid characters wherever she looked; and her last words to him were bitter, scornful, and false. No, she did not now dread that she would shriek or faint or weep. When life's cup of supremest bitterness has to be drained there is no escape or relief from the heavy, slow, intense throbs of the agonized heart. We are forced to be horribly vividly conscious of every moment that crawls by with the cruel slowness of a torture devised by the Spanish Inquisition. Whereas in the first moments when she only feared that Harleigh was wounded and in pain, Clare was oblivious of all external surroundings, she now seemed endued as with doubled and trebled senses. She took in every trivial detail without any conscious effort.

The narrow platform at the Barbaja station was crowded with a throng of men, women, and children. Clare shrank from asking any question. She went on for a little, one of the busy, hurrying crowd, not knowing where she was going or which way she should turn. She looked up and down at the long narrow rows of houses, at the brickfields to the right and to the left surrounded by mean grimy habitations, at the gaunt narrow-windowed mills and manufactories. Then she noticed a quiet-looking, poorly clad girl of thirteen or fourteen carrying a small bundle.

"Can you tell me where Mr. Harleigh is since—since he met with the accident yesterday?" Clare asked, her voice very low and shaken. She nerved herself to bear the answer, but it seemed like baring her heart to the operator's knife when the girl replied quickly—

"Oh, you mean the clergyman as was shot, Miss? I've heerd tell he is at Mrs. Barnwell's. Some says he's dead, but some says he's not; but, la! Miss, mother says you never know what to believe with so many people given to lying."

Clare slipped half-a-crown into the girl's hand, saying, "I want to go to Mrs. Barnwell's. Can you show me the way?"

"Oh, yes, Miss, thank you; I'll go within sight of the house. This way, please—this is a short cut. It's awful dusty here. Father says it's a real shame, all we pay in rates, and not a smell of a water-cart from one year's end to the other. If there were a few nobs living about we'd soon 'ave halterations, father says."

The loquacious girl poured out paragraphs of talk on the slightest pretext, or no pretext at all, while Clare toiled on, striving to keep up with her nimble unwearied steps. Though it was yet little more than half-past 7, and the sun had not long set, there were no lingering lights on the hilltops, no golden gleams of a summer sunset on the skies. There was an angry flush of crimson low down on the west, fading into a deep lemon tinge higher up. There were sure indications that the storm which had been foretold all day by the oppressively sultry thunder-charged atmosphere would soon burst. Round the horizon wide slow sheets of lightning now played almost incessantly, while all over the cloud-laden heavens a purplish darkness crept with startling rapidity.

"I fear I am taking you out of your way, and there seems to be a storm coming on," said Clare, in her slow tired voice.

"Oh! we're close to Mrs. Barnwell's, ma'am, and I can easy run into a neighbour's house," answered the girl cheerfully.

"I 'ope you ain't ill, Miss," she added in a tone of concern, struck by Clare's faint tones, and seeing that her face was painfully white. A low peal of thunder broke afar, and large heavy drops of rain came down, as if shaken from the wings of some Titanic bird in rapid flight.

"There, ma'am, that is Mrs. Barnwell's place," said the girl, pausing, and pointing to a neat-looking cottage a little way ahead, surrounded by a garden and several well-grown trees. Then she hurried away, and Clare, with weary lagging footsteps, gained the white garden gate in front of the cottage. The click of the latch as she lifted it, the sound of her footsteps on the shell gravel that covered the path, the swaying of the fig-trees and acacia in the wind that was rapidly rising from fitful moans into a high gale, the lightning flashing between the gloom of the distant woods, and the darkness of the threatening sky—all was vividly imprinted on Clare's memory, and made a picture which long years afterwards, in season and out of season, rose up in her mind with haunting persistence. There was a light in one of the windows, but no sound or sign of life was to be heard. This stillness smote Clare with a terrible conviction that all her worst fears were to be realized. Already she seemed to be in the very presence of death. Pale and trembling she stood for some minutes at the door. Before she could summon resolution to knock, it was softly opened by an elderly woman with a pale anxious face, her eyes red with weeping. When Clare tried to speak her tongue seemed to cleave to the roof of her mouth.

"Is—Mr.—Harleigh—here?" she asked in a low, hoarse whisper, with an odd pause between the words.

"Yes, yes. Please coom in," said Mrs. Barnwell, for it was she. "You are not well," she said in her gentle voice, as she noticed Clare's uncertain, faltering steps, and the excessive pallor of her face. "Sit down theer and rest," she said, and Clare found herself led into an easy-chair, in a room which was in partial darkness. The woman's thoughtful kindness broke down all artificial barriers.

"Tell me how he is," entreated Clare, holding out her hands, as if instinctively seeking for some support before the worst was told her.

The unhappy mother's tears overflowed. She clasped the stranger's hands in both hers.

"Oh, the doctors think there is a little hope o' his recoovery," she murmured in a broken voice. The room was illumined by a vivid flash of lightning, and a loud, long, continued peal of thunder crashed overhead. Then there was a silence, broken only by the mother's repressed sobs. As for Clare, she simply lay back in the chair. She did not become insensible, but neither was she capable of emotion or thought; least of all capable of considering that Harleigh's weal or woe was not after all the nearest interest of Mrs. Barnwell's life. Ordinarily Clare was far from being open to the reproach that her own joys and troubles made her insensible to the interests and sufferings of others. But in the pitiless mental and physical strain that now prostrated her she had no thought even for herself—no thought for anything on earth, for any human being—save one; that Harleigh was hurt unto death by the husband of this gentle, sorrowing woman, for whose sore grief she felt a vague compassion. Just then all was vague, terrible, and unchangeable. A stony, undisturbed stupor fell on her. She knew, after a little, that a subdued light was brought into the room; that Mrs. Barnwell bathed her temples with some pungent perfume, and slipped out of the room so gently that the most acute listener could not catch the sound of her footstep or of her voice as she passed into the adjoining room, where her son lay insensible. Harleigh, with his left arm bound up and in a sling, sat near the bedside, having just risen from a long refreshing sleep.

"Has the doctor been here since I slept?" he asked, in that hushed voice one unconsciously adopts in a sick-room.

"Yes, Sir; he called at 5. He said the signs o' fever had lessened, and that he would call again between 9 and 10 toneet. Theer is a lady in the parlour, Sir, who asked for you. She seemed suddenly taken ill after she came in. Happen she belongs to th' congregation."

The thought flashed through Harleigh's mind that possibly the lady was not one of the pewholders of St. Christopher's.

"I shall go and see her," he said, and quietly left the sick-room. At the first glance he thought—standing in the half-open door—the parlour was empty. There was a lamp on a small table in one corner of the room, but it was lowered; and the arm-chair in which Clare still lay passively stood between the fireplace and the door, and was partially concealed by the latter. Harleigh advanced into the room, and looking round he saw in that corner the outline of a figure, clad in a soft, grey silk, with creamy lace round the white throat, and the hands that lay nervelessly on her lap; he saw a white, still face with closed eyes, and his heart gave a great jump of mingled joy and fear.

"Clare, my darling," he said in a quick, impassioned tone, bending over her. He thought she must have fainted, but when he spoke she started up with a low cry.

"Oh, Harleigh!" There seemed to be no need for further words; all the agony, the suspense of the last few hours, the sudden, almost overwhelming rapture of this moment seemed to find expression in that exclamation and in the girl's eloquent face.

"Harleigh, I have heard nothing for an eternity but people saying that you were shot—that you were dying or dead; and for an eternity I believed it. I thought I might never again hear the sound of your voice or feel the touch of your hand." She looked into his face with a pathetic, unutterable tenderness. Then Harleigh knew that all the fears and terrifying doubts which Mrs. Hartingdale's words and Clare's own letter had roused were utterly groundless—idle as the visions of one who dreams that he is in a treeless desert strewn with bleaching skeletons, but wakens up to hear the sound of hidden waters and the song of happy birds. He knew once for all that Clare's fidelity was unshaken, and her love stronger than death.

"Harleigh, I have been so horrid," she said, lifting her head from his shoulder, and speaking in a voice which by reason of its meekness was hardly to be recognised.

"Did you come all this way to tell me that?" said the lover, with serene scepticism, "and did you really come all alone?" he continued, drawing her closer to him, and again laying her wearied, happy face on his shoulder.

"Yes. I was staying at Helena's, and she was away. I suppose it's really a kind of elopement. Oh, Harleigh, how can I ever be good enough to deserve such happiness; and you are not even badly hurt."

"Oh, no, my pet, only a flesh wound; a mere scratch in the arm. Poor Patterson is badly wounded, but I hope he will with care recover. His wretched stepfather, Barnwell, is the one to be most pitied. Why, Clare, you are not crying, are you?"

"I cannot help it," answered Clare, softly. "Why should I be so supremely happy when so many are crashed with misery? I seem now to see so clearly how selfish I have always been. I blamed my father for not sanctioning our engagement at once, but it was my own fault, I taught him to mistrust me."

"Hush, hush, my darling; don't you know this is Christmas Eve, and the first one we have ever been together, and that God is so unspeakably good to us that henceforth till death do us part we belong to one another?"

Without the storm raged with tropical fury, lashing the rain violently against the windows, and mercilessly fliching twigs and boughs from the trees that swayed, bent almost double before the blast. "Strange weather for Christmas Eve," people said querulously. But to these two it was a day to be remembered with infinite thankfulness and abiding content. What need to say that their gratitude and happiness found fitting expression in working for the outcast and the disinherited of the world; that their lives, enriched and completed by mutual help and family life, were bravely and faithfully dedicated to sowing and reaping in the harvest-fields of God, which stand ever in need of labourers meet for the toil?

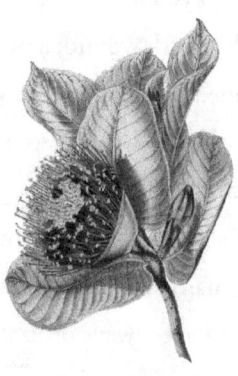

The Bushman's Revenge

Salian Muir

Chapter I

The older inhabitants of the wide and arid plains of Northern Australia to this day recall, with feelings akin to dread, the summer of 187–. The intense heat and protracted drought experienced during that disastrous season, and the consequent suffering in mind, body, and estate then endured, might well be compared to the terrors and inconveniences of the historic plagues of Egypt; not omitting that crowning visitation, the death of the first-born; for it, too, had its counterpart in many a sorrowing homestead on the Ballowie downs.

The crop failures, the loss of stock, the ravages of dingoes, rabbits and locusts, the plagues of flies and other tormenting insects, and, above all, the scarcity of that priceless necessity, water, were in themselves dire calamities, but when Death himself, utilising the ants and potent shafts of the sun, struck down, here and there, the weak and the unguarded, the persecution of an already sorely-stricken people was indeed complete.

It was the 24th day of December in this memorable year. The sun, which on each succeeding day for the past fortnight had striven to increase his record on the previous, had this day attained the climax, and beat down with fierce intensity. All nature—man, beast, bird and herb shrank in fear from his blighting ray: the spirit of living creation was broken and subdued. Yet not of all nature. The many and diverse members of the insect and reptile tribes held high revelry, and disported themselves in full enjoyment of the, to them, genial warmth. The lissom snake, whose multi-hued skin glittered in the shimmering haze, and his inveterate foe, the ill-favoured but harmless iguana, winked their gleaming eyes in bold defiance of the sun's best directed rays; the invisible grasshopper gaily beat his tattoo to the regulated march of that foraging soldier, the industrious but quarrelsome ant, while the homely-clad locust flitted leisurely abroad, vainly vying with the more gorgeously attired butterfly in attracting the admiration of her humbler kin.

But in other circles reigned distress and death. The once bright flowers and verdant herbage bowed their blighted heads in sheer enervation; the gasping birds were voiceless and inert, and the countless carcasses of the larger animals which strewed the plains, told only too eloquently their own tragic story; the bleached skeletons standing out like grim spectres mutely appealing for vengeance on their ruthless destroyer.

Bold indeed was the traveller who ventured abroad on the exposed downs on such a perilous day, and so thought Mr. John Maclean, J.P. the wealthy squatter and owner of Kangarilla Sheep Station, as he sat in the shade of his verandah, and saw in the far distance a human form trudging slowly along the track in the full glare of the midday sun.

John Maclean was a Scotsman born. He had arrived in Australia when a young man, and had now had some thirty years' experience of colonial life. Rising from the humblest position by sheer dint of hard work and thrift (generally termed "meanness" by those who knew him well) he had amassed a considerable fortune. But although financially strong, and a magistrate by Government appointment, John Maclean was not a popular man. He was the unfortunate possessor of an impulsive, irascible temper, which too often led him into excesses of speech and action of the most violent kind. Of pronounced vices he was notably free and in his commercial relations, although exacting, he was scrupulously honourable. But on account of his unreliable temperament, which varied suddenly, and on the slightest provocation—between fits of moroseness and outbursts of frenzied fury—the wealthy squatter was no social favourite. His servants feared him; his compeers were deferential but respected him not.

Now the master of Kangarilla was in no amiable mood as he watched the approach of the stranger. The knowledge of his blighted pasturage and of the decimation of his flocks was ever present to his mind, and the consequent loss to him, although it could not materially affect his solvency, was sufficient to cause his grave anxiety.

The traveller had now entered in at the panels of the home paddock, and his identity had slowly intimated itself to the eye of the master of the estate. With ill-restrained appreciation Maclean exclaimed:

"By heaven if it's not the loafing scoundrel Sundown Bill. I'll teach him and all the sundowning crew that Kangarilla is no haven for their idle, useless persons. 'If thou shalt not work, neither shalt thou eat,' is Scripture and sound common sense as well. At the last meeting of the Pastoralists I moved a resolution to the effect that these idle vagabonds should not be encouraged in their aimless wanderings by being housed and fed, and though my motion was not accepted I will, at any rate, give effect to my own principles. I'll give Sundown Bill a reception that he won't forget."

Sundown Bill it really was. A typical Australian "sundowner," one of the army of bush dead-beats who roam yearly over vast areas of the country, at first, doubtless, capable workers, earnestly desirous of obtaining employment. But the sundowner is a product of the country; such being the effect of this free wandering life, in a genial climate and under an almost perpetually blue sky, that ere long the second stage in the career of the graduating sundowner is reached—that wherein he outwardly seeks for employment and inwardly supplicates heaven he may not find it. From this stage to the third and last the descent is easy, and there is no mistaking the professional sundowner who has attained the degree of a master of the craft. The mission of the fully fledged sundowner is to traverse the country avowedly with no further aim or purpose than firmly and scornfully to decline, on all occasions, to accept proffered employment, and to live a precarious life by vagabondage and begging. To this class Sundown Bill belonged. He was a past master of the order of professional sundowners.

In appearance Sundown Bill, by which sobriquet he was familiarly known, was tall and gaunt. In age he was about fifty-four; his skin was tanned by exposure to weather and aversion to water, and his long, unkempt hair and beard were fully intermixed with grey. But Sundown Bill was by no means an ignorant person, and for his knowledge of men and politics, and his ability as a raconteur, he was usually welcomed at the camp fire, where to the amusement, if not the edification of his listeners, he discussed his subjects and related his experiences with a full and ready flow of forcible colonial "language." Yet, withal, he was a useless parasite, regarded as dangerous alike to the substance and the morals of the community—an unproductive being, who toiled not nor did he spin, and, in truth, it may be added, neither was he arrayed in any particular glory.

With "swag" and "billy" slung over his left shoulder, and carrying his water bag in his right hand, the bushman slowly approached, showing unmistakable signs of exhaustion, and thus greeted the master of Kangarilla.

"Good-day. Mr. Maclean; terribly hot."

"No doubt," came the ungracious reply, "but what brings you here?"

"Beg pardon, sir, but I'm passing through to Mr. Blake's, and I thought you wouldn't mind me resting in the shade until the cool of the evening."

"Now. Sundown Bill, look here. You know me. We've met before, and you know my opinion of you and all the other worthless blackguards like you who prey on this country. Clear out, and that very much faster than you came."

"But, Mr. Maclean, I'm dead beat. Don't turn me adrift on such a terrible day," pleaded the sundowner. "It's 25 miles to Mr. Blake's place, and I ain't equal to the trip until sunset."

"Don't you argue with me, yon loafer. Not enough to be ruined by my stock dying in thousands and eaten out by the cursed rabbits, but you scamps must prey on us as well. Get out quick, or by heaven, I'll kick you across the paddock."

"All right, boss; you're muster here; I'll go, but Mr. Blake don't treat me like this. Sundown Bill is always welcome at his place."

After a brief pause the desperate man pleadingly added, "For God's sake, boss, allow me to rest in the shade until evening, and I promise you I don't trouble you again."

"No! once and for all; no! If Blake's such a confounded fool as to harbour you scamps, you'll find my place no half-way house to Sundowner's Hotel. Clear out, quick."

"You'll do me one favour, boss; you'll allow mw to fill my water-bag at your tank," begged the sundowner.

Then John Maclean lost control of his quickly rising temper, and while refusing to grant the poor man's request to replenish his water-bag, strode up to him with evil intent. But Sundown Bill, with the strength inspired of insult and despair met the enraged man unflinchingly, and in a subdued and broken voice said:

"God help me, I'll go. Don't you touch me. I'm footsore and hungry; and my water-bag is nearly empty, and you turn me from your door on this awful day. You're a rich man, and I'm a poor worthless creature, but my word on it I'll be revenged on you yet for this cruelty."

Maclean approached menacingly exclaiming, "You stand there and threaten me you cursed hound."

"Don't; don't lay a hand on me," the bushman loudly entreated.

But John Maclean to his everlasting shame did, and with one firmly-planted blow, he sent the exhausted, defenceless bushman reeling against the fence.

With choking utterance the aggrieved and humiliated man, recovering his position, muttered, "You cruel coward," and bestowing a dark, revengeful look upon the squatter, he swung his swag on his shoulder, turned his back on Kangarilla Station and its owner, and continued his slow march across the open plain.

It was now two o'clock in the afternoon. The hot north wind, intermittently approaching on wings of fire, insidiously flicked the bronzed, sullen face of the wayfarer with stinging effect, but, suffering the acuter pain of wounded feelings, Sundown Bill felt it not. The ever changing currents met now and again in direct opposition, and, forming whirling eddies, caused columns of fine dust to envelop the form of the traveller, but blinded by passion, born of insult and injury, Sundown Bill saw it not. Consumed mentally by a wild desire for revenge, and physically by a burning thirst, the persecuted vagrant, with bowed head, plodded wearily on, and only once, until he had passed from sight, was he observed to pause for a minute to moisten his parched lips with a few drops from his almost depleted water-bag.

Chapter II

On the departure of the Sundowner, John Maclean withdrew to the coolest chamber of his house, and having partaken of a glass of cold whisky and soda, stretched himself upon his soft couch for his customary siesta. Conscious of having done his duty in so summarily disposing of the vagrant, Mr. Maclean set himself to think of a more pleasant subject, and found it in the personality of his son—his one child, Roy; the only creature on God's earth on whom he bestowed affection. And Roy Maclean was a boy to be beloved. Of a gentle, kind disposition, inherited from his mother, now these three years resting in the grave, the lad (by the very diversity of their natures, apart from paternal instinct) had entwined himself around the heart of his father. Roy was now thirteen years of age. He had spent the past ten months at school at the capital of the colony, and had returned for the midsummer holidays not a week previously. Being thoroughly at home in the saddle, like all colonial youths, Roy rode over on that evening to see his friends, the boys and girls of the Blake family, on the understanding that he would return home three days later. On the afternoon of the day before he was to return, however, the discerning eye of Mr. Blake saw what he regarded as unfailing signs of a coming change in the weather, and thought it prudent that Roy should ride home in the comparative coolness of that evening, rather than await the chances of the morrow morning. So shaking hands with his friends, after mutually expressing many good wishes Roy mounted his pony at five o'clock, calculating to be home by eight.

All went well with the lad until he dismounted at the boundary of his father's and Mr. Blake's runs for the purpose of opening the gate to admit of passing through. Having opened the gate, the horse was led on, but not having drawn him sufficiently far forward, the closing gate struck the heels of the animal, which, being a spirited beast, instantly kicked out vigorously, and, sad to state, struck the boy a violent blow, breaking his leg a few inches above the knee. Utterly helpless and in great pain, the youth crawled to the gate post, and there, with the best fortitude he could summon, awaited he knew not what. He was twelve miles from his father's house; and unexpected there; he was thirteen miles from Mr. Blake's residence, and on a track along which it was highly improbable any traveller would at that season pass. Two hours had elapsed, in which he had suffered excruciating pain, and was now passing off into fitful states of semiconsciousness. He must lie here all night and throughout the coming storm, or perhaps the dazzling sunshine and terrible heat of the morrow, should the expected change not come. The darkness was rapidly falling, and happily with it the darkness of unconsciousness was supervening on the mind of the afflicted youth. With closed eyes he lay, feebly moaning.

Now Sundown Bill kept the beaten track on his journey from Kangarilla to Mr. Blake's station, and being already fully six hours on the way, walking and resting, he approached the boundary gate of the two properties as young Roy Maclean was in the last stage of sensibility. The sundowner was not a little surprised to hear what clearly appeared to him to be the faint moans of a distressed human being. Arrived at the spot from which the sounds emanated, he was amazed to find the form of a delicate youth, with an expression on the face indicative of intense suffering.

"How's this," he queried. "What has happened, my lad?"

But no intelligible answer came from the boy.

Then Sundown Bill threw down his swag, and bending on his knees, peered into the face of the boy. With a start, he instantly drew himself back, a violent oath escaping his lips.

"Young Maclean," he cried. His wild eyes gleaming with satisfaction, the sundowner again bent down beside the prostrate youth in order to make certain of his identity.

"Are you the son of Maclean of Kangarilla?" he impetuously inquired.

And feebly the reply came "Yes."

"What's the matter? Are you hurt?"

"Yes," slowly answered the boy. "The horse kicked me as I was coming from Mr. Blake's, and must have broken my leg."

"Are they expecting yon home? Will they send for you tonight?"

"No; father doesn't expect me until tomorrow."

With this effort at conversation, the lad fell into a state of utter unconsciousness, and no further replies could be obtained to the questions of the tramp.

Sundown Bill stood up. A dark and dangerous scowl contracted his brow.

"His only son," he deliberately soliloquised, "and I've heard the very apple of his eye. What a revenge. It's no crime to do nothing. If he ain't expected home; tonight and tomorrow will do for him. Ha! ha! he refused me water that might have saved his own son. I'm only a hound to be struck and insulted and turned adrift to perish in the scorching sun. I know no better, and doing nothing's no crime. To act up to his father's opinion of me, I should kill the youngster where he lies. But no, I'll do nothing, but move on, and leave him to die."

And picking up his swag, Sundown Bill straightway walked out at the partially opened gate, an expression of satisfied revenge on his countenance.

Then, as if pierced by a dart, the indolent sundowner, the disreputable pariah, the abused and persecuted tramp stood stock-still, irresolute for a second. That instant the smouldering fire of inherent good, which lies latent in the hearts of the worst of men, suddenly touched by the quickening spark of pathetic opportunity, blazed out into brilliant activity. Sundown Bill struck the gate open with a violent swing, slung his swag on the ground, seized his water-bag and kneeling beside the prostrate son of John Maclean, he poured a small quantity of the precious liquid down the throat of the insensible youth, thereafter alternately rubbing the hands, and cooling the fevered brow of the sufferer with a moistened handkerchief.

Slowly the injured lad awoke to consciousness and pain.

"How do you feel now, sonny?" inquired the sundowner.

"I have been asleep, I think. A drink, please?" whispered the boy.

"There ain't much left, sonny, but you'll have what there is."

"Thank you. You're so good."

"Hush! Sonny; keep quiet now, till we see what's to be done."

And with a gentle touch, Sundown Bill examined and bound up the lad's fractured limb.

"You won't leave me, will you?" pleaded the boy.

"No, Sonny, not unless it's necessary."

"You know where we live?"

"Yes," said the bushman. "I know your father."

"Oh! father will be so glad, and will be so kind, to you. What is your name?"

"Don't speak no more, sonny. Keep quiet. My name's Sundown Bill. Ain't your name Roy Maclean?"

"Yes," replied the boy.

"Thought so. I remember your mother, my boy, when you were a baby. You're a brave little man, ain't you. I'm going to try you, sonny. I can't carry you home. I haven't strength to do it, and you couldn't bear it, anyhow."

"You won't leave me?" the boy pleaded.

Then Sundown Bill made the injured lad as comfortable as was possible under the circumstances and after vainly looking around for the missing horse, gave the last drop of water to the sufferer, encouraged him to keep a brave heart, promised a speedy return, and set off for Kangarilla. He hoped to complete the journey in four hours, summon aid, and return to the afflicted boy within two hours more.

To the lad the interim of waiting seemed eternity. To the bushman the distance to be covered was usually as nothing, but on this oppressively close night, in an exhausted state of body and mind, suffering privations of hunger and thirst, and, his mission being extremely urgent withal he felt an almost overpowering sense of weakness such as he had never before experienced. Yet Sundown Bill bravely struggled on. When well advanced on his journey it occurred to him that it was near the opening of Christmas Day, and he reflected that, once a shepherd himself, on that same morning many centuries before, the good shepherds of the East walked into Bethlehem to find the child Jesus, the angelic host singing the glad refrain "Glory to God, peace on earth, good-will to men."

With a pardonable conceit he imagined he saw points of analogy between his own mission and that of his brother shepherds of Judea. Perchance he, too, influenced by a beneficent unseen power to engage in his mission of mercy and good-will, might be rewarded with an approving smile from that same great Redeemer who, humbly born in a manger, and himself despised and rejected, would not lightly regard the good office of a poor sundowner.

These and other reflections, leading Sundown Bill back to the teachings and doings of his childhood's days, beguiled many steps of his tedious journey, and at what he guessed by the perpendicular bearing of the Southern Cross to be the tense hour of midnight, he espied the lights in the windows of Kangarilla home station.

Chapter III

That undefinable feeling of unrest which to some temperaments is the precursor of approaching storm in tropical countries had evidently seized Mr. John Maclean on this eve. Remorse, resulting from his summary treatment of the despised sundowner, in no way contributed to this disturbed feeling. In that respect the masterful squatter considered he had admirably performed his duty. But the disquieting effect of coming atmospheric disturbance was to some degree intensified by reflecting upon past instances of retaliation resulting from such condign treatment as he had that day meted out to Sundown Bill. Mutilated horses and cattle, poisoned dogs, and gross acts of vandalism and arson were not infrequently caused by malicious and retaliatory tramps. From whichever cause, or combination of causes, it was true that on this particular evening John Maclean was ill at ease. He walked to and fro in his verandah and around his homestead, until past the hour of midnight, relieving the monotony of his peregrinations by frequent libations of whiskey and soda, which increased his restlessness, and left him in an excited and reckless mood.

Suddenly his faithful sheep-dog following at his heels, stopped, and pricking his ears set up a prolonged low growl, which his master regarded as indicative of a stranger being in the vicinity. His thoughts rapidly recurred to the meeting with Sundown Bill, and who other than he, lurking in the neighbourhood until midnight, could approach the premises at this unseasonable hour, and with what purpose other than the sinister one of personal injury, incendiarism or theft. Grasping the dog by the collar Maclean quickly dragged him into an inner room, where he commanded him to lie still. He then extinguished the lights, seized his revolver, and issuing cautiously from the house, stood under an umbrageous eucalyptus tree, there to await the development of events. Nor had he long to wait. He soon observed a moving figure, slowly as if surreptitiously approaching the homestead. Nearer and nearer came the form, and with its approach the more firmly did the thought take shape in Maclean's mind that the object of the visitor was an evil one. Should it be Sundown Bill, his malicious intent was assured; for had he not that very day threatened him with revenge. Peering vigilantly into the moonlight, John Maclean presently drew himself quickly back, the visitor having come within the area of identification.

"It's Sundown Bill," said the squatter in a tone repressed but breathing fury, "I'll hold no parley with him this time."

And as the unsuspecting bushman painfully trudging along on his mission of mercy was distant a few feet from the concealing tree, John Maclean with a malicious grin on his countenance, raised his revolver and deliberately fired twice point blank at the body of Sundown Bill. With an agonising cry the latter staggered against the fence and fell prostrate to the ground, where he lay motionless, but faintly moaning.

Then John Maclean laughed aloud at his own astuteness in having turned the tables so unexpectedly on the sundowner, and in having so successfully circumvented him in his evidently nefarious design.

"When in doubt, play trumps," he to himself complacently said, "and I reckon I've scored this time, Master Sundown Bill."

He then walked leisurely towards the house, and summoning the men-servants from their abode, instructed them to carry the prostrate man to the wool-shed. This done, and lights having been brought, he ordered restoratives to be applied to the unconscious bushman, in order that, if not dead, he might be revived and prepared for transit to the near-est police residency, there to be charged with trespassing with malicious intent.

The second revolver shot had entered the left shoulder of the poor sundowner; the first had missed its aim. The attendants in their rough and ready manner did their best to staunch the flowing wound, and un-der the effects of the stimulants the injured man slowly recovered con-sciousness and feebly inquired:

"Where are we, mate?"

"Keep quiet, old man, you'll be all right shortly," replied the stock-man, Williams, not unsympathetically, for he knew the old sundowner.

"Ain't this Kangarilla?" asked the bushman

"It is," said Williams.

"Where's the boss? I must see him at once," said Sundown Bill.

"Look here, Bill: you know me, don't you; Bendigo Jack, and if you take my tip you'll leave the boss alone."

"But I must see him, Jack, it's urgent. Tell him to see me quick."

"Are you in earnest, Bill? You know the boss ain't violets on your sort."

"Never mind, mate, tell him to come here quick, or take me to him."

From the earnest pleading look on the sundowner's face, the stock-man assumed that the injured man had really something of importance to communicate, and went in search of his master, whom he found smoking in the verandah.

"Sundown Bill wants to see you, sir, very particular; he's something on his mind, sir, I fancy."

Now John Maclean had by this time come to the conclusion that he had gone, perhaps, too far in his drastic treatment of the wandering bushman, and had a slight fear that in his capacity of Justice of the Peace and Magistrate of the country, his summary action would not commend itself to the authorities of the Crown. It occurred to him that on whom magisterial honours are bestowed, from whom judicial and temperate action is expected; and John Maclean was in a more reflective mood when his servant summoned him to the side of the wounded man. He went without remark to interview the bushman. The latter had not realised, and had not yet been informed how and by whom his injury had been inflicted. On the entrance of his master, the sundowner, slowly and with difficulty said:

"You don't like me, boss, but; I never done no harm."

"You know I detest you and all your accursed fraternity. You're a dangerous, good-for-nothing lot, and I reckon you've got your deserts this time."

"Perhaps so, boss; perhaps I ain't no good. I reckon I'm not," and with this the poor sundowner's voice sank, and he groaned in pain of body and spirit.

"I'm shot, boss' ain't I?" he plaintively inquired.

"I reckon you are," said the squatter, and he smiled at what appeared to him the humour of the situation.

"Who done it?"

"I did; and I'm prepared to answer for it as a justifiable deed," emphatically responded the master.

"Perhaps so, boss—perhaps so," said the sufferer, in a low tremulous voice, and the tears welled up in his wild eyes and coursed down his bronzed and hairy face, "but I done it for the best, boss—I done it for the best."

"If you survive, you'll have an opportunity to prove that in court," was the brutal reply.

"There's no time for more talk, boss. Your boy Roy has broke his leg—kicked by his horse in coming home from Mr. Blake's. He's lying now at the side of the boundary gate. Put your fastest horses in the buggy, and go for him at once, and send some one to Ballowie for the doctor. Hurry up, boss; you've no time to lose."

John Maclean was struck dumb with amazement and horror. His countenance turned wan with shook, and he trembled in every limb. For fully a minute he stood speechless, staring vacuously at the prostrate man. At last he recovered his speech, and in a hoarse subdued voice instructed the stockman to harness the horses to the buggy without a moment's delay. He then bent down over the helpless man and inquired in the same constrained voice:

"Did you come back to tell me this?"

"Yes, boss; I found the little chap in a bad way; I done what I could for him; gave him the little water I had, and made him as comfortable as possible with my rugs, but he's in a bad way, sir."

"And you've walked back thirteen miles to inform me?" asked the master.

"Yes, boss; what else could I do; I'd have carried him back if I could, but he can't a-bear to be touched."

"God help me and forgive me," groaned John Maclean, and he moved away, bowed down with confusion and remorse.

The buggy was ready; rugs, pillows and restoratives were hurriedly placed therein, and, giving instructions to Williams to ride post haste for the doctor who resided some thirty-two miles from the station, and strict injunctions that Sundown Bill should have the best attention rendered him until the doctor's arrival, John Maclean entered the vehicle, and accompanied by a man and a maid servant, drove off furiously to the scene of the accident.

That eighty minutes' drive in the early Christmas morn was not a pleasant one for John Maclean. He had been unspeakably unjust and cruel in his treatment of a fellow creature, and his punishment was indeed severe, for what retribution so bitter as the requital of evil by good. Amongst a multiplicity of surging thoughts his mind reverted to one season years agone when his young wife, whose life had not been a too pleasant one, had taught little Roy to lisp:

"Peace on earth and mercy mild,

God and sinners reconciled."

Peace, mercy, and reconciliation! Heavens! what a travesty of the words had his unfeeling conduct been, for at this happy season, and on this day of all days in the year, with a violent discord that reverberated into heaven, he had clanged the odious death-knell in upon the sweet harmony of the blessed refrain sung on this glad morn by the heavenly choir. And verily, in boomerang fashion, the weapon of violence and malice which he had thrown had returned to him again, for there was no peace in the anguished soul of John Maclean.

At last the panting horses were pulled up at the boundary gate and having dismounted from the trap the anxious father, bending over the injured boy and passionately kissing him, cried:

"Roy, dear Roy, what has happened to you? Speak to me, Roy!"

"Father!" was all the reply the stricken youth could utter.

The maid hastily administered some brandy-and-water to the boy, who presently rallied, and with a faint smile on his wan face, said:

"Oh, father, take me home. My leg. Kicked by Diamond. It is so painful."

"I'll lift you gently, dear Roy, and take you home," answered the father.

"Where's the bushman, father? Did he tell you?"

"Yes."

"Where is he?"

"He's at the station."

"He was so kind to me, and gave me his rugs and his last drop of water."

"Yes, he's very good."

"He said he knew you, father."

"Yes, he knows me," said the father.

"And we'll give him such a merry Christmas, father."

"Don't talk too much, Roy, dear; it will tire you out," said the agonised man.

And for a time Roy was quiet. They placed him tenderly on the soft cushions and rugs in the buggy, and drove him carefully to his home. Arrived at the station, he was borne into a room and laid upon a couch, with every available comfort, there to await the arrival of the doctor.

The developments in the case of the bushman were such as to occasion grave concern to the inmates of the homestead, and to cause considerable alarm to the master of the house himself. The best unprofessional attention was bestowed upon the sufferers, but for both cases the advent of the medical gentleman was eagerly awaited.

Dr. Herne at length arrived, and immediately attended to the suffering boy. He set the fractured limb, gave strict instructions as to his treatment, pronounced him as in no danger, and predicted a speedy recovery. The doctor then proceeded to the case of Sundown Bill, and a few minutes' examination sufficed to show that the condition of the poor bushman was fraught with danger. The loss of blood and shock to the system, which already had been reduced to a state of extreme weakness by physical exhaustion and privation, were greater than the remaining strength could combat.

The experienced eye of the doctor quickly observed that the life of the unfortunate bushman was slowly ebbing away. The knowledge of this caused John Maclean extreme anxiety and anguish; to do him justice, not from any fear of the consequences to himself. He told Dr. Herne to spare no effort or expense towards alleviating and promoting the recovery of the sundowner. But the doctor's best efforts were in vain. The bushman was dying. Towards evening he rallied considerably, and to John Maclean this appeared a hopeful token, but to the doctor it was the rallying effort predictive of the end. Sundown Bill motioned with his lips, and the doctor approaching, slowly asked:

"How's the little chap, doctor?"

"He's all right, thanks to you; he's in the next room," said the doctor, who had had the whole of the facts related to him.

"You're Dr. Herne," said Bill.

"Yes; you know me, don't you? but you must keep quiet now and not talk."

"Oh, it don't matter, doctor. It's no go. I've gone on the wallaby track for the last time. Say, doctor, could I see the little chap before I go?"

The doctor mused. It would be a very unprofessional act to move either of the sufferers, but the circumstances were exceptional. He consulted Mr. Maclean, who left the matter entirely to the doctor, his own feeling being to gratify every desire of Sundown Bill. The doctor reluctantly decided to remove the sundowner to the adjoining room, and, as gently as possible, he was carried through and placed upon a couch a few feet distant from Roy. The boy was asleep, but a sad smile crossed the face of the bushman as he saw the pale face of the lad.

Soon the boy awoke from his fitful slumber. He recognised, with some surprise at first, the form of his friend and involuntarily his left hand was stretched out towards Sundown Bill. Smiles of recognition were mutually flashed from both, and the right hand of the bushman clasped the outstretched hand of the boy.

"How are you sonny—got home all right?" the Sundowner feebly inquired.

"Yes, Bill; your kindness saved me. If it wasn't for you I would have died," said the boy.

"It was nothing, Boy," said the bushman.

But John Maclean, seated in the shadow, his face tensely drawn, and mentally suffering the tortures of the accused thought it a noble deed, and in the absence of that ulterior motive of self-interest, which he always looked for in every man's conduct, to him Sundown Bill's was well nigh incomprehensible.

"Father and I will never forget your kindness," said the youth. "But what's the matter with you, Bill?"

"I've had an accident, Roy; and I'm dead-beat tired with the heat."

"Poor Bill! You've got that by being kind to me. How did it happen, Bill?"

"Oh, it ain't much, sonny! We can't help accidents."

"We'll have good times when we're better, Bill. You'll stay here and won't go on the track no more."

Then the doctor intervened, and kindly informed them that further conversation must be suspended for the present. Both sufferers gradually fell asleep, and the doctor, who had arranged to remain for the night, passed from the room.

But John Maclean still sat in the shadow.

Soon the doctor re-entered. About 8 o'clock Sundown Bill awoke, and the trained eye of the doctor observed that the bushman was slowly sinking, and that his hours, yes, his minutes, were numbered.

The dying man, turning his eyes to the boy, now also awake, stretched his hand towards him, and in it the lad placed his.

"Good-bye, Roy, I'm going," he sadly said.

"Where?" asked the boy.

"I'm going out on the track for the last long journey, Roy."

The boy was bewildered.

Then the doctor whispered to Roy to be a brave boy, and told him that his friend was dying. With a startled look the boy burst into tears, and cried "No! No!"

"Yes, Roy, I've got to go. I'll never see the blue sky nor the wattle blossom, nor hear the laughing-jack and the magpies no more. You'll get better and be master here someday. Think sometimes of poor old Sundown Bill, and don't be too hard on the sundowner who comes your way."

But the sobbing boy could not reply.

The doctor was touched by the affecting scene, and John Maclean, suffering unspeakable agony, sat still in the shadow.

Then the dying man said to the doctor, "Where's the boss, doctor?"

John Maclean heard and came forward.

"Good-bye, boss," said the bushman. "Will you shake hands with the old sundowner?"

His vexed spirit at last overwhelmed by the torrent of his feelings, John Maclean, taking the hand of the dying man, wept aloud, and cried vehemently, "Forgive me, forgive me."

"It's all right, boss. We've all made mistakes. Sundown Bill's life was a very big one."

"Forgive me," reiterated the remorse-stricken man.

The sundowner feebly pressed John Maclean's hand, and in a low tone said, "Don't tell the boy."

The dying bushman slowly withdrew his hand from the father and again grasping that of the son, said:

"Good-bye, Roy! Be a good boy. I knew your mother. She once spoke a kind word to me. When you get better you will write a letter to my old mother in the little home in Devon in the old country? I've not written her for twelve years now, but I know that every mail she expects a letter, and expects to see myself someday. You'll find the address in her last letter to me. I've carried it in my old pocket-book for the last eleven years. Tell her Bill is dead; died thinking of her, and say no more. Say nothing of his wasted, useless life. Poor dear mother!"

The boy sobbed bitterly, and clung to the hand of his dying friend.

Soon Sundown Bill closed his eyes, and faintly smiling, spoke incoherently of the good shepherds in whose company he imagined he came that morning to point out where the little child lay, and to bring a message of peace and good-will to the master of Kangarilla.

A deathly silence then ensued; the irresponsible lips ceased their motion, and the dying man slumbered peacefully for a time. Suddenly his features moved convulsively; his face finally assuming an expression of mingled fear and despair; and in a piteous, pleading voice he exclaimed: "Don't! don't touch me, boss; I'll go."

Then with a violent start he awoke in bewilderment, and gradually recovering consciousness, he bestowed a grateful smile on the doctor, and turning his eyes once again to Roy and slowly muttering, "Good-bye, good-bye," Sundown Bill fell into a calm deep sleep, from which on this earth he never awoke.

And long after Dr. Herne had pronounced life to be extinct John Maclean sat in the shadow, never uttering a word.

Next day the body of Sundown Bill was buried in the little cemetery on the estate, and on the same day, in his capacity as magistrate of the district, John Maclean forwarded a full and true account of the tragic occurrence to the Government Law Department. The doctor, who acted as coroner for that part of the country, also forwarded his report, referring therein to the admission made in his own hearing by the deceased, that his injuries were received as the result of an accident.

The law authorities decided that no further action in the matter was necessary.

It was many weeks after the death of Sundown Bill before Roy Maclean was permitted to leave his bed, but the first request he made, upon being able to step over the threshold, was to visit the grave of Sundown Bill. And great was his surprise upon reaching the spot, to observe a beautiful granite monument marking the resting place of his friend.

"Who placed this stone here?" he hastily enquired of his father, who had driven him thither.

"I placed it there," was the quiet reply.

And Roy, approaching the obelisk, read:

"ERECTED BY

JOHN MACLEAN,

to the memory of

SUNDOWN BILL.

"Greater love hath no man than this, that he gave his life, not for his friend, but his enemy."

***

Roy Maclean was intensely pleased with this mark of respect bestowed on the memory of Sundown Bill; for, during his long illness, he had silently cherished the idea of requesting his father to erect a tablet to the memory of the departed friend. John Maclean lived for several years after the death of Sundown Bill, but from the day of the tragic occurrence, he was an altered, a remorseful, and it is believed, a better man. It is certain that when a year or two later, a proposal was carried by the Pastoralists assembled, to discourage the visits of sundowners by refusing to give them food or shelter, John Maclean, to the surprise of all warmly opposed the motion, and voted with the minority. Moreover, and in proof of his sincerity, the homestead of Kangarilla had from that fatal day become proverbially known for its hospitality, which was duly taken advantage of and appreciated by all the nomadic fraternity of sundowners.

Some months after the death of Sundown Bill, the rural postman knocked at the door of a little cottage in a green lane in Devon, and the poor old soul who eagerly grasped the proffered letter with the Australian post-mark, fervently thanked God for his goodness in answering her prayers. The letter from her long lost son had at last arrived.

But her joy was soon turned into sorrow. Her son was dead; died bravely, nobly, the letter informed her. God be praised. To her the life that had been ended bravely and nobly, must have been nobly lived. Of that she was fully satisfied. And he had died thinking of her, his mother. Oh, blessed joy; and she wept tears of gratitude to God. The long, years of neglect were entirely forgotten. He was to her the child of her heart; her own son, who had lived and died nobly, and whose last thoughts were of her. It was enough; all she wished for now was to revel in the thought of it, and in her strong and simple faith, to prepare for that hour, which must soon come, when she would meet her son in spirit, and never part from him again. Blessed faith, glorious hope.

The letter proceeded to inform her that her son had bequeathed to her his money, to be paid in the form of an annuity so long as she lived. The bequest was more than sufficient to provide her in comfort throughout her remaining few years. John Maclean appointed himself testamentary executor, and remitted the first amount. To the aged mother, the legacy was further proof that her son had been an active and prosperous man in a far-away country.

But John Maclean is now dead, and Mr. Roy Maclean, M.P. and J.P., is master of, Kangarilla. Since attaining the age of manhood, Roy had learned the true cause of the sudden and tragic end of Sundown Bill, and in consequence his father's reasons for the erection of such an elaborate and costly monument to the memory of his humble friend. And he walks across to the little graveyard at frequent indefinite intervals during the year to mark his loving remembrance of his parents and his friends, his little children who accompany him reverently keeping the grass green and in season planting snowdrops and daisies on the graves.

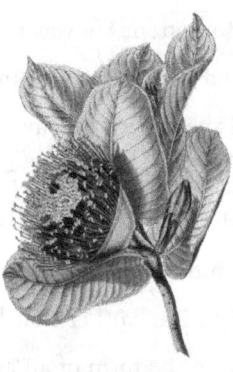

Uncle Tatbury's Ghost!
An Australian Christmas Story

F. S. Wilson

For over all there hung a cloud of fear,

A sense of mystery the spirit daunted:

And said, as plain as whisper in the ear,

The house is haunted!

– Hoc D.

Chapter I

M r. Tatbury's house was haunted!

You don't believe it? Of course you don't, dear reader; and why? Because your ideas of ghosts are always associated with rare old mansions in greatcoats of ivy, through which the sleepy-looking eyes of windows look drowsily down on the grassy court-yards beneath.

You can't realise a ghost sitting down cosy and comfortable in a warm well-lighted, modern parlour; but imagine that it must necessarily enter on the scene of the story through a pair of ancient iron gates, on whose rusty bars the shrieking blast plays a weird melody, as the shadowy visitant flits by.

Moreover, it must be a dull ill-humoured, teeth chattering sort of a night, accompanied with a slight sensation of snow and hail, to fill in the picture, just as a score or two of chubby urchins in short muslin skirts are stuck here, there, and everywhere, as a finishing touch to the closing scene of a pantomime.

Now, because this description of weather has always been considered "seasonable" for ghosts, and as this is Christmas weather in Great Britain (where, probably, you were "raised"), and as ghosts have formed part and parcel of Christmas stories from time immemorial, you won't believe that such a thing as a "haunted house" can be connected with the glorious sunny-faced Christmas-time of Australia!

Very well then, dear reader, please yourself. I seldom quarrel with a man (never with a lady!) for entertaining opinions contrary to my own; but if you will trace this sketch fairly to the end, perhaps you will then believe in Australian ghosts as much as I do.

Mr. Tatbury's house was haunted.

"But who is Mr. Tatbury?" You inquire, rather tartly.

Why, that is just what I'm going to tell you! Of course I shall begin at the beginning, for there's nothing like having a fair start; and if we commence unravelling a yarn at both ends we are sure to get it entangled before reaching the middle; so, having seen the gas "turned up," the performers grouped in their proper places, and the supernumaries all ready with the red fire for the finale, the bell is rung by the prompter, and the "green curtain" of 1864 rises on the New Christmas Story of "Uncle Tatbury's Ghost."

Tatbury Hall, as the residence of Joshua Tatbury, Esq., was designated, was (to use the words of the advertisement which induced its present proprietor to become purchaser), "situated in the delightful suburb of Paddington."

It was a structure of imposing appearance, though its exterior adornments were rather of a novel than picturesque character; but this must be attributed to Mr. Tatbury, who, on purchasing the building not only bestowed his own name upon it, but added such various "improvements" that its original architect would never have recognised his own offspring.

The fence encircling the entire premises was painted a vivid green; but the frontage palings had acquired a tint nearer akin to the red dusty road stretched out before them.

The portion of ground called by courtesy the front garden was laid out in trim flower-beds, of every imaginable shape; and a blighted-looking creeper franticly essayed to clamber up the trellised verandah, but being too weak to achieve its object contented itself with waving its half-matured buds in the glaring sunshine, sparkling on the drawing-room windows.

No doubt the garden had a deal of care bestowed upon it, but after the manner of road-side gardens in general, it never prospered; the "red" roses had no claim to their title, they would come out of a sickly brick-dust hue, instead of wearing the bloomy blush which healthy roses ought to wear; in fact, it was only after a thorough drenching rain that any of the trees were not of an "invisible green."

Then the outer gate had a bold polished brass handle, and the narrow walks were covered with a shelly substance that crunched under your feet, and suggested long rambles by the pleasant dreamy ocean. There was a formidable knocker, too, on the door (an iron ring in a lion's mouth), looking so fierce that it induced you to pull a deceitful bell instead, which refused even to tinkle until you gave it an extra jerk when it would rattle its tongue as if trying to alarm all the household, bringing the housemaid in a great hurry (and no pleasant humour), to answer the summons.

Then passing the rear of the building there was a dreary wilderness of an enclosure called the "back garden," which possessed a well and a pump and which supplied a consumptive cabbage about once in every three months—that is when they were in season, and the aphids didn't eat them; moreover the plot was almost surrounded by the straggling foliage of the "buddleia," which tossed its honey-scented flowers in the air, while a long gravel way led down to the extreme end, where a "summer house" of most wintry aspect was situated.

Retracing our steps to the mansion itself, and going in at the back door, we pass along the passage, and turning to the left, enter the dining room of Tatbury Hall.

It has been a warm sultry day (for remember, reader, it only wants three days to Christmas, this evening on which my story commences), but now the sun has gone down, and the southern breeze comes in cool gusts, bearing on its wings a grateful salty savour from Botany Bay.

Certainly the room wears a comfortable look, as the light of the table lamp flickers on the sparkling tea service, and falls on the faces grouped around it.

At the head of the table sits Uncle Tatbury, whose chief characteristics appear to be a limited supply of straight grey hair, a medium quantity of face, very red and very oily (suggestive of a newly boiled lobster in a fishmonger's window), and a superabundance of white waistcoat.

He had a severe and defiant way of propounding questions to you—questions which he never expected you to answer; in fact your inability to solve his inquiries always raised you in his estimation, and produced a rumble of satisfaction from behind the ample white waistcoat.

Mr. Tatbury had arrived in the colony twenty-five years ago and one of his most marked peculiarities was that he never failed to inform friends and strangers that fivepence-ha'penny formed his entire "cash balance" on-arriving in Port Jackson.

Now, if a man rises from wheeling a barrow to affluence, he is a man still, and may be a worthy man; but, if he perpetually wheels his barrow retrospectively before society he becomes a social nuisance.

So was it with Mr. Tatbury. His fivepence-ha'penny had borne him golden fruit and he loved to talk of it continually; but (so contradictory is human nature) if anyone, even in the bosom of his family, hinted at bygone days of poverty, Mr. Tatbury's red face grew as stormy as an angry sunset, and the white waistcoat produced any but jovial sounds.

Summing up his character in a few words, Mr. Tatbury was a "highly respectable man;" at least so the world said, judging from these reasons he always went to church once on Sundays (when it didn't rain), never put less than half-a-crown into the plate when he did go and kept his own carriage.

Mrs. Tatbury was rather portly, and what people generally term "a fine woman," but at the first glance her dress betrayed a want of taste that almost led her to indulge in the ridiculous. Mrs. T. "followed the fashions," and fell into the popular error, that the costume which suited a dashing belle of eighteen, would likewise "become" a matron on the shady side of five and forty. Under this delusive, but not the less pleasing idea, she followed her own tastes, and flattered herself that she looked as young as her daughter.

But if Mrs. Tatbury had an overmuch love for dress and fashion, she had little to spare for poor relations—a class whom she regarded with a most cordial detestation; in fact she would have parted with—ay! with one fashionable plume from her last new bonnet, rather than bestow one kind word on a relative so wicked as to be poor.

Her husband shared this dislike with her in a great degree. Certainly if a poor man applied to him for relief, and could prove that he was a worthy object of charity, that his wife was sick and his children hungry, then Mr. Tatbury had no objection to give him fivepence-ha'penny, and a lecture to the effect, that out of that identical sum he, Mr. T., made his fortune, and advised the applicant for relief to go and do the same.

Indeed, the only material difference in the tastes of wife and husband consisted in her devoting half her time to spending the money, in pursuit of which the major portion of the day found him engaged; but as long as Mr. Tatbury paid the draper's bills without grumbling all went "merry as a marriage bell."

Their only daughter, Angelina, was a tall, well-formed girl, rather pale featured, but possessed of sufficient beauty to claim the title of good-looking. Her eyes were very dark and brilliant and her mouth small and well-shaped; but there was a sharpness in her glance, and a scornful curl on her lip, that made you feel anything but comfortable in her presence.

A striking contrast did she present to the cousin who sat beside her, and upon whom devolved the task of presiding at the tea table.

Nothing remarkable was there in the little face of Agnes, Mr. Tatbury's niece—but oh! what a world of pure unselfish love, the very index of the peace and goodwill within. Such a quiet, yet withal such a merry good-humoured little being was she with her golden hair twinkling in the light, that she seemed sent, not for her own happiness, but to constitute the happiness of those around her.

Jonas Brooks, Mrs. Tatbury's father, was the only inmate of the room in addition to those I have attempted to describe. He was a white-haired old man with a very vacant expression of countenance but with a remarkably retentive memory—the latter involving him in continual bickerings with his son-in-law.

The servant had removed the tea-things, but the party still retained their seats—so quiet that the ornamental French clock on the mantel-place had nothing to do but to try and overpower the hum of the mosquitos buzzing in and out of the window.

Mr. Tatbury took up the daily paper. It wouldn't do. Evidently he had something to communicate. So looking round on the family group he inquired, "Who do you think I met today?"

As nobody appeared to know anything about it, Mr. Tatbury went on to explain that the person whom he had met that day was none other than a Mr. Frank Mayland, a name apparently familiar to all present.

The eyes of old Jonas twinkled as if his memory was busy with something. Mrs. Tatbury and Angelina simultaneously ejaculated "Oh, indeed!" and a shrewd observer might have detected a momentary flush on the cheek of quiet little Agnes.

"Yes," continued the master of Tatbury Hall, "the young scapegrace came down to my office this morning, and actually wasted twenty minutes of my business time in making me acquainted with his troubles—as if they interested me. It appears that his father was stabbed, or something or another, by the overseer of his station, four years ago, and that Yarranilla passed into the hands of the mortgagees. What little money remained, this young scamp has been amusing himself with; and now he has the assurance to apply to me for a situation, and even hints, something, about being in love with Agnes here; all on the strength of my knowing his father years ago!"

"Oh—ah!—in the old place, yes, yes!" exclaimed Jonas, looking round with a childish expression of pleasure on his face. "Ah, they say when people get old they don't remember things so well; but, bless you, I remember his father—Frank's father, I mean—when he used to come courting our Lucy more than twenty-two years ago! Why, don't you recollect some years before that how he advanced the money to set up that little shop in Whitechapel (that was before we came out here you know) and how the affair didn't pay, and—"

"There, there, father! that'll do," interrupted Mrs. Tatbury pettishly —"you always will bring in some nonsensical story about that ridiculous shop."

"Ridiculous!" cried the old man, shaking his head mournfully. "No, no, don't say ridiculous! I love to sit and think of old times and the dear old places, at home—sometimes it seems but yesterday that we quitted them; and if we did keep a shop, I often think we were a good deal merrier then than we are now;" and Mr. Jonas's face assumed quite a stubborn expression as he repeated, "No, no I say a shop isn't ridiculous, and there's nothing in poverty to be ashamed of."

"And I say there is!" growled Mr. Tatbury, as he threw the newspaper he had resumed to the floor. "You talk and talk, like the rest of them; but just answer me this—what business have people to be poor? Come now."

As this very defiant question seemed given as a decided challenge the old man looked helplessly around as if appealing for assistance, but finding none he at length ventured to suggest that "perhaps they couldn't help it!"

"Couldn't help it! Pshaw! I say they can help it," snarled his son-in-law. "Now look at me, Jonas Brooks; you know what I am and what I was. At ten years of age I was left without a parent—without a friend—to get my living, or to go without it! Well, I struggled on, and at twenty five married your daughter"—Mr. Tatbury nodded at his wife and looked about as amiable as a half-pacified hippopotamus. "You hinted just now, Jonas Brooks, at Frank Mayland's father rendering some trifling assistance. Well let that pass. I came out to Australia, and when I landed at the Circular Quay I was the possessor of fivepence-ha'penny. Think of that, sir! Five-pence-ha'-pen-ny!" and Mr. Tatbury looked so severely at his unfortunate father in-law, and so emphatically divided the miraculous sum, that Mr. Jonas flinched as if every syllable was a well-merited reproach.

"Now, Tatty, dear"—Mrs. T had a peculiar facility for abbreviating her husband's name—as a rule she used to bury the final portion, and call him "Tat"—but when high pressure coaxing was required his affectionate spouse habitually resolved his name, into "Tatty"—"Now, Tatty, dear; we all know about that, but don't—"

"Of course we all know about it, Mrs. T. with the exception, perhaps, of your father, here. I wished to freshen his memory respecting that particular period. You know what we were for a few years after we landed here, Jonas Brooks?"

Jonas inclined his head, and murmured something about "very poor."

"Of course we were!" cried Mr. Tatbury, triumphantly, "very poor! Now don't you think I could have remained so, if I had liked? Of course

I could—but I didn't like—so I worked myself up from nothing—or rather from fivepence-ha'penny," said Mr. Tatbury, correcting himself—and so might hundreds, if they chose, but they're an obstinate, mulish, pig-headed—"

How far his declamation against poverty would have extended I know not, but it was suddenly brought to a close by a little white hand placed on his lips: "Don't be hard with the poor, dear Uncle," said Agnes, throwing her arms round his neck, and kissing him.

"And why not pray?" rejoined Miss Angelina, giving her head such a toss that her shining ringlets shook again.

"The poor is hated of his own neighbour, but the rich hath many friends," answered Agnes quietly.

"She's right—she's right!" chuckled old Jonas, rubbing his hands briskly together, and rocking himself to and fro. "We weren't always as rich as we are now, but we never had so many friends before."

This was a fact which even the stubborn Mr. Tatbury could not controvert. His life's experience taught him that friends fluctuated with fortune, and that it was only when the marvellous "fivepence ha'penny" began to multiply exceedingly, that his acquaintances did likewise.

"I remember," continued the old man, reflectively, "a poor blind beggar, who was led about by a little dog; and every morning he used to come by our shop in Whitech—"

"Pish!" angrily ejaculated Mr. Tatbury. "Agnes may be right; in fact, I know she is—for I'm not such a heathen as to disbelieve the Book she quoted from, but if your confounded preaching isn't enough to make a man hate anything or anybody, I don't know what is!"

"Never mind, Tatty, dear," said his wife, in a consoling tone, as if soothing a refractory urchin; it's of no earthly use talking to father. Besides, what is the use of worriting ourselves about years ago?—we're happy and comfortable enough now, I'm sure."

But Mr. Tatbury wasn't quite so certain about it. True, he owned the house—and a very well behaved respectable house it was, in many respects but it sadly failed in one—it was haunted! A ghostly visitor defied its locks and bars, perambulated its passages, trespassed on the verandahs, and flitted about the garden beds.

Mr. Tatbury had tenanted the house some considerable time, but had only discovered that it was haunted a fortnight before my story commences. He said quite enough about it to alarm his wife, daughter, and servants; in fact, Bridget, the housemaid, reported having seen the ghost on two occasions; but as the spectre in one instance turned out to be a shirt left on the clothes-line, and in the other was proved to be the reflection from a neighbouring window, her testimony was not of much value.

As to Mrs. Tatbury, if the present popular inquiry of "Have you seen the ghost" had been addressed to her, truth would have compelled a negative answer, but she had seen and heard quite enough to render her uneasy.

Ever since Mr. Tatbury's revelations strange noises had been heard all over the house; the lights burnt in a most unaccountable manner, and there were perpetual scratchings, creakings, and scufllings, where there never had been such sounds before!

Doors slammed, and windows shook; as to the wind, it moaned most dismally, choking away in the chimneys as if each and all had a death-rattle in their throats; while in the middle of the night Mrs. Tatbury often fancied she heard that peculiar sound which Ingoldsby describes as "that of a coffin a-walking upstairs!"

All this (and much more) convinced Mrs. T. that there was something in her husband's assertion that the house was haunted; therefore she was not surprised when Mr. Tatbury shook his head mysteriously and remarked, "I can't make it out—it's very odd, very odd indeed! I allude to the—." Mr. T. didn't like the word ghost, so he looked more mysterious than ever, and nodded towards the door.

"You're quite sure you saw it?" inquired his wife.

"Am I sure I see you now, Mrs. T." interrogated Mr. Tatbury. Certainly something must have been wrong with the visual organs of anyone who couldn't see the portly figure so completely monopolising the ample arm chair.

"See it!—why, I've seen it a dozen times!—now gliding along the front verandah, now sitting in the back-garden, then melting away down towards the bay. I tell you I don't half like it, and if I had only known the facts of the case Tatbury Hall would never have got a coat of paint—or its rascally agent, the purchase money—out of my pocket."

"Well, it certainly is very annoying," coincided Mrs. Tatbury, "but you may have made a mistake, you know, Tat dear."

"What mistake could I make Mrs. T.? What could my imagination possibly shape into—into a—." Mr. Tatbury looked round nervously and the other inmates of the room glanced behind their respective chairs, and then at each other—as if each expected to find a spectral visitor waiting in the rear.

Despite the warmth of the evening, there was a clammy grave-like closeness to the air, and Mrs. Tatbury got up and moved her chair farther from the door.

As nobody seemed inclined to answer Mr. Tatbury's question as to the possibility of his being mistaken, Mr. Jonas mildly suggested "the pump."

"Moonshine!" growled his father-in-law.

Mr. Jonas explained that that was exactly what he meant! "The moonshine resting on the pump in the back-garden had suggested a ghost to the heated fancy—"

"Moonshine!—pump!—bah!" retorted the owner of the mansion. "Perhaps it was the pump I saw walking about in the front verandah, eh? Perhaps you'll suggest next that my 'heated fancy' was caused by an overdose of brandy, eh? Yes, if I had seen a couple of them you might have thought so! Pump! Humbug!"

Mr. Tatbury's face, grew fearfully red, and his white waistcoat rose and fell like the tide line when a steamer passes down the harbour. He picked up the *Empire*, and tried to fix his attention on the leading article, but the attempt was a miserable failure. The ghost not only haunted his house, but evidently haunted his mind, so he dropped the paper and continued: "I can't make out what the confounded thing comes into my house for!—and it is my house as right as law can make it. I've made every inquiry and can't find out that anybody's been drowned in the well, or buried in the garden. There was my old clerk, Jargs, who was found dead one morning with an empty brandy bottle for a bedfellow—but he had a cheque for his salary the day previous and even if he hadn't, he has no business coming out to Paddington. Then there was Tegsby, who shot himself, and Skimpinson, who broke his neck while riding—well, all our bills in their favour were taken up. I don't believe the firm owes either of them a farthing, and if we do, let them haunt the counting-house till the account's settled and not come out here to worry me. I'll tell you what, Mrs. T.; when a man comes to Australia with fivepence-ha'penny in his pocket, and after five and twenty years striving, gets a lift up and a house of his own, it isn't at all pleasant to have one more in the family than you bargained for."

"You never went up to it, to feel it, to touch it?" ventured Jonas.

"No, I didn't. I'm not a coward altogether, I can tell you; give me something or somebody I can lay hold of and I'll wager he won't trespass on Tatbury Hall again! But when you can't lay hold of it, what's the use of trying?" With this logical deduction Mr. Tatbury smote the table violently and added that he wouldn't mind giving the "thing" a hundred pounds if it would clear out of Tatbury Hall, and leave him in undisturbed possession.

"Then you really believe," said the old man, "the house is—."

Bang! went the door of a room upstairs; a gust of wind rushed through the fan-light; two or three hats fell down in the passage; and the table-lamp's flame gave a convulsive leap, and looked unmistakably blue!

Miss Angelica gave a faint scream; Mr. Tatbury glanced uneasily at the door; and Mr. Jonas hinted something about "never being troubled with ghosts in Whitechapel." Mrs. Tatbury advocated "getting ready for the party at Mrs. Crevner's," adding that "that dear man, Captain Chiselton," was to be one of the guests, and hinting at the admiration he had more than once expressed for "Angy"—as she fondly termed her daughter.

At Mrs. Tatbury's suggestion, Agnes preceded her aunt and cousin to the dressing room, not however to prepare to accompany them, but to assist at the toilette of the fascinating Angelina.

An hour afterwards the carriage rolled away with its burden of plea-sure-seekers; while Agnes drew a work-table from its recess, and was soon busily employed with the needle. Mr. Jonas Brooks sat in an old arm-chair, whose aspect suggested nothing but indolence and gazed sleepily out at the bright expanse of moonlight, as if in its flickering lights and shadows he could trace the well-remembered shop in Whitechapel.

It was a pleasant little picture; just such a stray glimpse of home and its attractions that quiet people love to look upon. The grey, bearded old man, and the fair-haired girl; he with fading memory peering down the misty avenues of the Past;—she, busy with the happy Present, and the no less pleasant Future!

Stitch! stitch! How nimbly her fingers plied the needle! How the gusty wind came whistling over the common making the leaves rattle against the casement as it rushed round the corner of the house; and what a tremendous effort it made to effect an entrance when the front door was opened and the family party took their departure for Mrs. Crevner's.

"Would you like Gabriel to come and talk to you, grandfather?" inquired Agnes (she always called him grandfather).

"Ay! ay! would I," assented the old man. "He seems to be the only one who remembers anything about old times and old places. Bring him in, Agnes, bring him in."

Agnes quitted the room and shortly afterwards returned with an individual, apparently older than even Jonas Brooks, who welcomed him right heartily, and rising from his armchair shoved the newcomer into the seat with such friendly force, that his breath took its flight as if it hadn't the slightest intention of coming back again.

"There sit you down there, Old Gabriel," cried Mr. Jonas in ecstasy, wheeling a chair so as to face his companion. "That's right, old fellow. Ah! this is as it should be."

A tremendous pull at the refractory bell and the sound of Bridget clattering along the passage to "answer the door," caused Jonas to give a guilty start; and the alarm depicted on the countenances of both old men suggested that the introduction of Gabriel to the parlour tended rather to make things as they shouldn't be.

"Bless me!—eh?—why?" exclaimed Mr. Brooks in a very ejaculative manner, "surely that's not Mr. Tatbury come back!—eh?"

"I think not, grandfather," replied the young lady, as she bent over her work; and whether from the reflections of the lamp we know not, the rosy tint seamed to deepen on her cheek.

"Is Mr. Tatbury within?" inquired a voice, as the front door opened.

"No, he bain't!" was the response of Bridget; who, after the manner of servant girls in general, paid little attention to correctness of language, and whose temper was acidulated by the energetic movement of the bell.

"Nor Mrs. Tatbury?" continued the voice.

"No, she bain't," answered Bridget.

"Dear me, how very unfortunate!—perhaps Miss Agnes is at home?"

In answer to this inquiry Bridget condescended to say that she "believed she was," and groping along the passage, thrust a head ornamented with a shock of very red hair, in at the parlour door, with the intimation that "a person at the door wished to see Miss Agnes."

"Show the gentleman into the drawing-room, Bridget, and light the table-lamp." And as Bridget departed on her errand Agnes put away her work, bent her rosy cheeks beside the withered face of old Jonas, and whispered something into his ear.

"Of course! my girl—of course!" he replied. "We'll have a talk about long, long ago while you're away. Won't we, Gabriel?"

Gabriel nodded.

"You remember the old shop, Gabriel—the place in Whitechapel?'"

"Lor, Master Jonas, I should say so! You don't think, surely, that sixteen thousand miles of salt water could wash away all recollection of home from an old fellow's heart!—eh, Master Jonas?"

Mr. Brooks protested that he never dreamt of such a thing; but leaving the old men in uninterrupted conversation let us follow Agnes to the drawing-room.

A gentleman rose from the couch as she entered, advancing to meet her, and addressing her by the simple yet endearing title, "Agnes!"

"Oh, Frank!" she whispered, as he retained her hand without the slightest apparent intention of releasing it, and drew her closer to him. "Oh Frank!—I feared that it was you."

"Feared? Surely Agnes, now that I have conquered my repugnance to cross this hated threshold, my visit is not an unwelcome one?"

Unwelcome not if an answer might be derived from the manner of Agnes, whose head nestled as confidingly on the newcomer's shoulder as if it had found its natural resting place at last. Indeed, the inquiry seemed to pain her deeply, for turning her tearful face appealingly to his, she whispered, "Dear Frank, do not blame me, you know how glad I am to see you, but my uncle—oh, I try to do everything for the best—indeed—indeed I do."

"Of course you do darling; I know you have enough to bear in your present position. As to Mr. Tatbury—"

"Don't blame him, Frank; indeed, he is often, very often, kind to me. He has little peculiarities of temper, but really he is very well, when you get accustomed to him."

"No doubt," responded the visitor, in a tone that implied much time and patience necessary in order to get accustomed to the little peculiarities of Mr. Tatbury's temper. "I'm not going to blame him dearest, especially as you seem retained for the defence, but I was just going to remark that if his behaviour at home matches that in his office a tiger robbed of her cubs is nothing to him. Why—but, never mind. Of course he is still inexorable?"

"I dare not, dare not, broach, the subject," she replied. "Even when your name is mentioned occasionally, I fear lest my agitation should betray the interest I feel in you. Why should this be? It is not, it cannot be wrong to give affection for your honest love; but still, I dread these meetings; surely to cause such fear, they must be wrong?"

"Wrong, Agnes?" replied the gentleman addressed as Frank—and who was, in fact none other than the identical "scapegrace" Frank Mayland mentioned by Mr. Tatbury.

"How on earth could such an idea cause you any uneasiness? Now, just calmly reason out the matter. In the first place there can be nothing wrong in giving your uncle his own free choice. He knows from my own lips that I love you as a honest man should love; he knows that opposition cannot move me, then it remains for him to decide whether I shall steal an interview here and there as an outlaw, or woo and win you as an honoured suitor. If he will not allow me to pursue the one course I can only resort to the other. Does not this seem reasonable?"

Now, taking into consideration that when love pleads with love, everything appears reasonable, we need not be at all surprised that this line of argument proved no exception to the rule, in the present case, and that Agnes confessed she thought it very reasonable.

"Do you think darling it is pleasant for me to be prowling round the house and grounds night after night as if I were thief? Yet thus have I been engaged for the last three weeks in hopes of getting a glimpse of your gentle face, and how often have I been rewarded? This is but the third time I have had an opportunity of speaking a few words to you. Sometimes I have crept into the front verandah—often for hours in the back garden, merely in hopes of seeing your loved shadow on the blind—and all this, remember, at the risk of being caught and treated as a trespasser.

"Our acquaintance has not been that of days, or weeks, dear Agnes. Your memory can carry your thoughts back ten, ay, twelve years ago when we were but children together. Don't you remember how our childish minds used to travel far, far back, and yet could never trace the time when our infant companionship began? At that time, my father was perhaps the most valued friend your uncle had, hence our acquaintance. My mother, who died when I was yet but an infant, I cannot image.

"I can well remember when ten years ago my father, enthusiastic in his ideas of country life, converted his business into cash, and purchased a small station in the Maneroo district. As vividly as if the parting had been but yesterday, I can picture my boyish frenzy at the idea of leaving you, perhaps for ever; I can remember your own tears and how you, a girl of eleven, and I, a boy of two years older, pledged ourselves never, never to forget each other. Of course, at the time, nothing could pacify me, but the novelty of the journey soon distracted my attention, and, childlike, my first great grief passed away with a few showers of tears.

"On reaching our new home, I found it very different from the one in Sydney, yet uncouth as it was in outward appearance, and ill arranged internally, the very novelty of its discomforts was a grand thing to a boy like me, and in a few months there was hardly a nook within five miles of Yarranilla that I had not thoroughly explored.

"Continually in the bush I, grew almost as wild and untutored as the animals that lurked in its recesses; and it was while lying on the verge of some mountain creek, listening to its soft gushing melody miles and miles from any habitation, that my boyish fancy for you, darling, grew into a deep, undying love—a love that has never swerved nor flagged.

"I need not thus detail every incident of my youthful life—suffice it, I was not suffered to dream on through a lazy existence. My father saw the necessity of education, and placed me under the charge of the clergyman stationed at the neighbouring township.

"At that time I was by no means averse to study, but while passing my days happily enough there, things went dreadfully wrong at Yarranilla. My father was totally unused to the management of a station. Blackfellows stole or speared his sheep—others died from disease. Most of the stock fell a prey to an organised band of cattle stealers, and in this extremity he secured the service of an individual named Mark Kingwood, to superintend the station. This man I never liked, and I believe he hated me thoroughly. He was my father's bane, and after his introduction things seemed to go on worse than ever. He was in league with those who had committed depredations among our cattle; he gradually drew my father into drinking and gambling till eventually the property was burdened with a heavy mortgage and one evening about four years ago I was summoned to Yarranilla, to find my father stabbed to the heart—lying dead—dead!

"The superintendent, Ringwood, and a shepherd known as Long Jim, were missing, and the place had been completely rifled. The police were immediately in pursuit, but returned after an unsuccessful search and from that day to this I have never set eyes on Ringwood or his companion—one of which I firmly believe to have been my father's murderer. Nothing remained for me but to sell the estate—pay off the mortgage, and try my fortune elsewhere.

"I crossed over to Victoria, and tried most of its townships, with various success, sometimes spending in one the little I had gained in the other. My object has been to attain such a position that I might come and claim the hand of my first and only attachment with confidence. I am sorry to say that success did not equal my expectations, and as a last resource I resolved to take passage to Sydney, and apply for employment or recommendation to Mr. Tatbury on whom I foolishly thought I could rely on account of his being my father's oldest friend and your uncle. I had written to him previously, and this morning's interview completely undeceived me. I left his office feeling insulted and degraded.

"Now I have no one to depend on—no one to love or to expect love from, save you. Dear Agnes, I shall be compelled to leave you and Sydney—but you will not desert me, darling?"

The only answer to this appeal was the single word "Never!" heard amid the fluttering sobs from the face upturned on his bosom, while the little hand mechanically tightened its grasp of his own.

"I ask you, dearest, because I have accepted a situation in Auckland, and leave by one of the New Zealand boats at daybreak on Christmas morning. I shall try and see you," he continued, "on Christmas Eve at all hazards, to wish you once more good-bye."

And then Mr. Frank Mayland seemed to dip the brushes of his imagination in the glowing colors of the rainbow, and painted such beautiful pictures on the wide canvas of the Future, that Agnes didn't know whether to give the preference to smiles or tears, and eventually divided it equally with a strange feeling of being very, very happy, and a vague fear of that happiness being too bright to last.

At all events it was near midnight when Frank took his departure which he was obliged to effect ingloriously through the back garden, on account of Mr. Tatbury's carriage driving unexpectedly up to the front door.

Agnes bade him a hurried farewell, and hastened back to the house.

As Mr. Tatbury entered his mansion, he exclaimed, triumphantly, "There, now! what do you say to that?" and not only he but also Mrs. Tatbury and Angelina, affirmed at the breakfast-table next morning, that they all had seen the ghost vanishing, over the back-garden fence.

Chapter II

It was Christmas Eve, and a beautiful, peace breathing, heart-soothing evening it was.

The day had been excessively hot, the sun throwing down his fervent rays till the air seemed to glow with a livid heat, and the scorching pavements had a quivering mirage dancing over them.

Later in the day heavy masses of clouds gathered in the west, looking very threatening, but very unwilling to come to the contest and an ominous silence prevailed, like that which precedes the crash of opposing armies.

It promised to be a bad night for business especially to the temporary stalls fringing the Haymarket; and the itinerant merchants in that quarter looked up anxiously at the sulphureous banks of vapour piled overhead.

At length it came! Such a flash of lightning! such a continuous cracking peal of thunder, rumbling and shaking till it died away at last into a weary grumble. As to the rain, it fell in great, distinct, spattering spots, each one coming down quite independent of its neighbour, as if it had a small private account of its own to settle with the parched earth below, and was determined to "hit him hard." Then the wind gave a gusty moan, in a sort of bass voice, just by way of giving the rain a spell—then it ran up the scale, touching the upper notes in this concert of the elements, and roared and screamed in a most dreadful manner. Then the rain fell in thick blinding sheets, the wind driving it in smoky mists along the house-tops—and then they went at it altogether—thunder and lightning, wind and rain!—flashing and crashing, and howling and spitting over the city to their hearts' content.

Like a man who gives unbridled license to his fury, who, during the few minutes of his passion, breaks everything breakable, and concludes by maintaining, "Well, if I am a little hasty—it's soon over!", such is our Australian climate during the summer months.

People were not at all surprised on this particular Christmas Eve when the rain ceased falling, the wind changed its stormy gusts into deliciously cool breezes and the sun sank in the west, leaving a crimson glare on the sky, as if blushing at the last hour's strife.

As for the stars! I shouldn't like to say how bright and jolly-looking they came out, winking and blinking at each other, as if congratulating themselves upon being high out of all the confusion that had reigned below. Why up in the clear sky overhead a regular jeweller's shop seemed opened, with glittering trinkets hung all about it; in fact, when I say that the stars shone, as stars only can shine in Australia—I need say no more.

Business went on brisker than ever—butchers chopped and sawed, and cut off giant joints. Joints that would persist in looking out of their owners' baskets, in spite of all endeavours to keep them confined; grocers made up dainty little parcels, giving the change, and the compliments of the season, to pretty girls, in a manner pleasant to behold, while the poulterer's shops exhibited lines of long-necked fowls, like rows of notes of admiration at the plentiful cheer provided for all—who had money enough to pay for it.

The erstwhile deserted stands at the Haymarket were re-arranged and re-peopled as if by magic—vendors with anything but musical voices, extolling the merits of the olla podrida of things new and old, and purchasers (with a good deal to buy and very little to buy it with) chaffering at the prices of the "thousand and one" articles offered for sale.

Leaving the Haymarket we pass down George-street towards the north—and look at the rich red blossoms of the Christmas bush, with its glossy leaves painted with raindrops glinting and quivering in the light flushing out of the public house doors.

Here is a blind man singing something, the words of which cannot be distinguished, and which hasn't the slightest resemblance to a tune! Never mind, for dear charity's sake throw a trifle in his old hat—it is Christmas Eve.

Earlier still down George-street and a man with a villainous expression of countenance—far too villainous for Christmas Eve!—passed, slouching down the road; pushing his way through the crowded thoroughfare in a very un-Christmas-like manner.

Turning up Argyle-street where the water, from the over-charged gutters of the streets above poured down in dismal little cataracts, he clambered the flight of stone steps, and emerged upon that dreary, unprogressive and generally disreputable region, known as "The Rocks," the most ancient portion of this city of Sydney. "The Rocks" as a locality retains much of its old vice and squalor. Advancement seems to have turned aside as it her golden footsteps shunned this particular point—this region of drunken men, wretched women, squalid children and quarrelsome dogs! In truth it is a desolate collection of miserable habitations, with inhabitants to match!

However its poverty did not seem to occasion any surprise to the man whom I have mentioned, for he pursued the sinuous turnings in a manner proclaiming that he had a thorough knowledge of the locality, and ended his wanderings before a low-browed house of shabby exterior, over which hung a sign-board announcing it to be the "Three Jolly

Reefers," and certainly, if happiness consisted in sky-blue jackets and ver-million faces, the three gentlemen depicted on the sign-board looked "jolly" enough.

As the individual paused beneath the flaming lamp fitted over the doorway—which appeared to be a sort of second entrance not connected with the bar—there was time to glance at his appearance. His clothes were of a character known as "shabby genteel," and were rather of a fash-ionable style; but what struck you at once as being very remarkable was the utterly hopeless expression of his face. Like a worn out coin, there was still the image and superscription of mankind upon him—but how de-graded and defaced! The demon Drink had set its glare in his eye, and its Cain-like stamp upon his forehead; had wound its enslaving coils around him, fettering body and soul, robbing him of everything that makes exis-tence sweet and holy and leaving him nothing but the reflection that the world would be a good deal better and wholesomer without him.

A low whistle soon gained him admittance—the portal being opened by an American negro, whose shining visage was surmounted by an old scarlet night-cap. This dusky janitor carefully chained and bolted the door, leaving the new arrival in the dark to shuffle along the passage to the inner room to which he was guided by the clinking of glasses and laughter within.

The company assembled in this apartment consisted chiefly of seafar-ing men who despite the horrible atmosphere of the place were roaring out some monotonous sea-song, the peculiarity of which lay in the repe-tition of certain "Tol de rol de lol's" at the end of about every four words. This choice melody was varied by occasional oaths and technical slang indulged in by the company.

"H'order! h'order! Gentlemen!—Mr. Glippery will oblige!" shouted a grimy looking man who seemed to have been constituted president of this convivial assemblage, and who enforced his remarks by knocking on the board with a tumbler, "Si-lence! Gentlemen! H'order for Mr. Glip-pery's song!"

Thus introduced, and having first smiled benignly at the company in general and frowned in particular at an impatient individual who cried, "Go it, Glippy," Mr. Glippery proceeded to invite his audience to "come to his mounting 'Ome," in a cracked voice which got through the song by periodical jumps forcibly reminding you of a barrel-organ with a severe cold settled on its lungs!

Immediately on the entrance of the man whom we have tracked to the "Jolly Reefers," and whose name I might as well mention, was Jim Badnidge, he was joined by a tall, gentlemanly-looking personage, the nicety of whose dress contrasted strangely with the rough attire of those with whom he was associated.

He at once drew the new arrival to an unoccupied corner of the room; and, without any of the common-place expressions usually form-ing the key to conversation, abruptly asked, "Have you seen him?"

Before answering this seemingly important question, Mr. Badnidge requested to be supplied with some liquor, which he metaphorically termed "a spider;" declaring that "until he had suthin' to drink he couldn't talk nohow, as his throat war as dry as a brickbat!"

"Well, be quick about it!" responded his companion. "I told you directly the steamer arrived to let me know, and here have I waited in this hole for your coming part of every night for a fortnight. Where have you been?"

"Hold hard, noble captain!" urged Mr. Badnidge apparently in no hurry to come to business. "Ah! that's suthin' like!" he added approvingly, as he transferred the contents of a capacious tumbler down an equally capacious throat. "If there's one thing I hate, it's water! I don't know when I tuk a drink of it before this last week or two, and then I couldn't help it. Now this 'ere 'spider' brandy dosed, with lemonade, ain't at all bad, but water ain't no business to be in a public-house, nohow! As regards where have I bin? Why in a variety of places, principally in Darlinghurst—cos' why?—I happened to turn into an auctioneer's shop, and just felt in my pockets to see whether I had enough money to buy a weskit, when what does I do but puts my hand into somebody else's pocket, and takes out a 'portmanteau' with five and threepence in it! Well, before I had time to explain the mistake, the cove collars me, and won't listen to nuffin! Of course I told the magistrate exackerly how it happened, but he said he thought as how if I spent a fortnight in Darlinghurst I wouldn't be missed by nobody! You see he didn't know as how you was a waiting along of me here!"

"And the young fellow?" inquired the other, who had allowed his companion to run on till want of breath compelled a stoppage.

"He's right," answered Mr. Badnidge. "He arrived here before I got into trouble. Yes, the Wonga came in the evening afore, and I had to carry my young gent's carpet-bag up a hill to the bus. First of all, you see he leaves his swag at the Post Office Hotel, and then out he comes, gits into a Paddington bus, I gits outside, and away we goes! When we gits out there I hears him arskin about a Mr. Fat-belly's house—"

"Tatbury—Mr. Tatbury you mean," interrupted the tall man.

"Ah—yes—I knowed it was suthin' like that! Well, he finds the house—a big place with green palins—round the front the goes, then down the back, thinks I, 'you're up to suthin' young gentleman!'— presently out come a young 'ooman—hurries down to the bushes in the back garding and shakes hands with the young feller o'er the fence—just like a scene in a Hopera!—then he gives her a paper—rubs noses and bolts off to the bus. I meant to come and tell you next night—when this misfortunate mistake goes and pervents me. That's all I knows about it." And as reward for this long piece of jaw-work (as he called it) Mr. Jim Badnidge drained his glass, and requested "Liza" to replenish it while he filled his pipe.

"Then he has arrived, has he?—curse him!" said the long gentleman, savagely.

"Oh! as much as you please, for all I care!" coincided Mr. Badnidge, "but I say Mr. Ringwood—"

"Hush!" hissed the other.

"Well—Chiselton—"

"Hold your fool's clatter!" growled the tall man, emphasising the request with an oath. "Neither of these names will do here! If you must have a name for me, call me Smith—that'll do—John Smith!"

"Just as you please," agreed Mr. Badnidge; "but now Mr. John Smith or Ringwood, or Chiselton or whatever your purser's name is!—considirin' as how the bird's bagged, or put into your hands (which is just as good)— what about the—?" And Mr. Badnidge slapped his trousers pockets.

"All right!" responded the man, whom I shall for the future name as Smith. "You're sure, you know where to pitch on him again?"

"As right," replied the other, emphatically striking the table with his clenched hand, "as right as ninepence!"

What powerful virtue is contained in this particular quantity of coppers to make it such a model of correctness I cannot pretend to say, suffice it that the simile appeared to have one weight with Mr. Smith, who took an old gold-bag from his pocket, counted out some silver, and pushed it over to Jim Badnidge.

That gentleman having carefully counted the money, as carefully stowed it away in his pocket and remarked "You hardly seem satisfied about its being the right cove, but you don't mean for to go for to think as how I could forget his likeness to the old chap at Yarranilla, as we—eh?— you know!" and Jim sharpened an imaginary knife on his boot, and made a stab at the air, by which pleasant little piece of pantomime he conveyed the idea of sticking a pig.

"Hush!" whispered Smith, looking round anxiously at the company.

"Blessed if I didn't think it was his ghost, as I watched him a coming over the Wonga's gangway; his eyes regular mates of the other—"

"Hold your tongue, will you!" hissed Mr. John Smith, with an imprecation which, if consummated, would have had a peculiarly blighting effect on the visual organs of Mr. Badnidge.

"Oh no, we never mentions him!" chanted that individual, "It's all serene, old fellow, it's the youngster, safe enough!"

"But now, captain, as that affair's settled, what's to be the next move—and what's the little game out at Paddington?"

"Well Jim," replied the other, "I want your assistance out there tonight. Since I last saw you, I haven't been idle, but under the name of Captain Chiselton, I have been introduced to more than one 'highly respectable' family. The one I have chosen for our operations is that of Mr. Tatbury—the place to which you tracked young Mayland—and I have managed to become thoroughly acquainted with the premises. I had intended to find a way to old Tatbury's fortune through his daughter, and regularly settle down till the money was spent; but I am afraid that plan won't work; besides the arrival of this youngster, who is somehow acquainted with the family, makes it dangerous for me to visit too often. Now, I've decided on making short work of it. Through the servants I hear that old Tatbury keeps a considerable sum in ready cash at home—that is to pay for our trouble tonight!

"He is dreadfully superstitious, believes in ghosts, and actually fancies the house is haunted!—this will assist us wonderfully. Acting the part of a ghost myself, I have no fear of any resistance on the part of Mr. Tatbury, if there should be"—Mr. Smith unbuttoned his vest and showed the hilt of a bowie-knife stuck in his belt. "If there should be, why I have something here that does its work well, and doesn't make any noise about it."

"You'll excuse me arksin such a thing," apologised Mr. Badnidge, "but I've always felt shaky since that 'ere affair at the station; there's no truth about the place bein' haunted, eh?"

"Haunted?—no!—but it will be tonight, and a rare couple of ghosts we'll make. I don't want to hurt old Tatbury, provided he won't make a noise but if I come across that youngster, who has hunted and tracked me for the last four years, down he goes, to follow his father. Now, Jim, you mustn't have any more of that stuff tonight—steady and sure is the motto; and the prize is too good to throw away, so no more drink tonight, I say!"

"All right, captain, just one more 'go' to steady a fellow's nerves, and then I'm at your service. How about the time?"

Mr. Smith consulted a handsome watch, and said that in an hour it would be time enough to start; suggesting the propriety of getting the "tools" together in the meantime—an idea in which Mr. Badnidge coincided, so draining his glass they left the public house together.

***

Christmas Eve and the night was far advanced—the stars looking quietly down on Tatbury Hall.

The moon was in her last quarter, and her silver edge was just appearing above South Head, throwing the bays into deeper obscurity, and gradually starting and shivering on the harbour's rippling surface, till it looked like a ragged crucible of molten silver.

Night quiet, quiet night—and the scrubby dwarfish trees in the enclosure rose up dark and wiry from the gloom. Night sombre silent night—and Tatbury Hall seemed like a mansion of the dead.

The family had retired early, each occupied with his or her own thoughts. Mrs. Tatbury thought of the grand dinner-party coming off on the morrow, and of fifty improbable things, any of which if they happened might mar the prospects of the whole.

Miss Angelina dreamt of the envy of all young ladies who should be introduced to the mysterious (and therefore charming) Captain Chis-elton.

Mr. Tatbury pondered on the probable expense of the forthcoming fete; and wondered whether the dreaded phantom would absent himself from Tatbury Hall for that occasion only. While old Jonas went to bed, and in dreams recollected bygone Christmas days in the little shop in Whitechapel.

There was one lonely watcher, however, in the silent house. At her bedroom window sat Agnes Tatbury—dear, pleasant-voiced little Agnes—quieter than ever as she looked out on the landscape bathed in the trembling moonshine.

Occasionally in our early years incidents take place that are indissolubly linked with the future. Years may pass away, and the trifling word, the insignificant act of our childish days, may be almost forgotten; but the seed has grown on silently yet surely, and we are suddenly surprised by seeing the flower burst forth in all its beauty. So with Agnes Tatbury; she had loved Frank Mayland when a child as children do love; after a few months' absence the image of her boy-lover gradually began to fade. Not that something more solid or real usurped its place. Agnes lived on single-hearted, shedding a halo of love on all around her, and when at last she received a letter from Frank hoping that her childish feelings were unchanged—yet fearing that they were—she felt that the love of the past had not lain dormant in her breast, but had grown with her growth and strengthened with her strength.

Accustomed as she had been to notice the want of genuine feeling displayed by the Tatbury family, her heart clung to this letter, recalling sweet recollections, and the whole tendrils of her affectionate nature seemed to twine around the writer.

She had anticipated little opposition on the part of her uncle, and was therefore astonished to find the visits of Frank Mayland not only discountenanced but entirely forbidden. Added to this was the thought of the rapidly approaching time of parting, for she knew that in a brief half hour the last fond word, "Good bye," would be spoken, and each fleeting hour of the morrow, would increase the distance between the loving and the loved.

Taking all this into consideration, we may easily account for tear-drops glistening on the cheek of Agnes, and imagine the haste with which she left her place of watching, to join a figure that stood out in the clear moonlight in the space below.

Throwing a dark shawl around her, and taking a hat from the hall-pegs, she passed through the little wicket leading to the back garden.

Upon her entrance Frank Mayland started from behind a rose bush, where he had taken refuge on hearing the door open, and the faint scream which this abrupt appearance elicited was prevented from more than half escaping by the application of a pair of lips to those of Agnes.

Of course there is no necessity for me to enter into the details of their conversation, as they sat in that rambling, wind-shaken, any-thing-but-summer-looking summer-house. We all have had some little experience of what is usually said on such occasions; and if I were to tell you how the tears of present sorrow fell fast, and how the sunshine of future happiness came bursting out of the darkness, until the beautiful rainbow of Hope shone glittering on the clouds, why, you would say, "oh, that's old!—I've heard and seen enough of that myself!"

However, I only want you to understand that there was a conversa-tion; and also that while it was going on, two fresh arrivals drew near the grounds of Tatbury Hall—being, in fact, no other than Mr. Jim Bad-nidge and his companion or employer, Mark Ringwood, alias Captain Chiselton or (as we have before spoken of him) Mr. John Smith.

"It looks quiet enough, but there ain't never a cloud to shut up the moon's cussed blaze!" remarked Mr. Badnidge, as he deposited a bundle by the fence, and looked up at the bright dome above. "Now, d'ye see, I think as how it would be advisable to try the front cos' yer see, this being Christmas Eve werry likely the servants'll be up a getting the grub ready for tomorrow and if we begin at the back, where they may be moving about, there's a chance of being interrupted in our work, which ain't by no means pleasant!"

"Well, there's sense in that remark, Jim, if you never make another!" answered his companion, who moreover directed Mr. Badnidge to bring the tools round to the front.

There beneath the shade of the verandah, they set to work and soon evidenced by the ease and quietness with which they cut through a panel of the door and withdrew the fastenings, that neither was a novice at his present employment.

"All right Jem," whispered Mr. Smith, as they slipped off their boots and stepped about, light as cats, in the passage. "Now for the ghost's dress—hand us the windingsheet!"

Jim unrolled it from the bundle—his hand shaking excessively as he did so.

"Why, what's the matter, man?" asked his companion. "You tremble like a leaf!"

"Hang it all!" muttered Jim, surlily, "I don't half fancy this affair since you mentioned about the house being haunted. In fact, since that 'ere job at Yarranilla, I've allers felt shaky, in the dark! I know as how 'dead men tell no tales,' and I ain't got no cause to be afeard on that account, but—"

"Afraid! of course you haven't! I never said the house was haunted—but if this old fool believes it is, why that makes it all the easier for us. Come, hand us the barker and let's have no more child's play!"

Thus adjured, Mr. Badnidge noiselessly rummaged out a revolver for Mr. Smith, as likewise a keen-edged weapon, which gave a dull sulky flash, and which Mr. Badnidge technically called a "tickler."

"Now then, Jem! all you've got to do at present is to follow me, and keep quiet. I'll manage the rest. But, if the old woman isn't too frightened to scream, and should pipe out, why, I leave that to you; only don't make more noise over it than you can help."

Up the broad flight of stairs stole the two men—lust in their hearts, and murder in their minds—on the holy peace breathing eve of Christmas!

The one called Smith led the way like one accustomed to the place; and halting before Mr. Tatbury's bedroom door (in order to adjust his grave-like attire) he quietly turned the handle, and glided softly into the room.

I said that on this particular evening Mr. Tatbury retired to bed early. He did so, but not to rest.

Mr. Tatbury couldn't make it out. He had not made a hearty meal before going to bed, so his restlessness could not proceed from his supper. He had not been annoyed or excited to any extraordinary degree—so it couldn't be that. At all events something lay heavy on his conscience—or his stomach—and scared "kind nature's sweet restorer" from his eyelids.

He thought of all manner of unpleasant things too! He cast up in his mind—like a long column of figures—the events of the three hundred and sixty odd days which had elapsed since the previous Christmas; and when he did add them up and saw "what they came to" he felt very dissatisfied with the result. In particular he felt that he had acted very ungratefully to the son of his old friend Mr. Mayland; and at last got so miserable over his reflections that he groaned aloud—then he tossed the bedclothes from him, and peered out into the dim half-lighted room.

The bed was surrounded with mosquito-curtains, and through these he could see but imperfectly—nevertheless something very white, started upon his vision; and his excited fancy speedily framed the dreaded spectre of Tatbury Hall, sitting in the corner!

Mr. Tatbury tried to "pooh, pooh" the idea but after some futile attempts to make something really definite and earthly of the quiet, immoveable thing from his then present position, he mustered sufficient courage to slip out of bed, and found to his great relief that the "ghost" consisted of some drapery hanging on the towel-horse.

Again Mr. Tatbury tried to woo fickle sleep, but his addresses were rejected. He buried his head in the pillow, dragged the bedclothes over it, breathed regularly, and tried to cheat himself into the belief that he was "going off," but the attempt was a wretched failure, and he thrust out his head and opened his eyes despairingly, at the very instant that the bedroom door slowly opened and a tall figure in spectral garments stole into the apartment.

There was no mistake about it this time! The thing glided along—noiselessly as though it were treading on clouds—towards a large rosewood object that filled, or almost filled, the further end of the room.

To say that Mr. Tatbury was frightened would convey but a slight idea of his feelings. The perspiration trickled in beads from his forehead, and poured from every pore, while he experienced a strange sensation all over his head, as if every hair was making "a long try, a strong try, and a try altogether" to shove his night-cap off! He was too much alarmed to move, and therefore made no effort to awaken Mrs. Tatbury; but lay watching with dilated eye-balls the movements of his unwelcome visitor.

Without the slightest noise, the cabinet opened its recesses, and the figure was gliding to the door by which it had entered, when a sound struck upon the ear of Mr. Tatbury that at once aroused him from inaction—that was, the rattling of his cash-box!

We heard Mr. Tatbury on a previous occasion assert that "he wasn't afraid of anything he could lay hold of;" and I must say that, however devoid of moral he was not destitute of physical courage. Now he no sooner heard the jingling of the golden coins together, than he reasoned instantly: "That box is too heavy to be carried by spectral fingers!" and with a dreadful roar, scrambled out of bed, and rushed at the figure, grappling as he did so, not with thin air but with real flesh and blood in the shape of long John Smith, the burglar!

"Thieves! Fire! Murder!" screamed Mr. Tatbury, as he snatched frantically at his cash box, and hung on to the intruder like a bull-dog.

"Thieves! Fire! Murder!" shrieked Mrs. Tatbury, whom the scuffle had awakened, and who, not knowing what was the matter, thought there could be no harm in following her husband's cry!

"Jim!" hissed Mr. Tatbury's assailant, "quiet the old woman!"

Jim appeared from the landing place; but quieting a woman (old or young at all times a difficult matter!) was on this occasion put out of the question altogether by the lady darting to the window, throwing it open, and screaming frantically for assistance.

Jim darted forward, but could not drag her from the casement. The blind was torn down, and a bright flood of moonshine shimmered through the room.

Mr. Tatbury still hung on to his cash-box, but was evidently growing weaker, the burglar pressing heavily on his chest with the sharp angle of his elbow digging into Mr. Tatbury's throat in a very unpleasant manner!

Mr. Tatbury's breath came and went in convulsive jerks, his hands relaxed and Mr. John Smith, having drawn the "tickler" from its sheath, had his arm raised to give the finishing stroke when the door was dashed violently open and he found himself in the sturdy grasp of Mr. Tatbury's Ghost!

Leaving his old, and now insensible, antagonist, the burglar grappled, for life or death with his new assailant.

Over and over they rolled, like wild beasts—but the new comer had the best of it, and as he held the other with face upturned in the moonlight, he ejaculated the single word "Ringwood!"

At the name Mr. Badnidge released the straggling Mrs. Tatbury—looked upon "Mr. Tatbury's Ghost"—gasped, "Mayland—Yarranilla!"

and with a terrific yell, darted from the room, and was heard rolling down the stairs.

And now other sleepy, and perplexed performers appeared on the scene—Mr. Jonas Brooks and old Gabriel, while the alarmed neighbours began to venture in at back and front and crowded up to the scene of battle.

Once the burglar managed to loosen his knife, but the stroke at Frank Mayland's breast was a faulty one, and the next instant the weapon lay at the other side of the room; then he clutched his revolver; and this time the chances seemed in his favour: there was a quick blinding flash, a ringing report and with a convulsive leap Mr. Tatbury's Ghost staggered back and fell at the feet of Agnes.

Before, however, the burglar Smith could regain his feet, he was deprived of consciousness by old Jonas, who struck him severely across the forehead with a chair—observing, as he did so, that "there wasn't any bushrangers in Whitechapel!"

***

Christmas Day—and the sun shone out, right merrily. Christmas Day—and the bells leaped for joy, to think of the peace and goodwill to men that came upon the earth once, and for ever.

Sunshiny, jolly-faced, heart-beaming, love-arousing Christmas Day!—on which if a man suffers an ill-humoured expression to dwell on his face, he ought to hang upon a gallows as high as that of Haman.

But Christmas Day has its influence on the hardest of hearts, and over the most ill-natured temperaments—a feeling pervading the crustiest of mortals, and tempting him to lay aside his peevishness "for this day only"—just as he hangs up his greatcoat and umbrella in the hall, until the sunshine again gives place to rain.

Well, when the burglar, Smith, on our Christmas morning came to his senses, he did so to find himself tied up hand and foot with a clothes-line; in fact there was such a superabundance of knots (every one having lent a hand to tie up this desperado), that it seemed an improbable chance of his ever being unloosed again!

As to Mr. Jim Badnidge, he had missed his footing at the head of the stairs, and had been precipitated down the whole flight, with such violence that his neck was broken there and then; an event which probably, saved it being done in a more scientific manner at some later period.

Frank Mayland, the Ghost of Tatbury Hall, awoke to consciousness and to the fact that somebody was standing at the bedside, with two tear dimmed eyes, looking down to his. Mr. and Mrs. Tatbury were there too, with old Jonas and the doctor, and even Miss Angelina (who had double locked herself into her bedchamber on the first alarm) mentally confessed that Frank Mayland was not such a bad-looking fellow, after all!

Of course Mr. Tatbury was profound in his expressions of gratitude—laughed heartily at the idea of having so long mistaken Frank for a ghost and urged him to make some request, the fulfilment of which would be an adequate return for the service he had rendered.

Some men—if they are warmed up to make a generous offer, feel sorry directly the offer has been made. Now, I should be sorry to assert that this was the case with Mr. Tatbury, but, certainly, he looked very much relieved when Frank asked him for the hand of Agnes—long-loved and long-loving Agnes!—as his only reward.

Some years have passed, and many Christmas chimes have rung since the time when these incidents occurred but never again has Mr. Tatbury had reason to believe that his house was haunted. He now lives on in undisturbed serenity (as far as ghosts are concerned), and is altogether as happy as a man ought to be, who made his fortune from fivepence ha'penny!

Old Jonas and old Gabriel still linger on, as talkative and stubborn as ever, and still possessing a firm belief in the merits of the "little shop in Whitechapel." As to Miss Angelina, she is still unmarried, and it is the opinion of all that her temper has not improved with age.

As to Agnes, she has been Mrs. Frank Mayland some years. Her husband has been fortunate in more respects than one—fortunate in business, as well as in marriage, and they are now residents in the Monaro district, Frank having repurchased Yarranilla.

It is there, dear reader, I would ask you to accompany me, before we wish each other the compliments of the season and say "goodbye."

It is Christmas Eve again, and the Australian bush is bright with a thousand hues, and merry with the whistle and clatter of birds with restless wings. The creek which in its windings nearly surrounds the station, is lined on either side with the "mimosa" or wattle-tree covered with gorgeous garments of scented golden flowers.

Now the sun goes down in haste, birds hush their clamour, and the creek tinkles onward into the shadows with a quiet gentle song.

Regardless of the closing night, two figures are sitting on the river bank, looking back to other times, to Christmas days passed long, long ago. And as Agnes Mayland thinks of all the grief that might have been, and of all the love that is, she leans back with a sigh and a smile on the manly breast of "Uncle Tatbury's Ghost."

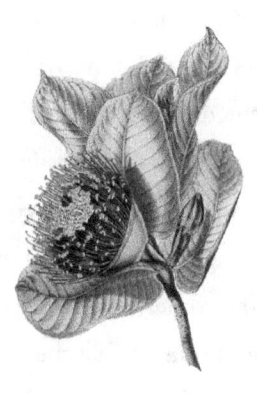

The Rightful Heir:
An Australian Christmas Story

Mrs. W. Morrice

Chapter I

In one of the flower-starred gardens that slope down to Woolloomooloo Bay, the bright sun was shining on a party of young people engaged in playing lawn-tennis. The gay dresses of the ladies made pretty patches of colour against the dark background of Norfolk pines and Moreton Bay fig-trees, and light, girlish laughter, mingling with the deeper tones of men's voices, rung pleasantly across the blue waters. Somewhat apart from the others were a lady and gentleman, who seemed so engrossed by each other's conversation that they paid but little attention to the game; and as these two persons are of more interest to us than any of the others, we shall, with the reader's permission, take a closer survey of them.

The lady was a tall, graceful girl whose fair beauty was set off advantageously by the pale-blue summer dress, its sweeping folds arranged with more artistic regard to the wearer's personal attractions than is usually the case in this present time of fashionable eccentricity. A broad straw hat, with blue ribbon and a bunch of forget-me-nots shaded a face which no beholder would be likely to pass by without notice, or, having noticed it, not turn to look at once more. The small, aquiline features were relieved, from their somewhat proud and resolute expression by the charming, dimpling smile, and by the soft light that beamed from the large, deep blue eyes shaded by dark, sweeping lashes. The healthy bloom on her delicately rounded cheeks, her abundant soft brown hair, and pearly teeth, were the envy of all her lady friends; and Marion Halstead rejoiced in the possession of her rare beauty, and was ready to enjoy life with all the zest, of youth and health. Whether she was as ready to make life enjoyable to others is a question to be solved. At present she was simply a thoughtless, light-headed girl of nineteen, fancy free, and ignorant of any of the higher demands of life. The purifying life of sorrow or love had not yet refined her inner life, and given it a nobler impulse towards self-renunciation for the sake of others. Her companion was a delicately featured, slightly-built young man about twenty-three years of age, a specimen of a well-bred Englishman with a pleasant, boyish face and refined drawl.

"And how do you like Australia, Mr. Northbrook?" asked the young lady as they stood together in the shade of a large magnolia, while the soft, warm air wafted the perfume from the gem-like flower-beds towards them.

"Well, you see, I haven't had a fair opportunity of forming an opinion on the subject yet," replied the young man, languidly.

"I have only seen Sydney and—aw—the suburbs as yet; and I must say Sydney does seem rather slow to a fellow who has been used to Rotten Row, and—aw—to Ascot, you know: but the harbour's stunning, and these gardens and villas can't be beaten—quite too, too, you know. I must say, however, I'm longing to get to my station: first-rate fun going after the kangaroos and emus, I believe. But now I shall take the liberty of asking you the same question, for didn't we come over in the same steamer, and haven't you been absent so long from your native land that you must feel awfully like a stranger?"

"If you want to know how I like Australia," replied Miss Halstead with a light laugh, "I must say like you that I don't care much for Sydney, but I feel sure I shall like being on the station, and, like you, I am longing to get there."

"I am delighted to find that we have some sympathies in common. Are you going to Queensland before Christmas?"

"Yes, we shall start for Brisbane in a few days, and intend spending our Christmas time at my uncle's station, Melangole."

"Then I hope to have the pleasure of seeing you frequently, for my station, Windemere, joins Melangole, I believe, and I shall make it a point of calling at once on Mr. Clovelly whose superior judgment and experience will be of great assistance to a new chum like myself."

"Oh, Uncle Clovelly doesn't trouble himself much about station matters; he has never been quite himself, since his wife's death. He leaves nearly everything to his super., a young man in whom he has unbounded confidence."

"Then I shall ingratiate myself with the super.," said Frank Northbrook, laughing; "anything, you know, for an excuse to be near you."

Before Marion could answer this complimentary speech the tete-a-tete was interrupted by the approach of two ladies, one of whom bore a striking resemblance to Marion, while the other was evidently young Northbrook's mother.

"Dear, dear," said Mrs. Halstead who was fair and slender like her daughter, but lacked the proud resolution that characterised Marion's face, "what a terrible heat. Marion, my dear child, you will be scorched out here; and no veil to save your face. The Australian sun is trying to fair complexions, don't you think so, dear Mrs. Northbrook? But I forgot, you have so little experience of the Australian summer, and you have no daughters to worry about their complexions, so there you have a trouble less on your mind. Dear, dear, you cannot imagine what a worry dear Marion's complexion has always been to me. So fair-skinned as she is, and so careless, and always running wild at the station as children will do. It was really quite a comfort to me in my bereavement when I lost my poor husband, who was killed by a fall from his horse, for he was head-strong, was my poor John, and never would listen to me, though times and times I've said to him—'John, I've a presentiment that you'll be killed off a horse someday,' but as I was saying it was quite a consolation to me to think that we would leave Queensland and live in England before dear

Marion's skin would be destroyed. I shouldn't wonder now," added the good lady, looking at Frank, "if your face should become quite blistered by the Queensland sun. I've known many young men just out from England—one man particularly—but I'm not sure whether he wasn't from Ireland: you remember Mr. O'Flynn, Marion?—no, that wasn't his name either; it was something with an O, I'm sure—it might have been Osborne—but it doesn't matter. Anyway, he was fair, like you, only I think his hair was very red, but his nose blistered, and all the skin came off—quite dreadful to look at, really: but cold cream is an excellent thing for sunburn. Let me recommend you to try cold cream, Mr. Northbrook, if your skin should get blistered."

"Thank you," said Frank, laughing; "I don't think I shall find it necessary to adopt such extreme measures."

"My son," said Mrs. Northbrook, a stately lady with a deep voice and clearly-cut features, "is accustomed to the exposure of sun and wind: he has been camping out with his regiment at the autumn manoeuvres. But it is a foolish thing in my opinion to spend Christmas at the station. Of course, I don't know much about station life, but from what I've heard, servants are very scarce, indeed, out there, and distressingly ignorant when you do get them. I have been told of a lady who actually was obliged to prepare the Christmas dinner with her own hands, owing to the scarcity or incapacity of servants, which is a truly lamentable state of affairs. It would have been much better to have spent our Christmas in England; such hardships as I have alluded to would simply kill me. My poor husband would never have exposed me to such a life: he always lived in England on my account. But Frank has taken the unhappy notion that, now his poor father's gone, he'll manage the station himself; so here we are, and God only knows what is before us." Mrs. Northbrook concluded her speech with a long sigh, and looked reproachfully at her son, who coloured, and fidgeted, and looked extremely uncomfortable.

"You might get the blacks to help you," said Mrs. Halstead, reflectively. "They are ready enough to work sometimes, only you must not give them anything to eat before they have finished their work, or else they will just lie down and sleep for the rest of the day. Do you remember Julia, Marion?—was it Julia now or Biddy who used to do the washing with her baby—piccaninny they call them you know—hanging on her back in a blanket? She was a splendid worker, but a sad thief—had a deep pocket in her blanket on purpose to slip in everything she could lay hands on. But if you did not mind this, and kept your eye on her, and locked away the brandy and that, and didn't object to the little piccaninnies rolling about the laundry floor, and the dogs—blacks are very fond of their dogs—if you could put up with all this, she would do plenty of work: and many a time I've been thankful to get poor Biddy—no, I do think it must have been Julia. Marion, dear, you take no interest whatever in my story. Try and remember now—was it Julia or Biddy who had the children, and pocketed the pound of fresh butter that day?"

"I really cannot remember, mother," said Marion, seriously, while Mrs. Northbrook remarked with a shudder that she hoped she would not be reduced to employing such savage, uncivilised heathens in her household.

"Don't look at the dark side of everything, dear mother," said Frank, coaxingly; "we'll get our Christmas dinner cooked somehow, without troubling you about it."

"Yes," said Marion, "I'll come and help instead of the blacks, and you and I, Mr. Northbrook, will set to and try and make everybody and everything as cheerful and comfortable as possible. I don't feel a bit afraid of work, do you?"

"Indeed," said Frank, "I shall only be too happy to do anything at all in your company, Miss Halstead; even to washing dishes, and peeling praties."

Chapter II

But now we must leave these good people to their pleasant small talk while we transport the patient reader to an inland station far on yonder solitary plains that lie beyond the stir and bustle of city life, beyond the demands of polite society and the fetters of civilisation; a lonely home surrounded by level tracts of unbroken plains, ringed by distant azure woods, haunted by the voice of ages, the sound of the breeze as it sweeps through the thick jungles and tall forest oaks and goes on wandering across the long, level exposure of grassy solitude till it dies away on the purple ranges in the east.

Before us lies the homestead of Melangole station; belonging to that uncle of whom Marion Halstead had spoken when she told Frank that she would spend her Christmas on the station. The simple weatherboard cottage is beautified by the delicate purple blossoms of the dallicus that creeps up round the wooden posts and smothers the low shingled roof. The garden is fragrant with the perfume of orange blossoms, and we can see the golden fruit peeping out from amid the dark leaves. Broad-leaved bananas wave in the breeze, and the homely sweet-toned magpie is warbling joyously in the feathery-leaved wattles. Beyond the wire-fenced garden lie the paddocks, with scattered outhouses and men's huts; farther off are the dim-green forests, an ocean of trees, the very impersonation of solitude. Westward the vast plains roll on towards the horizon, seeming to melt away into the undefined line where earth and sky meet; while towards the east, the level flatness is bounded by mountain ranges, the nearer ones clothed in the varied hues of blue-gum, hickory, pine, and cedar, and other cabbage palm; while the distant purple peaks reflect the changing aspect of the day, the shadows and lights of the shifting clouds, the golden sunshine of afternoon, the glorious radiance of eventide, the pale, mystic shimmer of the summer moon which floods the lovely landscape with a beautifying radiance.

A fine-looking old man with a long, white beard and gentle, care-worn face, is leaning over the garden gate; his old eyes, grown somewhat less keen of vision than in former years, are gazing fixedly at the distant plains. A solitary horseman is riding swiftly across them, and as he comes nearer we can distinguish first his tall, lithe figure, and then the keen, dark face, with eyes whose deep, lustrous darkness reminds us of the natives of Spain and Italy; so does also the clear, olive skin and crisp-raven hair; and so do also the clearly-chiselled features, regular as those of a statue. But when we look closer at that striking face we see that the jaw is too massive, and that the lips, shaded by a dark, drooping moustache, are too full and defiant for classic beauty. The eyes are full of slumbering fire, and as he takes off his hat to let the breeze sweep through his clustering curls, the low, broad brow is revealed, with dark, straight eyebrows meeting in a delicate line above the nose, and giving the face an expression of strong resolution. It is not a pleasing face just now, for it wears a look of gloomy despondency; and as the rider replaces his hat, and spurs his horse onwards with sudden impetuosity, he has the appearance of a man endeavouring to escape from the unpleasant companionship of some oppressive thoughts. Now he has gained the open forest land, and now he is in the paddocks near the house, and a few minutes later he has dismounted and is greeting the old man with respectful tenderness.

"Well, my boy," said Clovelly, for it was he, "how are grass and water standing out against the dry, hot weather?"

"Pretty well, all things considered," replies the young man, in a singularly deep, musical voice. "On the whole I think we are better off than most of our neighbours, and if we only get some rain after Christmas we shall pull through right enough. I believe Windemere is very short of grass and water, and the stock is falling off greatly. There has been another fire at the station, that was the smoke we saw yesterday."

"Those fires are not accidental ones, my lad," said the old man; "you may be pretty sure they had been laid on. Digby, the overseer at Melangole, is a hard man, and the blacks owe him many a grudge. The young master will find some ugly work before him when he comes. I reckon he'll soon sicken of station life under these circumstances."

"I suppose he knows nothing of managing a station," said the younger man; "he'll most likely amuse himself with shooting and hunting, like most Englishmen, and let old Digby go on driving the place to ruin."

There was a strange bitterness in the young fellow's voice that did not escape Clovelly's notice.

"Never mind, Norman," he said kindly, "never mind, my boy, some day we shall see you righted, and Windemere shall be yours to manage as you please."

"Someday," repeated Norman, impatiently; "someday, when will that be? It drives me wild to see the place that ought to be my own going to the dogs in the hands of knaves and fools. That lawyer, Dale, holds several mortgages on it already, confound him; and if this young Northbrook wants plenty of money, I suppose he will go on encumbering the estate still more. It is more than human flesh can bear to think that this Englishman and his mother are coming to take possession of my rightful inheritance while my mother's memory remains dishonored, and I am nameless in the eyes of man. While I think of it my blood boils and I feel afraid to meet my half-brother for fear of giving way to some outburst of passion."

"Steady, my boy, steady," said old Clovelly, laying his hand on his young friend's arm; "the young man knows nothing about your secret, and you must not feel angry with him for what is not his fault. You must have patience, and all will come right in the end. If I can only get that rascally lawyer to give up the certificate of marriage, which I feel certain is in his hands, we shall be able to go to work on a sound basis; but till then you must promise me to control yourself and not make matters worse by giving way to passion and folly."

"I will try," said Norman. "You are the only friend I have, and I will always be guided by you."

"That is right, and now let us speak no more about it. It is time you took the buggy into the township to meet the coach. You know my sister, Mrs. Halstead, and her daughter are coming today. You remember little Marion, don't you?"

"I remember her," replied Norman, absently.

At the same time he was wondering whether he would meet his half-brother in the township, and did not feel inclined to think of any woman except his dead mother whose wrongs weighed heavily on his heart.

Half an hour later, as he was bowling along in the buggy with a strong pair of fresh ponies, the strange history of his life came back to him with fresh vividness, and occupied his thoughts during the whole of the drive.

Norman's mother was a beautiful half-caste girl whom Mr. Clovelly had rescued from desertion and death as a little child, and had taken home to his wife to replace their own little daughter whom they had lost a short time before. Little May, as she was called, grew from a dwarfish, dark-eyed, uncanny child into a lovely girl, and Clovelly and his wife loved her as dearly as if she had been their own. It was not long before the girl's uncommon beauty attracted the notice of a certain Norman Northbrook, a wealthy squatter, residing at Windemere, and as he was a man accustomed to follow his impulses, and to gratify every desire, he fell madly in love with the half-caste girl and succeeded in winning her affections in return. When Clovelly discovered the state of affairs he gave Northbrook to understand that in this case there were only two alternatives—marriage or renunciation: and as the squatter was too much fascinated to think of giving up his love, he consented to the former, and the ceremony was performed at the station by an itinerant clergyman staying there on his way to the north. The only witnesses were Mr. Clovelly and his wife. Mrs. Clovelly died shortly afterwards, and the clergyman disappeared, no one knew whither. Mr. Clovelly was so shattered by his wife's death that he sunk into a state of apathetic indifference bordering on insanity, and for several years was to all appearance dead to all outward interests. By a strange fatality a fire broke out at the township soon after the ill-fated marriage, destroying the greater part of the buildings, among others the court-house containing the registering-office where the clergyman had registered the marriage of Norman Northbrook and the half-caste girl. Mr. Northbrook soon wearied of his young wife, and made business an excuse to return to England leaving her alone at Windemere. On hearing of the birth of his son he promised to return at once, but as weeks lengthened into months, and months into years, his departure from England was still delayed: his letters became less frequent, and finally ceased altogether, and the unhappy young mother began to think that she was deserted and forgotten. In the meantime Northbrook had met a handsome young Englishwoman of good family who appeared a most desirable match to the inconstant man. He regretted bitterly the folly which had induced him to fetter himself by contracting a marriage with that nameless half-caste girl, and as he went on pressing his suit with his new fancy, and maintaining the deepest secrecy with regard to his first marriage, he cast about in his mind for some way of freeing himself from the unwelcome bondage. Lawyer Dale, his evil genius and general confidant, advised him to ignore the first marriage which, according to the legal gentleman's opinion, could hardly be proved at present. There was no evidence save that of Mrs. Northbrook herself: one of the witnesses being dead, and the other as it seemed hopelessly deranged. The register was burnt, the marriage certificate safely in the hands of the lawyer—he having obtained possession of it by some means best known to himself—

and the whole affair had been conducted in so quiet and secret a manner in so solitary a part of the colony that scarcely anyone, save the parties concerned, were aware of a marriage having taken place. Mr. Northbrook might safely contend that there had been no marriage, and might please himself. Mr. Northbrook took the hint and pleased himself by marrying the English beauty: at the same time instructing Dale to pay the deserted wife an annuity, and to try and convince her that her marriage was illegal and void.

When Mr. Clovelly awoke, as from a trance, after years of mental darkness, he was greatly shocked and grieved to find how cruelly his adopted daughter had been treated. He used every effort to establish her rights, but soon saw that without some certain proof of her legitimate marriage there was no hope of success. He therefore resolved to wait his time, and meanwhile taking the boy under his care had him educated and brought up as befitted a gentleman's son. Nor were his kindness and fatherly care unrewarded, for as Norman grew up into manhood he proved himself of valuable assistance to his faithful friend, taking the management of the station almost entirely off his hands, and returning his affection with a loyal and staunch attachment.

The deserted wife did not survive her disappointment very long: she gradually faded away, and went down to her grave beseeching her son with her dying breath to make it his sacred duty to establish his rightful claims and to clear her name from ignominy and disgrace.

Such was Norman Northbrook's history, and it may be imagined that his thoughts were not pleasant ones as he drove into the township where he was likely to see for the first time that other Northbrook who was coming to take possession of his father's property. As his buggy dashed down the quiet street the coach drove up to the door of the inn, and Norman's keen eyes soon discovered Mrs. Halstead and her daughter whom he had both met when he was a boy. His attention was, however, more arrested by two other persons, one of them a proud-looking woman of middle-age, and the other a fair-faced, boyish young fellow, who seemed to be paying great attention to old Clovelly's niece. The blood surged up into Norman's face, and he felt it necessary to linger for some minutes talking to the landlord before he could recover his usual composure. This, then, was the second wife who had supplanted his mother—this was the heir of Windemere—his half-brother. He had promised to be patient, and to control himself, and he meant to keep his promise—but there was a fierce passion urging within him, a terrible, sinful feeling of hatred and jealousy as he stood, gazing gloomily at these two unconscious people who were about to make their home at Windemere, while he, the rightful heir, was nothing but Clovelly's super.!

When he had regained complete command over himself again he advanced towards the group, and no one seeing his impassable cold face would have guessed the storm that was raging within.

"Mrs. Halstead, I believe," he said with the peculiar graceful dignity natural to him (perhaps a heritage from those dashing chieftains from whom he was descended). "I had the pleasure of meeting you when I was a boy at Mr. Clovelly's station. I am Norman Northbrook, and have brought the buggy to take you and Miss Halstead to Melangole."

"Dear me," said Mrs. Halstead, shaking hands cordially, "how you have grown and altered to be sure. You were quite a boy when I saw you last—a shy, awkward lad, and now you have really grown so very much, it is quite remarkable. Well, well, how young people do grow up. Marion, my dear, this is Mr. Norman Northbrook, only fancy: your old playmate, you know. Only think, he has grown quite a man. It does seem strange to see you both grown up. Dear, dear, it makes me feel quite old, really."

The good woman might have gone on dribbling her commonplaces for the next half hour, but Marion interrupted, saying, as she held out her hand to Norman, "You have altered a good deal, and I suppose I have, too; you would hardly have known me again, would you?"

Marion looked charming in her plain grey travelling costume with a dash of pink here and there to relieve its sombre hue. She knew that she looked well, and was quite prepared to receive the admiring homage of this handsome, foreign-looking man in whom she should never have recognised the gloomy, shy boy of former years. But Norman met her arch look with a calm, steadfast gaze, and answered quietly:

"I should have known you anywhere, Miss Halstead; you have changed very little."

"The words might have been complimentary or not, as Marion choose to interpret them; the tone in which they were uttered was cold and commonplace: but what a voice he had, how deep and musical! What must that voice be when moved by passion and tenderness!

"Allow me to introduce your neighbour and namesake, Mr. Frank Northbrook," she said as Frank approached them. "How very singular that you should both have the same name," she added, innocently.

"It is rather strange," said Frank, with his easy, boyish smile, holding out a well-gloved, delicate hand. I hope—aw—that we shall be good neighbours. I'm awfully inexperienced, you know, in colonial life. You will be, perhaps, kind enough to—aw—to give a fellow some useful hints sometimes."

Norman's dark face flushed, and there was no answering smile as he just touched his half-brother's hand, and then turning hastily away, asked Mrs. Halstead if she were ready to start.

"I shall sit in front, mamma," said Marion in her decided manner. "You will be more comfortable behind, and you can look after your precious boxes at the same time. I know you would not be easy if you were separated from those bandboxes." With those words she sprang lightly into the vehicle, declining Frank's eagerly-proffered aid, and making a merry adieu to the young man and his mother was driven off with her mother, and was soon lost to sight by a turning in the road.

"I suppose this is our trap," said Frank as he turned away after gazing after Marion, and caught sight of a shabby-looking waggonette with a rawboned ill-groomed horse and a rough-looking driver in shirt-sleeves, an old "Jim Crow" hat on his shaggy head, and a short black pipe in his mouth. This worthy had a rubicund nose, a cowering, ill-favoured face, and a swaggering, insolent air.

"Mr. Northbrook, bound for Windemere, I guess," he said without removing his pipe.

"Yes, I'm Mr. Northbrook," said Frank, colouring. "By Jove, what a shabby turnout you've brought us: is that the best trap Digby could find for Mrs. Northbrook and myself?"

The man looked doubtfully at the lady who was surveying the equipage and himself with undisguised disgust. He made a show of taking his pipe from his mouth, but thought better of it, and muttered sulkily:

"Wal ye see, times is hard, young master, an' we're not over flash at Windemere. I'm old Digby himself, that's who I am. Everybody here knows old Digby, they do. I've been boss at Windemere ten year an' more; you can bet your life on that. But I reckon you'll be bossin' it now, eh? an' old Digby will have to knuckle under."

"Do you know my good man that you're—aw—infernally impudent?" said Frank, hotly. "You'll have to learn to speak differently to me if we are to get on together."

"I'll have to learn, eh?" said Digby, chuckling, and looking round to see if there was anyone near to enjoy the joke. Perceiving the landlord and ostler, and a few idlers who were listening to the dialogue with evident interest, he indulged in a series of knowing winks which distorted his face in a most remarkable manner; and taking his pipe from his mouth chuckled again, and continued addressing Frank. "Have to learn, eh? Come now, that's not a bad 'un. I reckon it's jest you who'll have to learn a dashed sight more than you know afore you're fit to manage Windemere. You'll find yerself finely at sea without old Digby, I reckon; for what with the rascally blacks an' the drought, an' no getting the stock to market for want o' water, things is in a deuce of a pickle; an' it'll take another an' wiser head nor yourn to pull through this season."

"Well," said Frank, choking down his vexation, "you see I've come over to see what's to be done; I daresay we shall understand each other after a while. Will you get in, mother?"

"Yes," said Mrs. Northbrook, icily, "when it is your pleasure to finish your conversation with that man. I am half dead with heat and fatigue, and anything will be better than standing here. Had your dear papa been alive, Frank, he never would have exposed me to such hardships: your poor father was always most considerate."

Frank made no reply to this admonitory speech, but busied himself with assisting his mother into the vehicle and making her as comfortable as possible. When they were seated and had left the township he suddenly asked Digby who and what this Norman Northbrook was; for having seen him driving off with Marion a faint tinge of jealousy had coloured his feelings towards the dark-faced stranger who had appeared most un-congenial and ill-mannered in his behaviour towards the young master of Windemere.

"Haven't ye heard of Norman Northbrook?" asked Digby, incredu-lously. "He's boss at Melangole: super. for old Clovelly, you know; and a knowing card he is. But there's no one as knows rightly what he is. They say his mother was a half-caste, an' likely enough, for he's allers taking the part o' them rascally blacks as no man would do as didn't belong to the tomahawk tribe hisself. But there's no one knows rightly who his fa-ther was. There's strange yarns about him. It's queer now that he and you should have the same name, ain't it? But I don't know nothing about him only that he's a cursed meddling feller as thinks he knows more about managing a station than old Digby."

Meanwhile Norman and his companions were driving along the plains which stretched out before them, a broad, yellow expanse dotted here and there with herds of browsing cattle that started away and fled at their approach in a cloud of dust.

As the travellers drove on they came upon a party of blacks camping on the red banks of a small water hole. The smoke of a small fire trembled up into the sunlit air, and women and children were busily engaged in preparing a meal from what looked suspiciously like the remains of a slaughtered bullock. A few lean, hungry dogs sniffed the inviting odour of the frizzled meat; and the braves stretched at ease beside their upright spears, smoked and watched the proceedings with evident relish. At the sight of the approaching vehicle they started to their feet brandishing their weapons and uttering loud yells, which elicited a little shriek of terror from Mrs. Halstead, while Marion moved involuntarily nearer to Norman as the savages advanced performing a kind of grotesque dance and uttering unearthly, yells and whoops.

"You need not be afraid," said Norman; "these are friendly blacks who know me well, they only mean to welcome us;" so saying he drew some parcels from under the seat, and stopping his horses threw his gifts to the blacks who caught them dexterously, and expressed their gratitude by renewed clamour and unintelligible gibberish, accompanied by lively gestures and sparkling eyes and teeth. Norman replied in the same language, the soft tones of which made his musical voice sound even more mellow than usual; then gathering up the reins whistled to his horses and dashed onward, leaving the wild figures in the distance.

"How grateful those poor creatures seemed," said Marion: "are they perfectly harmless?" She was wondering whether Norman objected to speak about these wild children of the forest and plains whose blood—

so rumour said—was mingled with his own. The young woman knew nothing of Norman Northbrook save that he had grown up at her uncle's station, and that he was a great favourite with the old man. She also knew that there was some secret connected with his birth, and had once questioned her mother on the subject; but Mrs. Halstead having only heard vague rumours which she did not consider quite fit for the ears of a young girl, answered evasively, and gave Marion to understand that the least said about the matter the better.

Of course all this was very romantic, and Marion felt deeply interested in the grave-faced man who had probably a sad history, and was certainly nobody, which was very unpleasant for him, poor creature. If, however, she thought that Norman might look sheepish or confused at her speaking about the blacks she was mistaken, for his face betrayed no emotion of any kind as he replied quietly:

"They are harmless as long as they are kindly treated; but some white men think they must punish every trifling offence with the utmost severity, and of course the black fellows retaliate."

"Do they ever spear or steal any cattle at Melangole?" asked Marion.

"No;—they did so once, but I went to the chief and complained, and he punished the thieves and promised that it should never happen again, and the promise has been kept. But at Windemere many depredations are committed, for Digby is hated by all the black tribes for his cruelty and meanness. The black man, Miss Halstead, is as capable of appreciating kindness and resenting injuries as his more cultivated white brother. The white man has come and taken what was the rightful possession of his weaker fellow-creatures, and now expects him to look on quietly while he enjoys the ill-gotten wealth. Is it a wonder that, maddened by misery and want, and goaded by the remembrance of his wrongs, the poor savage turns upon the pale-faced intruder with all the fierceness of his uncontrolled nature?"

He had spoken these last words in a voice of suppressed passion; his dark eyes flashed and his nostrils quivered, then, as if afraid of saying too much, he checked himself suddenly and urged his horses to a faster pace until the buggy flew along at a velocity that caused poor Mrs. Halstead to utter many exclamations of terror, while she grasped frantically at her leaping and tumbling bonnet boxes.

"How I shall enjoy a ride over those plains," said Marion, after a pause during which she had come to the conclusion that it would be wiser after all not to broach any subject respecting the blacks again.

"We have some pretty fair ladies hacks," said Norman, rousing himself from the reflections which had carried him far away from his charming companion. "Your cousin, Miss Clovelly rides a good deal, and always has some easy horses at her disposal."

"My cousin Lucy?" said Marion; "oh, yes, I had forgotten that she is now living at Melangole keeping house for uncle. I remember her as a child. She was not pretty, but very sweet tempered. I suppose she has grown up a pretty girl?"

Marion thought it very likely that Norman might be in love with Lucy Clovelly, who was the daughter of Clovelly's only son, and not only heiress of a considerable fortune by her father, but likely to inherit her grandfather's property which was one of considerable importance. Lucy had been a very plain, tiresomely well behaved child, always held up as a model to Marion; but she might have grown up to be pretty and interesting, and what more likely than that Norman Northbrook should be wooing her.

"Miss Clovelly is not pretty," replied Norman, quietly, "but she is one of the most unselfish and sweet-tempered girls I have ever seen."

This answer satisfied Marion on two points: in the first place it was evident that Mr. Northbrook was able to see for himself whether a girl was pretty or not: and secondly he was not in love with the plain but amiable Lucy or he would not have been able to speak of her in that evil and unconcerned manner. Marion felt suddenly quite kindly-disposed towards this cousin of hers, and resolved to cultivate her friendship. As for Norman, he was decidedly a young man of sense and discrimination, and it remains to be seen whether he would be as insensible to her attractions as he had been to Lucy's excellent qualities. Marion was not actually a coquette, she took no pleasure in breaking hearts, but she loved homage and admiration above everything, and thought it right that every man should look up to her as his queen.

Chapter III

A few days after Marion's arrival at Melangole a respectable-looking individual dressed in black, and wearing a tall, black hat—rather an unusual headgear in the Queensland station life—and mounted on a black horse, rode up to the garden-gate, and after dismounting, and fastening his funeral steed carefully to a paling, whipped the dust off his boots with his handkerchief, and approached the house with a slow and dignified step. The man was elderly, but it would have been difficult to have determined his exact age, for he had one of those grey, colourless faces that never seemed to have been young nor even appear to grow much older. His upper lip and chin were shaven, and his thin, grey whiskers carefully trimmed. His small, grey eyes—sharp as those of a weasel—seemed to have the power of reading the inmost thoughts of others, while never revealing what was passing in his own mind.

Lawyer Dale had been the late Mr. Northbrook's friend and counsellor for many years, and rumour unkindly had it that he had profited more by this friendship than his patron. Be this as it may Mr. Dale was at the present moment debating within himself whether it would be wiser to transfer his valuable friendship and services to the young heir of Windemere, or whether it would be more to his profit to offer his talent and knowledge of certain family secrets to the other Northbrook, the protege of old Clovelly. Dale was a clever, unscrupulous man, anxious to play a conspicuously genteel and respectable part in his neighbourhood; and there were certain ugly facts connected with the Northbrook history which, if made public, might reflect unpleasantly on his moral character. Besides this, he knew better than any other man—better indeed than Frank Northbrook himself—how that young gentleman's affairs stood, and felt certain that in case of the other side going to law the young master of Windemere would find himself unable to bear the expenses of a lawsuit. Therefore, on receiving a letter from Clovelly inviting him to a conference to discuss certain important matters respecting the rightful heirship of Windemere, Lawyer Dale felt that the issue of this interview depended mainly on himself, and was resolved to turn it to his best advantage. If he imitated the proverbial rats and abandoned the sinking ship he might be well paid for his trouble, and be freed from a load of anxiety which had weighed down his spirits for some time. There was always the likelihood, nay, almost the certainty of a lawsuit; when, having made a profitable bargain with Clovelly and Norman Northbrook, he might offer his services to Frank, and reap the harvest of legal quibbles and lawyer's briefs to his heart's content.

Mr. Clovelly was seated on his verandah, listening patiently to his sister's wandering conversation, when the clinking of the garden-gate caused him to look up and behold Lawyer Dale approaching with wincing gait and meek, respectable air.

"Good morning, Mr. Clovelly," said the gentleman, advancing, and taking off his hat as he bowed to the lady. "Good morning, Mrs. Halstead; allow me to recall myself to your remembrance—Jacob Dale, at your service, madame; I had the felicity of meeting you years ago, and your face is so fresh in my memory that I should have known you in a crowd. Time, my dear madame, has dealt very kindly with you. You do not seem to have changed at all during those long years, twelve or thirteen it must be, since we met last. I fear I have made too evanescent an impression on your mind to allow me to hope that you remember my poor person."

Lawyer Dale rubbed his nose gently with his forefinger as was his wont, and wrinkled the corners of his eyes into multitudinous wrinkles. He prided himself on his success with the fair sex, and was in the habit of saying that he could manage most women by adroit flattery and well-termed compliments, as he managed men by evil effrontery and imperturbable blandness.

Mrs. Halstead's faded cheek flushed with pleasure at the lawyer's words, for she was not insensible to complimentary speeches, having been a beauty in her young days and still possessing a graceful figure and delicate features.

"Indeed, Mr. Dale," said she graciously, "I have not forgotten you although I should scarcely have remembered your face had you not mentioned that you had met me, and I don't think I should have recalled your name had my brother not spoken of you several times since my arrival. I might have known your face, or fancied I knew it, without remembering your name, you know. Dear, dear, and it is really twelve years since we danced together at the bachelor's ball in Roma, or was it Brisbane? I think it was you I danced so much with that night. It was some gentleman with a name like Dale or Wood, and I think he was a lawyer; but he might have been a doctor: anyway, he danced most beautifully, and was a fine man; but now I come to think of it, he had sandy whiskers, and was very tall—no, I don't think you could have been at that ball—I must have met you here, at the station."

"We met in this very garden, Mrs. Halstead. I shall never forget our first meeting; your daughter was with you, a sweetly pretty child. I suppose she has grown into a beautiful young lady: she must appear like a younger sister beside you."

"Marion has grown into a very pretty girl, Mr. Dale. She is out riding with Miss Clovelly and Mr. Northbrook today: and would you believe it? she actually went without her gauze veil in this heat; she will be quite sunburnt. Young girls are so careless nowadays, Mr. Dale. When I was young I was never allowed out till sunset, and always muffled up with linen hoods and veils and gloves, for I had a fair skin like dear Marion, and my color was greatly admired; but that has gone like the rest of my good looks: we can't expect to remain young and pretty all our days, can we, Mr. Dale?"

"You have come on business, I suppose?" said Mr. Clovelly, stopping the complimentary speech that was trembling on the lawyer's lips.

"Yes—yes," said Dale, slowly; "on business, my dear sir, as you say. If you have time to spare I suppose we had better talk over this little matter at once: I am quite at your service. Excuse us Mrs. Halstead, business before pleasure you know; we must leave your charming society for a while."

"This way if you please," said Clovelly as he led the way into the house; and, opening a door, ushered his visitor into a small office.

"Are we sure of privacy here?" asked Dale, looking round suspiciously.

"Perfectly," replied Clovelly, closing the door and seating himself at his desk. "You received my letter?"

"I received your letter my dear sir. You inform me you are about to take steps to advance claims on behalf of Mr. Norman Northbrook as being the rightful heir of Windemere entailed by the late Mr. Northbrook's father on his eldest grandson. You say that you are all prepared to prove the legitimacy of Mr. Northbrook's claims: you are ready to give evidence that a de facto marriage took place in your presence at this house twenty-six years ago between the late Mr. Northbrook and an half-caste girl known as May Clovelly, your adopted daughter. You have doubtless the marriage certificate to prove the correctness of your assertions: excuse my speaking plainly, I am a business man, Mr. Clovelly."

"I have not the marriage certificate," said Clovelly, flushing slightly; "from what I can understand Mrs. Northbrook never saw the paper again after she had signed it. Blindly devoted to her husband she allowed him to retain possession of the important document, and I have strong reasons to believe that it has since passed into your hands, why and wherefore you best know yourself. In this case I should be prepared to give a reasonable sum to obtain this paper, which is of course of some importance to us, and the unlawful possession of which may become extremely troublesome to you in time."

"My dear sir, it first remains to be proved that it is in my possession: I acknowledge, however, that it is of great importance to you to obtain this marriage certificate: of supreme importance, Mr. Clovelly; in fact you haven't the ghost of a chance without this important document—not an atom of a chance," and Lawyer Dale rubbed his nose and looked searchingly at the old man who was struggling hard to repress the feelings of disgust and indignation that always rose within him at the sight of the man whom he held responsible for all his adopted daughter's misery.

"What do you want for it?" he asked, abruptly, now fully convinced that the paper was in Dale's hands.

"Mr. Clovelly," said the lawyer, rubbing his nose thoughtfully, "I am a most conscientious man—too much so in fact. I am a slave to conscience. You are aware that the late Mr. Northbrook was not only my client, but my most intimate friend, and during his lifetime I have always endeavored to serve him to the best of my abilities, although I did not always approve of his proceedings. Now that he is dead, however, I feel at liberty to follow the dictates of my conscience, and am prepared to fall in with your views providing you accept my terms."

"What are your terms," asked Clovelly, impatiently.

"In the first place," replied Dale, edging his chair a little nearer to Clovelly's, "I must request you to give me your word of honour that you will never reveal to anybody what has passed between us at this meeting. You see, Mr. Clovelly, I am a man holding a highly honourable position in society. I am received into the best families; I belong to every public committee; I am churchwarden, and have the honour of receiving the highest dignitaries of the church under my humble roof: in a word I am a man of position and prominence, and as such, must be careful to avoid anything that might give my enemies (for who has not enemies?) opportunity to malign my character. Therefore, my dear sir, I repeat before proceeding any further that I must request your word of honour as a gentleman to observe profound secrecy regarding this little business that we are about to transact."

Dale leant back in his seat as he concluded this speech, and wrinkling up his eyes observed his companion furtively while the old man sat in silent thought wavering between a desire to throw the lawyer out of the house and a conviction that he must sacrifice everything to obtain possession of the valuable paper. He regarded Dale as a cautious hypocrite and arch-rogue, and felt ashamed to make use of such a tool. But his love for Norman Northbrook, and the desire to see him righted, overcame his scruples and aversion, and after a while he said, coldly:

"I give you my word of honour never to mention what has passed between us at this interview. And now state your terms and let us finish this unpleasant business."

"My terms are two thousand pounds," said Dale, promptly.

"Two thousand; be hanged!" said Clovelly, hotly. "Are you mad?"

"My dear sir, consider what the possession of this document"—(here he tapped his breast-pocket)—"would be worth to your opponents. Why, they would give triple the sum to hold this certificate of marriage in their hands, and to be able to destroy it. Consider, my dear sir, the costs of a lawsuit, which would be a hopeless one, I can assure you—consider your young friend's prospects: I am certain the young gentleman in question would willingly give any sum to hold certain proofs of his legitimate birth: I know that Mr. Frank Northbrook, if aware of the existence of this valuable document, would give anything rather than let it pass into the hands of his adversary. It is only my delicate sense of honour—only my tender conscience—only the feeling that I owe your young friend some reparation for the unwilling wrong I have in some measure inflicted on him through my devoted friendship to his father—it is only because I am a slave to the scruples of conscience that I place myself at your disposal: all you have to do is to draw out a cheque for the trifling sum I have mentioned and you hold the fortunes of young Northbrook in your hands!"

"Two thousand is an impudent demand; really, Dale, you have the coolness of old nick."

"Not at all, my dear sir," said Dale, apparently rather flattered than otherwise. "Consider, I am a family man, Mr. Clovelly; I have an expensive household—seven daughters and a position to maintain."

"I will not give more than a thousand pounds," said Clovelly, resolutely.

"It is scarcely adequate, Mr. Clovelly; it is scarcely worth my while accepting so small a sum. However, as I feel it my duty to uphold the lawful claims of my young friend—I am a great lover of justice—and as you are such an old friend of mine I will really stretch a point and accept your offer. Here is the document; examine it at your leisure; you will find it correct."

Mr. Clovelly, having satisfied himself that this was the identical marriage certificate which he had signed twenty-six years ago, opened his desk, and writing out a cheque handed it to Dale who pocketed it, bowing politely as he rose to take his leave.

"Much obliged, my dear sir. I wish your young friend and yourself every success. Should you go to law and require an able advocate to state your case ex parte Northbrook, I shall be happy to place my services at your disposal. I need not, of course, remind you that I have your word of honour regarding this little secret transaction."

"I shall not require your services anymore," said Clovelly; "and you need not be alarmed at my breaking my given word—I am not in the habit of breaking any pledge. Allow me to wish you good morning."

"Good morning," said Dale, smiling pleasantly, and rubbing his nose with an air of exasperating self-complacency which made Clovelly's fingers tingle to pitch him out of the window.

When he was gone the old gentleman locked the document carefully up in his desk, muttering to himself:

"The greatest rascal unhung: a canting, dissimulating hypocrite. Ugh!. I hope I have seen the last of him; but as Will Shakspeare says:

'He that stands upon a slippery place
Makes nice of no vile hold to stay him up.'

"Thank God I have got what I wanted: and now we shall see who is to be master of Windemere. If all goes well little Lucy can marry Norman—for I really believe the little witch is fond of him—and he could not find a better wife. She will come in for Melangole at my death, and the two fine stations will be united."

This was old Clovelly's day dream. But alas! for day dreams and aerial castles, how seldom they are realised—how frequently they are dashed to pieces before we have seen any of their bright promises fulfilled!

Chapter IV

While Mr. Clovelly and the lawyer were transacting their business to their mutual satisfaction, Marion Halstead was enjoying that gallop across the plains, to which she had been looking forward with so much expectancy. The horse on which she was mounted was a beautiful, spirited bay. Norman and her uncle had wished her to ride the more subdued and gentle chestnut which usually carried Lucy, while Miss Clovelly, as a more experienced and careful rider was to be allowed to ride Lancelot. Marion had, however, set her mind on riding the beautiful creature whose arched neck, glossy coat, and large, soft eyes had won her admiration, from the first. Her pride was piqued at the thought that timid, gentle Lucy should outshine her by riding the horse she coveted, and in her wilful decided manner she had declared that she would ride Lancelot or not ride at all. Marion had ridden a good deal in her childhood on the station, and having resided in the country during her stay in England had found plenty of opportunities for cultivating her equestrian accomplishments: she possessed considerable nerve and felt fit to ride any horse on the station. When she was seated in the saddle on the back of the noble bay, she was triumphantly conscious of having carried her point as usual, and was inclined to be very gracious to Norman who was arranging her stirrups.

"You had better leave your whip at home," he said; "Lancelot is as quiet as a lamb, but he won't stand the whip. If you should touch him ever so lightly with it he is very likely to run away with you."

"I would not think of riding without my whip," said Marion, decidedly. "I shall not use it unless he requires it: and I hardly think he will require it," she added, caressing the horse's neck, as he stamped impatiently, on the ground, and pulled at the bridle rein.

"Allow me to take the whip," said Norman, stretching out his hand; but Marion, reddening with annoyance at his authoritative tone, replied haughtily:

"Pray, Mr. Northbrook, allow me to judge for myself in this matter," and set off at a smart canter, while the young man turning away in silence mounted his horse and followed with Lucy.

Marion felt slightly ruffled at this little incident: she was sorry to have spoken sharply to Norman, who had been so kind and attentive to her since her arrival at the station, and she could not help feeling a little mortified when he rode to Lucy's side and engaged in a conversation with her which caused the heiress's plain, good-humoured face to flush, and brighten with pleasure. But all these passing clouds were dispelled when the horses started together in a glorious canter through the open forest land, where the golden sunlight trembled through the white-streamed gum trees, and over the wild, lovely plains.

A fresh westerly breeze tempered the heat, and sent large, white cloud masses scudding across the sky, so that the level expanse of rippling, golden-brown grass was merry with the shifting lights and shadows. Large white butterflies chased each other among the flower-sprinkled grassy waves; the clear whistle and sharp crack of the "coachman" sounded from a gleaming pool half hidden by tall reeds and towering grass trees; and the air was laden with the perfume of wattle blossoms, borne by the whispering wind from the distant azure forests.

"This is glorious," said Marion, enthusiastically, as they halted on a slight rise to breathe their horses after a sharp gallop. "I don't think I have ever enjoyed anything so much in my life."

"But you often had nice rides in England," said Lucy, looking admiringly at her cousin, whose flushed cheeks and sparkling eyes added a new charm to her lovely face, shaded by the soft, dark Rubens hat with drooping white feather.

Poor Lucy sighed involuntarily as she gazed at that fair face, and then glanced at Norman, but his face was as impassive as that of a statue; and although his eyes were fixed on Marion, it was impossible to say whether he was admiring her or not.

"Yes, I had many pleasant rides in England," said Marion, carelessly, "but never across such plains, nor on such a horse," and she smiled at Norman, willing to propitiate him after her little outburst of temper.

"I am glad you like Lancelot," he replied, while his dark eyes met hers with their usual quiet intensity which Marion was always puzzled to understand.

Did those lustrous, grave eyes express admiring interest, or were they only criticising her coolly? She felt exasperated at the latter thought; she could not endure to be criticised; and she had a strange thought that all her powers of attraction were thrown away on this cold self-contained man.

"I suppose you will go to Windemere tomorrow evening?" she said, as they rode on quietly.

"I don't think so," replied Norman; "parties are not to my taste; I never dance, and it is very dull work looking at others dancing and flirting when one finds no pleasure in such things."

"Oh, surely you will go this time," said Lucy, eagerly: "it is so seldom we have any amusement of this kind, and it will be only politeness to accept the first invitation from our new neighbours. I am sure it would do you good, and you would enjoy yourself when you were there. Besides," she added, bringing out her concluding argument triumphantly, "you must escort us, you know, and act as our cavalier."

"Mr. Clovelly will escort you, and you will have plenty of cavaliers more fit to entertain you than I am," said Norman, coldly; and Marion, watching the pair narrowly, saw Lucy's face clouding with disappointment and thought: Mr. Northbrook does not think much of her, poor girl, and she foolishly cares a great deal for him. He seems to be a regular woman-hater; I must try what I can do with him. And aloud she said:

"I am sure you are only waiting to be coaxed to go. I cannot believe that you will lose the rare opportunity of enjoying yourself, unless, indeed, you are different to most young men."

"I am different," said Norman; my experiences of life have been such as to make me old and sad before my time; and I have no heart for light and thoughtless amusements."

"And you are really not going to Windemere tomorrow?"

"I think not."

"Not even if I ask you?" said Marion, dimpling, and driven to the verge of coquetry by his imperturbable calmness.

"Not even then, Miss Halstead. I have certain reasons which make me unwilling to go to Windemere—reasons more weighty than my aversion to parties."

His tone was as quiet as usual, but Marion fancied she detected a slight vibration in his musical voice, and there was certainly a sudden fire in his dark eyes, which belied the coldness of his words. Marion wondered whether she had touched some sensitive fibre in his nature. But she felt sure that she was totally indifferent to him—he cared no more about her than about Lucy or any other woman. He was outrageously ill-bred to meet her condescending prettiness with such a flat refusal; and augued and irritated, she hardly knew why, she gave Lancelot a smart cut with the whip which caused him to start violently and then dash away in a mad gallop.

The girl did not at first realise the danger she was in; the quick movement harmonised with her quickening pulses, and with the reckless feeling that possessed her at that moment she did not understand that her horse had bolted until she heard Lucy's cry of terror—she felt the powerlessness of her hands as she pulled desperately at the reins—saw the sunlit landscape flashing past with lightning speed—and heard the breeze whistling strangely shrilly in her ears. Then she determined to show that she could sit a runaway horse well and bravely, showing no signs of weakness or fear.

"Sir Lancelot will soon weary of this," she thought, "and Norman Northbrook shall see that I am not frightened."

So she settled herself firmly in the saddle looking straight before her as she was borne across the wide plains, and kept her hand tightly on the useless rein.

When Norman saw what was happening his first impulse was to dash after the runaway, but immediately foreseeing the danger of such a proceeding he reined-up his horse and said to Lucy:

"If Lancelot hears our horses behind him he will only run the faster. I must leave you to ride on quietly while I take a short cut across the plain and try to head him."

With these words he spurred his horse, and flew away in the hope of cutting off the fugitive's mad career before he went much further.

They had left the plain and were rushing along through the bush beneath tall pines and myalls, and gigantic blue gum towering up into the blue sky with straight, majestic stems and sparsely-leaved crowns. The dry, narrow bush road was bordered with bright flowers—the native fuchsia with its delicate, scarlet bells, the glowing waratah, the purple-fringed violet, and deep-hued, climbing sarsaparilla. Now and then a startled kangaroo bounded across the path, and tiny green and red parrots flashed past like a gleam of emerald and ruby. But now a sudden tremendous roar broke upon Marion's ear. What was that terrible distant thunder? Could it be that they were nearing the waterfall rushing down into the steep gully! Marion remembered the spot well. A few days ago they had spent some pleasant hours among the rocks and ferns, and now she saw those very rocks and their ferned sides, and the deep gullies with their waving tree-tops, and huge riven boulders festooned with blossoming vines and graceful fern-trees. She could see the placid dark stream that rippled so calmly over its pebbles fall suddenly with deafening roar and glistening spray four hundred feet below.

Her furious horse showed no signs of abating his speed—blinded by fear or rage he was rushing straight to his doom.

Past the marshy flats where flocks of wild ducks rose with wailing cries from the yellow tussocks—past the tall grass trees and giant ferns and rich blossoms—past the very spot they had sat a few days ago gazing down into the abyss where the stream seemed but a silver thread and huge rocks appeared, like small stones. She could see the rainbow playing in the cascade's spray; she could see the snowy, vapoury foam, leaping and whirling through the air; she could distinguish the varied rich foliage of sassafras and camphor shrub, and musk and cedar down in those wild depths; and she remembered even in that terrible moment how she had wondered laughingly whether if anyone fell over the precipice they would ever reach the bottom of that gully alive.

Lancelot could either not check his headlong course any more or was blind to the danger before them: he was rushing straight towards the brink of the abyss. Should she throw herself from the saddle? But no— she might be dragged by her stirrups, and that would be even worse than being dashed to pieces on those cruel rocks below.

"Poor, poor mother," sobbed Marion, as she pulled vainly with her last strength at the bridle. But at this moment, when they seemed to be within a few inches of the shelving brink, a figure suddenly threw itself between the gully and the maddened horse; and seizing the bridle forced him back from the yawning abyss.

Powerless and furious Lancelot struck out with his fore-feet, knocking off Norman's hat and grazing his forehead; but it was the last effort of passion. Trembling in every limb, covered in foam, with quivering nostrils and dilated eyes the horse allowed itself to be turned away from the fatal spot, and in another minute Marion felt herself lifted from the saddle and deposited safely on the ground.

Dizzy and faint she clung to her preserver, and looked up into his face which was bending down to hers full of tender anxiety.

"How shall I ever thank you?" she said falteringly; "you have saved my life at the risk of your own." But the next moment she gave an exclamation of terror as she caught sight of the cut on Norman's temple from which the blood was flowing down his cheek.

"You are hurt," she exclaimed turning deadly pale.

"It is nothing," he said, smiling. "Lancelot's hoof grazed my head, that is all; it is of no consequence."

"I am so sorry," said Marion, the tears starting to her eyes. "You might have been killed, and all through my foolish wilfulness."

She drew a handkerchief from her pocket and proceeded to tie up the wound with trembling fingers.

"Do not reproach yourself," said Norman, as he submitted to have the bandage knotted round his dark curls. "I was more to blame than you. I ought never to have allowed you to ride that horse. But I have never seen him so excited before. He is spirited, but gentle enough usually. Had you not touched him with the whip he would never have behaved so badly. Lancelot is like his master—he can be led by a silken thread in kindness; but a touch of the spur or whip maddens him."

"I can quite believe that," said Marion, looking at him with a return of her arch manner; but the dimpling smile suddenly died away and her eyes sank as she met the look of passionate tenderness in the dark face beside her.

"Do you know what I would have done had you gone ever that precipice?" he asked in a low voice.

"No," whispered Marion, feeling a new shyness and confusion that made her powerless to assume her usual self-possession.

"I will tell you," said Norman, still speaking in that low passionate voice. "Had you have been dashed over that fearful abyss, I would have thrown myself after you and have died beside you."

There was no mistaking the ardour of his words and looks, and Marion felt a sudden rush of mingled joy and sadness—a strange feeling of delight—a trembling timidity—a self-accusing sadness, which sent a flash of colour into her face, and made her heart beat wild and fast.

"I have been playing with fire," she thought; but at this moment approaching hoofbeats were heard along the road, and Lucy came riding through the trees, and, reining up her horse, sprang from the saddle and threw herself into Marion's arms with a burst of sobs and incoherent words.

"Norman saved you," she murmured; "I'm sure he did. I knew he would save you or die in the attempt."

Yes," said Marion, "he saved my worthless life, and narrowly escaped having his brains knocked out by Lancelot, who is an ungrateful, wicked creature to treat his master thus when he was in the act of saving from a terrible death."

"Are you hurt?" asked Lucy, anxiously.

"No, it is only a scratch," replied Norman, hastily, as he removed the saddle from Lancelot's back and placed it on his own horse."

"You will ride my quiet old stager," he said, looking at Marion. "He is rather rough for a lady, but there is no danger of his running away. Wombat is a famous stock horse, and can head almost any beast. But he is too sensible to think of bolting, and does not mind the whip. I always ride him when I go out with ladies, for I know I can depend upon him if anything should happen."

"I shall ride any horse you like after this," said Marion; "and please take my whip. Had I listened to you from the first I would not have been in danger of losing my life, and you would not have been hurt. It has been a lesson to me. I mean to be very obedient after this, and to give up my self-will and obstinacy."

She looked up at him with all the charming sauciness gone out of her face and with a new humility and appealing gentleness which was very touching in a creature of such rare beauty.

Norman flushed and then turned pale but he said nothing, and only busied himself arranging her saddle, and then lifting her on to Wombat's back, turned away silently and mounted his own horse. He felt sobered and saddened now that the excitement of the moment was over. He had not meant to let this proud beauty know that he had succumbed to the glamour of her loveliness and charm of manner. Not yet, at all events; for how could he expect to win her love? He, a poor, nameless man—her uncle's overseer: nothing more in the eyes of the world! His words had leapt up and betrayed his secret before he was aware of it. Perhaps it was as well; it would teach them both to be careful. And perhaps someday, when his rights were established, when his mother's memory was cleared from shame, he might venture to come forward and say boldly: "I love you," and ask her to be his wife, if some other had not forestalled him by that time.

They rode home in silence, each occupied with their own thoughts. Marion could not free herself from the picture of that terrible chasm on the brink of which she had been but a few moments ago. She still saw the gully with its tall tree tops and fern-clad rocks where, but for Norman's timely help, she would now be lying dead—crushed out of all human semblance. And he would have died too, so he had said: he must love her truly. And, again, she heard the musical voice murmuring those wild, passionate words, and saw the gleam of love and tenderness in the dark eyes.

She glanced at his face and wondered to see it so pale and cold. Everything seemed strangely unreal and dreamy; and with an effort to shake off her thoughts and fancies she turned to Lucy and endeavoured to engage her in conversation. But Lucy was sad and dispirited, and only answered in monosyllables. She was trying to realise that her vague foreboding had been fulfilled at last. The love which she had longed for for years had been given to another; and there was nothing left for her but to hope that she who had won so great a prize might prove herself worthy of it, and make the beloved one happy.

As for Norman, we know what his thoughts were, and how hope and despondency struggled alternately in his heart. One thing was clear to him: nothing should rob him of his love to Marion. Whether it proved his curse or his blessing, that love should be cherished till death; hopeless though it may be he would not renounce it. And when he reached home he unbound the delicate handkerchief from his brow, and held it next to his heart. It was all he might ever possess of the woman he worshipped, and he would treasure it as his greatest treasure.

Chapter V

Windermere was one blaze of light and colour on Christmas eve. Mrs. Northbrook had made up her mind to give her neighbours an entertainment in a style which should dazzle their eyes and impress them with the superior, taste and elegance of an English household. She had issued invitations to all the neighbouring gentry who had called on her, and from whom she had already received much kindness and hospitality. She had engaged an extra staff of servants, whose inexperience and stupidity had nearly driven her frantic; she had been distracted by the difficulties besetting her on every side; she had almost despaired of being able to procure musicians at the ball; she had been worried beyond all measure by the stolidity and obstinacy of old Digby, whom she had been obliged to consult on many matters; she had been rejoiced on securing the services of a first-rate female cook; and had then been reduced to abject despondency on discovering that this inestimable personage was a confirmed drunkard. In one word, poor Mrs. Northbrook had been fretting and fuming and lamenting from morning till evening until Frank had begun to wish that she had never undertaken what seemed so difficult to carry out, whereupon his mother had replied indignantly that she was always doomed to be misunderstood and undervalued, and all the time too when she was slaving herself to death for the sake of her son, whose arrival at Windemere she thought it her duty to celebrate by a little festivity, and hospitality.

In the mdst of this confusion and reign of general anarchy, Marion Halstead appeared a few days before the party and, true to her word, proceeded to do her best to make everything bright and comfortable.

Young hands and light hearts can do wonders, and Marion, with the aid and experience of Lucy Clovelly, managed to help Mrs. Northbrook through her difficulties in so fairy-like a manner that the good lady felt quite hopeful again, and saw her burden lightened in a very short time.

As for Frank, he was in a transport of delight, and committed all sorts of extravagancies for which he was soundly rated by the young ladies. And so, between laughing and joking and working, they succeeded in preparing Windemere for the Christmas festival; and when the evening came, Mrs. Northbrook was able to sit down and wait for her guests with the satisfaction of a hostess who knows that everything is well prepared to receive the expected arrivals worthily.

The night was warm and clear. The full moon hung high in the deep blue vault of heaven, flooding the garden and meadows and forests with a mellow radiance. Myriads of coloured lights twinkled on the verandah and in the dark shrubbery, vying with the moon and stars in brilliancy, and transforming the wilderness of untrimmed bushes and flower beds into a very fairyland of beauty. Beyond this glarish illumination lay the moonlit paddocks, through which a broad river rippled its deep waters beneath the sweeping swamp oaks and whispering rushes.

On a small island, surrounded by the washing tide, a red camp-fire flickered unsteadily amidst the tangled underbrush. Now and then dark, lithe figures could be seen leaping wildly around the ruddy blaze, while the night wind bore broken snatches of a monotonous, melancholy chant towards the house.

The blacks were celebrating their wild dances, and doubtless enjoying their corroboree as gaily as the white man his evening party under the lamplight.

Marion Halstead was standing on the verandah with Frank. She wore a simple white dress decorated with ferns and rose buds. A cluster of pink roses at her throat and another in the rich masses of her soft brown hair, and a hue of gold round her neck, with a small locket, were the only ornaments; and in this unpretentious costume she looked regally beautiful, the acknowledged belle of the ball-room. Marion told herself that she ought to feel supremely happy. Was she not the centre of attraction this evening: the queen of the festival? Had not her programme been filled at the first? Had she not been obliged to refuse a host of disconsolate partners? Had not the handsome young master of Windemere, himself the cynosure of all eyes, been her devoted slave all the evening, incurring his lady mother's displeasure, and almost neglecting his duty as host in the intoxicating delight of her presence? Six months ago—nay, even six weeks ago—all this homage and admiration would have filled her with unmitigated pleasure; but somehow tonight she felt wearied and dissatisfied. Everything seemed shallow and frivolous. For the first time in her life a dim perception of the worthlessness of a pleasure-seeking worldly existence began to dawn upon the girl's mind, and she was filled with a vague longing for something higher and purer than mere coquetry and vanity. A strange unrest filled her soul; a struggle against these new incomprehensible feelings was taking place in her heart, and she longed to fly and hide herself to try and understand the change that had taken place in her inner-life.

More than once during the evening she had been vexed at herself on finding that she was unconsciously watching the doors for the appearance of a tall, slender figure and a dark, grave face; and she had wondered at the heart sickness that had come over her as the hours slipped by and the expected one did not appear. Norman had promised to come after all. When he had placed her in the carriage that night he said in a low voice:

"I shall come before the evening is out just to catch one distant glimpse of you in your full glory." There had been a touch of bitterness in his tone as he muttered those words, and Marion had answered quickly:

"I hope you will really come. I shall be watching for you all the evening." Then his eyes lit up with such a sudden flash of joy that she was glad to hide her confusion in the depths of the carriage, and had felt thankful to her mother's unebbing flow of conversation which allowed her to commune with herself in silence.

"What are you thinking of, Miss Halstead?" asked Frank, breaking in upon her reflections.

"Oh, I am thinking of a great many things. It would not do to let you into all my secrets, would it?"

"I wish you would tell me one thing. I wish you would tell me whether you have any feeling for me. Listen to me—have patience with me," he added, pleadingly, as Marion started slightly and moved away with an air of surprised annoyance. "Marion I love you, and you must know it, although you always treat me like a boy. You know I am no longer a boy—I am twenty-one tonight, and have all the feelings of a man. Do you remember the night under the tropics when we sat on the deck together watching the moon shining on the sea? Then I told you how I loved you, and you only laughed and said, 'Don't let us spoil our friendship with such follies: love-making on board ship is always an inane, evanescent thing;' and so you silenced me, but I have not forgotten your words, and tonight I prove to you that my love has been true and lasting. I will have a definite answer this time. Answer me, Marion, will you love me and be my wife?" He attempted to take her hand, but she snatched it from him saying, petulantly:

"Don't make love to me; I can't endure it." And then, as if ashamed at her impetuosity, she added more gently, "I am very sorry; we have really been such good friends, and now you must spoil it all with this folly. It is only folly—you will think quite differently after a while."

Marion was thinking how mad she would appear in the eyes of her mother and the world in general to refuse such a good match as Frank Northbrook was considered to be. To be sure, he was believed to be a little involved just now, but one good season would set matters straight again; and she was a penniless girl, for her father had been unfortunate in his speculations, and had left his widow nothing but a life insurance, the interest of which was barely sufficient for her daughter and herself. They owed a great many comforts and pleasures to the kind assistance of Uncle Clovelly. Marion had been always taught from her earliest days that it was her duty to do a good match—that is, to marry a man for the sake of his wealth and position. But now that the opportunity presented itself to put her life lesson into good practice she felt that it would be impossible for her to do so. An intense disgust filled her soul when she thought of such a marriage. Even while Frank was speaking another face seemed to rise before her and another voice to whisper low, impassioned words in her ear. Why was it not different?—why was not Norman in Frank's place?

"You will give me hope—you will accept my devotion," said Frank, gathering courage from her gentler tone and apparent hesitation.

"It would be cruel to deceive you with vain hopes," said Marion. "I can never be your wife—never!"

"Then you love someone else," said Frank with a suddenly awakened jealousy. "Who can it be? Is it possible that Norman Northbrook is the happy man? He saved your life yesterday: I heard the romantic story. Has he won your heart by this simple act of gallantry which any other man would have been only too proud to perform. Do you imagine yourself in love with this Northbrook because he was fortunate enough to save your life?"

There was something in the tone of Frank's voice which roused all the girl's innate pride. A covert sneer, a supercilious irony which prompted her to meet his eyes with defiant resolution, and gave her voice a ring of triumph.

"You have no right to ask me such a question," she said; "but since you have done it I will show you that I am not ashamed to own my love, and that it is not merely an imaginary fooling prompted by gratitude. Yes, I love Norman Northbrook. I never knew it myself until this moment. I am proud of loving him; and although we may never be married I know this much, that I shall never marry any other man!"

"I wish I had known this sooner, by Jove," said poor Frank, looking utterly abashed. "I beg your pardon, Miss Halstead: I ought not to have asked that question; but I did I not for a moment believe that such could be the case. I see there is no hope for me now. It's awfully hard for me. It makes my life quite worthless;" and soft-hearted Frank hid his face in his hands while his voice broke into a sob.

Marion felt deeply grieved, and following her impulse of pity she laid her hand on his arm, saying gently:

"You will soon forget this and be happy again. I wish you every happiness, and we shall always be friends, shall we not?"

Her voice was full of low-toned tenderness, and Frank, taking her sweet hand in his raised it to his lips; but in the same instant he felt her start violently and withdraw it from his clasp; and following the direction of her eyes, which were fixed with startled apprehension on some object at the end of the verandah, he beheld Norman Northbrook standing there with folded arms and a face which looked pale and stern in the dim lamplight.

"Frank, Frank, wherever are you?" exclaimed Mrs. Northbrook's voice, as she appeared in the doorway and surveyed the pair with undisguised annoyance. She thought Frank was making a fool of himself with the penniless girl, and would be much better occupied paying court to Miss Clovelly, the heiress. "I want you to give me your opinion on the arrangement of the supper-table," said the lady in a significant tone, and

Frank, muttering an excuse to Marion, hurried away, glad at the interruption under these circumstances.

Norman advanced and stood beside Marion, looking down upon her with a look of resolutely-suppressed pain which gave his lips a rigid line and made his dark eyebrows frown ominously.

"I must apologise for interrupting you," he said, after a pause, speaking in a voice strangely unlike his own; "it was a mere accident. I was weary of the heat and glare of the rooms, and was looking for you when I intruded myself in this unwelcome manner."

"Don't mention it; your interruption was of no consequence, whatever," said Marion, feeling strangely tremulous. "What a lovely night it is, and how those blacks yonder seem to be enjoying themselves." She was endeavouring to speak in a light unconcerned manner, but the wild sadness in his eyes and the altered tone of his voice made her heart beat with sudden fear. "I really believe," she added, with a forced laugh, "that those wild creatures are as full of enjoyment, and feel as happy as the pleasure-seekers in Mr. Northbrook's drawing-room."

"They are happier," said Norman; "happy thoughtless creatures that they are, with no thought of what tomorrow may bring. Gay and light-hearted tonight—to-morrow perhaps lying at rest for ever, shot down by the gun of the revengeful white man."

"A sad life, and a terrible death," said Marion, with a shudder.

"Not at all. They are better off than we who, with a higher grade of civilization, have also acquired a higher capacity for mental suffering. They are like children, forgetting their suffering as soon as its cause is removed; while we unhappy wretches are doomed to brood over our griefs and disappointments until they drive us to madness and despair."

"What sad, wild-words," said Marion, feeling a dangerous tendency to sob. "Why do you talk like this?"

"Because I am in one of my gloomy moods," replied Norman, passionately—"because I feel fit to curse the day on which I was born—because I feel as if I could rush down among those savages, and burying their spears in my heart, put an end to my folly and misery. I came here tonight full of newly-awakened hope and happiness—one moment has shown me that hope and happiness will never more have a place in my life. The memory of this Christmas Eve will be madness to me, urging me on to recklessness and perhaps even crime!"

Marion was terrified at his wild words, but only for himself. She understood what he meant. He had seen her and Frank at the moment when she was trying to speak more words of comfort to her rejected lover, and when he had bent over her hand to kiss it and Norman had interrupted the situation. Her whole heart went out to him in love and pity, but she shrank back involuntarily from his stern face and flashing eyes.

Norman saw the movement and controlled himself by a supreme effort.

"Don't be afraid of me," he said in his unusual voice with the pathos of an agonised entreaty vibrating through it. "God knows I would not cause you a moment's suffering, nor would I hurt the man who has won your love. Fiercely though I may hate him, he is sanctified to me through your affection; and I would willingly sacrifice my life to save his if he were in danger. Forgive my wild looks; I am not master of myself, and scarcely know what I say."

Before she could answer he had turned from her, and bounding down the steps with the peculiar wild gracefulness that characterised all his movements was lost to sight among the bushes and trees!

Marion started forward with a half-stifled cry. She felt that she must not let him go from her in that reckless despair with that terrible mistake crushing all hope out of him. But he was gone! There was no answer to her cry save the melancholy cadence of a valse in the ball-room, and the monotonous, weird song of the distant black revellers.

Chapter VI

Norman strode away through the fragrant garden and across the silent, dewy paddocks until he gained the solitude of the forests where the forest oaks trailed their long, feathery boughs across his path; and the distorted trunks of the stunted white gum stood out pale and spectral in the moonlight like transfixed creatures in every attitude of agony and despair. The man's soul was wild with tumultuous passions and conflicting emotions. Wounded love and bitter jealousy, and burning desires for revenge, warred against the innate nobleness and chivalry of his disposition. Fierce longings to be face to face and hand to hand with his rival were counterbalanced by the all-absorbing tenderness for the woman whose happiness was dearer to him than anything on earth. The blow had fallen upon him unexpectedly at the very moment when he had begun to hope that he might win that sweet woman's love—just when it seemed that the one object of his life, for which he had waited with ill-restrained impatience since his earliest boyhood, seemed about to be within his reach—when he saw a hope of establishing his legitimate claims this sudden disappointment had come upon him, making his existence seem worthless and void of every interest. On his return from that eventful ride Mr. Clovelly had told him of Dale's visit, and had shown him the certificate of his mother's marriage. Norman could not help recalling with feelings of bitter shame how his first thought at this news had not been of his dead mother, who had gone to her grave in sorrow and disgrace; but of the beautiful girl whom he might hope to win if he were acknowledged as the rightful heir of Windemere. He had told himself bitterly that he had deserved his fate for setting this woman up as his ideal, and allowing her to occupy the place in his heart which till then had been consecrated to his injured mother.

But he would not allow his disappointed love to interfere with the fight for his rightful claims. He would claim Windemere and not the intruders. What a surprise it would be for that proud young Northbrook to find himself the poor, and nameless man whom he supposed Mr. Clovelly's super. to be! What a glorious triumph over the man who had robbed him of his love. But she herself—that dearly-loved woman, whose fault had only been that she was too lovable, too kind—what would her feelings be when she heard of her lover's change of fortune? Would she not grieve when cruel fate parted her from the man she loved? Could she help it that a mad, foolish fellow had for a moment believed her kind words and looks to mean more than gratitude and friendship? Should she suffer while he triumphed?

The momentary elation that filled Norman's soul at the prospect of his change of circumstances gave way to a rush of tender pity as he pictured Marion's young hopes blighted, and almost fancied he could see her reproachful, tear-stained face. Could he bear to make her suffer? Never!—he would rather die first. And yet, to be master of that beautiful station, the one object of desires since years—to be able to reform the abuses which he had noted with growing disgust—to restore his father's property to prosperity and order—to take his position among the squatters of the district, a man of importance and wealth with a power for doing good and for ruling beneficially as a little king in his own right, what a temptation for a high-spirited, ambitious man: and it was his right, his duty to claim Windemere!

Then the scene on the verandah flashed before him. Those two figures standing together under the lamplight. The woman looking up at the man with a face full of tenderness, while she uttered low words which the listener at the dim end of the verandah could not understand, and the man holding her hand and raising it to his lips. The memory of that picture maddened his heart and brain, awakening fierce thoughts and feelings from which he shuddered away with fear and horror; and rushing onward through tangled underbrush and thicket sought to escape from the spectres of his fevered mind by bodily fatigue and emotion.

The dewy vines showered sparkling drops on his head; the dingo started away from his feast on the slaughtered lamb; the flying foxes flapped their heavy wings above him; the curlew rose up from the scrub with long-drawn, melancholy shrieks; and from the distant swamps came the strange bellowing roar of the mysterious bunyip. The southern cross gleamed calmly above the misty ranges, and then as night wore on and the pearly dawn began to glimmer in the east, faded away with the other stars, while the moon grew white and ghostly, and then went down like a pale red ball into the rising river fog that hovered over the flats.

Exhausted with his wild wanderings, and worn out with the conflicting passions that had been warring all night in his breast, Norman flung himself down under a wide-spreading mangrove and gazed wearily towards the east where a few roseate streaks in the pale amber sky heralded the coming morn. The large blue convolvulus above his head opened their delicate, dew-laden petals to the dawn. The white clematis sent forth its soft perfume; the plainted coo of the wood dove sounded through the scrub; a few kangaroos were quietly nipping the short, dry grass on the plain; the magpie and thrush warbled forth their morning psalms. A faint breeze came sighing through the long yellow grass; the distant eastern ranges grew bright in the glow of sunrise; the sky flushed into a blaze of gold and crimson; and then the sun rose slowly behind the dark silhouettes of the mountain peaks, and the Australian Christmas morning had begun.

Norman gazed earnestly at the brightening landscape, and with the departure of night and the approach of a new day his gloomy thoughts and desperate passions seemed to melt away like the morning vapours, and a subdued, resigned sadness took its place. His better nature rose up triumphant from that terrible night's conflict; and as he started to his feet looking worn and haggard, but calmly resolute, he repeated to himself the words with which his mother had taught him to welcome the merry Christmas days of old:

"Glory to God in the highest; and on earth, peace and goodwill towards man."

Chapter VII

Frank Northbrook was seated in the little room at Windemere, which he chose to call his office, but which rather resembled a West-end boudoir than the office of an Australian squatter. The floors were covered with a heavy Persian carpet; the walls were hung with finely-toned copies of Landseer and Snyder's inimitable representations of animal life; the table was littered with the newest English magazines, periodicals, and novels. Meerschaum pipes, silver-mounted toy pistols, cigar-boxes, and a variety of ornamental and useless knic-knacs—many of them presents from disconsolate lady friends whom Frank had left in England—were strewn about in picturesque disorder. Easy chairs and lounges invited to idle repose, and the bright Christmas morning sun was shut out by delicate rose-coloured curtains; and the air was laden with the perfume of a large bouquet of flowers that stood in a hand-vase on the mantel-piece.

The owner of this cosy little den did not appear to be in a happy Christmas mood. He was lounging in an easy chair, smoking a cigar and gazing gloomily at an open letter which he held in his hand. A delicate, white spaniel on his knee was dividing its jealous attempts at attracting his master's notice with a noble-looking greyhound who rubbed his fine head against Frank's arm and growled ominously at the tiny favorite.

"I'm an unlucky fellow, by Jove," muttered Frank, tossing the letter on the floor and relighting his cigar which had gone out meanwhile. The letter was from Dale, informing him of unexpected claims which Mr.

Norman Northbrook was about to advance as the rightful heir of Windermere. The lawyer could not conceal the fact from his young friend that this Northbrook had a very strong case, but was ready to do everything in his power to assist his old friend's son. He was greatly shocked at this strange revelation; had always believed himself entirely in Mr. Northbrook's confidence; was deeply grieved to find that this had not been the case; hoped sincerely, for honor of his deceased friend, that the story was a fabrication; advised Mr. Frank Northbrook to go to law immediately, and was prepared to give him his services and do the best that could be done for him.

Frank's idea on perusing this letter was to believe the whole affair to be a deliberate invention of the lawyer's in order to extort money. He disliked the man extremely, and believed him capable of every mean action; but after he had read the letter several times and began to recall many little incidents, unimportant in themselves, but now suddenly invested with startling importance, his heart sank, and a sickening terror took possession of him. Could it be possible that his father had acted in so base a manner, deceiving his mother and himself, and deserting that other wife and child so cruelly? His suspicions once aroused, he began to remember many peculiarities about that father which seemed to give a semblance of truth to the lawyer's story: his aversion to return to Australia—his reticence about his former life—his fits of moody abstraction—his nervous irritability when the Australian letters came in—and, above all, the pitiful struggle to utter some words when he was stricken down suddenly by the hand of death; the vain striving to free his mind from some secret which weighed upon it, and which he seemed to long to disclose, but which was fated to go to the grave with him.

All these and many other circumstances came back to Frank's mind as he sat alone thinking over the startling communication contained in Dale's letter. It was strange that this Northbrook should bear his father's name; and if he were his half-brother this would explain the mysterious familiarity of his features, which had impressed him with a vague sense of having seen them before somewhere. This would also explain the oracular speeches with which old Digby was wont to exasperate him at times.

Good God! could it be possible that people suspected him to be in wrongful possession of Windemere, and that this Norman Northbrook was the rightful heir?

"I am a most unlucky and ill-used fellow," thought Frank with rising bitterness against this man who not only had won the love of the woman he had set his heart on making his wife; but who also seemed about to take his name and heirship from him.

"Good heavens! what am I to do if I lose Windemere," thought Frank, desperately. He had been brought up in luxury and idleness, and could not think of any occupation by which he might manage to support his mother and himself. What would his mother say when she heard of this fearful state of affairs?—such a proud woman as she was, and accustomed to every comfort. But when his reflections had reached this climax he was startled by a knock at the door, and on rising to open it found himself face to face with his half-brother. Frank's delicate face flushed, and his voice was constrained and cold as he wished his visitor good morning and invited him to be seated.

"I prefer standing, thank you," replied Norman. "I have called on business, but I shall not detain you long."

"Oh," said Frank, affecting an indifferent drawl. "Ye—es; I think I know what you allude to. I have—aw—received a letter from my lawyer, Mr. Dale, stating—aw—that you are about to advance some preposterous claims regarding the—the heirship of this station. I am prepared to hear your version of the affair."

Norman drew the marriage certificate from his pocket and opened it before Frank's eyes. "This and Mr. Clovelly's statements are my proofs," he said, quietly. "You will see that my mother was married to Mr. North-brook before he left Australia; and I may add that we have been successful in discovering the address of the clergyman who performed the ceremo-ny. Mr. Clovelly received a telegram from our lawyer to this effect this morning, so that we can produce a statement from this person regarding the truth of our assertions."

Frank's eyes wandered aimlessly over the paper without being able to grasp its contents, and then rested with a look of hopeless despon-dency on the dark face opposite with its statuesque beauty and worn expression.

"I suppose it's true," he muttered. "It's awfully rough on a fellow. Don't know whether to go to law or not. If you have certain proofs of your legitimate claims I don't see the use of running myself into needless expenditure for a hopeless case; and if we could settle the matter quietly it would be more pleasant for my mother and myself, inasmuch as it would prevent our private affairs being made public."

"I am willing to settle matters quietly," said Norman. "I wish to have my legitimacy established; but I resign all claim to Windemere!"

If a thunderbolt had fallen at Frank's feet he could not have been more startled and astounded.

"What do you mean?" he exclaimed. "Resign all claim to Winde-mere?"

"Yes," replied Norman, coolly. "All I desire is to have my mother's mar-riage made public—the rest is of no consequence whatever to me. I am about to leave the colony and to cast in my lot with the fortune-hunters and adventurers of New Guinea. Windemere would only be an encum-brance to me under those circumstances while it is a necessity to you."

"Am I to be indebted to your generosity then," said Frank, hotly, "or do you mean to bribe me into proclaiming your legitimacy because you are not sure of your claims?"

Norman's face flushed slightly at these words, but his tone was as calm as before.

"I advise you to be more careful of your words. You will have time to consider the matter and consult your lawyer. You will find that my claims are perfectly correct, and that I have no reason whatever to demean myself by bribery and double-dealing."

"I beg your pardon," said Frank, looking rather ashamed. "I ought not to have spoken in that way; but I am quite bewildered, I cannot understand this affair at all. It seems deucedly queer that you should be the rightful heir and yet give the property up to me. What reason have you for such extraordinary generosity?—and why on earth do you intend leaving the colony and throwing yourself into a reckless life of adventure and hardship?"

"I will tell you," said Norman, suddenly changing his calm tone into one of suppressed passion. "I am doing this for the sake of the woman we both love, and whose happiness is dearer to me than anything else on earth. You have been fortunate enough to win her love. Do you think I can stay here and see you marry her? the very thought maddens me! I must put distance and absence between us, and try to drown the sorrow which will henceforth be my portion in a life of recklessness and danger. Remember, Frank Northbrook, that Marion has lost a great price—the price of another man's happiness; and woe be to you if you ever undervalue the treasure you have won, and treat that sweet woman with coldness or neglect!"

He turned away and strode towards the door, but Frank started up with an impulse of generosity which overcame his wounded pride and resentment.

"Stop," he exclaimed. "You are mistaken—you believe that Miss. Halstead loves me—that I am her accepted lover?"

"Why do you ask me?" exclaimed Norman, fiercely; "did I not see you kiss her hand last night?—did I not hear her speaking to you in a voice the tones of which have been haunting me ever since? Do you want to drive me mad by reminding me of this?"

"You are quite mistaken," said Frank, blushing like a girl. "She does not love me at all—she loves you, lucky fellow that you are. She was only speaking some words of comfort to me when you came upon us."

Norman stood like one stunned for a moment, then grasping Frank's arm with a grip of iron he said in a low, stern voice:

"Don't trifle with me; I'm not in a humour for folly. Are you speaking the truth? Answer me—is this really true?"

"Go and ask her yourself," said Frank, shaking himself loose. "I have repaid your generosity and owe you nothing. You will not resign your claim to Windemere under these circumstances!"

Norman, who had been listening as in a dream to Frank's words, now caught his hand and wrung it with a fervour that well nigh crushed the delicate fingers.

"You are a fine fellow," he said. "I am proud to call you my brother. I should be worse than mean-spirited to deprive you of your only means of existence. Keep Windermere for your mother's sake; she could never bear a life of poverty and privation. I am able to fight my way well enough; and am satisfied to be the maker of my own fortunes."

"But if you marry Miss Halstead?" said Frank, falteringly.

"If Miss Halstead will not marry me as I am—a poor man, depending on his hand's work—she is not worthy of my love and does not love me truly. God bless you, Frank: I wish you a merry Christmas!"

***

The merry Christmas sun was shining brightly on Melangole, and throwing golden specks of light through the drooping leaves of a fine gum tree, beneath whose shade sat Marion and Lucy—that very morning when Norman was at Windemere with his half-brother.

Lucy had just been telling Marion the strange history which she had that morning learnt for the first time from her grandfather.

"How strange it all seems," said Marion. "Norman the rightful heir of Windemere, and poor Frank nobody. How glad I am that I did not know this last night; the poor fellow might have thought that I refused him because of his misfortunes. I am so sorry for Mrs. Northbrook; it will be a terrible blow to her."

"And are you not glad for Norman's sake?" asked Lucy, reproachfully. "If you loved him, Marion, you would not be able to think of anything but the fortune that has befallen him and you would have no sympathy with these intruders who have kept him so long from what was his rightful inheritance."

"Perhaps I think more of it than you imagine, Lucy. But I cannot help feeling what a sad Christmas those poor people will have, who were quite innocent of this wicked Mr. Northbrook's injustice, and on whom this terrible revelation will fall like a thunderbolt. It does seem hard that Norman should turn his brother out into the world without any means of subsistence. Frank is not fit for hard work, and is a stranger in this country; and Mrs. Northbrook has always been accustomed to every comfort and luxury."

"Let him learn to work for a living," said Lucy, hotly. "Let Mrs. Northbrook learn to lead a life of simplicity and hardship. Norman has worked all his life and his mother was left with a miserable annuity scarcely adequate to keep herself and her child. I have no patience with you Marion!"

Marion smiled at her friend's warmth, but in the next moment she turned pale and grasped Lucy's arm as a horseman came riding towards them from the direction of Windemere, and she recognised the tall figure and dark face of Norman Northbrook.

"That is Norman," said Lucy, rising hurriedly. "I must go and see how the preparations for our Christmas dinner are getting on." And disregarding Marion's whispered entreaty that she should remain, she disengaged herself from her cousin's detaining hand, and flew towards the house with the swiftness of a startled fawn.

Marion stood hesitating whether to follow her or not; but it was already too late, for Norman was within a few steps of her, and leaning from his saddle advanced to meet her with his eyes filled with a new gladness which she had never seen in them before.

"Merry Christmas," he said, holding out his hand; but when she returned his greeting and laid her hand in his, he retained it in his clasp, and looking down at her blushing face said gravely:

"I have just come from Windemere."

"Yes!," said Marion, "I have heard everything from Lucy this moment. I suppose I must congratulate you on being the future master of Windemere."

"No," replied Norman; "I am not going to deprive my half-brother of the station. I am able to work for my living, while he is not. I have resigned my claims to Windemere, and only wish to have my rightful claim to the name of Northbrook to be made known; I had a great struggle before I came to this resolution. I wandered away a mile last night before I conquered myself. It was a terrible night, Marion. I would not go through another one like it for all the Windemeres in the world!"

"You were mistaken," she murmured, looking up timidly. "I had refused Frank when you saw us."

"I know; Frank generously told me everything. Marion, is there any hope for me? Do you love me? and are you willing to share the life of a poor man, and help him to work his way up in the world?"

"You are a noble man," said Marion, proudly; "and I love you—is that not enough. What has poverty or wealth to do with our love?"

Chapter VIII

M r. Clovelly was very much surprised and annoyed when he heard that Norman had resigned his claims in favour of his half-brother; but finding all remonstrances useless he told Norman that he was a romantic fool; at the same time shaking him heartily by the hand, while his tears stood in his eyes.

It was a double disappointment to the old man; for as you know, he had hoped to see Lucy marry his favourite, and was not at all pleased at his preferring Marion. However, it was no use grumbling, and Lucy seemed quite happy and unconcerned. So the old man put on a pleasant face and did the best to comfort Mrs. Halstead, who was quite shocked at the thought of her dear child doing such a poor match.

"Such an idea, James," she said to her brother, pressing her handkerchief to her eyes; "such a mad thing of this young man to give up his claim to the station and then to want to marry my daughter: and Marion is bent on marrying him. Why, what are they to live on, I wonder. It is as bad really as a girl I knew who would persist in marrying a blind man; and if Mr. Northbrook is not blind in reality, he is blind to his own interests. I'm heartbroken over it—I am indeed!"

"Now, dear mother," said arion, who came in at this moment, "do not worry yourself about me. You are going to live with us, and have every comfort. Norman, you know, has an income of nearly four hundred a year; and uncle is talking of buying Windemere; as Mr. Frank Northbrook is going to sell it and leave for England; and we shall probably live there as Norman will manage the station. And now you must please try and turn your attention to my dresses, as Norman wishes us to marry as soon as possible, and we have no time to lose."

Mrs. Halstead's thoughts were immediately diverted into a new channel, and for the next few weeks she was so occupied with dressmakers, milliners, needlewomen, and ribbons, and laces and dress material, that she had no time for bitter reflections, and began at last to think that her dear child was not doing such a bad match after all.

As for the world in general—represented by the few families residing in the neighbourhood, and the inhabitants of the township in that district—the world shook its head, and whispered that Norman Northbrook must be mad, stark mad, to prefer remaining Clovelly's super. to being master of Windemere. But no one was more indignant at the turn affairs had taken than Lawyer Dale. Fully convinced that the issue of this transaction would be a most intricate, expensive, and interesting lawsuit, he had been busy preparing the facts of the case in favour of his client, Frank Northbrook, and foresaw a harvest of honour and glory, and more substantial rewards of his trouble, after conducting the case of Northbrook versus Northbrook: for whatever way the case should be decided, he was certain of his fee, and had a golden opportunity for displaying his talents.

Great was his disgust when he found how things had turned out. He was heard to use some very expressive language, and begged that the subject might never be mentioned in his hearing again as he considered it an offence against morality, conscience, and justice.

But the two who had pledged their vows of love on that bright Christmas morning cared nothing for the opinion of the world. Secure in each other's affection they stood before the altar a few months later and were united for life in the presence of a curious crowd who had assembled to see these two eccentric people married; and when it was all over, and Marion and husband passed down the aisle together, they were not thinking of the wondering eyes that rested upon them, criticising the bride's attire and appearance, and the bridegroom's proud, dark face— their thoughts were full of their own happiness, and of the Christmas eve when they parted in misunderstanding and sorrow to come together again in unfading trust and love on that happy Christmas morn that should bring new hope and happiness to every human heart.

And here we will leave them to continue their way through life, cheered by each other's steadfast devotion, and that kindly sympathy for the trouble of others which is the best anodyne against selfishness and worldly cares.